"Oh, God, we're mistresse[...]it."

"We really did it," Brooke echoed. They'd given up jobs, apartments, just about everything, to be kept by these lovers who demanded their time, their loyalty, and their bodies.

But they were also reaping the rewards. The clothes, the apartments, the allowances, the sex—these men had chosen them as their sexual playthings.

"I propose a toast to Brooke, whose imagination and foresight got us here," Delia said.

"To the Mistress Club," Brooke said, lifting her goblet. "And long may we keep our lovers."

Praise for Thea Devine

"[Devine] pushes the sexuality levels to the limits of the genre with an explicitness that practically sends the pages up in flames."

—*Library Journal* on *Seductive*

"A multilayered story that sizzles with sexual energy from start to finish."

—*Publishers Weekly* on *Seductive*

"Devine's deft plotting and searing sensuality wrap around you like a silken web . . . holding us captive with her prose and passion for her story and characters."

—*Romantic Times* on *Sensation*

His Little Black Book

THEA DEVINE

GALLERY BOOKS

New York London Toronto Sydney New Delhi

G GALLERY BOOKS, a division of Simon & Schuster, Inc.
1230 Avenue of the Americas, New York, NY 10020

Library of Congress Cataloging-in-Publication Data

Devine, Thea.
    His little black book / Thea Devine.
        p. cm.
        1. Young women—New York (State)—New York—Fiction. I. Title

    PS3554.E928175H57 2006
    813'.54—dc22   2006045594

ISBN-13: 978-1-4165-2415-1
ISBN-10:   1-4165-2415-0

This Gallery Books trade paperback edition October 2006

10 9 8 7 6 5 4 3

Manufactured in the United States of America

For information regarding special discounts for bulk purchases,
please contact Simon & Schuster Special Sales at 1-800-456-6798
or business@simonandschuster.com

For John, always and forever

Thank you, Nancy

His
Little
Black
Book

Prologue

Bowdoin College, Brunswick, Maine
December 2005

"No more of this shit," Brooke told Delia at the campus diner where she, Brooke, and MJ went for a coffee break every day. "I can't stand seeing you like this. He's not worth it! He was a pig, he treated you like swill. And he did it because he could. Do you *hear* me? Because he could. Because you *let* him."

But, Delia thought, Brooke just didn't understand. She had everything: confidence, looks, grades, money. Delia had nothing, she came from nothing, and her mother had told her she'd never have anything. She'd never find a man, never get married, never be anything.

But she had—she'd gotten into college, she'd found friends, and she'd found Frank. But now Frank was gone and she had nothing, just like her mother had said. And in the end, just like she always feared, she was still alone.

She was terrified of being alone.

"I can't," she moaned. "I want him back, I need him, I'm lost without him."

"You're lost, period," Brooke retorted impatiently.

But Delia didn't want to believe she was lost. She had just lost *something*—the man she loved. Who wasn't *so* bad. Really.

Brooke looked at MJ, who shrugged. For the past month, Delia had been mourning this impossible and destructive relationship, and they'd been trying to talk sense into her.

Brooke looked out the diner window that fronted the main street in town. It was a cute town, with lots of old brick buildings holding quaint shops, a nice college town if you wanted to be far away from everywhere—which maybe wasn't a good thing to be. The place was insular, the school population was too small, and you couldn't hide from your professors, your responsibilities, or your lovers when they didn't call.

This was the lesson that Delia had yet to learn, Brooke thought: You couldn't get so involved at this stage of the game. There was no point to *ever* getting involved, really. Involvement led to pain. You lost control. You lost self-respect. You lost yourself.

Better just to have sex wherever you could find it. Then you were in control. No one could hurt you; *you* inflicted any pain.

So much more satisfying . . .

Brooke twirled the spoon in her cold coffee, feeling her fury rising yet again at the thought of everything Delia had been through with Frank. Everything she herself had gone through, and MJ, too, whose businesslike demeanor protected that heart on her sleeve.

"We've given them control," she said abruptly. "We've just up and handed them everything and given them tacit permission to give back nothing. It started when we were young, because we were always pushed by the need to be popular, to be cool, to be part of the "in" crowd. And so we gave away everything precious in the service of not being the odd one out. Everything, including our virginity. Even now."

Just saying it out loud infuriated her even more. "Damn it—we're not baby girls anymore. We're not stupid. We know the ropes. Yet we fall into the trap every time: We fall in love. *We* invest in the relationship, and what do we get? Shafted. Dumped. Dropped."

"Excessed," MJ put in caustically.

Brooke made a derisive sound. "Enough of that. When do we learn the lesson? It's all about sex, anyway. It's never about anything long-term. It's about the five-minute future—as much time as it takes them to get it up and get it in. That's all they want: five minutes of pussy time. That's their idea of a relationship. And what do we get?"

They looked at her blankly.

"Time to weep and mourn every time they abandon us," Brooke answered her own question emphatically. "Well, hell—if all we have is time, then you know what? It's *time* to take control. It's time to make them pay."

Make them . . . *pay*?

An idea skittered around the edges of her mind. A delicious, salacious idea that, when she bit into it and savored how it felt, how it tasted, melted into her consciousness like the most luscious chocolate.

3

Why not?

Oh, God.

No. That would be—*what?*

Smart. Savvy. *Scary . . .*

How? What would they be doing that they didn't willingly do now?

I don't know, but it's different. There's something not right about it . . .

Like?

Like good times, good men, just rewards . . .

Like American Express Reward points?

Like—

Her breath caught. *Imagine it.* She saw it clearly: the three of them wrapped in luxury, swathed in furs, huddled in limousines with gorgeous, elegant, older men . . .

Why not? What was the difference, after all?

The difference was adult, mature, wealthy men who would prize them and treasure them and treat them like queens, as opposed to the lapping puppy boys with their hot hands, hot words, and horny bodies who would leave them with heartache and misery instead of jewels and gratitude.

"You know what—" she started, then stopped. This was crazy, they'd think she was nuts. And how could they even do it, anyway?

But MJ and Delia were both looking at her expectantly, hopefully; Delia, especially, with her lank blonde hair and haunted blue eyes glazed with unshed tears, her pale face fraught with longing.

Hell, it was better than anything they had now.

"We should form a mistress club," she said quickly, as if she were uttering dirty words.

"Oh, my God," MJ breathed, as if Brooke had opened a holy book at the page marked *epiphanies.*

"Oh, we couldn't," Delia protested simultaneously, but it was such a naughty, over-the-top notion that she was instantly seduced.

"No, listen. Listen—" To what? Brooke was still formulating the plan even as she spoke. "We've been giving it away to jerks who *allow* us to give them blow jobs, after which they blow us off. They're looking for thirty-second relationships when we're looking for thirty years. So what the hell are we doing? We're investing our emotions and our hopes in quicksand. This is not good business."

MJ looked awed. A business major, who looked all of fourteen this morning with her siren red hair in pigtails and her freckled face bare of makeup, she understood the bottom-line mentality. She got it, immediately and completely.

Delia looked shocked, tentative, interested. At least she was reacting and not crying. This was good. Maybe Brooke could sell this. It sounded good to her.

Hell, it sounded like a career.

"We should take our time about marriage," she went on slowly, conjuring her points from thin air. What did she know about mistresses or what it took to become one, anyway? But she liked the thought of it, the control, the power.

Of getting instead of giving.

Like interest. An investment.

"We should get the most we can *while* we can," she went

on. "Get what we deserve from men who will appreciate us and are willing to—remunerate us for our—skills and talents. I mean, if we're going to have sex anyway, wouldn't we rather have it in a luxury penthouse with an expert and mature lover on a mink-covered bed?"

"Oh, come on," Delia scoffed.

"Oh, my God, yes," MJ sighed.

"And the great thing about it is that it's no-commitment sex. They don't want commitment, and we don't want commitment. We just want everything they're willing to give us, for the thing we're most willing to give away. Doesn't that sound like good business?"

It sounded perfect to *her* as she uttered the words. Not a high-priced call girl. No, she meant each of them to be the chosen paramour of a distinguished man of means who could afford anything and who would shower them with all the luxuries and amenities a woman could want.

"Think about it. Equal power. Lots of sex, lots of appreciation, lots of little surprise gifts. Expensive gifts . . ."

She let them roll it around in their imaginations. Let them envision themselves on the arm of a wealthy lover, emerging from a long black limousine, or sunning themselves on a yacht cruising the Mediterranean. He would own a yacht, for sure. And go to Cannes every year. Or St. Tropez. Maybe he'd be a producer, a writer, a financier. The possibilities were endless for the kind of men any of them could attract.

Maybe Delia needed a little work. And MJ dressed a little too MTV. But that was easy enough to change. They'd figure out that part of the plan later. For now, it was enough to inaugurate the idea.

She loved the idea. *The Mistress Club.*

"I hereby call to order the first meeting of the Mistress Club."

MJ's eyebrows went up. Delia looked startled.

"Here's the deal," Brooke said firmly. "We three are the only members of this exclusive Mistress Club, and we are going to spend the next five months until graduation homing in on what it takes to become the most desirable woman in the world. Then, after we graduate, we'll give ourselves— oh, a year or so to . . . situate ourselves."

Delia looked confused.

"A year to find that gorgeous, wealthy lover who can't live without us," Brooke amplified. "We'll make it a contest: Whoever hooks up with the best, wealthiest, most generous man wins a prize!" She looked at them brightly. "What do you think?"

"What's the prize?" Delia asked.

"Shit, I don't know. A . . . a diamond bracelet."

"Ohhh," Delia sighed.

"So all it takes is the mention of diamonds to wake you up and shake you up?" Brooke grinned. "Well, diamonds would dry anyone's tears. Lots of diamonds, showered on us by appreciative men who only want a gorgeous, adoring bed partner. It works for me."

She was gratified to see they were both listening intently.

"We have to start now," she went on, winging it. "You can't just pluck a wealthy sugar daddy off the shelf. You have to first . . . first—work at it. Train for it. This is a competition, after all, and the prize is gold . . . and diamonds and furs and everything you could ever want! Just look at Melania Knauss and The Donald."

Everything that came to mind was so sybaritic that it seemed like a hedonistic indulgence rather than a preparation for a full-bore assault on finding a lover. Massages, pedicures, manicures, facials, trim bodies, great clothes, a fabulous job, perhaps a shift in their usual cynical hard-edged sensibilities into softer, more winning, and more willing personalities.

How hard could any of that be?

"You're serious," MJ said, awed.

"Tell me what's wrong with the plan," Brooke challenged.

"I can't see a thing," MJ conceded instantly.

"So . . ." Brooke took a deep breath. "We'll start now. Just as if we were gearing up for a job hunt. We'll do a spa track: weekly massages, steam baths, facials. Get ourselves tricked up and tricked out. We'll research the jobs most likely to put us in the presence of wealthy men who want to pay a good price for good company. We'll change the way we talk, walk, dress, and approach everything. We'll focus all our spare time on becoming the kind of women those men want and can pay for. We'll—"

MJ held up her hand, laughing. "Okay, okay, we get the picture."

"Do you? Because we have to change one hundred percent. Delia has to stop schlepping around like a hippie wannabe and start wearing bras, high heels, and makeup.

And you have to start dressing with more taste, more like the kind of woman to whom a CEO would be attracted—"

"And *you*?" MJ interrupted silkily.

"Me?" Brooke knew all her faults and failures, but they didn't include the way she looked or dressed. Her jet-black hair was naturally curly, her skin was flawless, her body was model thin, and her hazel eyes changed color with everything she wore. Still . . . "I need to stop bossing everyone around and acting like Miss Rich Bitch. And I probably could stand to tone myself down and dress more high end."

MJ smiled at her, catlike. "You're just lucky you came up with this insane idea. Because otherwise, given your good looks, size six, and trust fund, we'd have to kill you."

"It's a killer idea," Brooke said. "Don't you think, Delia?"

Delia's blue eyes, teary no longer, slowly focused on her. "Do you really think we could do it? Really, in your heart of hearts?"

"I really, really do," Brooke said gently, urgently. "But it's going to take time, and we have to be resolved and keep our eyes on the bigger picture, no matter what obstacles we run into. Because, my friends, we're aiming at living every woman's fantasy: We're going to become objects of delight and illusion, with no commitment and all the benefits. And we start right here, right now."

Chapter One

THE MISTRESS CODE

Get first, then give.

*Never waste your time on anything that doesn't get you
something in return.*

*Don't give it away: no itinerant penises, no pointless
one-night stands.*

*Never give it up at home: always his turf, because if he
takes you there, he wants you there.*

Always dress to kill, and always wear high heels.

Be discreet, aloof, mysterious, and elusive.

Do not not NOT fall in love.

Never get heavily invested in any man; let him invest in you.

New York City
Three months after graduation

It was one of those mornings when MJ just wanted to lie in
bed and wallow in her misery. Never a good thing, and

especially bad when she was lying next to a Big Mistake. And a wasted night. And a wasted fuck.

Wasted, period.

She didn't even know his name. He was a hey-baby-wanna-fuck-don't-need-to-know-your-name bull whose pumping power had diminished big time by the time they'd gotten to somewhere they could undress. The last sort of person she should have gone to bed with.

No *fuck 'em and leave 'em no-commitment bar-stool-romeo one-night stands* was, she thought hazily, rule number two—or one?

Commandment number three, rather: Thou shalt not fuck itinerant penises. Was there divine retribution if you sinned?

There certainly was earthly retribution: He'd gotten off, and she'd gotten nothing. And they were in her minuscule apartment, and there was a rule against *that,* too.

Shit. How stupidly careless of her. How brain-dead.

Brooke had cautioned them: Don't be led around by your G-spot. This is serious business, and it *is* business. We want to close the deal; we don't want to mess it up with distractions that detract from the main chance.

Well, she'd let in a big-time distraction last night, and while *he* had kicked it over the goalpost, she'd been handed off for his pleasure. Which just brought home the point that Brooke had been making for the last three months: It was better to get than to give.

She was tired of giving and not getting. She was tired that the short end of the stick always ended up inside *her.*

Brooke was right. Brooke was always right. It should be her mantra: *Get first, then give.* It was so simple. How the hell had she fucked it up so quickly?

She was a sucker for bad boys—the ones with that light in their eyes that said they knew you, but what they really knew was that you were a pushover for that first conning *I know you want to fuck* look they gave you. Stupid, stupid, stupid. How did she know what he was, really? Everything was on the surface: no feelings. Connecting body parts for the time it took to convulse and conquer.

Shit. Time to regroup. Time to get him the hell out of there and sanitize her apartment. Her tiny best-address place to sleep.

This was not working the way Brooke said it would.

No, you aren't working it the way Brooke said you should. The game plan. The right address, the right job, the right clothes, the right contacts.

They had been so cocooned at school. Everything seemed possible there, but the real world was merciless. And truthfully, she hadn't really been taking this Mistress Club thing that seriously. It was too much work.

She had been the first to come to New York, and just finding a job was hard enough. The rest was dominoes: If you didn't have money or a job, you couldn't get the address, the clothes, the contacts.

And she hadn't been looking all that hard for that perfect meet-the-moneyed-men job. She'd been working as a temp, which was the first step in Brooke's strategic plan, but she was barely scraping by.

Because she'd stupidly thought that maybe somewhere among the losers she'd been meeting she'd find someone seriously worth her time, seriously worth the effort, and she wouldn't have to do the work.

But the truth was, the only effort she was expending was to get her own orgasm before they jacked off and left.

They want sex with no strings and no investment, in case something better comes along.

Brooke again, in her infinite wisdom. Though bunny fucking got you temporary pleasure, it got wearing after a while. Either sex was just one more thing to get over with on a date, or you forced yourself to date someone just to get sex.

MJ yawned and stretched. She ought to write all that down. She'd keep her focus better that way.

Brooke checked on them like a worried mother hen, via their bimonthly meetings and email, that at a minimum they were keeping up the beauty regimen.

And MJ was. So she knew the bull had enjoyed stroking her silky-smooth caviar-infused skin. Had loved the scent of the lavender cream she rubbed on her body every night, and the sheen of her Louis Licari–dyed, avocado-conditioned hair.

But she lacked the clothes, the job, the resolve, the attitude. If she had any resolve at all, she wouldn't be staring at a snoring lump of limp muscle that had nothing to give her but grief.

Out, out, damned penis . . .

She lay wrapped in a sheet, her resolve reenergized, waiting impatiently for the moment when the bull would come to consciousness.

Shit. His penis was coming to consciousness.

Not going to happen. . . . I have been reborn.

That was the lesson. She got it now.

Get first, then give.

Rule number three? One?

Never waste your time on anything that doesn't get you something in return.

She'd better memorize those rules.

Never let a penis roam your territory—ever. You want to be on his territory, because that means he wants you there. Big time.

She nudged him with her foot.

"Oh, yeah, hi . . . baby—hey, gotta go . . ."

Predictable.

She watched with detached amusement as he scrambled into his clothes.

Get first, then give . . .

He probably had a wife, kids, and a boring nine-to-five job.

Get out . . .

You're wasting my time.

Get . . .

The door slammed. *Out.*

A new record: two minutes and gone.

Thanks for giving me that, at least.

And thank you, Lord, he didn't say he'd call.

Delia was ambivalent about New York. She had been here one month and the city seemed cold and heartless. It chewed you up and spit you out. You had to find your own way, skating on your own confidence whether you felt it or not.

She never felt it.

But if you could *get* that attitude, sometimes you could feel the energy here, feel that you were part of the swell of people who had places to go and things to get done.

She was getting something done today: She was prowling upper Madison Avenue looking for that potential meet-the-CEO job, although she hadn't figured out how you found such jobs when they weren't listed in the Sunday *Times*.

Maybe you just walked right in and asked.

Except she couldn't do that. How did anybody do that?

Thank God for Brooke. Superorganized Brooke had plotted the whole thing out, from rules to live by to a plan for getting them to their goal.

Everything so straightforward and simple that even she could follow through. The first part was to come to New York, get temporary jobs, and find inexpensive temporary apartments separately, so they wouldn't look like a pack of wolves on the hunt.

The apartment part was pretty rough. She had finally taken a tiny studio on Seventy-ninth and Madison, the cost of which was so astronomical she almost had to be earning six figures just to afford it.

She'd had about six cents left from her summer waitress job in Bar Harbor when she'd arrived here, and she'd maxed out her credit card just for air fare and the upfront money for the apartment.

Add to that the necessary trendy haircut at Sally Hershberger, and buying that one really great suit—on sale. And the sexy city-chic shoes.

God, she loved shoes.

But working as a waitress would not get her Jimmy Choos on a regular basis. And even though she was a really great waitress, her restaurant wasn't, as Brooke had pointed out, high on the list of potential places to meet a man with a black American Express card. They were looking for the kind of employment where they would provide a certain level of personal service—not sex—to a certain kind of clientele as part of the package.

Like a high-end, service-oriented department store like Bergdorf or Barneys, a jeweler like Graff or Cartier. A spa. A luxurious East Side hotel. A university club. An auction house.

Places where they would be seen, dressed for success, and interacting one-on-one with the clientele, taking care of them the way their would-be lover might like to be taken care of by a mistress.

Get the apartment, find the job, make the contact, and reap the benefits of being in the right place to make something happen.

They had to view Brooke's plan as an investment, and investments took time to reap dividends.

Delia knew that, but it was hard not to want things to happen instantly, very hard to take things slowly.

But Brooke had been firm. "Give it time; the effort will be worth it."

Delia wondered sometimes, given their competition: the

hordes of flashy, trashy twenty-somethings flooding Manhattan, ready to drop a dress at the drop of a dime, fucking in clubs, in cabs, on countertops, and in corners every night.

They had discussed all that at the first Manhattan meeting of the Mistress Club one week ago. Brooke had found the place—an inexpensive deli hard by Madison Square Garden.

A mecca for men and big, thick protein- and carb-loaded sandwiches that would choke a horse. *Man*-sized sandwiches. Perfect.

The competition wouldn't be eating those sandwiches, Brooke pointed out, but they did, cutting them up into manageable bites while they eyed the customers and discussed strategy.

"Here's how you deal with the competition," Brooke had said. "You target the market and sell to them. That's the first rule of business."

"A tough sell," MJ had commented, scooping up a forkful of coleslaw, "when they can have sex anytime and anywhere they want for free."

"Well, then, if that's true, why would a man take a mistress?" Brooke had asked.

"Because he can," MJ had said promptly.

"Because he's too old to get it up," Delia had put in.

Brooke had wrinkled her nose. "No—I'm thinking it's more like he's a certain age and income level, and he can afford to be particular and selective. He's not looking for a random fuck. He wouldn't want to risk making a random fuck his mistress for all kinds of reasons. So a mistress is someone he *chooses*."

"Sure," MJ had said caustically, "and all she has to be is young, beautiful, malleable, and uncritical, and adore him the way his wife doesn't. A trophy fuck."

"She is *us*, in other words," Brooke had said.

"She's a thousand of us pounding the streets right now," MJ had retorted.

"She's someone who devotes herself entirely to him and his pleasure," Delia had said suddenly.

Brooke had looked at her sharply. "You know, that's a good point. I mean, can a lawyer who's billing a hundred hours a week be a good mistress? Does a man looking for a mistress want a woman who's so busy at work she really has no time for him?"

"He wants someone whose sole purpose is to have time for him," Delia had said softly.

They had looked at her in awe, impressed that in one cogent observation, Delia had defined exactly what the mistress thing was about.

Someone young, beautiful, and multiorgasmic whose sole purpose is to have time for him.

"I can do that," MJ had said.

"I can't wait to do that," Delia had whispered.

But meantime, Delia thought now, she needed to find that job to turn the fantasy into a reality. Even though Madison Avenue seemed too full of women just like herself, well dressed, well coiffed, and on their way somewhere.

She paused at the corner of Eighty-fifth Street. This was somewhere. She chose a store, girded herself, and determinedly went in.

BROOKE'S RULES

No clubbing.
No bars.
Don't look or feel or be desperate.
Be mysterious and elusive.
Have no expectations.
Don't sleep around (unless there's a purpose).
Don't get scared, frantic, uncertain—the only urgency is
   finding a job.
Always be ready and wearing super-double protection.

Brooke liked to organize and manage. And she loved lists. Lists gave you control when things spun out of control—like men leaving you, or parents divorcing.

Lists focused your mind; they homed in on the important things and bypassed the garbage, the distractions, and the excuses. Lists were intimate and honest, and they allowed her to be herself and no one else had to see.

And making lists had codified the game plan: the rules to live by and how to get everything they'd ever wanted.

Minus the heartache and pain.

What was the Mistress Club, after all, but a way to manage their sex lives to their best advantage?

It made sense to her, and she believed in her rules.

Though she had discovered there *were* times when heels would not do, like when you were coursing up and down Manhattan on foot, scouting out where the would-be mistress should live, shop, and play. She wanted the three of them to radiate a certain old money glow, even though they didn't even have any money at all.

The uptown life: timeless designers, an apartment in an Old World prewar building, employment in a field where the wealthy traditionally worked, and a glamorous world that would provide them with opportunities to meet those uptown men whose lives were well-oiled machines run by their well-oiled wives, who were looking for full-bore penal immersion into a well-oiled trophy who had all the time in the world for *them*.

Perfect. On the money. Exactly where they were headed.

BROOKE'S MUST-HAVES:

The optimum job to meet wealthy older men.
The best designer clothes (Note: find that perfect resale shop).
An apartment at best address, even if it's in a closet.
The best hangout to meet men.
The best places to volunteer to meet men.
A place to network to get invitations.
The best sporting events to meet men (Note: cost out corporate seats but aim for skyboxes).

She was the last one to find an apartment. The building was on West End Avenue, on a corner just grazing the upper seventies. The tiny one-bedroom on the second floor had high ceilings, tall windows fronting the street, and barely any closet space. But it was drenched in Old World charm, and it had a tiny dining alcove (which Brooke immediately saw as a potential walk-in closet) and a fireplace. And it was *only* two thousand a month, with first and last months' rent up front.

"Cute," Brooke said. It might have been five hundred square feet, but what did she know about square footage, coming from a wealthy Chicago family with a luxury penthouse overlooking Lake Michigan?

This place was about as big as her room at home. And it cost too much.

But among all the obscenely expensive shoe boxes she had seen this past week, the apartment had the advantage of being in a desirable neighborhood and it had charm. It had, as the broker said, *potential.*

Although how much potential *she* would have, after writing the obscenely large check for rent, escrow, and adjunct fees, remained to be seen. She didn't like the feeling of being insolvent even before she'd written the check.

But she'd chosen to level the playing field, not to tap into her own money, her own clothes, her own previous life. Maybe to her detriment, since all these grand plans were costing more money than she had anticipated.

But that was the challenge, after all. And she loved a challenge.

"Someone is going to snap this up today," the agent said. She was slender, blonde, well dressed, well coiffed, and well done. She knew when to let a client alone and when to push a little. When to let the client's uncertainty about the outrageous cost percolate and when to initiate that moment of anxiety that would tip the client into *I must have it at any cost* mode.

"I don't doubt it," Brooke said. "Very small. But nice."

"Great address."

Brooke peered out the living room window. "But *so* close to the street."

"Some people like that aspect."

"Well, I'm from Chicago," Brooke said dismissively, as if that explained everything. "Hardly any counter space in the kitchen, either."

"The potential tenant of this apartment probably works long hours and doesn't really care about that," the agent said. "But of course the microwave comes with the apartment."

"Of course," Brooke murmured. It was a really nice apartment, but it cost half as much more than the one MJ had found the first week here, a studio on Park Avenue, and the one Delia had rented just last week, also a studio with a tiny balcony.

But it really *was* a nice apartment. And she didn't want anyone else to have it.

"Well, then—" the agent said, gathering up her purse and Maxx tote bag. "I see you still want to think about it. Don't take too long."

"Oh, no," Brooke said, opening her pocketbook. "I decided the minute I walked in the door. I'll take it. To whom do I write the check?"

A week later she found *the* resale shop, where the designer labels were top-notch and of the moment, where no item

23

was older than last year, and most weren't even six months off the runways.

Where the clientele was so wealthy and so in love with fashion they could afford to have what was new and one of a kind for as long as it remained one of a kind. And when they got bored or saw someone wearing their hot find, they brought it to Images so they could go in pursuit of the next new thing.

"We don't consign, we *repurpose*," Marielyce, the owner, told them.

And the racks were full, the labels were to die for: Marc Jacobs, Anna Sui, Prada, Bottega Veneta, Michael Kors, Celine.

The prices were expensive, but a bargain for those designers. Under a thousand dollars for a three-thousand-dollar Chanel jacket. Strappy snakeskin stilettos at five hundred dollars retail, under a hundred dollars there. Ralph Lauren, Roberto Cavalli, Pucci, Chloe. Missoni. Donna Karan.

A banquet of the best names, the most beautiful tailoring, colors, textures, and sparkle.

"We could only afford one item once a year," MJ moaned.

"One big shout-out item for starters," Brooke coaxed her. "Shoes, a bag, earrings—these prices aren't too out of sight."

"Shoes," Delia sighed. She was already trying on the snakeskin Bottega Veneta sandals. "These were in *Vogue* last month. I must have them."

"With what money?" asked MJ, ever practical, whose credit card balance was not skirting the edge of bankruptcy and who knew that Delia's was.

"I won't pay the electric bill this month. I'll give up cable. I'll—" Delia caressed the shoes. "I *love* these shoes."

"You shall have these shoes," Brooke said. "And I'll have this sweater and this skirt," a rose-scattered tea-length Ralph Lauren chiffon skirt with a coordinating cashmere sweater in deep chocolate brown. "And MJ will have—?"

"A bank balance," MJ said.

"And MJ will have that luscious Lauren emerald green silk blouse," Brooke said, ignoring her. "I saw you try it on, you loved it. It's the perfect color, perfect shape, perfect fit." She took it from the rack. "My treat, this first time."

"Don't do it," MJ said.

"Of course I'm going to do it. This is our new favorite store. The more we shop here, the better they'll get to know us, and soon we'll be giving them an ongoing list of our objects of desire, and they'll be calling us to come in. Just this once, to start us off. There's nothing like a designer blouse to add that *je ne sais quoi* to an inexpensive suit. You know I'm right."

She was at the register, flashing her credit card.

"How's your balance?" MJ murmured.

"In line with my dreams," Brooke said.

"Pretty big dreams."

"You have to see it as an investment. But you're still not sure, are you? MJ, you have to have *faith.*"

"It all could crash down around us tomorrow," MJ warned.

"Or the price-to-earnings ratio will make it a spectacular buy." Brooke handed over her credit card. "Plus, I get mileage for every dollar spent. By the time I'm finished, I'll get us all to Europe on mileage, or we'll treat ourselves to that trip to St. Tropez that we couldn't get any other way. So stop worrying, MJ. We're almost there!"

Chapter Two

Brooke became the cheerleader, the perky recreation direc-
tor who kept their minds off of the difficulties of job hunt-
ing and the expense of the apartments they didn't have a real
salary to pay for, and she occupied them with New York
things.

Bit by bit, they saw how her game plan worked to their
advantage. They learned the city. They saw they could do a
lot for very little money. And that Brooke was right—they
needed to keep occupied and interested, and in fact, everything she had found for them to do *was* interesting, had a
purpose, and made them glad they had made the decision to
come to New York with her.

"And here's the other thing," Brooke instructed them.
"You have to talk to people everywhere you go. You never
know when someone will have a connection you can use."

So they talked to people. And on their hourly wage jobs,
they made an effort to learn new things. And they went on
job interviews. On the weekends they got together and went
places and did things, and every two weeks without fail they
convened for a meeting of the Mistress Club.

"I call this meeting of the Mistress Club to order." Brooke rapped the little brass gavel that she'd bought on the table. They were meeting at O'Reilly's bar, located in the lower level of a town house just off Fifth Avenue, about four blocks from the Garden, where happy hour provided free hors d'oeuvres.

The place was crowded with well-dressed men just from work ordering burgers and beer and discussing the matchups for the evening's game.

"I love this place," Brooke said with satisfaction. She had come early to get a table just enough away from the crowd that they could hear themselves speak, but not so tucked away that they couldn't be seen.

A meeting of the Mistress Club meant full-armored dressing, head to toe. Brooke had been very specific about that—dressed to the nines, formfitting clothes, the highest high heels, and glam makeup, because you never knew when you might meet someone.

"We need to find a way to go to those games," Brooke said, making a note. "And don't tell me you're not huge sports fans. You can sit through a game if you're surrounded by interesting executive suits. *Interested* executive suits."

She tucked away the elegant leather Levenger case in which she made her notes. "Okay. We're here tonight to celebrate a lot of really good news. First, I got a job! I'm officially employed at the Peninsula Hotel as assistant to the concierge."

It was the perfect job for her. The wonder was management hadn't made her sign a confidentiality agreement—it was that kind of position, and the kind of hotel where discretion was the management philosophy.

But she knew they had thoroughly checked out her references, which meant they knew *everything* about her. What had lifted her above the other applicants of similar background and education was the fact that she really did love solving problems, a personal quality that she had stressed during the stressful interview.

After all, wasn't this whole Mistress Club idea a way to solve a problem? And hadn't her lists and plans gotten them this far?

She turned to MJ. "MJ?"

"I'm the executive assistant at the very exclusive Brioni's, as of two days ago," MJ said. "They hired me from the temp agency after I'd worked there four months. It's lots of personal contact, phones, fashion shows, meet and greet, travel arrangements, and possibly some travel for me in the future."

She threw up her hands. "Okay, so I was the skeptical one. I didn't believe your ideas would work, and I thought we'd drown in that tidal wave of competition gunning for the same things we want. But, I have to admit, you made it happen. You took three disparate college graduates and turned us into sophisticated city girls, with a game plan that's really working.

"I mean, who would have guessed that the fact I've been sewing since I was a teenager would make a difference between getting this job or remaining a temp? It's not your basic résumé point, unless you're after a career in fashion.

"But about two weeks ago, there was this very important client with an urgent tailoring problem during a really rushed lunch hour—and the rest is history.

"So thank you, Brooke, for making us persevere. And mea culpa for ever doubting you. Delia?"

Delia smiled happily. "Hostess, Time Warner Center. I just heard today. Lunch and dinner, formal dress, meet, greet, and seat. It was the Manolos, by the way."

Thank God she'd bought those shoes. She honest to God believed that the moment the manager saw her wearing those elegant Manolos, he saw *her* as the embodiment of his venue, the person he wanted to represent it at the front door.

She truly didn't care about appearances, but oh, she did love beautiful and expensive clothes. Brooke had helped her find job application clothes, dredging the racks at Images for the perfect dresses and suits that the perfect hostess would wear. Multipurpose outfits whose look could be changed by accessories or a little jacket, or some eye-catching, tasteful jewelry.

It had been a spending spree that she could ill afford, but she couldn't afford *not* to if she wanted to look the part.

"The hair is perfect." Brooke had approved, eyeing Delia as she swept out in a black chiffon gown. She'd gone a shade blonder, with the length shorter and cut at an angle to emphasize her beautiful facial structure. "The gown's great. You could wear a shrug over that one night, a beaded jacket the next week, and no one would ever know it's the same dress. Take that one."

They did—plus the beaded jacket, the sequined shrug,

the flowing crepe skirt, the bouclé jacket, the sensuous satin blouse, another couple of pairs of decadent stilettos . . . Delia was in heaven.

And in her place. She knew it was her place because she loved helping people.

And she owed it all to Brooke—for taking her out of her drab existence, for excising Frank, and for bringing her to New York, and for creating the game plan that had given them all a new life.

She lifted her Cosmopolitan and toasted Brooke.

"Welcome to our new lives."

Brooke lifted her glass and smiled happily. "How perfect is this? Did I not tell you everything would start to fall into place? Here's to us." They tipped their goblets and sipped. "How damned smart are we?" She felt full to brimming. "We did it. We're right where we need to be to find the kind of man who's looking for women like us."

And, she thought, MJ and Delia looked so beautiful. MJ, glowing in that emerald green blouse that leavened her business suit. Delia, so fresh and deliciously blonde and endearingly ingenuous.

How could any employer not have wanted to hire her? How could any man—one of her well-dressed, well-connected patrons-to-be—not fall for her instantly?

"Hear, hear," MJ and Delia said simultaneously.

"We worked hard and we didn't give up, and if we had come only this far, it still would be something, wouldn't it? But now we're on the threshold of something fantastic, and ready to thrust the door open."

"So to speak." MJ grinned.

"I wanted to meet here again to show you something I noticed at our last get-together. Look over at the bar," Brooke said.

They looked subtly, one by one.

"Nothing unusual there," MJ said. "The usual well-dressed, well-heeled middle-management crowd."

"No, no. It's what you can't see. I came in a couple of times in the last two weeks just to eavesdrop. We're talking bounty hunters here—those women are blatantly out to marry money, and they don't mind asking those guys right up front."

Delia blinked.

"Exactly," Brooke said.

"You mean they—"

"Ask a guy how much he earns, what kind of car he drives, that kind of thing. And if they don't like the answer, they just walk away."

"Wow," MJ breathed.

"Not our competition," Brooke added emphatically, "but I don't particularly want to step over their stilettos on our way to where we're going."

"They actually *ask*?" Delia said in disbelief.

"Actually ask. Like, hi, how are you, how much money did you make last year? Where's your apartment? Park Slope? Forget it. That kind of thing. Can you believe it? Trust me, the gentlemen who will want us are not hanging out at that bar. So we're out of here. And now that we're all gain-fully employed, we can afford to do something better, some-thing that will maximize our presence. I have a plan."

"You always have a plan," MJ murmured. It was rather awesome sometimes how Brooke's mind worked in plans.

Brooke ignored that. "Here's what we're going to do—we're going to choose one of the highest-end restaurants, one with town cars always parked in front, and we're going to lunch there regularly and often so that the staff and maître d' get to know us."

"Because . . . ?" MJ asked, already counting dollars.

"Because we'll become a presence. We'll become known. And maybe it will lead to something in a more discreet way."

"You have the best ideas," Delia said, her gaze still directed at the bar and the meet-and-greet do-si-do. "Because there's one redhead up there who just left the guy flat after talking to him for just two minutes."

"Well, that's not us," Brooke said. "I'll find the place, and I promise it won't cost the earth. And maybe it will reap some results. And there's one more thing I'm thinking, relevant to men and money. Now that we're in place, I don't see anything wrong with sampling. I don't mean bar guy, and I don't mean neighbor guy. And I don't mean random guy, either. But if someone approaches you through the connections you make at work, and he's the kind of man we're looking to attract, I say try him on."

"Oh!" Delia, sighing as if she were imagining it. "Oooh . . ." As if she could just feel it.

"I've been thinking along those lines, too," MJ said. "It's been way too long."

"Better a long abstinence than being shortchanged," Brooke said trenchantly. "And don't forget the mandates. Don't waste your time on anything that doesn't get you something in return. And don't sleep around without a purpose. Our purpose is to find that delicious man of means who is going to reward us for becoming his onsite round-the-clock fuck."

"I can do that," MJ murmured. "This is sounding better and better."

"Okay then, strategy."

There she goes, MJ thought. Brooke always made a list, and there was always a strategy. But strategy had gotten them this far, and MJ fully believed in it now.

Brooke opened her elegant leather folder again. "Don't be tempted the first couple of weeks on the job. It doesn't look good. *But*—if someone you've met approaches you outside the workplace, anything goes. Your discretion."

"No," MJ said, "I think I'm going to defer to you totally. You can take over my life anytime you want. Especially now that we have permission to fuck."

"Abstinence does make the dream a little sweeter, doesn't it? You won't settle for just any old shmuck who won't bust his balls for you, and show his appreciation on top of that. In fact," Brooke said, "I'll drink to that. To the lover who'll bust his balls for me . . . and you"—she tilted her goblet toward MJ first, then Delia—"and you." She looked around the bar, which was now empty except for a couple of guys in polo shirts and fleece jackets. "And one thing's for sure: That guy is not *here*."

Two weeks later, they met to celebrate their first paychecks and to audition the Park Avenue Café for their meetings.

MJ was already seated when Brooke and Delia arrived.

This was Monday, Delia's day off, but she had dressed in full Mistress Club style: hair, heels, sexy suit, jewelry. MJ was in a dark pantsuit with an ivory silk shirt and beautiful gold jewelry, her hair a shining red, her eyes sexy with makeup.

"This place is wonderful," Delia sighed as the waiter seated her.

"Perfect Midtown location. The best clientele," Brooke said, ticking off the points on her fingers. "How are you all?"

"Perfect."

"Good."

"Excellent," Brooke said, taking out her little brass gavel and rapping it on the table. "I call the Mistress Club to order."

"Wait till we order," Delia begged. "I've barely eaten all day."

"All right," Brooke said, signaling the waiter, who immediately brought water and fresh hot bread. "Check out the menu. Look at the prices. Not too bad."

They mulled over their choices for a few minutes and ordered.

Brooke said brightly, "So, here we are. Look around. Isn't this infinitely preferable to a bar or deli?"

They looked. It was still early so the tables weren't filled, but this was a well-known business lunch restaurant, and there were more than a few women in Armani suits in deep conversation at nearby tables.

"So," Brooke went on, "who has something to report?"

Delia raised her hand. "Everything's going great. I love my job. I just *love* it. So many nice people . . ."

"Nice men?"

"Lots of nice men," Delia said dreamily. "I'm giving it some time, just like you said. Not rushing into anything. Making sure they come back many times. I don't want to do anything that will rock the boat."

"Good. Exactly what we talked about. MJ?"

"I tip my hat to you, Brooke. This job couldn't be more perfect. Brioni's is Black Card heaven. And those men couldn't be nicer, or happier that I was hired. And I agree, we can't look like we're on the prowl. We have to make the job—and helping them—the most important thing, so we get repeat customers who ask for us."

Brooke made a triumphant fist. "*Yes!* You've come a long way, you nonbeliever."

"Huh," MJ said. "I should say so. Because being celibate is not my normal MO, I'll tell you."

"And I'm having the best time learning the secrets of the don't-ask-don't-tell set," Brooke said. "This is a dream job."

Oh, there were some restrictions—a dark suit was mandatory, plain pumps, discreet hair and makeup—but there was something about those constraints that was innately challenging and erotic.

And even better, she could leave the job at the door when she went home at night.

"And the best part is I have access to the concierge's go-to book, the one that tells you where to get anything anyone could ever want if price were no object. So in line with that, guess what? I was offered one ticket for tonight's Rangers game. I can't go, but I want one of you to attend. Either of you free?"

MJ looked at Delia, both of them clearly dreading the idea of three long hours in a crowd of screaming fans.

"Seat's in the reds," Brooke said, waggling the ticket in front of them. "That's corporate territory, my dears. You might want to check it out."

"One ticket?"

"Just one. I'm telling you, this is a fertile garden and one of us has to weed it."

Delia snatched the ticket. "I will. I'll do it for all of us."

"There you go," MJ said.

"Well, I'm all dressed up with nowhere to go," Delia said brightly. "And Brooke's always urging us to try new experiences."

"So you'll give us a full report next time," MJ said.

"I am totally there," Delia said. "This might be the best night out since we got here. And you all could be very sorry that you turned it down."

She had spoken with more bravado than she felt, because she was terrified of going into the Garden alone. Even after being fortified by an excellent lunch and a couple of Cosmopolitans after.

There were so many men, a lot of teenagers, fewer women, and no one dressed as she was, in a form-fitting Prada suit and superhigh Jimmy Choo heels.

Okay. I can do this.

She followed the crowd to the first door and handed her ticket to the ticket taker, who directed her to the escalators to her right. She went up two levels to the entrance marked with the seat numbers. Someone at the door pointed the way to her section, and someone at the head of the aisle directed her to her seat.

It was overwhelming. She had no idea how stunning a sports venue was—all those people; and the ice: clean, white, striped, logo'd, brightly lit; and some huge noisy machine wafting over it in concentric circles.

It was also cold. She hadn't expected that. And her seat was so close to the ice, to the action. The other seats in the arena banked upward in tiered sections, with the corporate boxes ringing the rink, floating above the crowd.

The noise was deafening, and the lights glared. She could see the TV booth hanging at mid-ice and the radio commentators down in the red seats across from where she sat.

This was definitely a men's club. They were all around her, they all knew each other, they were all well dressed and well heeled—executives entertaining clients, she surmised, well oiled and well funded.

There was nobody with half her style and elegance; the preferred mode of dress for women seemed to be team jerseys and jeans. She looked and felt way out of place.

Maybe this wasn't such a good idea.

"Hello. You look a little lost. Can I help?"

He was in the row behind her, a tall, nice-looking man dressed in Paul Stuart, probably in his late forties, with a kind of buzzed look in his eyes like he'd had a martini or two. Married, most likely, executive type probably.

This place was like Oz—nothing was real, and she'd be back in Kansas by midnight. So if he was trolling for companionship, well, anything was possible tonight.

"Maybe I am," she murmured. He was someone to flirt with, at least, to add interest to an otherwise boring evening. "I'm really new to this. A friend gave me the ticket; it's my first game."

"A hockey virgin. Well, that's a first for me, too. I'm Bill, by the way." He held out his hand.

"Delia."

"My pleasure." He held her eyes for a moment. "Really my pleasure. Look. I'll be frank. I was looking for some interesting company tonight. I have one of those obscenely expensive boxes up there and no one to share all the goodies with. So I'm wondering if you'd join me for a drink?"

"Join you? Or join *with* you?"

His gaze didn't waver. "You're pretty up front. Good. Let's say I hope something will happen, but I'd never press the issue. I mean, you're gorgeous. You could have anyone here."

"You're pretty honest, too," Delia said. "But I wasn't really looking."

She liked his style, though—low-key, complimentary, not too fast and rushed. She picked up her coat and handed it to him. "I'll tell you what. Let's have that drink. I'd like to see what goodies *you* have up there."

She was floating. The box was cantilevered out from the ceiling so that everything fell away and the only thing visible was the rink. Everything above them was dark, everything below lit by a penetrating bright white light.

In the box, the lighting was smoky soft and low, the furniture plush, the mood lush and sensual. In the anteroom, a chef was just finishing laying out a selection of hors d'oeuvres; he withdrew as Delia settled herself on the sofa and calculated the cost of doing anything with this man.

He's probably married, she thought. He's probably some highly placed executive in his company because he did have the key, and the chef knew him. He probably comes here solely to fuck—it's his clandestine hideaway, but he doesn't pick up the tab. He's probably fucked everyone from here to Park Avenue, so this isn't going to lead anywhere. And men don't make mistresses out of random fucks at a hockey game, anyway.

Those were the negatives.

She took the glass of wine he handed her and considered the positives. She was on *his* turf. He had approached her. He wanted her because something about her appealed to him.

But the question was, did she want to risk fucking a stranger and liking it too much, knowing she'd never see him again?

"Delia," he said softly, "why don't you take off your jacket?"

Move number one. Why not? She was wearing a satin blouse, sensuous to the touch, and no bra because she loved the feel of satin against her nipples.

And here she was, with a well-heeled and good-looking guy who was staring at her tautly peaked nipples like they were all-day suckers.

She leaned back against the sofa and let him look at the whole package—the tits, the curve of her body, her hips, her legs—while she sipped her wine.

It gave her time to think, to strategize.

God, she was beginning to think like Brooke.

The kiss would come next, and a lot would depend on how he kissed and what he made her feel.

Right now, she felt like a box of candy he wanted to rip open and devour.

The idea of it made her juices flow. She wondered if he had X-ray vision, if he knew she wasn't wearing underwear, either.

He set aside his wine and sat down next to her. "I don't want a drink. I'll have you . . . on my rocks." He kissed her, swooping over her body and into her mouth, his demanding tongue softening against hers as he found her willing, as she melted into the kiss, into his tongue, into his hand as he felt her nipples through the satin.

He was a good kisser, just enough wet and heat to make her body twinge with need. He had a way with a nipple, too—his fingers were expert at nipping the hard tip in a way that left her panting to feel more.

"I didn't know," he murmured against her lips, "when I saw you . . ."

"I'm not lost anymore," she whispered and took his tongue in a long, lingering kiss that was punctuated by the streaming pleasure of his tweaking her nipple until she almost came.

He knew it, too—too much power in his hands, she

thought dimly, as she gave herself to his tongue, which she loved. He clearly loved to kiss and probably had kissed a hundred women just like that.

But she didn't care. She missed kissing, she missed a man's fingers playing with her nipples, she missed everything—this was the reward for all her hard work.

"Delia—"

She made an instant decision. "Let me." She pushed him down on the couch, she pulled his pants open, she reached for his long, thick, scorching-hot shaft, and enfolded it in her hands as if she were worshipping it.

"Let me do this," she whispered. "Let me, please let me . . ."

"But—"

She licked the engorged tip and then suckled it, tonguing the precious slit. "You have to let me."

"I want your tits . . ."

"Have them." He immediately started unbuttoning her blouse. "But let me . . ." She nipped the head with her teeth, jolting him. "I need it . . . I need to do this . . ."

She loved to do this. To feed off of his pleasure, to do it for him—any him—something that would be so memorable, so prolonged and so pleasurable—for her even more than for him.

And he would remember her, would remember the night; how he met her, wanted her, kissed her; the way she begged, the feel of her nipples, her kiss, the fact that she put his pleasure above her own . . .

What better investment could she make tonight with this

man and his sex? And even better than that, Brooke would so approve—because she was on *his* turf, because he wanted her there, spending his capital, pumping his penis, both getting off *and* giving.

Chapter Three

"Oh, God, you had sex." MJ sighed in envy. It was the next meeting of the Mistress Club and they had settled in at what was now *their* restaurant. Brooke had paved the way, tipping the maître d' lavishly the first couple of times they'd come, and now he knew them and nearly always remembered their names.

"No, I *gave* sex," Delia said. "Way different. And better than that, I was on his turf, and I was in control, and *I* walked away, not him, after a very pleasurable evening. So I'd say that I *got*."

"Exactly," Brooke agreed.

"Did he ask for your number?" MJ demanded almost simultaneously.

"Oh, he asked. I refused. I followed the Mistress Club rules almost to the letter: I was elusive and mysterious, dressed to kill, on his turf, and now he'll have to figure out how to find me—if he's interested."

"Beautiful," Brooke approved. "Nothing like making a man work for his pleasure—any way you can. But what about the skybox set? Possible?"

"If you could get into the exclusive parties they hold up there during the big games," Delia said. "That's CEO territory. They like luxury. Bill just happened to get lucky that night: No one was using the company box, and I was at the game. Those ice-side seats are all about client entertaining and not nearly on the level of the private boxes. And frankly, there are women everywhere and the guys are just as ready and willing. The competition in the seats is fierce."

MJ looked askance.

"The players. The bench babes. The fan clubs. The locker lays. Bill told me all about it. Who knew?"

"You were perfect," Brooke said. "You did everything exactly right. You weren't desperate. You were gorgeous, discriminating, and available when the moment was right. You explored new territory for the Mistress Club, and we now can eliminate the sports arenas as a venue for finding the kind of man we're targeting."

"Maybe not wholly," Delia said slowly. "I mean, those men are there; we just need to find a way to meet them."

"Point noted," Brooke said, pulling out her leather notecase and writing something down.

"Ladies?" The waiter was beside them, poised to take their orders, which never varied: fish, salad, fruit, coffee. They never looked at the menus, as he was coming to know, and he deftly removed them as he made note of their orders and withdrew.

"Guys like Bill aren't in a position to make anyone an offer," Delia went on. "He just doesn't make that kind of money. At least that was my impression."

"What would you do if he's able to locate you?" MJ asked curiously.

"Well, it would mean he went to some trouble to do it," Delia said brightly. "That should count for something."

"And that's your call," Brooke said. "But keep reminding yourselves that we're not desperate, we're not out to grab the first likely candidate, and most important, we're *not* comparing ourselves to anyone else. We are gorgeous, gainfully employed, available, and *particular,* and we want to find a potential lover as discriminating and meticulous as we are. And that doesn't happen in a week or a month. Maybe not even a year. But I guarantee you, it *will* happen."

"Guarantee?" MJ said skeptically. "How?"

"Because that fastidiousness is one of the most important things that will set us apart from the crowd. You have to be as mysterious and unobtainable as a noire heroine. Particular isn't the word for it."

"So you call Delia's encounter being particular?"

"No. That was Delia assessing the situation and deciding if she had something to gain. And she did. She got a luxury seat for the event, upscale food, great wine, and good company; she was in control; she was where *he* wanted her to be; and best of all, she left him wanting more without giving up her phone number and giving him the advantage. She gave up nothing, but he gave it up. Didn't he?"

"Yes." Delia sighed. "And he had a lot to give, too . . . Oh! Our meal's here."

"Thank you so much." Brooke smiled at the waiter. "It looks lovely." She flaked off a forkful of salmon. "Oh, God, that's good."

After a couple of minutes, Delia pointed her fork at Brooke. "You could network an invitation to one of those fancy skybox events. Some guest at the hotel, perhaps, who's an avid sports fan? Or . . . oh, I don't know . . . just a thought."

"You just want to go back there and see if Bill comes looking for you," MJ teased.

"Oh, I think he will," Delia said confidently.

Brooke was amazed at how far she'd come in such a short time. All she'd needed was some structure within which she could pursue what she had always most wanted: a sex life where she had some control.

Theoretically, the rules were meant to supply that, but Brooke saw them as a moral touchstone as well. Perhaps it had initially been an intellectual exercise for her, but she saw no reason why those guidelines wouldn't eventually get them everything they wanted.

Delia was proof of that right here, right now—glowing and beautiful, no longer sad and downtrodden. She was confident now of her appeal, her value, and of the goal of their quest.

If MJ was still a little cynical, well, she had come along anyway because she couldn't stay away. Eventually, after enough trial and error and bad bed, she'd see the big picture with more clarity.

Just the fact they were here, in this lavish high-end restaurant, able to afford a pricey lunch, looking as glamorous as any model, was proof they could do anything, if they had a plan.

And Brooke prided herself on the fact she always had a plan.

But she had no plan for the day *he* walked into her life. She was enjoying that life too much. Her apartment had taken shape nicely with the help of some savvy thrift store shopping, and she liked her job enormously.

A bustling hotel was the perfect place for someone who was as brazen, organized, and curious as she was a woman of mystery and discretion.

Brooke was in heaven. Spring was coming, and there was that certain earthiness in the air. The new crop of college graduates would soon descend on the city, and everything would be fresh and blooming—including love and possibilities and her certainty that they were streetwise enough to handle any sensual situation.

So when *he* approached her desk that afternoon when she was busy coordinating a theater trip, Brooke was utterly unprepared for the shock of recognition and need that zinged through her body.

And then he was looming over her, impeccable in a Savoy suit, Thomas Pink shirt, Burberry tie, Chopard watch—and she wasn't just impressed by the labels. It was *him,* the entire package—his height, his elegance, his utter comfort in his skin. He wasn't handsome in the classical sense, but he knew who he was and that he commanded attention, and he had the confidence, impeccable manners, and cool grace to wait until she had finished her task before he spoke.

"If I may . . . ?" His voice was rich, fluid, infusing her senses.

She gathered her wits. "Of course. How can I help you?"

At that instant, between them, it was a leading question and she knew it—and so did he.

He smiled and she smiled back, happy as a child.

"Hello," he murmured. "Well, it seems I need tickets."

"I'll be happy to see what I can do," she said, and even that common response seemed double-edged. "Tickets for . . . ?"

He consulted a notepad. "Spamalot, party of four."

It didn't even sound incongruous spoken in that ineffably elegant accent. She made a note, her hand shaking. "Any preference for a date?"

Oh, God, had she said *for a date*?

"Tomorrow."

"Of course." She couldn't look at him. She had to ask his name, but the words stuck in her throat. She felt as awkward as a teenager and it utterly threw her because it wasn't supposed to happen this way. "Your room . . . number?"

He handed her his card after he added that information.

"Mr. Steffen," she murmured. "I'll see what I can do."

"Thank you." Then he was gone, without prolonging the exchange, which to her now felt stilted, prosaic, and commonplace.

And yet—

Under the surface, it felt like her life was about to change, and she hated that it had sounded like the opening of a bad confession story.

Mr. Steffen . . . Hugh Steffen.

His elegant vellum card held only minimal contact information. British, by the sound of him. Oh, God. He'd be out the door and back in London before she knew it.

Where was her grand plan now? *I need some rules.*

She hadn't expected this. She hated this feeling of wanting to tell everyone she'd met someone, *the* one. Well, maybe the one . . . whom she couldn't wait to see again.

So obviously, she must not see him again.

She could delegate the tickets. No, she was the keeper of the secret black book. She'd get the tickets and have someone else deliver them. Cool, calm, and removed, that would be *her* ticket. He was probably here for only a day or two. He could be leaving tomorrow, which would be perfect.

Or here for weeks.

She was falling to pieces in the blink of an eye. She felt giddy and light-headed at the thought of seeing this man again, even from a distance. She'd go anywhere with him if he asked, even into the nearest closet for a wham-bam moment. *Anything* . . .

This wasn't supposed to happen. She was supposed to be the one who was above it all. The one with style, sense, and the skeptically skewed view of men and mating. The one who always had a plan.

And now she could plan nothing. Now she felt no more sophisticated than a horny girl grasping for the one unexpected moment she might see *him*—even at a distance—who had to restrain every impulse to be someplace where he might see her.

I need to formulate some rules of engagement.

No—I don't care . . .

This was insane. She'd never gone over the edge like this before. And he wasn't even remotely a contender for a penthouse, pearls, and a life devoted to his pleasure.

What am I thinking?

Later that day her secret source came through with the tickets; she had them in her hand late that afternoon.

Don't do it . . .

He won't be in his room. He will be out doing things with whoever will be sharing these tickets. He's at a business meeting. He's at an elegant lunch at the Gotham. He's . . .

She stopped just short of leaving her office. She forced herself to ring for the bell captain instead, handed him the envelope with the tickets and Hugh Steffen's card, and watched him walk out the door while she suppressed every instinct to call him back.

Be elusive and mysterious . . . Follow the rules . . .

This was ridiculous. She was as fluttery as a humming-bird just thinking about him. She was the very embodiment of the Mistress Code, and she had to fight to regain that calm center.

Do not not not fall in love . . .

. . . at first sight.

She couldn't tell anyone. It was her secret, her vice, to want him so ferociously in the face of everything she had ever said.

Dear Lord, let him come . . .

At this moment, nothing else mattered.

Her sanity returned once she was back in the safe haven of her apartment. Okay, it had been a lightning-bolt attrac-tion, but lightning was evanescent. She'd thought she was impervious to visceral instantaneous attraction, but she wasn't. So she had to be on her guard, because capitulation to sexual hunger would destroy every plan, wipe away every goal, and leave her out of control and alone.

The last thing she could bear was to be out of control. She'd had enough of that in her life, between her feckless mother and vindictive father and their years of trying to best each other after their divorce.

She didn't mind being alone, but it was important to be aware of her direction, her choices, her feelings.

Today was the first time ever she had wanted just to chuck everything with no thought other than to make a man notice her, desire her, and come after her.

I have to stop this. I will be completely ineffective if I let myself drown in this swamp of lust.

Her cell rang. *Him?*

"Hey, Brooke."

MJ. "Hey yourself." She did not want to talk to MJ right now. "What's up?"

"I need some advice . . ."

Oh, shit. Brooke felt that caving that told her this was going to be about a *man*—and she didn't want to talk about some stupid man, and she couldn't share anything about Hugh Steffen because she'd sound like a fool after all her careful rules.

She *was* a fool.

"Shoot," she managed to say. But she knew what MJ was going to say: Someone had come into the store, someone whose eyes met hers, and lightning crackled and—

"What color is his credit card?" Brooke interrupted MJ's breathless narrative.

"Platinum. He's been back a couple of times. We've talked. He asked if he could see me."

One up on me ...

"See you how?" Brooke asked, feeling envious. "Naked? For fast food and a fly-by fuck? For his convenience and your need? For ever and always?"

"I—"

"What are you *getting,* MJ? Not desperate again, I hope. Those guys can scent desperation like a tiger on the hunt."

She hated doing that, but it was as much for her as for MJ. If they weren't careful, they would both sink into the must-have-a-man muck and then the never-ending dissection of why the bastard walked out on them.

"I just want to try him on," MJ said, undeterred. "I think you said that's okay under the Code."

"Is he possible?"

"I don't know."

"How old?"

"Late forties, I'm thinking. Nice, fit, tall, well mannered. Married."

"They always are," Brooke muttered. "So what did you think I was going to say?"

MJ was silent for a moment. "I don't know. Experiment. See if he makes an offer."

"My guess?" Brooke said. "One dinner, one all-night session. He'll promise to call but he won't. And he'll shift his business somewhere else."

54

As would Hugh Steffen, under the same circumstances. He would book another hotel if he ever got involved with her, and she would have lost her hotel all those lovely dollars and massive premium charges for platinum services rendered. But she should keep her mind on MJ's problem, not the potential services that could be rendered to Hugh the God Steffen—by her.

It wasn't a big problem. MJ could have her date, and MJ could have her week of anguish and angst if she must.

"I will adhere faithfully to the Code," MJ promised.

"I'm sure you will," Brooke replied. *She wouldn't.*

"He could be the one," MJ said.

"He could," Brooke agreed. *He couldn't.* It just wouldn't happen that easily. At least as she envisioned it. They were novices still.

But MJ, as always, must learn the hard way.

I should listen to myself.

But this is different.

"Let me know what happens," she said.

"You sure?"

"Sure. I love a good soap opera as much as the next girl." *I'm about to live one—and I don't care about the rules . . .*

Oh, dear heaven, what was she thinking?

MJ was furious with Brooke after she hung up the phone. Brooke had explicitly said that they had permission to try someone on. And MJ had already decided she was going to take full advantage of any man who walked into her life and wanted to treat her right.

She was playing by the rules. Her gentleman had made arrangements to come pick her up. Then he'd asked her to name the restaurant, and she had chosen Le Bernardin.

She'd obsessed for two days over the dress, until she happened on a restrained little black silk Stephen Burrows dress with a sexy oval split at the bodice that had just come into the resale shop. She'd wear the simplest jewelry: a pearl choker—weren't pearls always correct?—with a flash of gleam at the ears. The shoes, strappy silver Christian Louboutin sandals, and a bag to match with a glittering buckle to mirror the earrings.

And then the makeup—how did you look like a lady who wanted to be fucked? She settled on smoky eyes with a more nude, not-so-obvious lip gloss. Sleek hair. No paint anywhere else, toes or fingers. She thought the look was dead-on—smoldering but not trashy, sensual but not flashy—beautiful, elegant, and sexy—everything she felt, while she waited for the urbane and sophisticated Mr. Dallan Baines to come for her.

But two things hit her as she opened the door of her apartment to admit him. The first was that this was a *man* she was dealing with, not some randy, grabby college frat boy. And the second was, this was grown-up stuff. She was dealing with a man of experience and charm who knew how to control his libido and how to play with a woman.

And if he wanted sex . . . ?

Up to you . . .

The thought scared her. What if he really left it up to her whether they tumbled into bed or not? Except he would make it a long, slow, sensual dance of two consenting partners with parameters fully defined—she was certain of it.

Her body felt creamy suddenly, and she went breathless with longing. She yearned for sex with someone who knew what he was doing and how to do it.

"So," he murmured, taking her chiffon shawl and wrapping it around her shoulders. "Charming place."

"Thank you." She didn't know what else to say. When in doubt, be polite and silent.

"You look lovely."

"Thank you."

He had a car waiting.

Oh, God, this was so out of the realm of her experience, her knees went weak as he helped her in and settled her into the luscious tactile leather seats. He guided her from the car and into the restaurant. They were seated immediately at a very nice table.

This was so far beyond her expectations, she felt like swooning. But it was so much better to act as if this were nothing unusual and let him adore her over dinner.

"You are very beautiful," he said as he gazed at her over the menu.

She gave him a faint, shy smile. "So are you."

That made him smile, and he consulted the menu for a long moment. "May I order for both of us?"

"I wish you would," she murmured, afraid of ordering something too expensive. She was pleased to see a look of satisfaction flash in his dark eyes. That was a clue that he liked being in charge and liked that she had immediately deferred to him.

He ordered dishes that she could manage without complication, as if he knew this was all new to her and he was enjoying her moments of delighted discovery.

All the while he made light small talk about business—he worked for a Wall Street law firm quartered uptown—about her life, her interests, things of interest in the news, the newest hit on Broadway.

They ate companionably, leisurely. He fed her some snapper, some foie gras, some wine. He ordered champagne, Krug Clos du Mesnil, and poured for her, toasting the beginning of what he hoped would be a mutually satisfying relationship.

He dipped his fingers in the champagne and brushed her lips with them. She shyly licked them, her excitement mounting. Then she sucked them hard, and that sensual, knowing look flashed in his dark eyes again. He wanted her. She knew that, although with a man like this, she didn't know where the lines were drawn.

This was the moment, as dangerous and fraught as any first date, but with many more levels to the bargain. This was the moment for her, as well—her body was open and creamy for him, and if he touched her, she thought she would just clot and pour into his hands.

He smiled gently. "Let's get the important things out of the way before we go any further. Yes, I'm married, and my family lives up in northern Westchester."

"I see," she murmured. What did she see? Nothing was different, really.

"MJ? Is that a problem?"

"Not at the moment." She sipped her obscenely expensive Krug.

"And beyond?" he pressed her.

"Why?" she dared to ask, her hands shaking slightly. This was way outside her experience, this was a scene she might have imagined, or might have swooned over in a lush 1950s movie, but it was never something that was ever going to happen to her.

"I want to sleep with you—"

Oh, God, little darts attacked her vitals as he said that—

"—and I know these things always start out with good intentions that nobody gets hurt, but they always wind up raw. Especially with someone you've met in a business context. It destroys the business relationship and it kills the personal one. Even if you go into it understanding no one is getting divorced, and this will never lead to anything more permanent, it will happen."

"So why do it?" MJ asked curiously.

"Because I want to sleep with you. And you want to sleep with me." And the unsaid: *Because I can* . . . "And because there's something about you that's irresistible."

This was more familiar territory—the come-on she knew, the one calculated to reel her into his arms, into his bed.

She tilted her head and gave him a considering look. "That's a wonderful line, Dallan. I don't believe it for a moment."

He grinned at her, his eyes lighting with that pure smug male certainty. "*That* is what we must explore, then." He summoned the waiter and the dessert menu over her protests. "You must have something sweet and luscious, MJ. Mousse for the lady." The waiter bowed and withdrew.

"Mousse is for controlling hair," MJ said tartly.

"Let's talk about it," he said practically. "What if we did, what if we slept together—what would be your expectations?"

Oh, Lord, there were no Mistress Club rules for this. Brooke had better make some guidelines; MJ felt like she was drowning in an ocean of *don't knows.*

"What would be yours?" she asked, desperately throwing the question back to him.

He gave her the compliment of seeming to give it some thought, but she was almost certain he'd worked every detail out well before this evening, perhaps even before he'd decided which of all the women he met or worked with he would propose to take to bed—tonight.

"I shouldn't see you at work. I'd give you enough notice so that wouldn't happen."

"That sounds fine." And it would also minimize him seeing her after the affair crashed and burned. Fine with her.

"I consider a relationship like this happily ever *now.* I expect that you will not be looking for a happily ever after from me, because there won't be one."

Anger flared at his presumption and his callousness. "And I don't want one. I'm too young to tie myself down to any man this much older than me. I'm looking to experience everything I can, with as many men as I can. If it seems as if you're growing too attached, I won't hesitate to walk out the door."

She was almost certain he didn't quite like the *as many men as I can* or the *this much older than me,* but all he said was, "Then we understand each other."

She was trembling so hard she could barely think. But she had to feign a sangfroid she didn't feel. "Is there anything else?"

"I want all your free time and your naked body—exclusively."

Did she really want that? Limited to one man with no reciprocity? This minute, she wanted that desperately. The thought of being the exclusive lover of this gorgeous, elegant man made her insides melt. It had been so long . . . And at least he had clarified what he wanted beforehand to avoid misunderstandings.

Or was it just verbal foreplay? Her body was responding as if it were.

But he was dictating all the terms, and that was bad Mistress Code form. How would Brooke want her to respond to that?

"We'll negotiate that after I try you on," she whispered.

He raised an eyebrow. "Try me *on?*"

She was shivering now with her daring. "Dear Dallan, if we don't fit . . ."

"I assure you, we will fit."

She liked the tone of pique in his voice and plunged on. "But I won't know until I have you naked and tight between my legs, Dallan. That's the only way *I* can know."

"So you want my naked penis, do you?"

"To try *on,*" she emphasized. "That's one of my requirements—the fit of a prospective lover is very important to me."

"And what happens if a penis doesn't *fit* your expectations?" he asked silkily but with a slight edge.

She shrugged. How on earth could she be so laissez-faire with this tiger of a man who looked like he wanted to devour her.

"What else?" he growled tensely.

She thought a moment, trying to dredge up the Mistress Code and failing miserably, because the thought of his naked penis reaming her sent every other consideration out of her head. "I expect that you'll have arranged someplace luxuriously comfortable where we can be together, if you meet my expectations."

"That's already been arranged. And my penis *will* meet your every expectation."

"I hope so." Again that little edge to his tone. This sex talk was ramping him up as much as it was her, and she didn't know where she'd found the nerve to say these things to him.

Something in his eyes. Something in her? Maybe the thing he'd seen in her that she knew nothing about, but he did?

Things that made her feel reckless and hot and mindless of what she said to him, as long as she kept his interest piqued and his desire stoked?

She felt . . . powerful. She slanted a considering look at him, playing for a moment to pull herself together, and decided to pitch in and damn the consequences.

"I think we should go now, because any further discussion is useless until I feel you between my legs."

"Oh, this discussion has been very useful, MJ. You've shown me many hidden facets I never expected."

He signaled for the check. "I can't wait. Come. My apartment isn't far away."

Chapter Four

Of course he had an apartment—*that's already been arranged*—close by where he worked and played in the city.

MJ didn't care. She was shaking with her audacity at taking on this man and obliquely questioning his sex, his penis, his vigor.

But she would be on his turf. She'd already gotten the dinner, and if things worked out, perhaps there would be more.

"Do kisses count?" he murmured in her ear as he steered her to a high-rise, high-end apartment building in the east sixties.

"Not as much as other things," she replied daringly.

"Do you kiss penises?"

"I kiss them, suck them, play with them . . . blow them . . ." Words were easy, so easy that they were on the elevator before she grasped fully and for real that she and Dallan Baines were going to have sex, and that she was going to play bitch because she'd started this game and she couldn't let him win that easily.

He had been erect practically since they left *her* apartment, and he had removed his jacket before the elevator stopped, had his key at the ready and his arm firmly around her waist as the doors opened to a plush, subtly lit hallway.

He propelled her toward a door at the end of the hallway, inserted the key with all the care and sensuality he'd use to insert himself into her moments from now, and then he flung open the door to a little jewel box of an apartment overlooking Midtown.

She barely had time to register the details of the designer-furnished living room, the galley kitchen, the vestibule that connected those rooms to the entrance to the bedroom, before he nudged her in.

The room was washed with backlights, the bed was king-sized, covered in Ralph Lauren suede and piled with pillows.

She had made the rules, and she would accept the consequences.

He unzipped his fly and eased out his jutting penis; its shadow sprung out against the wall and it was as if there were two penises seducing her.

"So tell me, MJ—tell me this penis won't fit. Tell me you won't feel me spreading and penetrating you. We may well find that you don't fit *me*. So maybe you should beg me for it."

"Not until I try you on," MJ said firmly. Inside, she was shaking with anticipation, fear, lust, excitement. She had never tormented a lover before, she had never had a lover this sophisticated or this erotically verbal.

"You should be on your knees in gratitude to have a penis this hard at your disposal."

"We don't know that yet, Dallan."

"I know that," he said, easing onto an overstuffed chair and positioning himself so his shaft was limned in the low light.

Her body was already butter soft with need. He was so all there, a thick, long, rigid pole of pure male power beckoning to her to climb onto him and embed him deep inside her.

She slowly stripped off her dress, letting it slide down her naked body into a fluid black puddle at her feet.

His eyes blazed with undisguised lust. She sat on the bed, leaned back on her elbows, and spread her legs so her waxed slit was in full view.

"So Dallan . . . I'm here," she murmured. "I'm naked, I'm ready for you, but," she added coyly, "your penis isn't here."

He made a growling noise. She saw him spurt, and then jack himself out of the chair and onto the bed, still fully clothed.

"What a bitch," he growled in her ear as he mounted her fast and furiously, ramming his hot, throbbing head between her legs hard and deep. "What a tease . . . I like that, I like this game. But I'm going to win . . . am I deep enough yet?"

"Deeper," she breathed, lifting her body agilely against his so he could thrust harder into her.

"Tell me how it feels, tell me if it fits . . ."

"I can't tell." She was panting. "Hold still."

"I can't. Yes or no . . . *now* . . ."

She bucked as he drove into her. "Be . . . still . . ."

"*Tell me* . . ." He poled harder. "*Does it fit?*"

She made a pure animal sound as he jammed himself into her even tighter.

She drew a sibilant breath. "It's perfect," she breathed, arching up to take him even deeper. "Fit, feel, heft, hardness . . . perfect."

"I knew it." He drew back and she braced herself for one last blasting drive. But instead, he pulled away from her spread legs, sat back on his haunches, and looked at her creamy pale body, her hard pebbled nipples, his juices seeping between her legs, the pearl collar around her neck, her tousled red hair and her sex-flushed skin. She was perfection except for that cock-sapping challenge he hadn't expected. "But because you doubted that, you'll have to beg me for it, MJ—or you can just leave."

She stared up at him, at his thrusting shaft still wet with the essence of her, at his hard, adamant expression and simmering eyes, and she felt as disoriented as if she had fallen down the rabbit hole. "*What?!*"

"You have to beg for it now, MJ. I don't give it away to any cock tease I happen to be interested in."

"Are you interested in me?" she breathed.

"I look at that creamy skin of yours and that body and your succulent mouth, and I ache to stuff myself between your legs and live there. I want to be your teacher and your master. I never thought you'd question my prowess. I thought you wanted us to fuck as much as I do. But apparently *only* if my penis fits."

"It fits," she whispered. "I'm hot for you, I'm ready for you."

"*Are* we on the same page, MJ?"

"Anything you want, Dallan, I want it, too," she whispered

tremulously. This was the edge, the brink, and she would never know what he might have planned or proposed. Stupid of her, playing games in which she didn't know the rules when she was horny as hell. He was gorgeous, sophisticated, and well hung, and what the hell was she doing?

"I'd like to believe that." He stroked himself consideringly, and her whole body twinged with yearning.

"Dallan?" That sounded desperate.

"Come and get me, then," he said, "on your hands and knees." He rolled away from her and onto his feet at the foot of the bed.

She lay there, rimming her dry lips with her tongue, considering for one fraught moment whether she wanted his penis *that* much, and then she curled her legs under her and got on all fours.

At that angle, everything that made him a man, she wanted. She didn't care what penance he demanded of her. She moved forward slowly, undulating her hips, her head held high, until she had crawled to the foot of the bed and was within licking distance of his throbbing shaft.

He waited, his hands on his hips. "So . . . ?"

She slanted her head, ducked under his thundering erection, and sucked his scrotum into her hot mouth. She felt the give in his body as she swirled her tongue around his firm balls and sucked and scraped at them with her teeth.

She felt his hands at her shoulders, trying to ease her away, and she burrowed deeper in between his legs, balancing on her haunches now, grasping his stone-hard thighs as she reached beneath his balls to that smooth, secret stretch of skin between his legs and began kissing and suckling at it.

His body went wild under her succulent tasting. She felt the erotic surrender of his hips, and her excitement escalated as she covered that enticing secret part with her hot saliva, her hot sucking kisses.

She heard him growling low, words of resistance, of encouragement. It didn't matter—nothing mattered but that she had him now.

She had him . . . she furrowed deeper . . . she had him—she had him—

And suddenly he had her. He pushed her ruthlessly back on the bed, turned her over onto her hands and knees to cant her derriere upward, and mounted her with a long, low animal growl of pure possession.

"Oh, God . . ." he spurted ferociously and barely got himself under control with iron will. "MJ?"

"Dallan . . ." Her voice was soft and silky with satisfaction.

He pushed deeper and settled his body tightly over hers, so she felt the heft of his sex and the weight of his body on hers. "This is how I want you, MJ. Completely mine and wholly dominated by my lust to possess you. You love being completely at the mercy of a man's sexual appetites. I knew it the first time I saw you. And I knew mine was the penis you've been hungering for. Feel it, so long and strong inside you."

He flexed it and she felt it so deep it touched the nerve endings of her vagina. "You've been aching for a man like me," he whispered in her ear. "You've always wanted to subsume yourself into a man who's stronger than you, and you'll do anything for the pleasure he can give you."

She made a soughing sound. She couldn't move, he was mounted so masterfully on her, wedged so tightly against her, so deeply within her.

He undulated and poled still deeper, as he lifted her more tightly into the cradle of his hips and fucked her with short tight strokes.

She was helpless; she was enveloped by him, utterly consumed by him—and she loved it. Every breathtaking minute of it, every stroke, his total possession, his out-of-control lust for her, his power subjugating her strength—she sank in the thick tide of his cum in his utter greed to fill her with his essence.

Then there was that long lush silence in the aftermath of his release. He covered her wholly, his throbbing penis still in possession of her cunt, his fingers between her legs idly dipping into the thick cream that oozed from between her legs. *His* cream.

"I can't get enough of your cunt." Barely a breath in her ear, but she shuddered at his hunger for her and the feel of him rolling his hips to shove his iron penis still deeper. "I love that you waxed your pubic hair."

She writhed pleasurably and he probed deeper with his fingers.

"I have to wonder how many other penises you would have *tried on* before you found a masterful lover like me, MJ."

"I was waiting for you. I only want you." She felt his deep satisfaction in that response, in the convulsive push of his body.

"Show me." Challenging, sex-charged words, barely audible and in tandem with his fingers smearing her liberally with his cream.

She whispered, "Tell me how."

His body rippled. "Ah, the magic words, MJ."

"Anything you want, Dallan."

"Your naked body open to me in any way I want . . ."

Her body heated up at the lusty implication of his words.

"I want what you want, Dallan," she breathed with a mounting excitement exploding all over her.

"You've always known precisely what I want," he growled as he drove into her. "I knew what you were like the moment I saw you . . ."

He was lusty and raw with her, holding her down so he could splay himself over her body and completely envelop her with his nakedness.

He rode her tightly, with a controlled greed that was utterly consuming. She loved his being in control, taking what he wanted, demanding that she keep him completely enfolded deep inside her.

"I never want to leave," he growled. "This is just the beginning . . ."

She never knew she could feel so much in this obverse position. She never knew a man could ejaculate semen like that time after time. She was drenched in it, bathed in it, rubbed with it, perfumed with it, head to foot.

He wouldn't leave her alone. When she went to relieve herself, he came and took her against the bathroom wall. And on the easy chair with her legs spread over the arms so that she was wide open to him; he buried his mouth, his face deep in her sex, and he held her wrists as the price for her pleasurable silence as he pleasured her with his tongue.

On the floor after, he went into her hot, quick, and hard. Over the edge of the bed, on her back, with her legs on his shoulders and her body canted like a slant board to take his hard, driving possession.

He licked her ear. "You're just the kind of woman I've been looking for."

"What kind of woman is that?" A touch of coyness? She shouldn't.

"You're sensual, compliant, willing, malleable, complicit in your submission to me. You want a lover completely in control."

Did she? "I—" She didn't know.

"Never mind. I'll say it for you. You do. And I'm the man who can exploit that need for our mutual pleasure. I'll give you all the sex you can handle if you give me authority over your body. I think you crave that. But maybe you don't. However, that's how it has to be for me. So, do you want that, MJ?"

She could hardly breathe; every organ in her body went weak. A dominating lover? She felt stifled and overpowered, and she reveled in it. He wanted *her*, to command *her*, to occupy *her*, and to empty himself into *her*—

"I want it," she whispered tremulously.

"Want what?"

She couldn't stand it. "Your beautifully hard, thick, long, luscious shaft possessing me."

* * *

She couldn't share him or their sex with the Mistress Club. Things had escalated so quickly that she didn't know quite where she was anymore. She was seeing him exclusively every spare moment, most of which was spent with his penis deep inside her and her quiescent body taking his hard, driving fucking to her glorious spasmic pleasure.

That meant before she went to work, she went to his apartment for a stand-up quickie. Lunch was more leisurely, but still with that nearly out-of-control edginess with which he took her. And evenings were long hours of food and fornication.

He preferred that she await him naked if he was late. He bought her a set of pearl choker necklaces to wear as a thrall collar to symbolize his sexual authority over her. She was his sex object, his malleable sex doll.

Sometimes he reprimanded her for not keeping his lust for her foremost in her mind, her life, topmost on her list of important things to do. *Run to Dallan whenever he calls, whenever he wants to do you*—first item in the BlackBerry every morning, last thing to do at night, and any five minutes she could find in between.

Her daydreams were full of him, his lust, their pleasure. His sex was addictive. Her need was all-consuming. His possessiveness was engulfing.

She floated in the haze of her enslavement, grateful to be wanted by this strong, commanding, elegant, and desirable *man*.

* * *

Brooke was feeling restless and a little edgy, maybe because it had been three weeks and her Mr. Steffen seemed to have disappeared into thin air.

So much for him.

But even worse, it had been three weeks since MJ had had her first date with Dallan Baines, and she had been mysterious and coy ever since.

She'd blown off yet another meeting of the Mistress Club, the previous two of which had been postponed because she couldn't make it.

"Nothing is happening in our mistress careers. We have to step this up," Brooke told Delia as they lunched without MJ. "I just haven't figured out how."

"I'm not in any hurry," Delia said. "This is fine. This is great, actually. Besides, I don't need another Frank in my life right now. I need a guy who's going to value me."

Brooke stopped eating in midmotion. "Wow," she breathed.

"I know. This has all been head changing *and* life changing."

"So forget the diamond bracelet?"

Delia made a face. "Oh, no, you don't get to change the rules. I'll always take diamonds, whoever's handing them out."

"Let's hope it's that wealthy lover we want to attract. Let's hope MJ's man can give her diamonds. But I think there's something really off about this. MJ's been so evasive. I mean, I understand wanting to keep him to yourself, but she's been supersecretive about him. Which means we'll hear too much about him when it ends."

But, she thought, the longer MJ and Dallan Baines were a couple, the more hope there was that Hugh Steffen might eventually seek her out—a similar casual acquaintance choosing to become something more.

In your fairy tale . . .

The search for the ultimate man would continue. No matter how this turned out, it was way better than bar-bopping, navel-flaunting, mindless, go-nowhere one-night nooky. With a new crop of bare-bellied, Botoxed, size-zero girl graduates swarming all over the place, man-hunting season was on, and they were all baring their breasts and dropping their pants.

But Brooke was as certain as she was of her name that this was *not* the way to go. They had to keep above that. There had to be some other way to get where they wanted to go.

"Well, hello there."

She was so deep in contemplation that she didn't even hear the words.

"Brooke?" Delia's voice penetrated her haze and she looked up.

Omigod. Her blood ran hot. "Mr. Steffen. You're in town." *A stupid, banal comment.*

"Indeed. Booked at another hotel, as it happens."

"So nice to see you," she murmured. What could she say with Delia sitting there with that avid look on her face.

"Definitely good to see you as well," he answered, then nodded to Delia and went on to his table.

"Oh, my goodness," Delia breathed. "*Who* is that?"

"A guest who stays at the hotel," Brooke said. "And sometimes not."

"Well, his eyes sure are staying with you."

I hope so. "Nonsense."

"Still," Delia whispered.

Good. "He's here for business, obviously."

"But he's just the type . . ."

"I know."

"Well?"

"I don't know."

Delia stared at her for a moment, her eyes flashing. "*I* know. You want him."

"Yeah, I do." In spite of everything, in spite of all reason and how stupid it would be.

"Good, because I'm telling you, Brooke, he wants you, too."

So maybe that *had* been a productive lunch, Brooke thought later, sitting at her desk and rifling papers. She had decided that she needed to reorder her thinking. That she was going to stay out of MJ's mess—because she had no doubt it *was* a mess, and that even though Hugh Steffen was in town, she was going to ignore that fact.

Except right now, the eager teenager in her wanted to call every hotel in Manhattan to discover where he was staying.

Oh, my God, cool down! MJ wasn't the only one running amok. And that could put her exactly where MJ was going to wind up eventually.

Except she was much more levelheaded than MJ, and she was much more savvy . . . maybe. MJ's silence about her new situation was making her antsy. Either MJ had come to an accommodation with Mr. Baines, was not seeing him anymore and didn't want Brooke to know, or was having mind-blowing sex and didn't want any of them to know.

But Brooke was certain that if he'd made MJ an offer, they *would* know. So this silence was definitely worrisome.

As were her own hormones, doing belly flops over a distinguished-looking fifty-something Englishman who had no interest in her. Maybe.

I need a plan. I need more rules to cover unexpected men . . . unexpected desire.

Brooke's Contingencies for the Unexpected Man

If you want to sleep with him, sleep with him.

That one's for me . . .

And then what?

Damn. How long did you give the unexpected man to come up with some kind of proposition?

Three weeks. So, MJ—get out.

And what if his proposition didn't include all the things they wanted?

Drop him.

What if you were stupid enough to fall in love with him?

Fall out.

Harsh. But that was for her—for her unexpected man, the one in some hotel not so far away that if she just picked up the phone, she could find out where he was.

Her face burned.

The phone rang. "Guest Relations."

"Perfect." *Him!*

"Mr. Steffen." Her insides instantly heated up, warm and melting in the center. Was that light and disinterested enough? "How can I help you?" she asked, forcing the tremor out of her voice.

"Have a drink with me after you're done there."

She caught her breath, waited a beat before she answered to give it the legitimacy of a quick think over. Why play coy? His time was limited, and in some respects, so was hers, because this could go nowhere. Except—to bed. Tonight. Oh, my heaven—*heaven* . . . "I'd love to."

"Excellent. The Waldorf, the Cocktail Terrace. Six-thirty, say?"

"Sixty-thirty." She slowly hung up, feeling like she'd turned to mush. How efficient he was. How certain he'd been she'd say yes.

No, don't impugn his motives yet. Don't believe that he has a list of ladies he can summon whenever he's in town.

Let's just say he's a very nice man staying at a very nice hotel and he's taking me out for a drink. Period.

Not. This day is never going to end!

She made it end on the dot of five-thirty and raced home to engage in the what-to-wear writhe-and-wriggle. Black was always good. Lauren, always classic. Hair down, up? Makeup—Stila? Smashbox? Restrained? Sultry? Shoes— Manolos? Not so obvious? Bag? He would know a designer clasp at thirty paces, she was sure of it.

This was too short notice. Too fast, too soon. Too delicious. Oh, God . . . jewelry . . . gold was always better than anything. Restrained. Ladylike.

Follow the Mistress Code and you can't go wrong.

Flash your legs, not your belly . . . must remember to write that down. Cleavage, not carnality. Oh, this was good. Hurry.

She raced out of the apartment and grabbed a cab. "The Waldorf." Oh, God, it felt so grown up, so ineffably right to be saying that.

Traffic was awful. If she hadn't had those shoes, those major Manolos, a major weakness, she would have gotten out and walked. As it was, she had to get out on the west side of Park Avenue and cross the street rather than wait for the cab to maneuver through the sea of traffic going toward Grand Central.

Of course, she was late. Not good mistress form. Must add that to the list of "must nots."

Into the cool, exquisite lobby. She looked up and saw him watching for her, leaning over the balcony railing. Her breath caught, and she thought, oh, my God, my heels had better not catch.

To the elevator, and then—there he was as the door opened, tall and elegant, his eyes lighting up at the sight of her. He took her arm and led her as gracefully as Fred Astaire to the terrace and their table overlooking the lobby.

Only when she was seated did she feel even remotely herself. No major mishaps. Just a major assault on her heart as Hugh Steffen smiled at her.

"Hello."

Breathless again. "Hi," she managed. Up close, he was no less a god. Flawless, even with the amusement lines crinkling around his eyes, and that iron gray hair.

"So happy you could make it."

"I'm happy, too," she murmured.

The waiter hovered.

"Shall we have the Cole Porter champagne toast?" He nodded to the waiter. "So my dear, here we are, and you are more beautiful than I imagined."

Melting again. "You imagined . . . ?"

"You have to admit, uniforms are very conducive to fantasizing, especially when someone as lovely as you is wearing one. So bland and constraining. It makes a man wonder . . ."

Oh, this was going so fast, so quickly. Did she want that? *Yes.* She'd thought about him too much over the past weeks. And this was not the time to play games if she wanted him. "And what did you wonder, Mr. Steffen?"

He smiled again. "Hugh, please. I wondered how you would look dressed just as you are now, in silk and stilettos . . ."

The champagne arrived.

"And how you would look *un*dressed . . . in silk and stilettos . . ."

Her body creamed as he looked at her with that light in his eyes. The waiter popped the cork, poured, let him taste, approve, and then poured two flutes and moved aside so that the accompanying hors d'oeuvres could be served.

"Thank you," he murmured, and the servers withdrew. He lifted his flute. "To silk and stilettos, my dear."

She lightly tapped her glass to his and sipped, her body taut as a cello string and playing low notes in her nether parts.

"Here, taste this." Seafood forks had been provided with the hors d'oeuvres; he nipped a small round of puff pastry and held it out to her.

She let him feed her, closing her lips around the tidbit in an unconsciously sensual way. "Umm. Melts in your mouth." She took another as he watched her intently and said, "*I* would like to melt in your mouth."

Oh, God. Darts of desire zinged everywhere. She closed her eyes for a luscious moment, then opened them and met his gaze directly. "I'd like that, too."

"Good, because I haven't been able to get you out of my mind."

"Nor I you."

His eyes lit again. "Good. Let's drink to that."

She knew instinctively there would be no negotiating tonight. Tonight was for celebrating that they felt the same, that her need was as strong as his, and that they would explore that territory—tonight.

She went weak with anticipation. He had fine hands, a fit body, a sensual mouth; the expression in his eyes veered from amused to appreciative at any given moment, and he always seemed to be relishing that moment.

"Come." He nudged her, holding out a forkful of scallop and bacon.

She took it obediently, knowing the look in her eyes said *she* wanted to come—and soon.

"Anticipation is the best appetizer," he murmured. "We have all the time in the world."

You're my *appetizer—delicious and filling and just as quickly gone . . .*

But she shook off that thought and smiled at him, feeling that same delight as the first time she saw him.

Why couldn't it be him?

She knew it wasn't him.

"We know everything we need to know, don't we?" he asked after a moment.

"We do."

"Yes, I rather thought you'd feel that way." He tipped his flute to her. "You're an utter and delectable surprise."

"I'm happy you think so."

"Then shall we . . . ?

She loved how he phrased it, so delicately that it made her breathless just thinking about everything to come that he had not said. She nodded.

He kissed her in the elevator as it rose to the highest floor, whispering against her lips, "Let me melt in your mouth," then did with an expertise that caught her by surprise. The way he licked her and then slowly insinuated his tongue between her lips; his kiss was exquisite, so gossamer in its demand of her.

"We have so much time," he breathed, and she didn't contradict him.

He was quartered in a luxury suite with a sitting room, where he settled into a chair and pulled her down into his lap.

"Time to kiss and fondle." He claimed her mouth again, he stroked her silken thighs, ran his hand all the way down her leg to her toes, slid his hand upward to the hem of her dress and pulled it up over her hips to find what he knew he would find— that she was naked beneath her dress and her body was hot for him. "And to feel the nakedness of you between your legs . . ."

She moved against his stroking hand and made a sound.

"I need to feel your cunt now . . . say yes . . ."

He was so coaxing, so playful about it. His mouth was so seductive and his fingers so caressing, she breathed, "Yes," and canted her body so that his finger could rim her nether lips, part them, and she sank down onto them as he entered her heated body.

Two fingers, three—she gasped as he inserted the fourth, as he pushed into her, twisting and pumping until she was mindless with need.

"There . . . now this pretty pussy is all mine . . ."

Oh, God . . . she rocked against the hard, probing pressure of his fingers, her body wild with rippling pleasure. He could stay there forever—oh, dear Lord, this was a man, with a man's hands, and a man's firm, demanding mouth; it was so outside anything she'd ever experienced . . .

"Pretty pussy . . . so wet for me . . . come for me, pussy, purr for me—"

She could feel each finger separately as he bore into her, could feel his thumb braced on her mound, felt the lushness of her body and the start of the sharp, steep climb to orgasmic oblivion, and she let herself go, let herself slide into a long, slow swoop of molten pleasure.

"Ah . . . ah . . . ah . . . ah!" Him? Her? Both of them, as her orgasm broke over her like a hot pummeling wave?

She pushed at his hand but he wouldn't move it.

"Come, come, come," he crooned, settling her, still with his fingers inserted between her legs, against his erection. "That was so good, pretty pussy. So good."

"Mmmmm," she groaned, writhing away from his invasive fingers.

"No, no, don't do that. I like my fingers in your cunt. Kiss me."

She kissed him, but he instantly took over, his lips settling hard and sensuously on hers as he delved into her mouth and her sheath with simultaneous movements of his tongue and his fingers.

She was on some other plane, a place where only sensation existed, honed to two fine points of pleasure—her mouth and between her legs. All she could do was hang on and let him do what he wanted to do, let him call her his pretty pussy, let him pleasure her however he would. The carnal gratification was that intense, that necessary, and she didn't know how she was going to live without it.

No more unexpected men . . .

Except if they want to fondle and feel your buttocks, those expert fingers sliding up and down her crack, caressing her, feeling her, testing her there—

He was teaching her the prime pleasure points of every part of her body, back, front, inside, outside . . . her body was all honey now, every part of her thickening with uncontrollable lust for him.

He kept kissing her, whispering to her, caressing her bottom and easing downward into her cunt, and then just as slowly and sensuously withdrawing from her and feeling her up to her anus. She swooned as he held her buttocks apart in the most expert way while he felt and probed her there.

"Oh, you are a pretty pussy, just melting in my hands," he breathed against her lips, "purring with pleasure, the perfect pussy." He calmed her as she surged to his seeking fingers. "No, no, no—we have all the time we want . . . come to me, pussy—like that . . ." as he thrust his fingers back into her creaming cunt—"like that . . ." as he penetrated her from the obverse position . . . "like that—and that . . ."

And that and that and that and that—her orgasm didn't stop, her body expulsing her pleasure almost of its own volition. His fingers were everywhere, probing, penetrating, pumping. . . . His mouth devoured her, taking her pleasure deep into himself, not letting her pull away, back away, turn away from what his fingers pulled from her wildly undulating body.

"No more," she gasped.

"But I have to, my pussy."

"No . . . enough . . ." Her voice was barely there; her body was shell-shocked with the shivering aftermath of her racking orgasms. She couldn't move, could barely breathe or respond to his kisses.

He stroked her thighs gently, sensually. "Don't move. Now I get to look at the pussy that produced such a thunderous orgasm."

"Oh . . ." All she could focus on was the feel of his hand fondling her thigh, her buttock.

"It was good for me, too," he whispered as he kissed her again.

Oh . . . uh-oh . . . he was playing with her buttocks again, his fingers sliding and stroking and gently probing her exactly where she wanted him to open her.

"Come, pretty pussy, I'm not done yet. Let's play some more . . ."

Chapter Five

He wanted nothing from her, just the mindless eruption of her pleasure as he explored her cunt and her bottom. Nothing for him—but she felt him pulsing, elongating, poking, almost as if his shaft were an entity separate from him, yearning to get at her.

Hours passed in a haze of lush, wet kisses and hot, thick orgasms. She never knew she was capable of such voluptuous hedonism.

His hands were magic; he knew everything about a woman, everywhere to touch and fondle to prime her. And in between, he held her against his chest, kissing her, murmuring to her, assuring her there was time, so much time.

His penis didn't feel like it wanted to waste much more time. It was making itself felt as he parted her legs yet again to explore her creamy depths.

"Let me . . ." she begged him, sliding her hand along his iron shaft.

"No no no, we have time, I promise you." He penetrated deep again and she bore down on his fingers, giving him what he wanted, giving him her complete surrender to this pleasure.

He had shown her so much more than she knew about herself, about a man, about pleasing a man. This was Mistress Prep 101, she thought. And as long as he wants this, or anything he wants of me, I'm his . . .

"So, my pretty pussy," he murmured after another explosive orgasm, another long, luscious kiss. "Here we are . . ." His fingers still rooted between her legs; she had closed her thighs, trapping them there, and she felt him stroking her deep deep deep, melting her again deep inside. "And I haven't even gotten to your nipples yet."

The words made her cream again. "Get to them."

"Next time."

"When?"

"Tomorrow, straight after you finish at the hotel, if you desire."

"I want it now, Hugh."

He seemed pleased. "Not yet."

She wriggled against his embedded fingers, and he kissed her as he slowly withdrew them. His kiss deepened, taking her down hard against him as he removed his hand from between her legs. He grasped her thigh, he pulled her tighter; his kisses grew hard with a compulsive need he would not give in to.

Not tonight. Tonight was to learn her, to test her passion, her limits, her capacity for pleasure. It caught her by surprise when he finally penetrated her from behind, rimming, inserting his finger, suddenly *there*.

She stopped her assault on his mouth with a startled gasp, her eyes wide.

"Perfect, my pussy. You are perfect."

It was so strange. It was like his finger was the center of the world. The pleasure was so unexpected there, so odd, so—right . . . because it was him, his exploration of her, just one more part of her that now was open to him, for him, and accessible for his pleasure and for hers.

"Don't move. Just feel."

She looked into his eyes and sank into a swamp of voluptuous pleasure as he fondled her cunt and anus, and into his heady satisfaction that she was so willing, so open, with an appetite for every carnal act he performed on her.

"I'll have wet dreams about you tonight and all day tomorrow," he murmured.

"Me, too," she whispered. "Don't stop."

"Not until you explode in my hands one more time."

"It's coming."

"Love it. You have the most luscious pussy. Come for me—*now*."

Powerful words, for her. She was on her hands and knees, with his fingers penetrating front and back so that she could undulate her hips against two powerful pleasure points, with him watching her face as his caresses built in her body, each distinct, sharp, in opposition and the same, coming coming coming . . .

. . . one long last thrust hard against the finger in her anus and she was gone—writhing hard and fast as a belly dancer, seeking the hard rock of her orgasm as she succumbed.

Down down down . . . it was a white water of sensation, rushing gushing flushing her down through the rapids until she sluiced through on the other side.

He pulled her close again, slowly withdrawing his fingers, ignoring the heat and thrust of his penis, kissing her forehead and stroking her shoulders.

She felt bereft without his penetration.

"Tomorrow we'll dine first," he said on a breath.

"I want to dine on *you*," she whispered shakily.

"Strange pussy." There was laughter in his voice. "Adorable, amazing pussy. Gorgeous, delectable pussy. But I'd best not start that again, or I'll be rooting in your cunt and we'll be hours at it and no work will get done tomorrow. Which is problematical now, since I've found you. My pretty pussy will occupy all my thoughts tomorrow. I don't think I can wait till evening—do you suppose you could do lunch as well as dinner?"

"I'll do whatever you want," she whispered.

"You know what I want, pretty pussy."

"I want it, too."

He took her again, front to back, held her in the steamy aftermath, then helped her dress and right herself, and sent her on her way with a car service.

At her apartment building, she stood watching the limousine lights recede, and only then did she enter, moving slowly, sensuously, feeling every inch of her body.

What exactly had happened tonight?

The unexpected man had happened. New ideas, possibilities, sensations had happened.

Beyond that, she didn't want to explore. Didn't want to share.

Now both she and MJ had sexual secrets, and had willingly, knowingly, defiantly hooked up with men whom they already knew were bound to leave them.

Delia loved her job, and if the Mistress Club never got off the ground, if she never found someone to keep her and shower her with orgasms and offerings, she wouldn't much care.

She couldn't have imagined a life this exciting even a year ago. Then she was hanging on by her fingertips to her sanity, her scholarship, and the last vestiges of her futile love for the emotionally abusive Frank.

Thank God Brooke had dreamed up this fairy tale. Delia wasn't a dumb blonde—she understood, even in the depths of her despair, that finding a wealthy lover in Manhattan was every bit as much a fairy tale as Sleeping Beauty.

But the idea had galvanized them, had given them something to hook their imaginations to that would drive them toward an end. And Brooke was a genius for how she'd sold it to them. Control of their sex lives, getting something for what they routinely gave away—it had made perfect sense.

Their quest had given them focus, gotten them super jobs, nice apartments, and entrée to the coveted single life in Manhattan. Life that could swing in twenty different directions depending on what you wanted and how fast and how far you were willing to go.

She had had her share of propositions since she'd been at the restaurant. She'd heard her share of stories about the *beyond* night life, the secret sanctums where everything was possible. She knew, having shamelessly eavesdropped, where celebrities converged, wound up, unwound, danced, and drank, and she'd had invitations to join the orgasmic floating party.

But she hated partying. She was a homebody, a nurturer, even though she was the first of her family to attend college. She'd realized early on that she couldn't fix her family, she only could fix herself; but it had taken her longer to comprehend that she couldn't have fixed Frank. But back then, she'd been so desperate for any morsel of affection that she had held on to her idealized vision of their relationship like a lifeline.

Thank God for Brooke. Brooke had given her a life.

"Good evening. Do you have a reservation?" She was wearing a floor-length vintage gown tonight that she'd found in the East Village, which went surprisingly well with her up-to-the-minute hairstyle.

She smiled at the customers, took their names, showed them to their table, and settled them in. Nice people, elegant people, people who were getting to know her—people who were regulars, who never failed to stop for a moment's conversation with her.

God, she loved this job.

The phone at her station rang.

"Good evening, how can I help you?" She knew she sang into the phone, but she'd been told customers loved the lilt in her voice.

"Is this Delia?" a strange male voice asked.

She stiffened. "This is she."

"This is Bill."

Bill? It took her a moment. Bill of six months ago in the skybox? "Bill—?"

"The Garden, the skybox . . . I hope you remember . . ."

How could she not remember? All that luscious head cream. "Bill, how nice to hear from you. But I'm at work now, so I really can't talk."

"Where *can* we talk, and when?"

He was eager and that was promising. But she hadn't thought he was Mistress Club material. Obviously he'd been thinking about her, and he'd gone to the effort of finding her. All good things. And she'd really enjoyed blowing his penis.

"Well, I'm here until midnight. If you're willing to wait until then, we could have a drink at the Cellar Bar."

"I'll wait. When?"

She looked at her watch. "Twelve-thirty is the earliest I could get there."

"Can I come there?"

"No."

"All right. Cellar Bar, twelve-thirty."

"Good," she said and hung up. Better than good.

So he really wanted to see her again, even if it had taken him this long to find her. And he had a really long, hard penis. And she *was* feeling like she wanted some again. So Bill's call seemed fortuitous, destined even.

Maybe.

You never knew, when you blew a guy, what he was thinking. Not that it mattered when it was a one-shot, one-night blow. But wow . . . six months later—

She saw him immediately when she walked into the bar. He was dressed well in a Brooks Brothers suit, and he was nursing a beer. He must have felt the shift in the air because he looked up, got up, and came to greet her.

"Delia."

"Bill." Like they were long-lost relatives or something.

"Let's get a table and some privacy."

When they were settled in a far corner and had ordered, he leaned into her and said, "You're even more beautiful than I remembered."

"I think what you most remember is that I gave you a beautiful blow job," Delia said.

He nearly choked. "Yeah, that I remember."

"So because of that, here we are. How did you find me?"

"A lot of trial and error. I found out who held those seats and called the hotel office, but no one knew you. I left a message that if someone did know you, would that person call me back. Did that for about two months and finally heard from an assistant there. And all she'd give me was your work number."

Good for Brooke. Delia smiled at him. "You went to a lot of trouble."

"You're that kind of woman."

The drinks came, beer for him, club soda for her.

"What kind of woman is that, Bill?"

"Beautiful, seductive, aware of your power. You know the score. You're easy to be with."

Meaning I'm easy, Delia thought.

"I'd like to be with you sometimes."

Delia felt a familiar sensual twinge. She knew what it meant, too. It meant she could very easily succumb to wanting to take care of this guy's needs. She felt the urge; it had been too long since she had a penis of her own. But *be with you sometimes* was about as vague as a married guy on the prowl could get. He needed to put something on the table.

She twirled her straw for a moment, then looked at him from beneath her lashes. "How would that work, exactly?"

"Dinner now and again. Sex . . ."

"Where?"

"I get the skybox to myself every month or so—you can't get more private or luxurious than that."

"It was nice," she agreed. "I really enjoyed that."

"Let's enjoy it on a regular basis, then, no strings. I'll call when I'm available; you decide if you want to come. So to speak."

I'd love to come. Just not like this.

"We could see how it goes," she said, opting for having *some* sex.

"That would be good," he said instantly. Whatever she wanted, however he could get her there. She saw it in his eyes. He wanted a sex partner on call; more than she wanted to give, for the return she'd get.

Not good Mistress Code.

He wasn't offering her anything, really, except a cool environment in which to have sex—*now and again.*

It wasn't enough. But maybe she'd choose to have one more encounter with him. One more encounter with his already engorged penis.

If she looked at it that way, she'd still be getting something; she'd still be on his turf, and at least she'd have some satisfying anonymous sex.

Maybe that was exactly what she needed at this moment.

"Dallan . . ." MJ's back was against the wall, and his penis was deeply embedded in her while he simultaneously suckled and tweaked her nipples.

He grunted. "Shhhh . . ." He pulled on the hard tip and her body convulsed. "Such a sweet hard tit. Love that tit . . ." His mouth grazed the other one as he pressed himself even deeper.

MJ moaned and held him tighter as he stroked the hard tip with his tongue, exultant in the knowledge that he invariably lost his iron control when he fed on her nipples. This time was no exception—his bucking body swerved out of control, pouring his thick, hot semen into her in the long dark hallway to his apartment where he had taken her fast and hard because, yet again, he couldn't wait.

They were both panting when he finally got back in control. "I can't believe what you do to me," he muttered, pulling up his trousers and tucking in his shirt. "Look at what you do to me."

"I love everything you do to me," MJ whispered.

"Good. Let's fuck again. Come on—"

They raced down the hallway to his apartment door, and he grabbed her suddenly and pushed her down to the floor. ". . . *Here.*" He ripped open his trousers. His penis erupted, hard, hot, and ready.

"Spread your legs." It was a command.

She raised her skirt and parted her legs and let him drive into her mercilessly, the way he always did after the first fuck when he always lost control in her.

Now he was in control, the way she adored him—heavy and hot, thick and filling. She was bound by his desire, a slave to his hunger for her nakedness. Theirs was a mutual surrender into a thick, lulling swamp of on-demand sex.

He lay over her, heavy, panting, his release trickling out around his still embedded penis. "God, MJ."

"I know," she whispered. This was too much and too good.

She willingly subsumed herself into his limitless and incessant desire for her. She loved being *his,* loved his naked body, his thick bulbous member, his luscious honeyed kisses, loved his desire to walk the razor's edge of exhibitionism and defiance with her body.

She loved his sweat, the scent of his sex, the taste of his cum, the feel of his hefty shaft penetrating her.

"God, I can't stop . . ." His body always went wild, his hips grinding and pushing into her, as if he wanted to shove the whole of himself between her legs.

She feared he'd consume her utterly, his lust was so blindingly overwhelming sometimes. She didn't feel the friction or the heat, she felt only his engorged penis taking and taking, until she could give no more. Only then did he allow himself to let loose, when she could have sworn he didn't have a drop left in his body. And yet there it was, trickling between her legs, leaving her sapped and limp.

She would be so clotted with his cream, so satiated that she never wanted to move, and all the while his shaft moved, stretched, and elongated again.

"Oh, look, MJ. Erect again, just looking at your creamy nakedness. Spread those cunt lips."

"Dallan," she started to protest; she was raw, she was tired after hours of copulating. But he was her unbelievably expert and commanding lover, and she couldn't deny him her body. Nor would he let her.

He eased himself into her precisely at her vaginal opening, just to let her feel his thick erection. "It's insane how you do this to me."

"I love that *I* do it to you," she murmured.

He cupped one taut-tipped breast. "And your tits get so tight and hard every time. I never get tired of fondling your nipples."

I do. What? What was that insidious thought? No, it was just that they got irritated with all that tweaking and compressing. But she loved his bulbous head tucked into her just *there. . . .* That aroused her almost as much as his passion.

Not.

Nonsense!

Don't move. I can't take another lunge into my insides. No, I love his shaft kissing my cunt lips.

Not.

She shook her head. *What am I thinking?*

"MJ?"

He had said something and she'd missed it. Damn. "Yes, Dallan?"

"You heard me. I'm ready to fuck." He rolled onto her and shoved deeper.

"Yes, Dallan," she murmured, bending her knees to accommodate her lover, who was wild for her sex, her heat, *her*. Yes, Dallan. Whatever you want, I'm totally yours to do with what you will. Yes yes yes . . .

BROOKE'S RULES FOR THE UNEXPECTED MAN

Sleep with him if you have to.
If he offers nothing after three weeks (two weeks? one
    day? one night? one hour?), lose him.
Do not not not fall in love.
If you think you're falling in love, fall out.
If he persists, tell him what you want.
If he thinks you're nuts, leave.

Brooke stared at the list on her computer screen. *Could I be that callous with Hugh?*

Never.

Nevertheless, there had to be rules. You had to have a plan, because nothing ever worked out the way you thought it would, no matter how you planned for the contingencies.

Look at *her*. Affluent family, always enough money, the best schools, reasonably popular, had a social life, was academically superior, parents divorced when she was thirteen, but they'd stayed together for *her* sake.

Her sake? Hardly.

They'd lived at opposite ends of their huge apartment

overlooking Lake Michigan, never seeing each other. One of them could've died and the other not know it, living in that hell they'd created for themselves. And her.

Trapped in the middle, she had escaped into alcohol and fumbling teenaged fucking. Thank God she'd had a friend who was aware of which doctor to go to for protection from her worst instincts.

She had been in an alcoholic haze most of her freshman year. She'd slept with most of the football team (but so had everyone else), and then she woke up one day and found the good sense finally to straighten out her life, realizing that she was the only one she could rely on to save her.

So she'd taken control, making lists so that everything was planned out with a reasonable supposition of what the outcome might be, so she couldn't ever be blindsided again.

That was how she'd run her life for the last six years: setting goals, attaining them, and crossing them off her list.

Sleeping around wasn't high on that list. Going to college far away was. Coming to Manhattan was. The Mistress Club was an idea out of nowhere that shunted her onto an entirely different track.

And who could have planned for the unexpected man? That had been totally off the radar, too. How did you deal with him? You fucked him and then bid him farewell, because he'd do the same to you.

A man who has no commitment to you has no investment, she thought. He has nothing to lose, and he's been getting you in exchange for nothing.

How stupid.

So what determined when the unexpected man became the meaningless man?

Three weeks? Three weeks, you're on call, he's not, and he's getting everything, and you're getting foie gras, fucked, and no future?

Dumb.

And he's told you that in advance?

Even dumber.

Hugh Steffen hadn't yet told her so, but she knew. And even knowing that, she'd gone back to his hotel room the following afternoon, dressed in her hotel uniform that so captivated his imagination.

He met her at the door in his dressing gown, barefoot, his shaft protruding long and strong from the silk of his robe.

"Oh, my dear pussy, I can't wait to strip you."

"I can't wait to see you." She reached for him.

"No, no, not yet. Come, food first."

"Let me eat you first," she begged him a little breathlessly. His tantalizing penis poked out like a tent pole.

"You're a brazen pussy, my dear. How can a man resist? Especially when time is of the essence . . ." He led her to the chair where he had so expertly fondled her the previous night, sat and spread his legs slightly, and opened his robe.

His shaft jutted out, thick, throbbing, and hard, more of him than she could have imagined. His scrotum sacs were taut and bulbous. His body was sleek and toned.

She knelt between his legs and took his pliant head in her mouth and pulled on it, hard. His body jolted with pleasure, and she took him then—fast and hard, sliding, pulling, nibbling at the shaft, the head, sucking him with lip-smacking sounds of lustful enjoyment.

He spurted and she took his spunk into her mouth, then pulled mercilessly at his head until he surrendered, spewing hot and creamy into her. She held it in her mouth for as long as she could, then she let it seep back onto his pulsating shaft.

She climbed onto his lap, raised her skirt, and straddled him so that her nakedness fit tightly onto his cream-coated shaft, and she guided his hands to her bottom, to her crease, to her newfound point of pleasure. He inserted his finger there, and she rode him in rhythm to his stroking to a melting, molten orgasm.

"Such a versatile pussy," he murmured in her ear.

"We don't have much time."

"There's always time," he assured her. He shifted her onto her knees and guided her over his rigid shaft; she eased herself onto him, deeply down onto him, until he was so perfectly embedded that she felt his head touching home.

When will time run out?

Not today . . .

They rocked together like longtime lovers. He kissed her creamy mouth, stroking her with his tongue, tasting himself on her, tasting their scent, their sex on her lips and deep in her mouth.

The feel of him between her legs was indescribable. He was so long and strong, she felt as if he were her center and she was undulating around it and over it. She rubbed it and bounced on it and cradled it deeply and lustfully between her legs, and she never wanted him to withdraw from her.

He angled his hips up, poling into her in an unexpected tight thrust that caught her just as her body craved that—and she shot up into a rocketing orgasm that was a series of sharp, hard explosions of pleasure into which he shot his wad.

Time is running out.

Time enough for him to savor his staying power within her. "Such a luscious pussy. I need to caress it and kiss it."

"I need to go back to work," she murmured.

He sighed. "Ever the way."

"But not quite yet." She needed to keep his penis embedded in her for a few more minutes.

"You'll let me pay homage to your incredible honeypot tonight."

But what about all the nights after tonight?

A forbidden thought. Tonight would be enough.

Was it?

Now she was panicking. How long was he here for, anyway? What if he were leaving tomorrow? What would she do?

She wanted him insanely. He was everything a would-be mistress desired. He had to want her that much, too, or she would die.

Now she was hysterical. No one died from losing a lover whom she never really had in the first place. What did she really know about him? He was handsome, elegant, amusing, English, and he knew exactly a woman's secret pleasure points.

So she had handed over her power and her sex to this irresistible man with his irresistible words and his irresistible penis.

Against everything she had advised everyone else to do, because she couldn't resist the opportunity to have a distinguished older lover with potential and a still lusty desire to copulate.

The *potential* part was the problem.

We don't need to know anything more, do we? he'd asked almost immediately, effectively cutting off any questions and demands.

What a canny man. He'd worked her slowly, sensuously, bringing her to a sinuous, explosive pleasure that was so alluring, so voluptuous, any woman would instantly capitulate.

Meantime, he got all the sex he wanted and he got to walk away, unexpected man morphing into meaningless man, leaving her with memories and postmortems.

A man like Hugh Steffen, with resources, charm, wealth, and a hardy need for sex, *ought* to make a commitment to a mistress. Yet why would he need to? Women were too ready to be screwed over. Even she, for all her good sense and her lists and her plans for every possibility, even she had succumbed to his beguiling charm, his smile, his mere presence in the world.

She hated herself for it—but nothing was going to keep her from going back to his hotel room that night.

Bill called Delia again the next day. She wondered how hard he had worked his corporate partners to make the skybox available that night. It was amusing to picture him going through his office, promising the earth to anyone whose turn it was to attend the game.

No, it wasn't. It was kind of sad, actually. And it wasn't what she wanted, and it certainly did not fit with the Mistress Code. *Get, not give . . .*

She must clamp down on those instincts to take care of someone needy.

Just this night. And she would ask him his intentions. Brooke was so right: A place of one's own, an adoring lover who put you there, true appreciation for what you were to him and what he was to you—that made sense. No emotional nonsense, just a mutual connection with no mess on either side.

Tonight, she thought, was going to be messy.

Nevertheless, she met him in front of the Garden sign, already thick with fans, scalpers, and rushing-home commuters by six o'clock. He wanted to give them time to "get comfortable," he said. Talk a little, have some food, a drink. Get to know each other a little now.

She thought not. She'd thought perhaps she could reject him on looks alone, but he was as attractive as ever, and so keyed up that this luscious blonde in her tight Calvin suit and Manolo stilettos was with *him* tonight.

She was not immune to his excitement; it stimulated every sensual nerve in her body, and she felt that twinge of arousal that she had to ignore. She was just too susceptible to the thought of sex, and especially sex with a man whose penis was as strong and robust as his.

She couldn't let it happen. She'd fuck him, if matters

came to that, but unless there was something else for her after this encounter, she'd bid his penis good-bye.

They waded through the crowd and up to the upper tier of the Garden. The seats were already filled, the noise was deafening, but once he got her in the door of the private box, everything was quiet, muted, sexy.

The lights were low. Finger food was already set out and the bar stocked.

He'd been up here already, making certain there would be no interruptions.

"A drink?"

"Club soda."

"Come on."

She smiled. "I need to keep my head clear."

"I'm hoping to make you lose your head."

He poured a beer, handed her a club soda, and guided her to the couch. "So here's to—"

"Let's just toast to the moment, Bill."

"To the moment." They sipped, and he set aside his beer. "I want to spend this whole evening with you naked."

Damn, that twinge again. "Me naked, or both of us naked?" she asked, stalling for time. The thought made her hot.

He was shucking his jacket, his trousers. "I'm there." His shaft thrust out at her, long, deliciously rounded and swooping upward, tactile and seductive. He stood and moved in front of her to place himself directly at her mouth.

Too irresistible. She had to touch the head, had to stroke the smooth underside of it, just *had* to take his pliant bulbous head in her mouth—because she loved when a man ejaculated from her sucking him off.

"You are amazing." His voice was raw with need and pleasure. "You are—I want to fuck you. I want you naked on the sofa. I want—"

"I know," she crooned soothingly. "Let's rest a minute, let's get you protected." She dug for the rubber she always carried with her. No foreplay necessary; she was already primed.

He undressed her, she dressed him for action, and in three minutes she was on her back, and he was slowly and sensuously pushing himself into her, her body arching involuntarily with pleasure as he squeezed between her legs and held himself there for a long erotic moment.

And then he drove and she met his thrust and exploded. She hadn't expected such a highly charged coupling that she would orgasm in thirty seconds. It was going to make it much harder to deal with him in the aftermath.

She felt as if she were standing outside herself, watching as he reared back so that their bodies remained connected solely by his penis inserted into her. He looked like a crowing warrior, and she was the spoils of his conquest rather than the seductress who had subjugated him with her sex.

This coupling was his victory, not her seduction, which left no room for any negotiation. Bill had already put her down in the charge column that read *convenience:* free for the asking when it was good for *him,* with his company picking up the tab.

It killed her ardor faster than a gallon of cold water.

She wriggled out from under him with a pang of regret that she'd never get to fondle him again.

"What? What's wrong?" He reached for her and caught her ankles as she was swinging her legs over the edge of the couch.

"That was very nice," she said. "But I'd like to discuss my needs before we go any further."

That deflated him. "What do you mean, your needs?"

"Well . . ." How did she put this nicely? "If we are going to have sex on a regular basis, I need things. An apartment. A clothing allowance—"

"Why?" he sneered. "You'd always be naked."

She ignored that. "A schedule of when you'd be available. A diamond bracelet, dinner out . . . Perhaps we could travel together."

"I'm married," he growled through gritted teeth.

"Yes," she said soothingly, "I know that. And while this is a lovely place to screw around once in a while, it wouldn't do at all if we were together. I'll need a place just for us if you want to continue to have sex with me."

"You're a whore."

"No, but I know my value, Bill." She began putting on her clothes in a way that she hoped made him horny, just to show him what he was giving up. Just to show him she had some power. That his name-calling, his disappointment, his rage, meant nothing to her.

"In this situation, you have all the nuts," she went on, daintily sliding on her skirt, her jacket, her sky-high heels. "I need some nuts, too, Bill, and those hanging between your legs, while they're lovely and quite delicious to suck, aren't commensurate with the value you're getting from me. And that's not even counting the fact your company's paying for the food and accommodations."

"You stinking whore."

She shrugged. "Whatever. I really enjoyed having sex with you, Bill, but I think we're done."

"Cock tease. Bitch!"

She sent him a leveling glance, picked up her pocketbook, and paused at the door. "I *am* sorry. You're so cheap. I really enjoyed sucking you off, if that makes any difference to you."

She walked out into the roaring crowd of fractious fans just as the Rangers scored.

It was an apt finish. After all, what had this been but a game? And Bill had scored and she had not.

Chapter Six

Delia called Brooke the minute she got home. "I need an emergency meeting of the Mistress Club. I did something awful, stupid. Maybe it wasn't, I don't know, but I just have to have input. Brooke, *call me back*."

Brooke was lying in Hugh Steffen's arms after hours of sensuous foreplay and no foreskin action. But this was perfectly fine, cuddling in his big hotel bed in the dark, feeling, licking, sucking, teasing, kissing.

She had worn a slinky Randolph Duke halter dress with nothing beneath and ankle-strap stilettos, which were the only thing she still had on. The rest he'd taken off thirty seconds after she entered the room.

She had eaten dinner naked. Not that she'd eaten; he was more appetizing than the appetizers. He did naked very well, indeed. He was engorged to bursting and she wanted to smear the crème brûlée and caviar all over him and lick it off. She wanted to do a hundred sensual things to him, and he just sat there eating and making small talk while her lust for him escalated exponentially.

How sadistic was that?

"Hugh."

"Yes, my pussy?"

"Didn't you say something about—"

"Later, my pussy. We have all the time in the world tonight."

She felt as if time was slipping away and there was no time for sex, to get things straight, or to come to an arrangement.

Maybe that was why she felt antsy tonight. This man was so out of her league that she didn't know how to handle things.

She took a sip of wine. She was breathless with a voluptuous yearning to feel his penetration. She didn't care where, which way, or how.

"Come to my bed, my pussy. It's time."

He sat against the headboard and motioned her to straddle his legs facing away from him.

"Spread your legs for me so I can feel up your pussy," he whispered in her ear. She angled her legs, pulling them up tight against her body. She felt his shaft thick and throbbing against her buttocks, felt both his hands sliding down either thigh, felt her body melting like chocolate as his fingers grasped her nether lips and parted them. Felt him dip into her with two fingers, three, four, thrusting, dipping, sliding, feeling . . .

"My darling pussy is thick with honey," he breathed against her heated skin. "I've never had pussy so clotted with honey as yours."

The words thrilled her, aroused her, made her push to feel his fingers deeper and deeper still.

"Let me just play with your pussy."

"I can't . . . I can't—I need . . ."

"I know, my pussy needs her penis. But I need to dip into my honeypot, I need to feel the honey you make for me."

"Yes-s-s-s . . ." as he pumped her between her legs. "Oh, yes . . ." And she went mindless, seduced by the feel of his fingers, the sensations he provoked, the sibilant sex sounds he whispered in her ear, the feel of his tongue licking the curve of her neck, and his fingers pulling her cunt lips still farther apart . . .

So good—such insane pleasure . . . feelings as thick as molasses coursing slowly through her veins, through her, becoming her until all there was of her was her hot, slick, pulsing center.

She rode his fingers, pumping her in the moist heat of her cunt. And then—*now now now* . . . the firecracker of an orgasm caught her by surprise. Hot lights exploded all over her body, inside her body, and she frantically wrung every last flash point of pleasure from his thrusting fingers.

He wasn't done. His fingers still played with her between her legs, but *she* was done. She needed nothing else from him.

Except—

He knew. There was a hot peak when he could no longer withstand his own need, and then he rolled her onto her back, mounted her and took her, sliding into her aroused wet heat like it was home.

"There's my pretty pussy, the best of all the pussies," he crooned, swooping in for a long, breathless kiss. "I adore luscious, hot pussies like yours."

He rode her hard and high. Unbelievably sensitized by all his fondling, she felt everything more intensely, more keenly, more pleasurably, and her orgasm broke over her like the tide, radiating long and slow from deep in her womb until it cracked all over his pistonlike thrusts and brought him home.

Perfect.

So perfect.

. . . What did he say about pussies?

Don't think. Just hold him, just feel him.

Tomorrow I'll think . . .

She couldn't think anyway, with his penis nudging her, thick with lust.

"More," she whispered. "Lots more."

He licked her lips. "Whatever my perfect pussy desires."

Brooke lost count. Four times? Five? His stamina was impressive. Time flowed into timeless hours. She was going to be late for work. She'd have to sneak into the office and change into her spare work suit. And she absolutely needed to examine those comments of his, though she didn't quite remember what they were.

It didn't matter. He still held her in the aftermath of this final coupling, his shaft resting in his lap.

The quiet was soothing. He wasn't sending her away, not yet. He would propose something; how could he not?

What had he said about pussies?

He stroked her hair, murmuring sensually . . . *pretty pussy, perfect pussy, the best of all the pussies . . .*

There.

That. *The best of all the . . .*

How *many* pussies?

Don't think about that . . . yet . . .

"I'll be leaving tomorrow," he murmured into the darkness.

"What?" she murmured drowsily.

"I'm going back home tomorrow."

"Oh. Oh?" Her heart started pounding. The moment was here suddenly, sooner than she expected it. Maybe he wasn't going home—maybe he was just ending this, maybe there was someone else in the wings. Or in another town. Or coming to him right here hours from now . . .

Damn. How could he end it? They were extraordinary together. She didn't want to lose him. But there was nothing she could say; he'd forestalled that.

We don't have to know anything more, do we?

And now she wanted to know everything.

It was a fifty-fifty moment—he'd make an offer, or it was over.

"It had to come, my dear."

"Of course." She kept her tone as neutral as possible.

Ask me . . .

"Of course I'll be back stateside again, though I don't know when yet."

"Of course."

"So—may I call you when I come?"

Everything tilted, and Hugh Steffen morphed into meaningless man.

She gathered the last shreds of her pride. "Of course," she

said calmly. "I'll always be happy to consider having sex—if I'm available."

"That's perfect," he murmured into the darkness. "Just the way it should be."

"I totally agree," she said. "A recreational penis can be just what a woman wants sometimes."

"I knew you were that kind of pussy. I'm so happy I found you; I really enjoyed fucking you. A young woman's sex is just luscious."

Did he think that would appease her? She was shaking with anger and something she couldn't define as she gathered up her clothes.

"Shall I send for the car now?" Always the gentleman.

"If you'd call a cab, I'll be fine," she managed through gritted teeth.

He flicked on a light and called the concierge. "Ten minutes, pussy dear. Take your time dressing."

She headed for the bathroom, closed the door gently, sat on the toilet, and refused to cry.

MJ, it's Brooke. We're having lunch tomorrow instead of next week, and it's mandatory you be there. We have things to discuss. No excuses.

They had just walked into her apartment, and Dallan had settled himself on the couch and was looking around while MJ listened to her voice mail.

"Who the hell is Brooke?"

She closed her eyes wearily. This would involve long, detailed explanations.

This was the first time she'd brought Dallan back to her place since they'd started seeing each other. No, sexing each other.

No, since Dallan had taken over her life.

She took a deep breath. "My college roommate. Before you and I met, we used to have lunch once a month."

"Your only standing lunch date is with me."

"I know that, Dallan."

"So how can this Brooke think you can just drop everything for some *mandatory* lunch because she has, or maybe *you* have, *things to discuss*?"

MJ swallowed. "Maybe she's in trouble, or Delia's got some problem. I won't know unless I go."

"You have no need to go. I'm all you need."

"Yes, you are, Dallan. No one could ever want more than you, if she were fortunate enough to be the woman you chose."

"Then why would she want to abandon me for her friends?"

"She wouldn't. She just hasn't seen them recently. It might be nice to—"

He grasped her wrist. "No, I don't think that's nice. Nice is not abandoning me and my needs to take care of someone else's needs. Nice is not wasting my cream when I'm hard for you every day, all day. You know what would be nice? If you just took off your clothes and sucked me off right now."

And she did it. She shucked her suit and her underthings, and she knelt between his legs and willingly swallowed his cum as he jerked off in her mouth.

"Nobody does it like you," he growled. "Come—let me fondle you."

She climbed onto his lap and let him run his hands all over her body, let him penetrate her and stroke her and calm her. This was a gentler Dallan—the one who was considerate and kind, who was always sorry when he spoke too roughly to her or was too abrasive.

She loved these moments when he was soft like this.

But the voice mail message had distracted her. The words still sat in the air between them. He knew she was thinking about it. She couldn't help it: Brooke was never that preemptory, Brooke didn't demand.

Something was up.

Dallan's shaft was *up*—again.

"Cunt time—*now*."

She got up obediently, straddled his legs, and sank onto him as he pulled her tight against his chest and rocked himself deeper into her.

"This is what's important," he said. "My penis, your cunt, my pleasure. Who can give you what I give you, MJ? Not your so-called friends—unless they have penises, and if they do, then you're a fucking bitch, a brazen liar, and a whore-cunt, and I *will* wash my hands of you."

"No, no—it's not like that, Dallan. Honestly, it's just my college girlfriends. Brooke and Delia."

"You know what?" He pushed her off his shaft, pushed her away altogether. Got up, leaving her curled on the sofa, all righteous irritation because this one afternoon he couldn't fuck her, and he gave her permission.

"You go to that lunch, MJ. You enjoy that lunch with your so-called *friends* and then come back and tell me all about it, and *I'll* decide whether it was a waste of your time and the ejaculate I could be spending in you."

"I hereby call this meeting of the Mistress Club to order."

They were ranged around their table at the Park Avenue Café, and the maître d' was kind enough to say it had been a while since he had seen them.

Brooke felt exhausted, MJ looked weary, and Delia looked troubled.

"We have lots to talk about," Brooke said, "and not nearly enough time. So we had better start fast and finish soon. Delia?"

"Well, the thing is, I don't know if I did the right thing—about Bill, I mean." She looked at Brooke. "You gave him the phone number, right?"

"I did. I figured it couldn't hurt."

"Well, I hurt him—I think. Maybe not. I mean, the Mistress Club is kind of a theory, right? So when you get down to it, when you have someone interested, then what do you do? Especially if he's made arrangements for the rendezvous and expects you just to fall in with his plans and his convenience."

Brooke said, "Well, I've been formulating some rules for that because I've become painfully aware that we have to deal with that problem. But—what happened with you?"

Delia told them, in explicit detail, including the jaw-dropping maintenance requirements she'd outlined to

Bill—"honestly, right off the top of my head"—and his reaction.

"You *rejected* him?" MJ said, awed.

"I did, but in the bitchiest possible way. And now I'm feeling—"

"Don't," Brooke said instantly. "You did absolutely the right thing. The thing I wish *I* could have done it the minute . . ."

Their eyes swerved to her in unison, and she saw she couldn't hide, couldn't dissemble about her own experience. "Okay, confession time. I was approached by one of our hotel guests—the gentleman who stopped at our table, Delia, during our last lunch?"

Delia caught her breath. "Oh, but he was—"

"Yes, he was. A very well-traveled and well-troweled businessman from England who collects gullible women. I fell for him like a lead balloon. I thought the sex was so mind-blowing over the course of our two-day affair, that he'd be scrambling to make an offer."

"And did he?" Delia asked.

"No. He made a fool out of me. He just wanted another number to call next time he's in town and he's horny. He collects pussies. Loves his pussies. Said I was the best of all his . . . He actually *said* that during—" She let out a distressed sigh. "He probably says that to everyone. God, but he was good. I was so naïve. And he's not nearly worthy enough if he needs the novelty of a new body every time he's stateside." She thinned her lips. "It won't be me next time. But then, he probably never calls any of them again. What a bastard."

The waiter arrived and they ordered their usual fish and salad, with iced tea. Nobody was hungry. MJ looked miserable.

"I know you have a story, too," Brooke said to her. "Dallan Baines hasn't offered you anything, has he?"

"He's freaking because I'm having lunch with you guys. Usually we're going at it hot and heavy this time of day."

"Usually?" Delia breathed. "Like—every *day*?"

"Morning, afternoon, and evening," MJ said.

"Jeez . . ."

"He's married. And he's got a glorious apartment in town, but he hasn't invited me to live there. I sleep there, I can have sex there, but I can't live there."

"I see," Brooke said. "Please tell me you're not in love with him."

MJ hesitated. "I don't know. I need him. I can't run my life without him."

"What does that mean?"

"He's the boss. And that's how I want it. A strong, decisive man who runs everything—do you know how rare they are?"

"Do you love him?" Brooke asked again.

"Yes," MJ said defiantly. Then, "Maybe. I love that he's taken over. But that's everything, down to the last detail, and it's exhausting sometimes. Sex is exhausting sometimes. He just wants it all the time, and expects . . . Of course, I want it, too. He's so virile, I *do* want it all the time, just like he does. Only not so much."

"And he's offered nothing?" Brooke demanded relentlessly.

"He adores me, he wants me endlessly—that's not nothing, Brooke. He doesn't want anyone else. I own *his* body, too."

"Or he owns *you*." Brooke looked meaningfully at MJ's thrall collar.

"It's a sex thing," MJ said.

"But you're at his beck and call all the time. You do whatever he wants, whenever he wants it. And he's made you believe that you want it too, MJ—only he's getting it all for free."

MJ said nothing.

"You're getting nothing, he's getting everything."

"I'm on his turf," MJ shot back. "He pays for everything."

"Does he take you out? Buy you things?"

"When did we become mercenary?"

"When we decided the guys were getting everything, and they had the idea they didn't have to give back anything. Delia's the only one strong and brave enough to tell a guy she wanted something in return. God, Delia. You make me ashamed of my cowardice."

"Not me," MJ said staunchly. "Dallan is my man, and I'm happy."

Brooke gazed at her a moment. "Okay. But let me tell you some thoughts I've been having on the matter."

"You made a list," MJ muttered.

"Oh, you bet. Because we got hit like thunder by these unexpected guys, and I didn't provide us with any strategies to deal with them. Both Delia and I had run-ins with unexpected men who turned into meaningless men. So this is what I thought." She took out her Rules for the Unexpected Man and gave them out.

"Three weeks? Three *weeks* and then you dump them?" MJ squeaked. "Forget that, Brooke. I'm not giving up Dallan."

"You will," Brooke said.

MJ snorted and tore up the page. "I'm wasting my time here. I can still get home in time to have sex with Dallan. I just hope he'll let me in the door."

"Hey, it's your body, your self. Just be careful how much of it you're subsuming into him."

MJ thrust back her chair. "You have no idea how amazing it's been."

Brooke stared at her pale, tired face. "Oh, yes I do," she said softly. "I'd have given myself to that son of a bitch Hugh Steffen *exactly* that way, if he'd asked me to. And I wonder how long it would have taken me to realize I had to get away from him."

MJ stalked off.

"You scared the hell out of her," Delia said into the long silence that followed.

Brooke felt like hell. "I know. But everything she said about that man scared me. He'll isolate her and keep her from her friends and maybe from her work, and become more and more possessive until there's literally nothing left of her. Shit. I wish I'd never started this whole thing. I never thought any of us would be that susceptible to bastards like these guys."

"Don't do that, Brooke. How could you know?"

"Frank was exactly like that, wasn't he? Doesn't it all

sound so familiar? He hasn't begun chipping away her spirit yet, but he will—and I bet she still won't listen to anything we tell her. You know that even better than I do."

Delia closed her eyes and nodded. She knew. Sex was addictive with a guy like that. He made you the focus of his world, knowing you'd never had a possessive lover like that ever in your life and that you'd die for one. They traded on your fear, your need, your desperation; they fed on it, on you, until there was almost nothing left.

She blinked and opened her eyes. "We'll save her," she vowed. "I don't know how yet, but we'll save her. And soon."

MJ had to beg him to let her in. It was too late, lunch was over, he wasn't in the mood, she should just go back to work and he would call her later.

Finally, he'd relented and let her in. He was stark naked and highly aroused, but he wouldn't let her near to touch him or console him over her behavior.

So she phoned the store and feigned some disaster, then she sat gingerly on the sofa arm and watched him prowl back and forth in front of the window and around the sofa, waiting for the moment to have her say.

"So . . ." he said some twenty minutes later, gesturing to his engorged penis. "This is what you wasted this afternoon. *What* was so important?"

"It was stupid," MJ said. "Our friend hooked up with someone who really wanted to have sex with her, and she rejected him. He had a place, he made his intentions clear, and she *rejected* him."

"Bitch," he muttered. "Women are all bitches."

"And she wanted to know if she'd done the right thing."

He paused, suddenly still. "Do you think she did?"

"*Dal-lan.* He went to all this trouble to find her because he couldn't stop thinking about her after they hooked up. She agreed to meet him, so he set up a private place where they could be comfortable and have sex. And she went there with him, she let him take her, and then *she* rejected him."

He went very, very still. Then: "Absolute bitch whore. *All* women are bitch whores." He came around to where she perched and speared his hands through her hair. "Except you. My loyal cunt understands all about a man's penis, doesn't she? That's why you came back this afternoon, MJ. Because you have your own man to fuck you whenever he wants you."

"Yes," she whispered. "I couldn't take that talk another minute, knowing you were here, and I could be naked with you."

"Yet when I told you I didn't want you to go to this lunch, you were reluctant to follow my wishes. It turned out just as I said. I'm hard for you and you cut short your lunch, and it's wasted because I just don't feel like fucking."

"Whatever you want, Dallan. I made a mistake, seeing those . . . those bitches. Anyone who rejects a man that way can't be a friend of mine."

"You don't need any other friends but me, MJ. And my penis."

"You're absolutely right, Dallan. You're my best friend and I wasted our sex time together and I had to get back to you as soon as possible to make it up to you."

He made a low growling sound.

"I'm not going to see them again. I made that clear."

"Good." He stood in front of her and stroked himself. "You made the right choice to come back to me sooner than later." He stroked harder, sliding hard and rough until a pearl of semen oozed from the tip of his shaft. "And you finally understand that. So you can lick that. Just that drop. And we'll say my afternoon cum hasn't been wasted since you learned something important today."

Brooke was having a crisis of conscience. "We know nothing," she told Delia two days later, when they met after hours at Park Blue for a good bottle of wine and some food from the small plate menu. "There's something I'm missing, and until I figure it out I'm declaring a moratorium on the Mistress Club."

Delia shook her head. "You're just upset about MJ."

Brooke nodded. "She's never had that kind of attention before. She used to be tall and gawky and flat-chested and ignored; now here's a sophisticated older man panting for her body. What woman wouldn't give herself over to that kind of possessive lust?"

"She'll figure out what's really going on," Delia said. "She'll look in the mirror one day. She's too thin, too pale. I was shocked by how she looks. She'll see it; she'll get it; she'll break away."

"God, I hope so. And we need a new strategy, or we're going to be dragged right down with her. These are strong men with hard needs, and we have to learn to deal with them.

"The problem is, they can have anyone they want. I was flattered when Hugh Steffen called. He looked at me like he wanted to devour me, but all he wanted was a young female body to spend himself in. So how do you separate the spunk spenders from the splurge spenders?"

"We have to train ourselves to remain distanced. This is not for love, and it's not forever," Delia said.

Brooke nodded thoughtfully. "You're right. Listen, I had a thought."

"Ye-e-e-s?"

"Belly-dancing classes."

Delia burst out laughing. "How do you go from controlling men to belly dancing?"

"What's more seductive than undulating moves that are as explicit as sex? We can learn how to entice, how to keep our distance until we get what we want . . . and it'll tone and exercise our bodies, besides."

"Only you would think of that," Delia said, clapping her hands. "I love it. Where? When?"

"There are belly-dancing classes at the Broadway Dance Center, during the week and Saturdays."

"You're kidding."

"Nope. So let's start tonight."

Tonight was a deprivation. MJ knew it because Dallan wanted her on her hands and knees in the most subservient way.

She didn't care. Whatever way he wanted her tonight was fine. She climbed onto the edge of the bed, following his di-

129

rections. He wanted to stand behind her, to just jam himself into her and let his orgasm rip.

But I didn't reject you . . .

The thought dissipated as he mounted her forcefully and the pleasure of his possession radiated through her. She lived for this, she existed for this—this hard-driving, hard-pumping lust that he expended so violently in her body. *Her,* not some voluptuous bottle blonde or mindless bimbo. *Her.*

He held her bottom tight; he thrust at her body in short, hard, pistonlike bursts, grunting in rhythm with his movements. One-two-three-four . . . MJ found herself counting . . . two-three-four . . . coming . . . She could feel him stiffening deep inside her, getting ready, hotter, harder—one last ramrod thrust—one and two—and he blasted his thick cum into her.

He stood there, still grasping her buttocks, still embedded, still as a tree.

He *was* a tree—strong, tall, thick, and mighty, every inch of him everywhere. MJ couldn't move. Her nipples grazed the bedcover. Her body felt fragile with emotions that would crack wide open if she moved.

"This is nice," he said. "I like this. It's just me, my penis, and your cunt."

MJ winced. She felt panicky, she didn't deserve this. What could she say that would make him enfold her body with his again?

"If a man just concentrates on cunt, he's much better off," he went on. "What else does a man need but a tight, moist place to occupy? Of course, there's no such thing as *nice* cunt. If a man could just buy himself one without all the crying, complaining, and rejecting, he'd be a lot happier. But they're attached to bitches, so what can a man do?"

"He can have me," MJ whispered. "He can have me any way he wants me."

He rocked against her, flexing himself inside her as if he were flexing his power. "Except when your bitch friends make demands."

Exhaustion. "That's over."

"We'll see."

"Dallan . . ."

"Or maybe that fucker should have been more forceful with your friend. A man doesn't let a cock tease blow him off."

"No. She shouldn't have done that."

He undulated his hips, pressing deeper. "What should she have done, MJ?"

She took a deep breath, girding herself to pacify him. "She should have made an accommodation with him. He probably would have discovered she wasn't as good as he thought. Brilliant of him to arrange their assignation where he did. She'd be forced to leave if he'd rejected her."

"You do understand a man's penis pride, MJ. At least, some stranger's penis pride. It makes a man wonder. And I can't fathom what you understand about mine after this afternoon's debacle."

"But I learned my lesson, Dallan. I'll never abandon our sex again, I promise."

Are you sure you want to make that promise?

WHAT?

"How do I know you mean it?"

How do I know?

WHAT AM I THINKING?

She knew what it was—it was Brooke's comments, and Delia's strength in telling Bill what she wanted. But she couldn't picture saying those things to Dallan.

Things like: We're together morning, noon, and night, why can't I just move in? Why can't we go out to dinner? Why am I not happy, when I always wanted a commanding man to take charge of things? When I love giving myself wholly to someone much stronger than me?

Why are you always punishing me?

STOP IT!

She took a deep breath and forced herself back to the moment. She was on her hands and knees on Dallan's bed with his shaft still embedded in her. Just what she yearned for, longed for. A big, strong man with a thick, hot root to fill her in all ways and take her away.

She *was* a mistress, the lover of a man who liked to be in control, who possessed her in every way imaginable and whose jealousy was proof of how much in thrall *he* was to her body.

Or how gullible I am.

WHAT?

Get back to *him* now. Answer him.

God, this was tiring.

"I mean it, Dallan. Tell me what to do to prove it. Anything, I'll do anything."

He slowly withdrew his shaft from her hot tunnel, yet another deprivation. "I'm glad you feel that way, MJ. Actually, I rather thought you would."

Chapter Seven

She was not made for belly dancing, Brooke thought disgustedly. There was something about the way you had to undulate your hips that she just couldn't fathom when she was vertical.

Not that she was the only one. There were a dozen other women who couldn't get the rhythm or the ripple. But that was small comfort when Delia immediately swirled and shimmied like she'd been born to it.

"Don't give up," Sharla, the instructor, encouraged. She was barefoot, dressed in a gauzy costume festooned with bells and beads, and she remained enthusiastic in spite of the fact that half the class was dancing off rhythm. "It'll come, it'll make sense. Practice at home."

And on they went, twirling and swirling as best they could to the exotic rhythm of the insinuating music.

"Why didn't someone tell me?" Delia demanded breathlessly when the class ended.

"Me, too," Brooke groaned. "I never should have started this. How do you get your hips to bobble like that?"

Delia grinned. "I've got bobbly hips. You know what? We need one of those tapes, so we can practice at home."

"Terrific idea. Then I'll never have to humiliate myself in public again."

"We're not coming back?"

Brooke looked at her face, alight with her exertions and something more—enjoyment, accomplishment, arousal? "Sure—Saturday."

"Good. You're right, this was a great idea." Delia bobbled her hips.

"Show-off."

Delia grinned. "I'm *so* flaunting it."

They walked in silence for a while along Broadway, still crowded and teeming on the cusp of midnight.

"Delia . . ."

"What?"

"Try to talk to MJ."

They came to the corner where they had to separate.

"She's not answering anything, not her cell, not texting. Nothing," Delia said.

"I know. Me neither. Shit."

"Yeah. I keep trying, I don't know what else to do."

"Short of kidnapping her—which is not a bad idea," Brooke said.

"You've just got harems on your mind. She'll figure it out," Delia said. "Didn't I?"

They hugged and Delia turned east and grabbed the first cab that turned the corner. Brooke waited until the taillights were out of sight, then slowly walked to her apartment, feeling a pinprick of hope.

* * *

Saturday's routine was for touch-ups and takeout, clothes and culture, manicures and man-watching. All the good stuff that Brooke loved about living in Manhattan. Everything she looked forward to after a week of problem solving at the office.

By Saturday, she was also feeling a little less upset about MJ and by her own experience with Hugh Steffen.

"Maybe we just have to get through some of these meaningless men to prepare for the men we're meant to be with," she told Delia after another belly-dancing class that afternoon. "We just have to remember that this is not about falling in love."

"I'm not so sure about that," Delia said slowly.

"No. That is *totally* against the Mistress Code."

Delia shrugged. "I'm not so sure; I just won't argue with you about it. I'm feeling pretty powerful after my showdown with Bill."

"We need to raise a toast to that. We're pretty near the river. How about we go to the boat basin café for a drink?"

"Sure." As they headed to Riverside Drive, Delia added wistfully, "I just wish MJ were with us. I tried to get her this morning, about the tenth time I've called her at work and on her cell. This is ridiculous. Why can't she be with us?"

MJ was tucked in Dallan Baines's arms, wrung out from yet another draining bout of sex, while he lay sound asleep, finally worn down by lust.

Thank goodness.

What? I didn't mean that.

Yes, you did.

The familiar weariness swamped her. It usually crept up after sex, when *she* was depleted, tired, raw from penetration, and emotionally exhausted from trying to pacify all Dallan's irritations.

But he's perfect. He wants me. He's mine.

Is he?

Shit—stop that.

If anything, he'd become more possessive, more demanding. Wanting things, different things, new things, things that involved her body—like dressing her naked torso in leather strips, cuffing her wrists and ankles and then spreading her and holding her captive as proof of her devotion to him.

The excitement of this new component of their sex life was interfering with her work and her real life. *What* life? She spent more and more time with him, placating him, servicing him, except when he decided not.

Sometimes he called and told her not to come.

There was a whiff of the sadistic about it, almost as if now that he had trained her and absorbed her, the point of the exercise was done.

But that was impossible. He wanted *her* with an intensity that thrilled her.

Today's session was unusual. It was a Saturday, one free of family obligations for some reason, and he'd called her suddenly and imperiously to come to the apartment. Called her early, so they could have the whole day. That had to mean something.

But why today, really?

She didn't dare ask.

Did you hear yourself? You didn't "dare" ask. She lay quietly, keeping everything she really knew skating lightly on her consciousness.

He's mine.

That was all that mattered. And that for the first time in months, she was not spending a weekend day alone.

Brooke's solution for lurking lust was to keep them busy. After their weekly mandatory mistress maintenance sessions, belly-dancing lessons, movies, and shopping the sales listed in *New York* magazine, neither she nor Delia was thinking much about men.

Just about MJ.

And MJ was thinking about the fact that she missed them. About the fact that Dallan had laid out such stringent rules that she couldn't even pick up the phone to call them, which she'd strongly wanted to do after that abortive lunch.

Why did Brooke have to be so critical? Brooke thought she was the queen just because her parents were wealthy, and because the Mistress Club had been her idea.

Well, she, MJ, was the only one of them who *was* a mistress. The first of them to snag a full-time lover, despite Brooke's peculiar ideas about *getting.* Giving was what it was about. And she was giving like crazy.

Right. You give and give, and what are you getting?

The greatest sex of my life.

And you're so happy, aren't you?

Yes, I am. I *am.*

Not.

She wondered what Delia and Brooke were doing. She wondered if they had found anyone yet. She missed their Saturday routine, because Dallan didn't want her hanging out with her girlfriends even when he wasn't there.

Why not?

If she went out with them, he wouldn't know.

But she'd cut them off after that last lunch. Had sided with the unknown Bill over her girlfriend because it was what Dallan wanted. Feeling that somehow he would know she'd been disloyal.

That's crazy . . .

I can't lose him.

Why not? What's he got, besides an inexhaustible penis?

All my secrets.

So what?

All my *secret* secrets . . .

So what?

She lay beside him the next night, staring at the ceiling.

I'm not happy. She couldn't remember if Brooke's formula for them becoming mistresses included being happy. But a mistress's job was to keep her man happy, and Dallan certainly couldn't deny that she was available, willing, enthusiastic, adventurous, orgasmic . . .

He never says a word, except to constrain you somehow.

But she'd had this argument with herself before. It was true that Dallan was not a man to give compliments or appreciation lightly. Or ever. But the fact he was still with her said volumes.

140

Didn't it?

"MJ?" Dallan's voice, clogged with sleep. "I need a fuck."

Not *I need you. I want you.*

I love you . . .

She made a small sound. *Don't.*

"MJ." His tone was peremptory now.

She heard herself say in a pacifying tone, "Yes, Dallan. I'd love to do you," and she wondered, what am I doing?

But she knew—she was rolling onto her back and spreading her legs for her lover, the man who wanted *her,* her body, her sex, her secrets.

Early on Saturday morning two weeks later, Brooke settled in at her favorite spot, the window overlooking West End Avenue where she'd placed her dining table, to take stock.

She was not happy with how things were progressing. Work wasn't working. Their outside social activities had yielded nothing. Memberships in museums and volunteering were not producing any results.

She was certain now that the kind of man who could support a mistress was not to be found at any of those venues. So where were they hiding, and how could she root them out?

Maybe they needed to buy a box at the ballet. Or rent a roof in the Hamptons. Or worm their way into one of those despised clubs and get tight with whoever was the hip party producer of the moment. Those guys collected the trendy and terrific to populate their parties; maybe that was the entrée to the more rarified circles of the hip and horny.

Or maybe the Mistress Club was a dumb idea altogether.

How naïve of her to think they could take the mistress world by storm. Those women probably cat-fought their way to their positions of power. Or maybe there was something like a mistress matchmaker . . .

She went very still, her heart beating like a drum. *Oh, my God.*

She felt absolutely stupid and utterly brilliant at the same time.

She had said all along that men who were seeking a mistress would be very discreet. They'd never take their lust to the streets or anywhere public. They were too well-known, for one thing. Their wives were probably seen and photographed everywhere that the fashionable set partied.

So, if she were the CEO of the world, had unlimited resources, and wanted a beautiful young paramour, where would she look? Understanding of course, that the CEO of the world would want the cream of the young, beautiful, and available women—and probably not those who regularly made the headlines.

I'd want her checked out before we even met to make sure she wasn't a reporter for Page Six or the Enquirer.

I'd want her checked out medically so I wouldn't be letting myself in for any sexual surprises.

I'd want to know her requirements before we met and maybe I'd want them presented by a third party so monetary aspects could be handled out of sight.

I'd want to meet her somewhere neutral and private, to see if we were compatible . . .

I'd want some guarantees . . .

Exactly! These people could afford to be as particular as a king; they didn't fuck just anybody.

Only—mistress matchmakers didn't run ads in *Town & Country.* If such a thing existed, it was something in the ether, something people *knew.*

So she had to find someone who knew. She had to listen when people were whispering. She had to get them to places where they could "hear" who was available and where to find them.

Sure, I can do it.

She'd figured this much out. She could do anything.

I'm tired.

Tired of what? Tired of sex? Tired of Dallan?

Stop it. She could never be tired of an indefatigable lover like Dallan.

He's mine. Is he? He was by her side every night, yet she still had to go home.

"MJ, I need some tunnel time."

"Yes, Dallan." *NO, Dallan. How about wanting ME for a change?*

She obediently spread her legs, feeling disconnected from her body, her needs. It was always *his* needs. He'd taken over completely, just as she'd wanted.

That *had* been what she wanted, right? Then why was she so unhappy?

She took his pummeling, standing outside herself, watching, feeling a ticking clock inside her. Bam bam slam . . . she didn't even fake it this time.

"What, you can't get it up tonight?"

"I'm tired," she managed to say.

"I didn't give you permission to be tired."

"Okay," she muttered.

"Whenever you're tired, I want to fuck again just to wake up your cunt."

"Not tonight."

"I'm sorry—not tonight? You have a headache or something?"

He's all mine, don't forget that . . .

"No, Dallan. No. Let's do it again. I'm ready now."

What am I saying?

He plunged into her again and she girded herself to fake it, to make him feel that she was with him now.

Afterward, he collapsed on top of her the way she had always loved. But now she wished he'd get off of her, that he was far away from her. He was heavy, sweaty with his exertions, and she didn't like how he'd used her tonight.

How he always uses me.

He does *not* use me—

No? Does he come when you call?

I never call.

Does he ever ask what you want?

He's mine. That's all that matters. I'm his mistress.

You're his whore. He'd have to pay someone else to do the things he does to you.

Nooooooo . . .

"Time's up, MJ."

She heard his voice from far away. That was what he always said when he wanted her to leave, as if sex with him was therapy. For whom? Him or her?

And why did he want her to leave? Tomorrow was Saturday. They had a Saturday precedent, so why couldn't she stay?

She didn't dare ask. *Listen to yourself: You don't "dare" ask. You have to leave.*

No. I have to go.

Deep inside, she knew the difference was real, and crucial. And that, scared as she was, she was ready to make that choice.

Tonight.

Oh, God ... Tonight?

Tonight.

Chapter Eight

The next morning, Brooke's doorbell buzzed urgently and interminably. No one should have to wake up at dawn on a Saturday, she thought fuzzily as she fumbled to see what time it was. Seven AM, for God's sake. The world had better be ending.

She stumbled to the intercom and barked, "Who?"

"MJ."

"Oh, Jesus . . ." The world *was* ending. She buzzed MJ in, unlocked the door, and immediately made coffee. She was setting out bagels and cream cheese as MJ walked in the door and into her embrace without saying a word.

MJ looked awful, her eyes hollow and damp from crying; she was too thin, looked too fragile, and felt like she would break from the consoling hug.

"Go sit down."

"My bags are outside."

"I'll bring them in." No questions; this was a crisis. "Go sit down and let me take care of you for an hour."

"Okay."

She took off her coat and curled herself into one corner

of the sofa. Brooke brought in her suitcases, then finished getting together a tray with the coffee and bagels.

"Have some coffee."

"Okay."

Brooke poured, added sweetener and milk, and handed the cup into MJ's cold hands. "Don't even talk."

"Okay." MJ sipped, and Brooke smeared some cream cheese on half a bagel, then cut that in half and gave one piece to MJ.

"Just a bite," Brooke said coaxingly. "You'll feel better."

"Yes, Mom."

"Should I call Delia?"

"Not yet. I just—I need . . . I decided last night . . . I'm scared."

Brooke took a deep breath of relief. "Okay, let me guess. You're done with him, right? That's all I need to know right now. Let me get dressed and you finish your coffee and that little bit of bagel, okay?"

"Okay." MJ wearily thought that she didn't even have the strength to keep herself upright on the sofa. But that was all right—Brooke had enough will and strength for both of them. Enough so that MJ didn't have to sort through her emotions right now, or to castigate herself for her weakness and her god-awful need to be controlled. Look where it had gotten her: trapped with a bastard who'd taken the power she'd willingly handed him and masterfully crushed her with it. She didn't know how to get over that.

Brooke came back, dressed now. "You okay, MJ?"

"Yeah."

"Do you want to talk? Or sleep?"

"I don't know."

"What happened?"

"Nothing, actually. I just suddenly saw . . . what you've been saying. I'm getting nothing, and he's getting everything. He sent me home—he always sends me home—but tomorrow—I mean today—is Saturday and I thought since I was so tired, I could just . . . stay the night. But no. Weekends are for his family, except when *he* says they're not—and so he sent me home. Again.

"And I thought, this is nothing to break up with him over, but for some reason it was really critical. Like *this* was the moment I had to make a decision—because I'm not happy and I feel like I'm losing . . . something. Because it was all about him and nothing about me. So I told him, and then I went home, packed, and came here."

"Whoa," Brooke murmured. "That's huge."

"It feels small. *I* feel small."

"You did the right thing, coming here, leaving him. What did he say?"

"He laughed."

Brooke said nothing. There was nothing to say. That arrogant bastard had had MJ under his control far too long. How he'd deal with that loss was his problem.

"Does he know about us?"

"Kind of. He heard that message about the lunch, but he doesn't know where you guys live or work, or your last names, nothing like that."

"Good. All right, we have to make a plan."

MJ shook her head. "Maybe there are things you can't plan."

"Never," Brooke said emphatically. "First, we're calling Delia. Second, we're not allowing you to wallow in regrets today. We're going out, and I don't care if you want to or not. I have a theory I have to test, and it can't wait for you to stop mourning Dallan Baines. So hang in there, MJ. We've missed you, the Mistress Club needs you, and we're just starting to ramp up my plan."

It took less than an hour for Delia to appear on the doorstep with Zabar's chicken soup in hand.

"It's good for everything else. Why can't it cure *the thank God I got rid of the overbearing bastard* blues?" She hugged MJ and then set out bowls. "Come on, let's drown the memory of that shit with some soup."

MJ reluctantly pulled herself to the table. "He's not a shit. I just want to sleep."

"No, you don't," Brooke said decisively. "Here's the drill. You're going to stay here. I'll go to your apartment and get your things." She waved her spoon at MJ as she started to protest. "You couldn't handle a flea right now. We have work to do, and I need the skeptical, stringent MJ back on our team. You don't ever want to see him again, so you're going to take some vacation days and keep out of sight for a week.

"Next, I had a brainstorm." Brooke banged her spoon on the table. "I hereby call this meeting of the Mistress Club to order. All are present, I'm happy to say. Eat your soup, MJ."

MJ shot her an irritated look.

"We've missed you," Delia said.

"Me, too," MJ managed around a spoonful of soup.

"Okay, the brainstorm," Brooke said briskly. "I had this off-the-wall idea that there's probably such a thing as a mistress matchmaker, like a broker. Someone who screens prospective mistresses, maybe guarantees they are who they say they are, and that they're disease free and a bunch of other stuff like that.

"Because of privacy issues and paparazzi and their wives being in the public eye, a mistress isn't something they find at the Garden horse show or a Hamptons charity event."

She looked at them brightly. "Don't you think?"

MJ looked dumbfounded. Delia said, "Honest to God, how did you come up with that?"

"I was trying to analyze why we weren't getting anywhere."

"And—um—where does a well-intentioned girl find these brokers?"

"I have no idea. That's today's mission. We're going shopping and we're going to eavesdrop. I was listening to this life coach on TV, and she said there's always someone who knows what you need to know. Our job is to find that person."

"Bro-ooke . . ." MJ looked disgusted.

Brooke shot her a quelling look. "Really. So, who knows more about what's going on between the sheets than the fashionistas who shop the same bargain places we do?"

"Who?" MJ muttered.

"Oh, it's so good to have MJ back among us," Brooke said

kindly. "Or maybe the salespeople. In fact, particularly the salespeople. That's a genius thought. MJ, you're going to shower and change. It's a jeans, cami, and stiletto day, and if you don't have any with you, you can borrow mine. I'll figure out which shops we're going to hit. Delia, you make sure MJ doesn't lock herself in the bedroom."

They were out within the hour, MJ grumbling every step of the way. "Can't I just submerge myself in misery?"

"No. You can step into the light and let every man we pass ogle you," Brooke said. "Much better strategy, much better on the ego. That shit wasn't worth your time, but don't get me started on that. We're not doing a wailing wall day. Okay, we're going to two hospital thrift shops, and a new resale shop I found called Second Take. Ready?"

She didn't really have an idea of what she wanted them to do, other than browse and shop and listen. Talk to the salesperson. They couldn't just ask if there was such a thing as a mistress broker and where could one be found.

They went out to dinner afterward at Sel et Poivre, having gleaned nothing but a couple of pairs of shoes and some jewelry.

"I just couldn't spend the money," Delia said regretfully as they did a thorough postmortem on everything they didn't buy over a trio of Manhattans.

"A waste of time," MJ said sourly.

"We can't leave her alone tonight," Brooke told Delia.

"Don't you feel better?" Delia asked MJ. "Without that psychic pressure you always used to feel from him? Remember, I lived it, too."

"Not like this," MJ whispered. "He isn't a boy. He's a very strong man."

"Not so strong, if he didn't know enough to value you." Delia turned to Brooke. "I'll stay with her."

"We'll both stay with her for the next couple of days. I'll take a day off—you arrange to work a couple of nights. We'll get her through it." Brooke eyed MJ. "I don't think it will take long."

"About as long as it will take to find this mythical mistress broker," MJ said a little snidely, because she felt as if Brooke were rolling right over her.

"Oh, that," Brooke said airily. "I bet you I'll know everything I need by this time next week."

MJ was a mess, but she'd walked out at the right time. The real problem was the neediness that glossed over the bullying and the complete abnegation of self. She'd lost herself in her eagerness to please him.

And what pleased him changed moment to moment on his whim. That was one of the many things that Delia would make her understand, with her tact, her empathy, her own experience, and her hard-won resolution. She would have an answer for every "but," an answer for every excuse.

Brooke sat in awe that first evening after they returned from dinner, listening to Delia handle MJ, preventing her in the most delicate way from calling Baines and handing herself over to him again.

"If you felt tired and weary before," Delia said gently, "you will feel crushed by him altogether if you give in now.

He will lord it over you that he won, and that he didn't have to do *anything* to bring you back to him.

"That's the whole key to everything, and you know it already. He has never had to do anything. He knows you will do it all for him."

"No," MJ protested. "No."

"You're doing it now. *Listen to yourself.* He doesn't have to do anything to make you crawl back to him. *Nothing.* That's what he knows, and you don't. Nothing."

MJ shook her head . . . but in her head, she heard: *I need cunt.*

No, he needed *me.* Didn't he?

Let's fuck . . .

She went very still. *Time's up.*

That's what he knows, and you don't . . .

"That's how they bully you," Delia said in her gentle voice. "I believed it, too. That Frank loved me. That I wasn't doing enough. That he was really a great guy. And omigod, he chose *me*! And all I had to do was be a little better, a little more submissive, a little more deferential. A little more . . . *dead.*"

MJ looked at her with hollowed-out eyes.

"That's what they want. They want to kill your spirit and destroy your life—and they *know* you'll help them do it."

MJ shook her head again.

"Just think over your time together."

Yes, Dallan. Whatever you want, Dallan. . . . Don't dare ask anything of Dallan. Can't I stay, Dallan?

Time's up.

I have to go. I'm not coming back.

He'd laughed. You will. You need me. You need this. You'll be back.

She'd been complicit in her own spiritual demise.

No, I won't let you. At that moment, she'd been certain.

Yet not even a whole day later, she couldn't bear to think she'd never fuck him again.

I need . . . you. He'd never said so. *You need me.* He'd explicitly said that.

That's what he knows—you'll do it all for him.

Say that over and over and over. He doesn't have to do anything, you'll do it all for him. All he wants is cunt, anyone's. It didn't matter to him whose. Hers just happened to be the cunt of the moment.

She looked at Delia.

Delia nodded. "Don't do it for him, MJ."

It doesn't matter to him . . .

She felt a cold anger. She felt the hot tide of all the months she'd held herself in rigid check slowly melt away. *It had never mattered to him.*

Only to her. And he'd known that. It was his weapon, but she was the one who wielded it, punishing herself for his inconsistencies.

Doing it for him.

She wasn't there yet, but she felt the release of the godawful fear of never seeing him again. *Not nearly there yet.* But she knew at that moment that she would not willingly and metaphorically obliterate herself for his sadistic pleasure.

* * *

Sunday, Brooke went out, leaving Delia with MJ, who looked a lot less like a refugee from the village of the damned.

Had *she* looked like that, after she realized what Hugh Steffen was up to?

I will not analyze what happened with him. What's the point? He's a practiced charmer, and I'm a babe in the city and he got me. He got me big time.

She headed east. Maybe Saks or Bloomie's would be fertile fields today. And Images, their favorite resale shop. Where she'd bought scads of things that MJ and Delia didn't know about, so that the owner, Marielyce, now knew her by name and taste.

Maybe today she'd ask questions. There is always someone who knows the thing you need to know, the life coach had said, and Brooke liked the idea that any friend, any random stranger, might have an answer she needed.

She headed down to Saks, where she spent a lovely hour wandering around haute couture, trying on unaffordable Carolina Herrera dresses and listening to interesting but unproductive conversations.

She loved this floor, with its respectful and hushed atmosphere of uncompromising service. This was where the elegant CEO wives would shop. This was where the salespeople knew you by income level, and maybe even handpicked outfits for you to choose from. Or sent them to your home, if you had a personal shopper. They probably all had personal shoppers. So what clever question could she ask a salesperson to ferret out what she needed to know?

But the salesperson was too watchful, subtle as she was, as if Brooke might walk away with the store if someone weren't looking. Could salespeople discern who was there to spend serious money?

Now and again a well-dressed woman came in and went off in deep discussion with the salesperson to more private quarters.

Maybe that was the tipping point.

Show your bank account at thirty paces.

Her bank account didn't even total thirty pesos.

So Brooke decided to cut her losses, even though she loved the luxe silk blouses and the rich bouclé Chanel jackets that felt custom fitted but were not working-girl friendly, pricewise.

This is where I'm going to shop when someone wants to buy me nice clothes.

Okay, to business. Outside, she flipped her cell and called Delia.

"We're doing fine," Delia reported. "What about you?"

"I haven't found the right opportunity, the right venue, or the right question," Brooke said, "but I'm working on it."

"You go, girl," Delia said. "We'll be fine."

Reassured that MJ was coping and not crying, Brooke headed downtown to Images.

The shop was quiet on a late Sunday morning. That could either be good or bad, there was no way to tell.

Marielyce greeted her like a long-lost friend. Or maybe she was just lonely for some company.

"Brooke. It's been a while since you've been here."

Marielyce was older, elegant, totally fashion savvy, and had a faint accent.

"I've been busy," Brooke said. "But it's time to update. What wonderful things are lurking on the racks?"

"Look—just turned in, I have a Chanel suit, a mere four hundred fifty dollars—a pair of Luca Luca shoes, under a hundred. An Hermès bag—but don't even think about a Birkin. Everyone's hoarding them. And—this the best—La Perla lingerie. This is how you know a man is serious about you."

She opened the display case and brought out an extravagantly embroidered set of lace and stretch tulle thong panties, bra, and bodysuit. "Never worn—the tags are still attached. Someone must have been very angry to dispose of such beautiful lingerie. Look at the way the embroidery covers everything, yet glimmers to catch the eye. See the deep vee of the thong, so it sits just below the small of the back, inviting a lover's touch? And the bodysuit—all nude except in strategic places. The lace, so soft. Touch it."

Brooke touched and imagined a lover touching her.

"This would fit you," Marielyce said, eyeing her speculatively. "One hundred fifty dollars for the set, a third of the retail price. Some customers are a little leery about such items. But for you, if you're interested . . ."

Brooke's imagination ran wild. It was almost orgasmic, the thought of wearing this for a lover. Of getting a gift like this from a lover.

"If you're looking . . ." Marielyce murmured.

Brooke brought her attention back to Marielyce, something prickling at the back of her neck.

"What if I'm looking for a nice, wealthy man who wants a fresh, young, unspoiled, well-educated, and beautiful mistress?" she asked impulsively, yielding to a feeling that Marielyce was talking about something entirely different from lingerie.

"Oh," Marielyce murmured. "Well . . ."

That sounded . . . hopeful.

"The set, shall I wrap it for you?"

Brooke took a deep breath. No help there. "Absolutely." Now what? She watched as Marielyce folded the pieces reverently.

She handed over her credit card, signed the slip, and watched as Marielyce tenderly wrapped the set—*her* set—of La Perla in tissue paper.

"What you want," Marielyce said softly, "is entrée to the Mistress Club."

Brooke's head snapped up. "*What?*"

"The Mistress Club. This is the place you find the man who can truly afford to support a mistress."

Brooke's heart started pounding. There was another Mistress Club? A *real* Mistress Club?

"How does one obtain entrée?" she asked, fighting for calm.

Marielyce gave her that speculative look again. "One is referred," she murmured.

"And who might make such a referral?"

Marielyce smiled and handed her the bag. "Not everyone is suitable."

"That is understood."

Marielyce continued staring at her, almost as if she were trying to *see* her.

"I am so empowered," she said finally. "If you truly mean what you say."

Brooke let out her breath. "I do."

"Then you have everything you need to know," Marielyce said. "I hope to see you again, Brooke. And soon, so you will tell me how it goes."

"I will." Brooke took the bag, restraining the urge to ask where the "everything" was. Maybe there was something in the neatly wrapped package, because Marielyce had given her only the receipt. "Thank you."

"My pleasure," Marielyce said just as another customer came in the door.

. . . *everything you need to know* . . .

She had to get home, fast. Marielyce must have given her something in that package that would open the door to getting everything she wanted. She stepped into the street and hailed a cab.

There was bouzouki music coming from her apartment, with low thumping drums underscoring the sensual beat. She opened the door to find MJ and Delia in the middle of the living room, moving in rhythm to the belly-dance tape she had bought after the last class.

And MJ was smiling. MJ was moving sinuously and effortlessly to the music as Delia encouraged her, neither of them having noticed Brooke.

So this was why Delia had said they were fine. She'd gotten MJ off the couch and away from the bedroom, and encouraged her to take out her *well buts* in a sensual exercise that made her shake her butt. Delia was a genius.

"Hey, you all," she called finally.

They stopped simultaneously. "Hey," Delia said. "C'mon, we're having a bellyfest here."

"I can't compete with you guys. I do those moves better on my back."

Delia stopped the tape. "I'll get some coffee."

"Great. I have lots to tell you."

They each took a cup and settled on the couch.

"You really do that belly thing well," Brooke said to MJ.

"That's my endorphins on overdrive. I like it. I wish I'd been able"—MJ stopped and looked at Delia, who obviously had been pushing home how Dallan had been isolating her—"to take the class with you," she finished slowly.

"She's a motion-commotion," Delia put in.

MJ smiled faintly. "Anyway, what's your news? You look like you're about to burst."

"Frankly, I'm leery of what I'll find when we unwrap that." She motioned to the package she'd placed on the coffee table.

"What is it?"

"Lingerie—gorgeous, luscious lingerie, the kind men buy for mistresses. Someone had just put it in for resale."

As they drank their coffee, Brooke told them what had happened at Images.

"You're kidding," Delia said. "There really *is* something called the Mistress Club?"

"I was floored. I never would have thought there was such a thing."

"Sounds to me like a version of that mistress matchmaker you were theorizing about," MJ said.

"Yeah, it does. But that wasn't my question—that was the answer to where to find the kind of men who can support a mistress. So this proves that the universe knows the answer to everything—you just have to ask flat out."

"A mistress club," MJ said, shaking her head. "Like the Playboy Club or something, a place a man would go specifically to find a mistress."

"That's what she said. Where men who can support mistresses find them. I guess anything's possible in this city."

"So what, exactly, did you receive in this answer from the universe?" MJ asked with a touch of her usual skepticism.

Brooke grimaced. "I'll know when I unwrap that package."

They stared at it like it was radioactive.

"Open the damned package," MJ said.

"Okay." Brooke pulled off the tape and slowly unwrapped it.

Right on top, tucked into the low-cut double-strap bra, was a small vellum card.

Brooke held her breath and extracted it. She handed it to Delia, who handed it to MJ. On it was a name—Maîtrise—and an address in tiny raised letters and nothing more.

Chapter Nine

The address was one of the most exclusive neighborhoods in the city.

They looked at each other in dead silence. This thing was real. The address was real. The Mistress Club was real.

And it could happen. If they wanted it to happen.

"Omigod," Delia breathed.

It scared the hell out of Brooke. It was one thing to talk about it and fantasize about it. But to willingly hand yourself over for the hedonistic pleasure of a choosy, high-powered sophisticate who could afford to keep you as his plaything, and who operated on a whole different plane with a whole different set of rules?

They would want perfection, total immersion, and other things she couldn't even imagine.

She'd be walking in blind.

"Are you going to do it?" MJ asked in a hushed voice, ever practical.

"I don't know." But she was the one who had been given the entrée, she was the one who had dreamed up the idea, had pushed and prodded them to this point, had cheerled them into believing they could achieve the goal of having a mistress lifestyle. So how could she back down now?

It was just that her two-day affair with Hugh Steffen had been an eye-opener. To be so seduced by such a totally worldly man who got off on coddling, cuddling, and petting you until you were butter in his hands, and then lapping you up until he was sated, and you began to nurture *hopes* . . .

Of course he'd needed no more. He had no dearth of women willing to sleep with him. He was attractive, amusing, sexually magnetic, and just elusive enough to make an irresistible package. But to him, she was now a memory, one among dozens, even hundreds, a passing fancy to while away the time between business meetings.

So why was she hesitating? A mistress club at least guaranteed the possibility of a result, if you got past the door. She should jump on this instantly.

No. She should scope it out, investigate it, take her time.

Or just ignore it, and everything Marielyce had said to her.

She was usually fearless, but this was outside anything she knew: This was TV movie stuff. Fantasy novel stuff. This was entrée to a *sex* career in Manhattan, the equivalent of an actor's big break.

Because what was a mistress but an extremely facile actress?

Then she noticed the flushed and absorbed look on MJ's face. MJ wasn't weeping over Baines now; she was as deep into this bombshell as they were.

Brooke felt like the fairy godmother who'd waved the magic wand, turning mice into mistresses.

So how could she back out of it?

She rubbed her hand over her face. "I still can't wrap my brain around it."

"You have to see what it's all about," MJ said. "You can't *not*."

Delia put up her hand. "You do what you think is best."

Brooke looked at MJ. "You think I should go for it."

"Sure."

Delia leaned forward. "We should look at that address tomorrow. It could be a warehouse or something."

"In that neighborhood?"

"Well, you never know."

"I know," MJ said. "She has to take off from work and she has to do it."

They stayed up nearly all night discussing it.

"What do you think the girls have to do, the ones who are referred to this Mistress Club?" Brooke asked. "What do you think *we* would have to do?"

"Maybe give references, take physical exams, that kind of thing?" MJ suggested.

Delia laughed. "It's probably like school—you start with Mistress Mandates 101."

Brooke grabbed the reins. "Maybe they test you to see where you are in the pantheon of prospective mistresses. How smart you are, how cultured you are, how street smart, how fashion savvy." Really, what did she know about what supernova men wanted in a mistress? "So how would anyone determine that?"

It was a question they turned over and over, with no answer. *There's only one way to find out.*

"You just have to lead the charge," Delia said sleepily, thankful for her evening shift the next day.

"Uh-huh, and we know what happened to the four hundred." Brooke yawned. "That's one for me in the *educated* column. Any knowledge of the Boer War gets fifty points on the mistress intellect scale."

Monday morning they dressed for Midtown meandering, and grabbed a cab to the East Side.

"Oh," Delia breathed as they emerged on Fifth Avenue, a stone's throw from Central Park and several blocks from Fifty-seventh Street, where mansions and prewar co-op apartments sold in the millions of dollars. The number they were seeking was in an exclusive turn-of-the-century building on the corner. "Oh . . ."

Brooke looked at the card. The address was right. The name, Maîtrise, cryptic and mysterious both, still meant nothing to her.

"Let's walk," Brooke said, turning toward Fifty-seventh Street. They fell in three abreast. "So what did we learn?"

"The address is real," MJ said.

"And Tiffany's and Harry Winston aren't too far away," Delia added.

Brooke shook her head. "You're impossible. But you know what, you could be right. Let's go shopping."

Because there was nothing like browsing at Tiffany's to put a girl's priorities into perspective. A diet of diamonds and Dean & Deluca was not to be sloughed off so cavalierly.

But MJ, after about an hour and half, started looking a little glazed. MJ was making comparisons between herself and the thin, elegant Fifth Avenue fillies who were ruminating on and rejecting engagement rings right and left as she, Brooke, and Delia scoped out the showcases.

"I think it's time to go home," Brooke whispered, motioning to MJ.

Delia nodded. "I'll take her back to your place." She took MJ by the arm, and MJ didn't resist. Brooke thought she was looking rather zombielike right now, like some evil spirit had inhabited her thoughts.

Brooke waited until they had crossed Fifty-seventh Street before she headed uptown.

But she should be dressed to the teeth and wearing that new lingerie, rather than just a striped silk wrap top and a flowing moss-colored chiffon skirt.

Monday was not a good day to start the process of becoming a mistress.

Oh really? If not now, when?

It couldn't hurt to take another look at the building. It couldn't hurt just to go inside. But she walked around the block twice, procrastinating.

Okay. This is it. This is to save MJ. The sooner we're involved in the mistress world, the sooner she'll forget that son of a bitch.

She took a deep breath and pushed open the ornate front door.

It was like a castle inside the entryway, with a thick, plush Persian carpet, stone walls where an ornate wall-sized tapestry hung above an upholstered bench, an antique chandelier shed soft subtle light, and another ornate door was set opposite the entrance.

Almost instantly a doorman appeared there.

"May I help you?"

She had the card with her. *All for MJ.* She extracted it from her bag and gave it to him.

He barely gave the card a glance before he handed it back to her.

"This way, please."

He opened the door and motioned her into a marble-floored reception room with a carved fireplace. There were club chairs comfortably situated around it, a similar Persian rug on the floor, and console tables along the walls on either side, with crystal vases full of fresh flowers and lovely gilded mirrors above them.

The doorman's station was cleverly tucked away to the right of the door. He picked up the intercom, murmured a word, and then said to Brooke, "Go to one. The elevator is to your left."

No backing down now.

She was trembling as she walked slowly to the left. There were two elevators. One, paneled in rich walnut with brass fittings, was open as if it had been sent for her. Maybe it had been.

She stepped in and pressed number one, and the door closed.

This is for MJ. The elevator door slid silently open, on the next floor.

She didn't know what she expected, but it wasn't this haute hushed elegance, this *Architectural Digest* layout of the perfect Manhattan living room done in earth tones and off-whites, sparkling crystal, accents of brass and burgundy.

And the perfect hostess coming toward her, dressed perfectly in a youthful black Chanel suit with white satin cuffs, a matching top, and black and white shoes, holding out her hands as if Brooke were an honored guest.

"Welcome to Maîtrise. Come, sit. Let's talk."

Her hostess was a woman of a certain age and blondeness, with that ineffable chic that comes only from years of living at a certain level with lots of money to indulge yourself.

She led the way to two chairs and an ottoman covered in toffee suede by a bay window, and motioned for Brooke to sit. A butler immediately appeared with a coffee service, which he put on the ottoman and then withdrew.

Her hostess leaned forward. "I'm Vanessa."

Brooke's voice stuck in her throat. "Brooke."

Now what?

Vanessa looked at her expectantly, then held out her hand.

The entrée! Brooke took the card from her Kate Spade tote and handed it to Vanessa, who scrutinized it as if there were a message written in invisible ink.

But the only thing on that card was the address. And it was a little bent at one corner. Vanessa said, "Very well," and tucked the card away.

She poured two cups of coffee and handed one to Brooke. "Now tell me why you're here."

So this was the test. A casual conversation with a worldly woman assessing and deciding if you were a candidate for the Mistress Club.

Was there a right answer or a right type? Did she even want to try to get past this first dragon? She could say anything, and tell MJ and Delia that she'd tried.

No. This is everything I wanted, exactly how I imagined it.

Brooke sipped the coffee to give herself some breathing room. The goal was so close and so far away. And she was on a tightrope, trying to keep a balance between fear and hope that this would work out exactly the way she had always imagined.

Vanessa waited. She wore diamond earrings, a beautiful diamond ring, gold bracelets, expert youthful makeup, and a trendy chignon.

I could be Vanessa—minus the blonde hair—in ten years. What do I really, really want?

This was the moment, right now, in her hands.

"I'm here because I'm young, a little experienced, and I'm not jaded yet. I'm fairly new to the city, I'm beautiful, educated, intelligent, and I want to control my sex life."

Vanessa smiled. "Do you know what Maîtrise means?"

"No."

"Control."

Brooke felt a thrill of recognition. How eerie was that, that this name would mirror her whole philosophy in dreaming up the Mistress Club?

"Maîtrise is a very exclusive spa," Vanessa continued, "where a very select group of hand-picked young and beautiful women take control of their bodies and their lives, and our discriminating male clientele comes to relax and rejuvenate themselves in that fountain of youth. So let's get the basics out of the way, shall we? Where you're from, where you went to school, where you work, when you came to New York, that kind of thing."

Brooke told her as succinctly as possible, awed that Vanessa took no notes. Vanessa asked polite but incisive questions that delved into Brooke's experience, her wants, her needs, her secrets, her desires.

"You are very beautiful. Stand up, let me see how you carry yourself."

Brooke stood, walked around the room, then sat down again.

"Size six?"

Brooke nodded.

"I need two things from you today before we can go any further. One is references, and the second is your agreement to have a physical exam at our expense. You're smart enough to understand why. I'll give you the name of our doctor, who will report back to me alone. Are both of those conditions acceptable to you?"

Brooke didn't hesitate. "Yes."

"Excellent, then." She produced a card. "Make your appointment this week, please. And I'll take the names of your references now."

Brooke gave the name of her superior at the hotel and a friend in Chicago who had known her since she was a child.

Vanessa stood, and Brooke took the signal and rose also.

"I'm very pleased that you accepted the invitation to come to Maîtrise," Vanessa said, holding out her hand. "I hope it proves beneficial to both of us. When you return next week at the same time, the doorman will admit you."

"Thank you," Brooke murmured. They were at the elevator foyer by then. She felt a brief squeeze on her elbow, then Vanessa was gone.

Delia was frantic, both because MJ was fighting her to call Dallan, and she had no idea where Brooke was.

So when Brooke walked in the door, Delia was fuming. "You could have called."

"I wasn't anywhere I could—"

"MJ was in such a state today, I had to physically keep her from the phone. I took out the phone jacks and hid her cell. It was a little nuts. Was I ever like this, so out of control, my-life-is-over-if-he-doesn't-love-me crazy?"

"Some nights, but the details are dim. And who wants to remember all that, anyway? I'm really sorry, Delia. That must have been awful, to see MJ go over the edge again like that." She paused, then said in a rush, "Delia, listen. I went there."

"Oh, my God. To the Mistress Club?"

"Yes. It was a conversation and two conditions, and that was all until next week."

"Oh, my God. Shall I wake MJ? She's got to hear this."

"Have you guys had lunch? Want a pizza?"

"Sure. But—you went there?"

"Yep, I went there."

"Holy shit. That took . . ."

"Balls. I know. I was scared to death, too. But I was thinking about MJ, and I did it."

Delia looked up from her cell. "You should've called me! I'll go wake MJ."

But MJ was already in that fuzzy-awake state. "Hey," Delia said. "Pizza's coming, and Brooke's back. She went there!"

"What?" MJ yawned. "*What!*"

"She went to Maîtrise. Come on; let's go hear the details."

After they'd settled in, Brooke told them what had happened: the apartment building, Vanessa's appearance, and a blow-by-blow of their conversation.

"Wow," Delia breathed.

"I did it for you," Brooke told MJ. "I did it so we can all have some options. And so you can shed the notion that there's only one love and one kind of life, and you somehow trashed it. That son of a *bitch* trashed it by treating you like shit, and now we're going to meet men who will treat us like treasures."

MJ's face clouded. "Maybe."

"Well, I'm committed to seeing their doctor, and you *know* he's going to poke and pry everywhere. That's sacrifice."

"It really was that simple?" MJ asked.

"I think it must get harder from this point on; they have to be pretty stringent about who they accept. The doctor will undoubtedly be testing me for drugs, alcohol, estrogen levels—God, anything you can think of. And I wouldn't be surprised if there's some kind of confidentiality agreement to sign, and some form of remuneration if things don't work out."

"I'd love a monetary bandage," MJ said wistfully.

"Then I guess we'll see what happens. In the meantime, tomorrow we all have to go to work—though maybe MJ should take some time off. I'm worried about Baines's reaction when he finally realizes that MJ is no longer at his beck and call."

Brooke found out two days later when she went to MJ's apartment to pick up mail and clothes, and the doorbell rang violently.

Oh, shit. The voice mail was blinking madly, and she instantly knew why. Baines had most certainly been calling and now, frustrated by no return call, he had shown up.

She tucked MJ's clothes and mail into her tote, hoping that MJ hadn't given him a key and he would just go away, or that the neighbors would call the police. But she could also sit there all night while he stubbornly waited for MJ to show. He was that kind of guy.

Not good. She had her doctor's appointment in two hours at a fancy address on Park Avenue, but not if this idiot kept ringing the bell and banging on the door downstairs.

Time to put an end to that.

She saw him watching through the windowed door as she came downstairs. Damn. He could push his way through that door in two seconds if she opened it. MJ never should have rented a walk-up; it was too damned dangerous.

"Hey!" he shouted through the door. He was a tall, elegant man, but there was something mean and calculating in his expression. "You—where's MJ?"

This was not going to work. Brooke resolutely walked up

to the first-floor landing and knocked on the first door, hoping someone would answer quickly, and that it was a guy and he would be furious about the aggressive pounding on the door downstairs.

"Yah—?" It was a sleepy bald man, rubbing his eyes as if she had just woken him.

"There's this really angry guy downstairs, looking for your neighbor, MJ Branden. I have no idea who he is, and I didn't want to let him in. Do you think you could just . . . back me up . . . so I can get out of the building?"

The guy looked her up and down. "I don't know you."

"I'm a friend of MJ's. She'll be away for a while; I was just picking up her mail and some clothes."

The banging grew louder.

"Yeah, I hear him now. Okay. I have a baseball bat."

"That might be useful."

She waited while he got the bat, and he followed her down the steps, where his appearance silenced Baines.

"Step away from that door," Brooke called out, "or we'll call the police."

He stepped back, far back, and Brooke was grateful that a little crowd had gathered, and someone had flipped a cell and was talking into it.

She turned to the neighbor. "Thanks. I think it's okay now."

She eased out of the door, making certain she locked it securely behind her.

Baines looked around him at the curious crowd, then came forward and grasped her arm.

"Excuse me!" she said and pulled away.

The crowd moved in.

"Where's MJ?"

"I don't know who you're talking about. I'm just subletting here."

"Yeah, like I believe that. Who are you?"

"Mona Lattimore," she snapped, naming a recent guest at the hotel. "Who the hell are you?"

"None of your business," he growled and wheeled away. "You just tell MJ that I'll find her, wherever she's hiding or whoever she's sleeping with."

Hot fear coursed through Brooke's body. With a man like that, you didn't take his threats lightly.

MJ couldn't ever go back there, she decided, as she wriggled onto the exam table an hour after the encounter. MJ probably should quit her job, too—damn it. Jobs like that were hard to find.

She needed a plan. MJ needed protection.

"Hmmm," the doctor muttered as he inserted a speculum. "We must check everything."

"Fine."

"Nice, nice. Sit up—"

He'd measured everything, including how deeply she could be penetrated.

Lord, the things they wanted to know . . .

But maybe some men needed that kind of accommodation. The thought of a shaft that hard and long made her shudder with longing.

It's been too long . . .

He examined everything: her vagina, her breasts, her nipples, her hair, her mouth, her hands and feet, her anal area. She felt like a piece of raw meat. And she was never going to get the feel of the doctor's invasive hands out of her memory.

"You have to stay here from now on," she told MJ that night, after describing what had happened at her apartment.

"But," Delia asked, "if Bill could so easily track *me* down, couldn't Dallan find us, as well?"

"No one in my work life knows about you guys, and I assume that's true of you, too, Delia. So I think we're safe here."

"Good," Delia said resolutely. "Men like Dallan and Frank don't like to lose."

"Ummm . . . can I have a say?" MJ asked warily.

"No!" they answered simultaneously.

"Look," Brooke said, "my idea is to get us hooked up with the Mistress Club as fast as possible—and then *everything* will be possible."

MJ sighed. "And you've got a plan, I bet."

"Actually, I don't. Yet."

"Good, because I don't want the Mistress Club. I want Dallan." She stared defiantly at them.

"You really don't," Delia said gently. "You want someone kind and strong, who will appreciate you the way you deserve to be appreciated. Do *not* give yourself over to him again."

"I have to," MJ whispered.

"No, you don't."

"But he's the only one—"

"He's *not*."

"—who understands . . ."

Delia moved a little closer. "Understands what?"

There was a long pause. "Me."

Delia sighed. "That was what *I* thought. That Frank was the only one who knew all about me."

MJ's eyes were damp. "Exactly."

"But you guys showed me that his only interest was himself."

"Yes . . ." MJ whispered.

"And he didn't care about *me*."

MJ started to cry.

"Only, he knew things . . . Well, there are lots of men who treat secrets with reverence and respect, rather than something you should be ashamed of. Whatever the secrets are," Delia added kindly. She let a few beats of silence go by so MJ could absorb what she was saying.

"What's your secret?" MJ asked tearily.

"I'm a plain old vanilla, missionary-position farm girl," Delia said. "Pretty dull for some guys, Frank included. He always wanted me to do things I didn't want to do. So now I know some things I didn't used to, but that's not *me* in bed. And he made me feel like shit, on top of it. I much prefer the idea of a lover showering me with attention and gifts, and making me feel like a queen.

"And that's what this is all about—value. We have value,

and there are men who want that. So let's find them. And let's leave the garbage in the street where it belongs."

MJ took a long shuddery breath. "Maybe . . ."

Brooke stepped in. "He said he's determined to find you, and while I doubt he can, we'll take precautions. Then once I'm in the Mistress Club—"

"*If* you're in," MJ corrected in a watery voice.

"That's my old MJ," Brooke said encouragingly. "*When* I'm in, I'm going to refer you both as quickly as I can. Baines will seem like a deposed dictator in comparison to the men you'll meet there."

Chapter Ten

She had been woefully underdressed last week when she'd impulsively gone to Maîtrise, and Brooke was determined that this time she would positively reek high maintenance.

"Thank goodness for recycle shops," she said as she discarded this outfit and that before settling on the La Perla underwear, and a top-to-toe white Carlisle ensemble consisting of a puckered jacket, obi-waisted crepe trousers, and a silk tank, a Chanel-like drape of gold, beads and pearls, Celine pumps, and a Prada python bag.

She left her long black hair wild and tumbling, kept her makeup subtle, and her mind on the goal: that coveted membership in the Mistress Club.

She was nervous as hell as she hailed a cab and gave the address of Maîtrise. The doorman appeared the minute she pushed open the door and immediately ushered her into the reception foyer. The elevator was waiting.

It felt very different, as if she were *there* already, in that rarefied stratosphere of the kept and cosseted.

Oh, Lord, I'm too inexperienced for this . . .

But, she reminded herself, the alternative was equally un-appealing; marriage and matronhood were not for her just yet, and being a frantic single dancing the fuck-and-farewell fandango all over the city was a huge waste of her time.

This was so much better: It was clean, neat, elegant, with the parameters mutually understood and emotions packed away for the duration.

The elevator door opened, and she stepped into the hushed and elegant living room of the Mistress Club.

A minute later, Vanessa entered from a door on the left side of the room.

"Brooke."

She wore an Italian-made cream-colored jacket today, with a matching whisper-thin jersey pullover and a chiffon skirt in a subtle matching print. Her hair was again pulled into a chignon, her jewelry was minimal, her shoes a coordinating cream color. Everything about her was polished and put together.

She took Brooke's hand and motioned again to the chairs. "Let's talk."

That didn't sound good. Damn damn damn. Brooke held her head high as she seated herself.

No coffee today. That didn't bode well.

"Brooke?"

She turned her distracted gaze on Vanessa.

"Everything is fine," Vanessa said with a smile, and Brooke had the feeling that by *everything*, Vanessa meant more than her references and her physical well-being. Of course, they would take no chances here. Probably everything was vetted, from the hospital where she'd been born to whether she paid her bills on time.

Vanessa was still speaking. "We can go forward with your membership."

Brooke blinked. *Membership?* A weight dislodged from the pit of her stomach, and she smiled.

"If you're ready," Vanessa added.

If? What did *ready* mean? Better not to ask. Just dive in headfirst, and swim. Brooke squared her shoulders. "Of course."

"Then let's get started." Vanessa rose and led the way to that side door, through which they entered a hallway and then a beautifully paneled office where there was a desk and leather side chairs, a suede-covered sofa, and matching tables.

Vanessa indicated the sofa, and Brooke sat while she gathered some papers, pens, and a sleek walnut clipboard from the desk before she joined her.

"As you know, we are extremely particular about our membership. Our goal is to protect all our clients while providing a luxurious and sensually relaxing interpersonal experience in a spa setting, where our members feel utterly pampered, valued, and totally secure.

"To that end, we require some guarantees from our new members. This is a privately owned concern, so any mention of Maîtrise in any context in any tabloid publications would warrant legal action. I'm going to ask you to sign our standard confidentiality agreement, which is to protect *all* our members."

Brooke read it quickly. It was a Sturm and Drang contract between her and the corporation that owned Maîtrise, with dire consequences if anything of a private or personal nature pertaining to the guests of the spa or the spa itself were divulged in a public way.

She signed the agreement.

"Excellent," Vanessa murmured. "Now, with membership, you are provided with your own dressing room key, so you can come and go as you wish." She handed Brooke a filigree key on a gold chain. Brooke promptly put it around her neck, and Vanessa nodded.

"You may use all the facilities freely. There are no constraints here, no rules. Do whatever feels comfortable to you—it's your choice. However, we do take some precautionary measures of a different nature."

She handed a sheet of paper to Brooke. "We'd like to get to know you better. So here, you can indicate some of the things that will give us a clearer picture of your personality. Your likes, your dislikes, your hobbies, your interests."

Brooke scanned the sheet, her hands shaking. This was it: the go-between moment, the negotiation of privilege and perks, couched in a generic lifestyle questionnaire.

Circle as many as apply, get as much as you can. Nothing specific to mistresses, everything pertaining to monied men looking to protect their interests while they indulged themselves with their own private playthings . . .

I am: happy, ambitious, easygoing, hard-driving, loving, attentive, affectionate, adaptable.

I like: books, music, sports, theater, shopping, clothes, travel.

My hobbies are: sports (tennis, riding, biking, golf, swimming, running), shopping, crafts, cooking, fashion, antiques, reading, art, travel.

I'm attracted to men who are: successful, older, handsome, rich, athletic, eclectic, self-made, elegant, bookish, take-charge.

In the best of all possible worlds, I would love: beautiful jewelry, a lovely apartment, a catered dinner every night, my rent paid for a year, a luxury trip to Europe, someone to take care of me.

Vanessa took the finished page and scanned it. "Yes. Exactly as I thought." She tucked the page into a file with the confidentiality agreement. "Now, we like all our new members to experience all the lavish indulgences available at Maîtrise. So this is your day, Brooke. I'll take you to your dressing room so you can change. I'd like you to consider a partial Brazilian—you'll love it, and our staff are very skilled at that service. After, we'd like to take pictures for our membership roster. But take as much time as you wish before that and enjoy *all* the benefits of your membership at Maîtrise."

The dressing rooms were on the second floor, just off the elevator. Hers was as large as a bedroom, with a walk-in closet, a chaise lounge, tables, paintings, soft lighting, and a lovely old Oriental rug.

"This will be your dressing room," Vanessa told her. "Please . . ."

Brooke disrobed and put on the diaphanous gown that was hanging on a padded hanger in the closet. It covered nothing; she might as well have been naked. She had the distinct impression, as Vanessa eyed her with approval, that most members chose to be.

Up to the third floor. Here there was a long corridor with two sets of folding doors.

"Our male clients enjoy the gentlemen's club"—Vanessa gestured to her left—"while our ladies choose from a variety of spa treatments designed to enhance and beautify their bodies. This aspect is not co-ed. Welcome to Maîtrise, Brooke."

She pulled open the door to the spa and Brooke had the instant impression of light. Everything at Maîtrise seemed to reflect bright, soft light and sybaritic comfort. No salon chairs here; only plump overstuffed club chairs and thick padded benches. Ethereal privacy curtains. Mirrors reflecting back the beautiful surroundings inhabited by beautiful people.

Every spa service she could conceive of was available here, and a half dozen women her age were already enjoying them.

And every practitioner was male, nearly naked but for a silk loincloth wrapped around his waist.

Vanessa brought her to Baskhar, who had extremely capable hands and musculature to be envied. "Baskhar is our waxer extraordinaire."

He motioned her onto the padded bench, and Brooke hesitated. On a table beside him were the implements of his trade, disguised in expensive stone jars to prevent his clients from knowing exactly what they were in for.

Don't think. Be a woman of the world, even if you feel like a babe in the woods.

She hoisted herself onto the bench and lay back. Baskhar gently pushed apart her legs to examine her thoroughly. "Very nice. We expose lips."

Almost instantly, she felt warm wax being painted onto her exposed cleft, and she forcibly quelled her panic. It was just a wax job, for heaven's sake.

Then he pulled sharply. And it hurt.

Baskhar denuded only her vaginal opening; he left the hair between her thighs but trimmed it.

"Men love mystery," he said impersonally. He spread her legs wider and grunted.

"Nice. Let me see arms, legs."

The torture went on. But it was soothed afterward with a honeyed oil massage between her legs. She'd never had such a thing, or such a dispassionate treatment of her nether parts as Baskhar stroked and patted her mound with a magician's touch.

"Beautiful," he murmured, when Vanessa reappeared. "Take picture. Lie still."

"*What?*" Brooke struggled to sit up.

"Be still. Men love to see before they buy." Baskhar spread her legs, and a minute later her nakedness was digitized close up.

After that, she gave herself over to an afternoon of pampering. Every service she could possibly want that enhanced, perfumed, and softened her body was hers for the asking.

And she asked. For MJ's sake, she had to experience everything.

She took a hydrating steam bath, had a hot-stone massage, an herbal facial.

They did her hair, her makeup, her hands, her feet; then she was pulled, pummeled, and polished on top of that. She could have stayed there forever, luxuriating, but Vanessa came for her.

"Our lounge is on the fifth floor," she said, "where our members love to relax after a day of pampering. You might enjoy a drink, some conversation, some quiet time. Leave your gown here, I have some adornments for you."

Adornments proved to be dangling gold earrings, a thin gold chain to drape over her hips, and gold stiletto sandals.

Oh, God, Vanessa really was going to make her parade around naked? She couldn't do naked. She could do modestly revealing. She could do transparent dressing gown. But naked—?

"This is all you need to wear," Vanessa said. "This, and your hard, pointy nipples. Come."

Brooke looked down at her breasts, faintly appalled by the notion that her erect nipples were *adornments.*

How awful could it be, to walk around naked and talk to people?

Vanessa was waiting. Brooke tripped down the hallway after her to the elevator on those four-and-a-half-inch wobbling stilettos.

"I trust everything is fine," Vanessa said, pressing the number five on the brass keypad.

"Everything's lovely." *Not.* But she owed it to Delia and MJ to follow through on this. And to redefine her own boundaries—because she'd breached them a half dozen times already at least.

But *naked?* She hadn't expected that.

The elevator doors opened. Once again, her first impression was light—the huge room was sun-flooded from skylights and windows. Everywhere there were plush sofas and chairs scattered around, with men and women occupying them, engaged in conversation, relaxation, or lustful petting.

There was a bar along the far wall where guests were ordering drinks, doors on the opposite wall, and a pool table at the far end, and opposite, a long table full of canapés for nibbling.

"Here we are. Enjoy yourself, Brooke."

The doors closed on Vanessa, leaving Brooke feeling as if she'd been caught with her pants down.

No one was looking, particularly. The women here were all dressed in variants of Brooke's adornments: ankle bracelets, golden cuffs, thrall collars, wispy cutout bras, or thongs, everyone in sky-high strappy sexy sandals, every woman as sleek as a purring kitten and treating her nudity as if she were fully dressed in subtly sexy clothing.

Brooke didn't know quite what to do, so she edged her way into the room and over to the bar.

"You're new," the bartender said. He was bare-chested, but she couldn't see whether he was bare all the way down.

Probably he was wearing that loincloth; most of the male guests were in silk dressing gowns.

He looked way too young to be working in a venue like this, but she had the feeling he was inured to it. He'd barely given her body a glance, and he kept his gaze determinedly on her face.

"Yes, as of today." She ordered a Perrier with lemon. "I'm Brooke."

"Well hello, Brooke. Welcome to the wind-down room, where your mission is to rev up the guests. My advice: Find someone who looks likely and start a conversation. You're never more interesting than when they think someone else wants you."

She took the goblet he handed her. "Thanks."

She looked around the room. The men were older than she'd imagined, some of them reading the paper, some just sitting with their heads back, one or two deep in conversation, another on his cell phone.

The women were either talking to each other or to the gentlemen, or cuddling with them in a dark corner.

None of the men were particularly handsome or fit, the way she'd always imagined they would be.

Reality check: Powerful men who have the means to support a mistress do not necessarily look like Hugh Steffen. They looked like every man, and Brooke didn't know if she was disappointed or relieved.

She made her way to a grouping of chairs near the window, where one of the men seemed nicely absorbed in his *Wall Street Journal.*

So here I am . . .

She studied the man opposite her, who was so intent on his stock figures. He was wearing a dressing gown; he was tall, swarthy, with thinning gray hair, thin lipped, barrel chested and long legged: And there was something about him. She didn't want to call it magnetism or charisma, but she had the feeling he didn't suffer fools and that he had a very strong, controlling hand on whatever boat he was steering.

What about someone like him?

What about *him*?

He looked up, almost as though he could hear her thoughts, and his eyes glanced off hers. Hooded eyes, thick brows, strong nose, high cheekbones. An aura of controlled power. A nod and then back to his paper.

I failed.

She felt a touch on her thigh and looked up. It was her silent companion. She looked inquiringly at him.

"You're new here?" His voice was deep and gravelly, his demeanor casual.

"First time ever," she answered lightly.

"A virgin," he murmured, his interest palpably sharpening. "As it were." He held out his hand. "I'm Thane."

His grip was firm, hard, and very hot. This man pulsed with so much energy that just a handshake threatened to swallow her up.

"Brooke." She felt consumed already, because there was something predatory in his sudden intense interest.

Oh, Lord, right out of the box . . .

"Do you mind?" He patted the chair next to her.

This was the crux of the matter, the moment she couldn't say no—and how she handled him would determine everything that would come later.

"Please," she said, and he set aside his paper and shifted his large body into the chair next to her.

"You're quite beautiful."

"Thank you."

"So this is your first day. What do you think?"

She didn't know *what* she thought. Couldn't remotely divine what *he* was thinking, except for the obvious. "It's rather overwhelming."

"That it is," he agreed. "I love how pointy your nipples are. I'd ask to fondle them, but this is your first day, and I don't want to . . . overwhelm you."

"Do you think you could?" she retorted sweetly.

"We could explore that option," he said, "but you're not ready."

Not ready? When her body was reverberating like a bowstring, with a Brazilian pulsating between her legs, and naked nipples that responded to words that were as arousing as an evening of foreplay? Why would she have a moment's hesitation when the goal was already in sight?

"Maybe I am." She smiled.

He put his hand on her thigh. "I have a feeling you're not."

She couldn't let this opportunity go by. At best, he was attracted to her enough to pursue her; at worst, she could practice on him.

"I'd like to find out," she said. "Otherwise I wouldn't be here, would I?"

"Point taken, Brooke." He ran his hand up her thigh.

"So how does that work?" Oh, there was a brazen invitation if ever there was one. Not a very elegant approach.

"We'll just talk for a while," he said. "I'm not in a big hurry."

Damn, she'd rushed that fence. "That's fine," she said. "I'm not, either."

"But I like the fact you're brand-new. I'd like to be the one to try you out."

What a sly fox, chastising *her* for being too forward, then taking the bit and running with it. That told her something about him.

That, and the sudden spurt of his sex underneath his robe.

"I'd like to try you out, too," she said, slanting a covert look at his bulging erection. He was so *big* and working heroically to keep it under control. She couldn't avoid looking at it, and she had the distinct feeling he wanted her to.

She imagined him penetrating her, felt that luscious liquefying of her body that presaged arousal.

He smiled and squeezed her thigh as he watched her face, aware she was creaming for him. She couldn't hide it, didn't want to. All her preconceived ideas had condensed into a tight nub of unexpected desire.

"Brooke?"

"Yes, Thane?"

"What are you thinking?"

She laughed. "Exactly what you think I'm thinking."

"Tell me about yourself," Thane said.

"I would think the fact that I'm here would tell you everything."

"You are one sassy lady, Brooke. What else should I know about you?"

Why would he want to feel her out, when he so obviously wanted to feel her up? There was no answer to that, so she told him about herself, her college years, her decision to come to New York, about Delia and MJ, and about her job. She omitted any mention of her desire to become a mistress.

The fact that she was sitting there naked clearly told him that.

"And no one's claimed you?"

She shook her head, puzzled. "No. No. This is my first day here."

"Good." He ran his large rough hand up and down her leg possessively and felt the convulsive movement of her body in response. "I think—yes, I think I'm going to claim you for my black book."

Dare she ask? "And what does that mean?"

He was looking at her nipples almost hungrily, she thought.

"It means that until I decide what I'm going to do about you, no one else can have you."

"*Do* about me?" Did she have no control? Did she really want this, want him? Or just the excitement of sex and arousal?

"Brooke," he murmured just a little reproachfully as he

got up. His massive erection jutted out enticingly from under his robe as he looked down at her. He leaned over her suddenly, bracing himself on the arms of the chair, maneuvering the heft of his penis toward her mouth. Waiting to see what she would do. Daring her to . . .

She eyed the shaft head so close to her lips and slanted a look at him. "Really, Thane, is this—?"

"It's whatever *I* want it to be," he said roughly. "What do you want it to be?"

Was this a test?

She closed her mouth around the pliant head. It was huge, it invaded her mouth like no other penis she'd ever sucked, just filled her right up almost to the back of her throat, deep and hard, the way it would fill her up between her legs. Sucking him took all her energy; she pulled at him and licked him until she felt his body tighten and the lush reward of a spurt of semen at the very tip. She swiped it off with a hot lick of her avid tongue.

He jerked his shaft from her greedy mouth. "I'm interested," he murmured, his voice rough. He reached for her right breast and compressed her nipple between his fingers.

She grasped his shaft, her body arching upward in a shock of pleasure.

"I'm *very* interested." He didn't remove his fingers, and the naked feel of him enfolding her nipple like that made her body go insensate with pleasure.

"What about you, Brooke?" He squeezed gently and she felt his penis elongate. "Are you interested?"

"Yes," she breathed.

"Good." He compressed her nipple again just to see her body jolt at his touch. "Go see Vanessa. I'll call you—soon." And he was gone.

She was barely aware of anything, she was so swamped by the lush feelings in her breast. Why didn't he stay, why didn't he keep on—?

"Omigod."

She shook herself out of her sensual haze to see that one of the women had taken Thane's place beside her.

"Do you know who that is?" the woman asked in a hushed, awed voice.

She shook her head.

"Thane Bohansson, the media mover and shaker. The power behind the power. The man who out-Sumners Sumner Redstone."

"Oh!" She had heard of him, and maybe she'd have been more on point if his sex hadn't been so enticingly close and in her mouth. "Oh. Well."

"Yes," the woman said, extending her hand. "I'm Lonita, by the way. You're new."

"Yes. I'm Brooke." She shook hands, noting that even though Lonita had a beautifully toned body that was enhanced with a cutout bra, a thin chain around her thigh, and the requisite stilettos, her face was a little less doll-smooth than the other girls lounging around.

"Hi, Brooke. So he . . ."

"Said he's interested. What does that mean?"

"You *are* new. Actually, he broke a few rules with you right there. They're dead set against doing anything sexually overt on the floor. That's what the dressing rooms are for. And they'd really prefer that any fucking is done off premises, since this isn't a bordello. Or so they say.

"*Interested* means he wants to see you outside of Maîtrise. That's what he meant by *claiming*. It's the first step to deciding if he'll make you his mistress. So go for it. Why not? He can afford you."

"But he's not—" Brooke started to say and broke off.

"They never are perfect," Lonita said, instantly intuiting Brooke's objection. "They're short, heavy, balding, they're tall, too dark, or disproportionate in size—what do you care, as long as they have a fat penis and a fat wallet? Everyone is the same height horizontally, anyway. And looks aside, Bohansson is pretty magnetic."

"I guess," Brooke said hesitantly and wondered why she was reconsidering anything right now. How fast did a woman usually get picked as a mistress, anyway? And Lonita, who'd been around the park a few times, probably wasn't anyone's first choice for a plaything now.

"So what happens is, Vanessa will enter your name in his black book, and no one else will be permitted to approach you until he's decided whether things will go further. Then he'll call you. Wine and dine and fuck you. If you're good, if you're smart, if you're accommodating, there's a good chance he'll want to keep fucking you—with *all* that entails. So be smart."

"Okay," Brooke said. "I can do smart."

"Good. You should go see Vanessa, since she's the keeper of the fabled little black books. They all have them. It keeps things orderly. Prevents any misunderstandings."

Brooke blinked. "That's good to know. Thanks."

"Good luck. Hope I don't see you back here anytime soon."

"So." Vanessa set aside an envelope she'd been about to open as Brooke entered the office. "You've been claimed. Sit down, Brooke."

Brooke sat.

"Mr. Bohansson . . . very special. And so quickly. Well, a man like that is always attracted to what's new and fresh. From now on, your relationship with Mr. Bohansson is solely your business. I've given him your number and he'll contact you privately. Meanwhile, you're welcome to continue coming to Maîtrise. In fact, I recommend that you do, if only for Mr. Bohansson's pleasure. A man like him likes it when a woman is well cared for in every way.

"If there is ultimately no accommodation—and these things are not guaranteed, Brooke—then I will lift Mr. Bohansson's claim on you, remove your name from his little black book, and you will be free to mingle again with our guests. Do you have any questions?"

"No, that's clear."

"Congratulations, Brooke. It isn't often a newcomer to Maîtrise attracts the interest of a man like Mr. Bohansson. He is one of our treasured guests."

"Then I'll treat him like a treasure," Brooke murmured.

"Excellent. I'm looking forward to seeing you back here soon for your regular regimen."

It was more a command than a question. And maybe it

made sense: They wanted to be certain that those who were chosen maintained that perfection in every way.

"I'll be here," Brooke said.

"Good. It's important, Brooke." That was pointed enough. "Till next time then."

Brooke felt her eyes on her back as she carefully closed the door.

Vanessa waited until she heard the lock latch, then reached for the envelope she'd set down.

She knew what was inside—Thane Bohansson's usual gratuity for calling his attention to *the one ingenuous beauty in the whole city who doesn't want to be a model or an actress, isn't drugged out or in an alcoholic stupor, or involved with some stoned-out deadbeat.*

It was ever the way with high-powered, controlling men like him, she thought: They liked the untainted, the innocent, the untouched. It was her job to find those girls for him. And they were few and far between, these days.

Maybe this Brooke would turn out to be *his* treasure.

She carefully opened the envelope, glanced at the enclosed sum, and smiled.

He'd been unusually appreciative this time.

Chapter Eleven

On the way back to West End Avenue, Brooke was bothered by one thing: It had all been so quick. It just wasn't a given that a man like Thane Bohansson would lust after her on first glance.

Oh, but he'd lusted for her nipples.

She shivered. She could almost re-create the feeling of his fingers on the one taut tip, squeezing it, rolling it between his fingers, sending her body into sensual orbit. She could envision his sex, the taste and smell of it . . .

Why shouldn't it have happened that fast? Why not? And why not to *her*?

She knocked on her apartment door to signal she was back. Delia and MJ instantly converged on her with a hundred questions.

"Was it . . . ?" "Did you . . ." "Were they . . . ?" ". . . any men?"

Brooke laughed and fended them off. "Let me change, at least. I can't tell this story unless I'm in my come-home jeans and T."

"Oh, but look at you," Delia said, touching her hair. "And your makeup—they did your makeup?"

"They did every possible thing you can think of. I mean, they're grooming mistresses, right? I have to change."

"I've got dinner in the oven," Delia said. "Spaghetti and salmon, whenever you're ready."

Ten minutes later, Delia dished out the food, plopped on her chair, and demanded: "I can't stand it anymore—*spill*."

Brooke gave her a crooked smile. "Well, a lot of it was pretty much how I guessed it would be. Someone who's zillionaire rich owns that place, and really wants to keep it under cover. It was made very clear that I'd be in major legal trouble if there was a breath of a mention about it or its clientele in any media anywhere on this earth."

"Whoa," Delia murmured.

"And then the fun began." She described the disrobing, the spa complex, the waxing, the massages, the stations for hair, makeup, manicure, pedicure. "It was like being at a wedding buffet. Line up for whatever you're hungry for; your every wish is served up by a hunky, near-naked guy."

"Ooh . . ." MJ breathed.

"Exactly. And that's before you get to the lounge on the top floor of the building. There's a bar and nibbles, billiards, reading matter, conversation or quiet, your choice, but you know you're expected to mingle with the male guests. The women are naked"—Brooke paused to enjoy their reaction—"except for certain *adornments* that Vanessa supplies. Mine were these," she flipped her earrings, "a pair of mile-high stilettos, and a thin gold chain around my hips."

"Did you—" Delia began.

"Hey, I took one for the two of you. I mean, we had to know, and somebody had to do it."

"So what happened?" MJ asked.

"I managed to sit down by a real bigwig CEO type."

"*And . . . ?*" MJ and Delia together.

Brooke sniffed. "He's interested. When a client is interested, your name goes in a little black book, which is his claim on you, and then no other man can approach you until that's lifted."

"And that was *it*?" Delia asked. "What about the guy?"

"He'll supposedly call—but where have we heard that before?"

"Who is he?" MJ again, always practical.

"Thane Bohansson. Have you ever heard of him?"

"Hol-ee shit!" MJ said. "Are you serious? You're talking *that* stratospheric? He's said to be the power behind a multitude of media, and no one knows much about him otherwise. You'd have to read the *Wall Street Journal* to find word one about him, and then it's usually about some company he's alleged to own."

"But—you found him in this lounge," Delia recapped, "and you're stark naked and . . . he's *interested*?"

Brooke put down her fork. "Well, I might have blown him just a bit."

"*What!*" Delia and MJ shrieked.

"He was right in my face, and I thought, this is the moment of truth. And his head was so plump and ready to blow, so . . ."

MJ sat back, shaking her head. "My God, this is wild."

"Yeah. But the thing is, this guy is no cover model. He's big, he's kind of pirate dark, he's sixty-something, and he's obviously trolling. I didn't know what to expect. I was flying blind, so I just went by my instrument panel."

"You sucked him off," MJ said, still in disbelief.

"No . . . I kind of sucked a spurt out of him. I guess it was enough—for the interest part. What would *you* have done?"

Delia blew out a breath. "I don't know. But you hooked him, so . . ."

"Well, that's the thing that kind of bothers me."

"Shut *up*—what about that could possibly bother you?" MJ asked.

"First, he hasn't offered anything. And second, it happened too damned fast, which makes me nervous."

Delia looked at MJ, who shrugged.

"You know what you'd tell us?" Delia asked. "You'd tell us to go with the flow, and that we're almost where we want to be, so who cares how fast or slow it was, and why ruin it by overthinking it."

Brooke sighed.

"Just get us an invitation to the Mistress Club," Delia said. "That's my kind of wet dream."

Brooke shook her head. "These guys have seen tits and slits forever. So how does a potential mistress stand out?"

Delia thought for a moment. "Someone new and fresh probably raises a flag."

"Yeah, and someone willing to jack a guy off in public, that's pretty enticing," MJ sniped.

"Oh, but I didn't mention the part where he fondled my nipples."

"I'm having an orgasm!" MJ said. "What's *wrong* with you, girl?"

"I was in the moment? Anyway, I'm told Maîtrise means control. But who has the control if a woman is claimed and she can't make contacts until a client decides if he wants her or not?"

"Those men don't make idle choices, though," Delia mused. "They don't walk into those situations without a lot of preparation."

MJ looked at her defiantly. "Well, I love that idea: being claimed by one special man."

Delia jumped in encouragingly. "Then you'll find him there. Because someone there right now is looking for someone just like you."

He called at the end of the week. "Brooke."

She was in her office at work, her cell at the ready, a complicated theater and dinner city tour plan spread out before her. Her heart skipped as she recognized his voice. "Thane."

"Busy tonight?"

Be smart, don't play coy.

"No, I'm not."

"Good. I'll send a car. Seven o'clock. Don't wear anything that will impede me in any way."

Her breath caught, but he'd rung off. The tour plan was forgotten; what to wear instantly became paramount.

She called MJ. "He called."

MJ made a little sound, almost as if she had been the one waiting for the call. "And?"

"He's sending a car. Tonight. He wants me naked under my clothes."

MJ made another sound. "Sounds like he knows exactly what he wants."

"MJ, this is so not you."

"A big, monied hotshot who wants to sex you up in public—sounds fun to me." It sounded more than fun, it sounded heavenly, like someone taking control again. Someone better, who would adore her and do things to her and with her wherever he wanted to. But she'd just have to live that life vicariously for now, until she was claimed by her own all-powerful man.

"Come as soon as you can. I need help with this."

Delia was working the night shift, so Brooke and MJ met at five and made a shambles out of Brooke's closet.

"How do I know what to wear if I don't know where he's taking me? How casual, how glam?"

"Let's be logical. The clue is no impediments. If you wear jeans, he can't get to you. If you wear a bra, he can't get to your nipples. If you wear panty hose, he can't get between your legs—but stockings and garter belt could be very arousing."

"O-kay."

"So, some little black slink he can slide off of your body in two seconds."

"I have to be that easy?"

"A man like that wants fondling time, you give it to him." *I would.*

"But—that damned Brazilian—I have never felt so *naked* as I do now. Every moment, I'm aware of how bare I am down there."

MJ made another sound of longing. "Fine. But that doesn't solve the problem of what to wear."

Brooke rummaged some more and pulled out an empire-style slip dress of brown silk overlaid with mitered stripes in a deeper cocoa color.

MJ was speechless for a moment. "Wow. Those stripes sure are suggestive. The one at your thighs points right to nirvana."

Brooke sent her a scathing look. "Only you would think that."

"Oh, your Mr. Bohansson will think that, too. Trust me."

"All right. I don't need a bra with this dress. I'll wear gold sandals, my Maîtrise earrings, and some gold chains. Enough?"

MJ agreed, and Brooke jumped into a quick shower, applied a rich moisturizer all over her body, a subtle cream perfume, a spray of tanner on her legs, a dusting of glitter powder across the low-cut bosom of the dress, and had MJ curl her ends as she applied makeup.

"Okay?"

MJ nodded.

"Okay." She grabbed a small gold evening purse fitted out with money, a credit card, protection, a folding brush, a multipurpose makeup pencil, and some breath mints.

"Nervous?"

"Scared to death."

The buzzer rang.

"Go get him," MJ said. *Get him for me.* "I want to hear every juicy detail later."

The limousine, long, sleek, black, and luxurious, delivered her to the TriBeCa Grand Hotel. Thane was waiting dressed in businesslike gray, imposing and impressive if not elegant. She allowed him to help her out, admire her, and tuck her arm under his as he guided her to the exclusive Sanctum nightclub.

Here they would have drinks, a little conversation, listen to the hottest DJ playing the group of the moment, while he showed off his accessory of the moment: *her.* She understood that. Her job was to look beautiful and make certain heads turned as they walked by. When they were seated, he ordered the Calvados 75 champagne cocktail for her, a bourbon for himself.

They watched trendies and hotties dance and drink, and at just the right moment, when there was a subtle pause in the noise, he signaled that they would leave. It was as if she rose from the sea with Neptune alongside her.

Every eye was on them as they exited, and the noise rose behind them in a crescendo as they stepped into the hotel lobby, where his chauffeur was waiting.

Inside the limousine, he relaxed. "I can only stand so much of that. How important is it to you?"

Showing off for her? *Be smart.* "Not at all."

"Good. I like that dress. Come here."

A man in control, understanding his purpose and hers. He slipped his arm around her shoulders, covered her breast with his hand, and leaned in to kiss her.

She let him kiss her as the limousine plowed through the night life traffic of lower Manhattan, and he fondled her tongue and nipple simultaneously until she was squirming. Squirming because that nakedness between her legs instantly creamed with arousal.

He was a direct and blunt lover; his kisses weren't so much arousing as conquering. But the caressing way he fingered her nipple beneath her dress put her in a near orgasmic swoon.

He removed her strap to bare her breast. He sank into her mouth, he kept at her nipple, rolling it and compressing it, until she almost came.

"SoHo, sir."

The chauffeur's voice came from a distance, and Thane eased his mouth from hers, but not his possession of her nipple. "Thank you." He went back to her mouth, sucking at her tongue, stroking her nipple. Her body arched, seeking the pleasure point, bucking against his kisses, his incessant fingers.

"Brooke . . ." Somewhere in there, she heard her name as he maneuvered his thigh between her legs and she ground her waxed nakedness down onto his leg, onto that indecently expensive suit, and indecently creamed her orgasm all over it.

He held her nipple quiescent, he kept his tongue in her mouth. Somehow, the driver knew to keep driving.

It took a long time for her to become sensate again, to become aware of his thick tongue still occupying her mouth, to feel the hypersensitivity of her nipple, to feel the slick residue of her orgasm between her legs and on his trouser leg.

He didn't seem to want to relinquish the kiss, so she deepened it, seeking *him* this time. *Be smart.*

She let him dress her; smarter still. She didn't try to talk—even smarter. And the more she kissed him, the more reluctant he became to remove his tongue.

Very smart.

She was the eager lover now, lusting for his kisses and caresses as if she couldn't live without them. Maybe she couldn't—that had been one rocking orgasm out of nowhere.

And because she was still straddling his thigh, she knew how thickly erect and how hot he was. She had to get to his shaft in a nonobvious way. She eased back on her kisses, murmuring, "Oh . . . I'm so sorry—I'm . . . It's so much . . . and it's just our first time together . . ."

"No, no, no," he whispered, stroking her hair.

"I ruined your suit."

"I can buy another."

"So generous," she breathed. "Let me get out of your way . . ." She started to climb off of him, but he shifted his leg and pulled her onto his lap so that she straddled his bulging erection.

"That's where I want you."

She smiled. "That's where I want to be."

He kissed her again, a long, thick kiss that made her as hot as he was, made her squirm and ripple against his throbbing shaft.

She never would have thought . . . not *his* kisses, not his overpowering tongue. She moved restively and he slowly broke the kiss.

"Thane . . ."

"You want dinner," he said bluntly. "At least dinner."

"I was going to say . . . I'm a little tender down there— they only just waxed . . . Could you . . . would you? unzip and let me . . ."

He cupped her face, stared into her eyes. "Say it."

Be smart. ". . . let me dine on you."

"You are either damned smart, a damned con artist, or a goddamned wet dream. You can't be real."

And smarter still. "Your penis is very real, Thane. I know."

He looked deeply into her eyes again and then called out to the driver: "SoHo, *now.*"

He held her face, nipping at her lips. "We'll eat later. I want to eat you first."

"Not before I eat you," she whispered, flicking her tongue against his thin lips and catching his snaking tongue.

The limousine drew to a stop. "SoHo, sir."

"Brooke . . ."

"It's so hard to stop . . ."

"Five minutes and you won't have to stop . . ."

She shimmied against his erection. "Thane . . ."

"We have a big room overlooking the river. Room service, anything you want. So the sooner we get there . . ."

She felt as if she couldn't stand to leave him. How had this happened so quickly, so soon? "Not now?" *So smart . . .*

"Five minutes."

"Promise?" She climbed off of his lap.

"Brooke."

She wrinkled her nose at the reproach; not smart.

He took her arm and led her inside the hotel, wholly ignoring the splotch on his trousers. A stop at the desk for the key. The chauffeur following with his designer luggage. Everything quiet, hushed, expectant, respectful. The elevator silent as it whisked them to the highest floor.

The room was as big as a house, with an expanse of windows overlooking the Hudson River and the twinkling lights of New Jersey.

The bed was old and carved by hand, and the bedding was five-hundred-thread-count Egyptian cotton with silk pillows and a satin duvet. There were lush curtains for more privacy, a glamorous bath, a sitting area with a luscious leather-tufted sofa, chairs around a glass dining table, an armoire, and all the latest electronic connections and equipment.

"Less than five minutes," Thane said.

She looked at him from under her lashes. He was waiting. She had been so eager, and he was waiting for her to act on her sexy little promise—but that walk through the entrance of the hotel had doused the heat in her. They should have stayed in the close confines of the car, in the dark, with the mystery of his rampant sex between them.

Now, she didn't know quite what to do. And there were too many lights, which reminded her of how *not* like a movie star lover he was. The elegant room seemed out of sync with his raw physicality, the reality of his sixty-something body, and his sharp, blunt looks.

So, what—she wanted him to be the unknown lover, with a paper bag over his head? For some reason it had been easier in the dark of the limousine, easier to concentrate on the physical pleasure.

He walked around the room turning out lights until just the dots across the river were visible. She heard him removing his jacket, his tie, his shirt.

Then he took her hand, led her to the leather sofa, and pulled her down onto his lap, back to front. "Let's say that we're still in the car."

He couldn't have guessed. He couldn't have.

"Your nipple, Brooke."

Be smart. She pulled down one strap, he pulled down the other one, all the while licking and sucking her neck and shoulder, then turning her head commandingly to meet his kiss.

She wasn't ready, but his tongue quickly overpowered hers, and his hands cupped her breasts possessively. She felt swallowed by his interest, by his lust.

She felt him harden again as he fingered her nipple, felt his shape, his length. Felt her own body begin to liquefy as the thick pleasure of his fondling coursed through her.

I'm so easy . . . in the dark.

He maneuvered her onto her back on the sofa and climbed over her.

She made a distressed sound—he pushed himself up to rip off his trousers and put his sex into her eager hands. *Smart.*

She guided him between her legs, never breaking the kiss,

skimming her hands over his length and thickness, making luscious little noises of adoration at the back of her throat as she spread her legs and brought his shaft head to kiss her nether lips, then canted her hips upward to take him just inside her.

Connected. That one breathtaking moment when a man's sex breached a woman's most intimate, most voluptuous, and vulnerable part.

He didn't push into her, just let himself be enfolded by her for one inimitable lust-locked moment.

And then she squeezed and he made a sound, and he thrust into her like a piston, taking her hard and hot and hurried in tandem with his hard, hot kisses.

"Brooke—" His voice was thick against her lips. "I'm . . ."

"Yes," she whispered. It didn't matter if he jacked off first. *Smart.* "Come—I want you to shoot everything you have into me."

He groaned.

"And then, I'll eat . . ."

He bucked, he tensed—

". . . your delicious hardness . . ." she promised on a sultry breath ". . . in my mouth."

He reared back and let go a long, hot spume of thick semen.

And collapsed onto her.

"You're goddamned good," he muttered in her ear.

"You, too," she whispered, being smart.

She slept a little, then awakened to find he had ordered from room service. An array of appetizers and finger food awaited on the glass table.

He was prowling the room, barefoot and dressed in just his shirt, his penis quiescent for the moment, dark, long, and massive.

"Food," he said, gesturing to the table.

"I know what I'd rather nibble on," she said. *Smart.* "Why don't you come here?"

He set down his drink and came over to her.

"I haven't forgotten how deliciously plump and thick you felt in my mouth," she whispered, looking up at him as she grasped his thighs.

His penis jolted and hardened.

"So succulent."

And lengthened.

"I want more," she whispered and closed her mouth around him and sucked. She felt his hands in her hair, felt him shoving himself deeper, knew she was going to take the full brunt of his cum. So, let him listen to her pleasurable noises as she sucked him off, let him ejaculate all over her mouth, let her drip with his cream. Let him . . . let him . . . and *let me be the one who does this for him . . .*

She took him voraciously, endlessly, not allowing him a moment to gather himself. This was what she wanted now, in the dim light where he was a prince with an incomparable erection and she could care for him in the way that a mistress should.

Then she felt that moment of release coming. She pulled back to his head, she lapped and sucked it avidly, and a moment later he thrust hard and gave her his cum.

She sucked it out of him, letting some flow down onto

her, until he wrenched away and dropped onto the couch.

She lifted her dress and smeared his semen on her mound, massaging it into her cunt lips as he avidly watched.

"Take off that dress."

She smiled, stood, and let it slide off her body, followed by the necklaces, but she kept the sandals and the earrings. "No impediments."

"I noticed. Sit. Back to front."

She sat, her buttocks cushioned by his spent and softening penis. She leaned back against his naked chest. He curved her face to his so he could kiss her, while his other hand stroked her naked body, exploring all the curves and secret places he had not begun to discover.

She gave herself to his questing hand, relishing the pulsating heat of him, the thick softness of his exhausted penis, the precision with which he felt her up.

She closed her eyes, luxuriating in his unexpectedly soft and arousing touch. As his hands slid downward, she felt herself go limp with pleasure at his expert stroking. When he parted her legs and draped them over his thighs, she barely moved.

When he began stroking between her legs, she loved it. When he parted her nether lips and spread them, she began to squirm. Every part of her now was open to his very knowledgeable exploration of her secrets. She didn't like that he had control now and all she could do was lie back, the most naked part of her laid bare for him. But she was smart.

And he had a light, commanding touch. He dipped and stroked and rimmed until her whole body went weak and she was all his, to do with what he would. And he did; he used both hands, driving his fingers into her with one hand and fondling her clit and outer labia with the other.

The feeling of being possessed like this was indescribably luscious. Her body felt thick and molten hot. She arched and bucked as he pumped deeper; riding his fingers, riding the rolling thunder of her climax as it poured out between her legs, onto his hands, onto his shaft . . .

She couldn't stop; he kept humping her with his fingers, pulling out her pleasure even when she thought she was done, even when she wanted to be done. And then she *was* done, utterly spent, with him still elongating under her buttocks and his hands quiescent on her mound.

He silently gathered her into his arms and turned her so that her head was on his shoulder and she was cuddled in his lap. Then he began caressing her buttocks and exploring and playing lightly with her anus. Whatever he wanted, she let him.

He suddenly breached her from the rear and she gasped. Then he breached her between her legs again so that he held her imprisoned with his fingers, front and back, tight against his hammering chest and his massive, throbbing erection.

First she went rigid with shock, then she melted into the feelings, the pleasure, and finally she melted against him.

"Stay the night." His voice was rough in her ear.

But then there would be the morning. So far she hadn't given away much that she hadn't given away before; the stakes were just higher.

"Do you want me?" she whispered.

"Do I?" He nudged her with his penis. "What about you?"

"I . . . yes."

"Yes, what, Brooke?"

"I want whatever you want to give me." *Smart.*

"Stay, then. There's more."

She nestled against him as he began pumping her again, front and back, and whispered, "Good. I can't wait."

He finally made her sit down and have some food. She made him stand beside her so that she could play with his relaxed penis.

"We don't have all that much time together, even if I stay the night," she pointed out. "So why should I give up even one minute I could be playing with you?"

"No reason I can think of."

So she held it and fondled it as she nibbled on the nibbles, and periodically kissed it and tongued it and avidly watched it grow and thicken and become aroused for her. Then she nibbled on it and sucked his balls as he stood there, sucked him until he was weak with need, and before she knew it, she was straddling him and he was pumping his spunk into her like a geyser. She sank onto his depleted shaft and ate some more of the appetizers, delicately feeding him as well.

In the muted light, he was a big old bear with more stamina than she would have guessed. What was not to like about him on that level? That was the point of *her* Mistress Club.

He was nibbling her nipple now. He'd smeared caviar onto the tip, and he was flicking it with his tongue and making her crazy. When he began sucking, she felt him thicken and elongate to fill her.

She undulated her hips in belly-dance rhythm with his sucking, she held tight onto his shoulders, and she gave him the sounds of her slow, spiraling pleasure. And down she went, the sensation curling sinuously from the center between her legs to the deepest part of her and gently bursting there.

He lifted her head and stared at her.

"I don't know what to make of you."

"You make me come, Thane. Isn't that enough?"

"Is it?" He kissed her roughly, thrusting his hips upward. He couldn't stop. Her lips, her nipples, her tight, hot, waxed mound, his stone-hard erection—he couldn't stop pumping, even when he barely had anything left to spew.

He wrenched away from her mouth. "Is it? You didn't answer."

She was on delicate ground here. She was still mounted on him, and she had no idea what he was getting at, no idea what he wanted her to say. The safest thing was to keep impressing on him that it was his sex, his vigor, his virility that were important, not anything she wanted.

"Isn't it? Hasn't all this been enough for you?" She watched his face, the pirate dark skin, the hooded eyes. "I guess not." She started to dismount, and he held her back.

"Don't leave my penis."

"I never want to," she whispered without thinking. Shit. *Not smart.*

There was a long beat. "You're good."

She said nothing. What could she say, when she was naked and still straddling him? Whose pleasure—his? Hers? Right now, she didn't know. But on some level, after all this sex, she couldn't bear the thought of not having him inside her again.

He was the one who broke the sexual connection. He lifted her gently from his lap, away from his semen-slick shaft, and stood up. She stood, too.

"You meant it?" he said suddenly. "You don't want to leave my penis."

And now, a roll of the dice.

"I *never* want to leave your penis," she whispered. "I want it right now, again. It's too much for me—it's so thick and hard and demanding. It's everything you are, Thane. And it isn't gentle. But—"

He came toward her then, his erection in full thrust, pure and naked man power that was irresistible. She backed away as he moved implacably toward her.

"But what, Brooke?"

"I'm obviously not enough for you."

He kept coming at her and she backed up against the door, with nowhere to go and no response from him. He kept looking at her as if he were gauging her, because he wanted to believe she meant everything she said, that it wasn't a game of take him for a ride.

He planted himself directly in front of her, his shaft nudging at the juncture between her legs. "Maybe you're too much for me, Brooke. Maybe I can't understand why I can't get enough of fucking you, when I don't have a centimeter of semen left in me. But goddamn it—spread your legs."

He thrust at her, blundering his way into her body, pinning her hard, hot, and tight against the door. In that instant, he owned her, occupied her, and left her no room to move, to react; the only thing she could do was feel. And she felt—she was full of him, every inch of him, the thickness of him, the weight of him.

He lifted her legs and wrapped them around him so that she was supported solely by the door and the heft of his penis jammed into her.

"That's all," he breathed into her ear. "This is all I want. Just to stuff my penis into your hot, moist cunt." He pushed deeper. "I have nothing left, and I need to fuck you. Tell me how a man can get that hard again after every fuck. God almighty . . . I will not give this cunt to another penis."

"Then don't," she whispered.

"Tell me what you want."

Be smart. "All I want is what you're giving me now."

"You can have my penis . . ." he pushed her tighter against the door, ". . . if you meant it about never wanting to leave it."

"I meant it."

He groaned and his whole body shuddered with a spurt of release.

"Twice a week. Overnight. Anything I want, any way I want it."

She caught her breath. This was it—the mistress moment. And you didn't bargain or try to dictate the terms.

She compressed her vaginal sphincter to give him a tight little kiss on his shaft.

"I'll do anything," she whispered.

"I thought you'd say that," he growled, then caught her mouth in a hard kiss. "I'm taking you to bed."

She buried her head in his shoulder as he carried her to the oversized, beautifully made up bed, laid her down and followed her down, covering her masterfully while remaining inside her.

And then he just rocked her gently, pressing himself deeper from time to time. He kissed her in his blunt, hard-tonguing way, and all of that was prelude to the growing excitement as his body gathered steam and hers began to cream.

And the lights were so low, and he was so thick, filling, and deep, and her body was so soft and pliant with the satisfaction of having achieved her goal. . . . It was a rainfall fuck, like hot little drops dancing all over her body as he thrust and drove and she belly-danced around the thick core of him, and made this moment her own.

Chapter Twelve

MJ called Delia early the next morning from Brooke's apartment. "Guess what? Brooke hasn't come home yet."

"Hmm. That's a good thing—isn't it?"

"God, I hope so. I hope her elusive bigwig had sex with her all night, but I'm on pins and needles. Oh, Delia, she looked absolutely *gorgeous* last night! So I was thinking . . . maybe we could go to Images today."

Delia knew what MJ was thinking: that maybe Marielyce would offer them the same entrée as she had Brooke. Delia wasn't ready for that yet, but maybe MJ was. She'd been more her old self this week, but even though distance had given her a clearer perspective on Dallan Baines, she still had that doubt that any man could want a woman with her "secret."

Delia knew what the secret was; she had gone through that same struggle over whether she was the kind of woman who wanted to be dominated and controlled. She wasn't, but MJ was a different person.

"Okay," she said, "let's do it. We'll go to Images and see what turns up."

* * *

Brooke was prowling around the room, dressed in Thane's white dress shirt, while he watched her from the bed, his naked shaft flexing playfully in invitation.

In the daylight she was wholly aware of him, the not Prince Charming who was lord of all he surveyed. *What have I done?*

Twice a week. Mistress Club heaven.

Looks don't matter. Big pockets and a big penis do.

The penis part actually made her salivate; that part was heavenly. And he was everything that she had specified, except handsome and built.

Well, one part of him was built, that was for sure. And that was the most important part. She also liked the way he handled her, and what price could you put on that?

"Brooke?" His voice was thick with need and exhaustion.

"I'm here." She climbed back into bed and nuzzled his slack manhood.

He eased her away and slipped his hand under the shirt to play with one taut nipple. "Nice and pointy. Did I tell you I'm hot for pointy nipples?"

"I get hot for *your* point." She ran her hand over his shaft.

"Not now. I'd rather do your nipples."

"Oh, please *do* my nipples, Thane." She moved so he could reach both of them, her body tight and aroused, her breasts arched toward him. He took both nipples at once, squeezing and rolling, pulling at one, then the other, as she melted like putty.

"Such hot nipples."

She straddled him while he played with her. She loved this part, she loved it too much, she couldn't tell him how much she loved how he manipulated her nipples as she undulated and ground her hips against him in passion.

"I think I'll call you Nipples."

Her orgasm exploded at those words in a straight, hot melt from her nipples to her vagina.

"Nipples." His voice held such pure male satisfaction that she wondered hazily if his doing her nipples twice a week would be enough for her.

Delia and MJ set out fairly early from Brooke's apartment, MJ shimmering with an anticipation that made her cheeks flush and her green eyes bright.

She'd dressed in the emerald silk blouse with a Tahari suit, subtle makeup, and her red hair slicked back in a sophisticated, trendy style.

"Don't anticipate too much," Delia warned her. "Marielyce will not pounce on us the minute we walk in the door, and neither of us is brazen enough to ask her anything flat-out."

"We'll play it by ear," MJ said. It was the perfect city morning, with a bright blue sky, clean air, and a pulsating sense there were places to go and she was going there.

For the first time in a long time she felt hopeful, as if she were on the threshold of something explosive and exciting.

The shop had just opened when they arrived, and Marielyce greeted them and asked what their pleasure was today. MJ slanted a look at Delia as they followed her down the aisle to see the new items she had taken in since their last visit.

"Handbags, ladies. Handbags are the accessory of the season. Vuitton, Prada, Chanel. One of these would update anything you're wearing this next season."

She had an array of barrel bags, satchels, messenger bags, and shoulder bags, all with prominent hardware, and MJ was instantly tempted.

Delia preferred the shoes. Chanel, Louboutin, Luca Luca—she was in affordable heaven there.

She was aware of Marielyce's covert interest in them as they tried things on, made suggestions, and offered opinions. That had to be because of Brooke. Marielyce knew they were friends, so she was probably curious about what had happened with Brooke. But she wouldn't—or couldn't—ask. *I'm imagining things.*

Suddenly, there were *the* shoes: burgundy suede, Hugo Boss, a Mary Jane strap across the instep, pleating across the vamp, four-inch heels. Delia grabbed them and didn't even look at the price as she preened in front of the mirror. "I'm taking them!"

"Nice choice," Marielyce said, as a little bell signaled that the last customer had left the store. "Another one of those brand-new gifts that some fortunate woman chose not to keep." She sent Delia a meaningful look.

She meant some fortunate *mistress,* Delia thought, stroking the suede shoes. I never would have done that if someone were generous enough to buy something like these for me.

"How is Brooke?"

Delia blinked. "I'm sorry?"

"How is Brooke doing?"

"She's fine—"

"—and otherwise occupied today," MJ put in. "We hope," she added playfully.

"Hmm." Marielyce murmured and drifted away.

Delia sent MJ a reproving look. "Not good mistress form, MJ."

"A little too bold? But maybe it subtly sent the message of *our* interest."

MJ's interest *should* be encouraged, Delia thought. They were here; why shouldn't MJ pursue the coveted entrée to Maîtrise?

What to do? Maybe nothing. Maybe that little hint was enough to clue Marielyce in.

She picked out a beautiful winter white Kenneth Cole coat from the rack, slipped her arms into the coat, and walked to the mirror. The store was empty except for her and MJ, and Marielyce was folding garments that had been disrupted by the previous customers.

"Beautiful coat," she said as Delia turned in the mirror. "It's from this season's collection, another discard from yet another unappreciative—"

"Mistress," MJ finished for her.

Marielyce didn't blink. "Indeed. Well, there has to be a place where they can get value for their assets."

"It seems rather cavalier," Delia said, stroking the material, "to give such an extravagant gift away for a third of its cost. I would think the giver would be devastated."

"You are very caring, very sensitive to the feelings of the man," Marielyce said. "Most aren't."

"I wish I could buy the coat," Delia said regretfully as she slipped it off, "but unfortunately I can't."

"Perhaps there will come into your life a gentleman who could afford to buy it for you," Marielyce murmured as she hung it up.

Delia felt prickles all over her body. "I would love to find such a gentleman," she said carefully.

"And such a gentleman would love to find you. Perhaps I could be of service in that regard."

"It would be deeply appreciated," Delia said.

Marielyce looked at her for a long moment and then nodded. "MJ—what have you found that has enticed you today?"

"The idea of being a mistress," MJ said brashly.

Delia felt a little trill of horror go through her. Marielyce was so formal, so circumspect, that such a frank statement could put her off.

"Many are seduced by the thought," Marielyce said. "But there is so much to consider. How little time your lover might have for you; how tightly you will be reined in, to be available for his pleasure; what he might demand of you and the use he will make of your body, his little quirks and jealousies . . ."

She was watching MJ's face as she listed all the things that others might define as negatives, which were all the things MJ wanted. It was in her eyes and the avid look on her face.

"Are you really truly prepared for that, MJ?"

"I would love that," MJ whispered.

Marielyce nodded. "Then tell me, what you have chosen today? The shoes, Delia? MJ, a pocketbook? Lovely choices. Let me wrap them, and in time you will know everything you need to know."

She lay on her belly, her naked bottom canted upward. He had straddled her thighs and was sliding his shaft into her crease, pushing and prodding at her anus and her womanhood alternately as she shimmied her hips to entice him to penetrate her.

He didn't speak much during sex, she was discovering. When he wanted, he took, and he took her now in a thick, driving swoop, his hands grasping her buttocks tightly as he embedded his taut, throbbing length deep inside her.

He ejaculated fast, almost as if he couldn't control himself, coming coming coming in thick, rhythmic blasts as he collapsed onto her.

"God," he muttered. "I goddamned want more. I want to rub my milk into your nipples . . ."

"I'll do that for you, Thane. I'll massage your cum into my nipples."

He groaned and eased himself out of her, and she sat, her legs spread, her body arched, so he could see everything.

Giving him a sultry look from under her lashes, she reached down between her legs, swiped her fingers into her cleft, and then massaged his thick ejaculate all over the hard, pointy tips of her nipples.

He was stroking his shaft and almost came again, watching

her slide her slick, semen-coated fingers all over her nipples.

"I want a picture of your nipples."

"Thane!" She pretended to be scandalized. Was she?

"I want those nipples with me all day long."

"Let me think about it." Smart to hesitate? She didn't know.

"Just your nipples."

"Disembodied nipples?" She giggled.

"I'll know whose nipples they are." He pushed her back on the bed. "I can't stop fucking you." He pushed his shaft slowly and maddeningly into her.

She reached out her arms for him. "Don't, then."

"Two days, Brooke. It's all I can give you."

"It's enough," she whispered.

"It won't be enough for everything I want to do to you," he growled as his hips ground against hers. "But it's what I'm offering."

"That's what I want, too," she whispered.

"Do you?" he asked sharply.

"Yes," she said, suddenly unsure. One moment he was thinking entirely with his sex, and four beats later he was a hard-nosed businessman. "I'm not a scheming bitch, Thane. Yes, I know who you are, but I don't know anything more. You probably know more about *me*."

"I do," he said, his head cocked as if he were listening for something in her voice as well as her words.

What could she say that wouldn't sound rehearsed and calculating? Or was everything with him some kind of test, just to see how she responded?

"That's all I have to say, Thane."

"It's enough."

"You do have a thing about *enough*," she said without thinking.

"I have to."

"*Am* I enough for you?" Was that too coy?

"My penis thinks so."

"It's most discerning," she murmured. "I think I like it a little more than I like you."

"Probably very wise of you in the long run. My penis likes your cunt."

"And I like him rooted there, so—"

"So he'll root." He brushed her mouth in a brisk kiss. "And I expect he'll take over from there."

"You know what," Delia said as they were waiting for the bus, "I'm thinking exactly what Brooke was thinking last Sunday."

Traffic was heavy on Sixth Avenue, and MJ was in a fever to get back to Brooke's place so they would be there when Brooke returned. "What was Brooke thinking?" she asked.

"That it was too fast too soon. Didn't you think it was too easy? Almost like Marielyce was expecting us?"

"Well, why wouldn't she assume we'd be as interested as Brooke? Especially now that Brooke is with someone. Maybe she knows."

"Hmm," Delia murmured as the bus drew up and they boarded. "But we don't know if Marielyce did refer us."

"She said the exact same thing to us as she did to Brooke."

"That's true. So we should find one of those cards tucked in the tissue." Delia looked out the window at bustling Broadway as they passed Lincoln Center. Every block had a different feel, a different pulse.

"It's *Groundhog Day* redux," MJ said. "Didn't we play this scene last week?"

Delia gave her a faint smile. MJ wanted this way more than she did. But that was a good thing. Dallan Baines couldn't compare to the possibilities of the Mistress Club, especially if Brooke's overnight was successful in enticing Mr. Bohansson to see her again.

"So who goes first?" MJ asked after they had returned to the apartment and were staring at their wrapped purchases.

"You do. For suggesting we even go to Images today."

MJ carefully unwrapped hers, a dark-brown pebbled leather Cole Haan satchel with brass fittings. "I *love* it," she murmured. "But will I love it more if . . ." She looked at Delia.

"Go on."

"I want it," she whispered and opened the bag. Marielyce had stuffed it with a huge wad of tissue paper and MJ removed it, then looked a little stricken when she found nothing.

"Any pockets inside the bag?" Delia asked.

MJ brightened. "Yes!" She bit her lip, held her breath, gently unzipped the pocket on the back wall, then dipped her fingers inside. "It's here!" Her heart started pounding. "Oh, my God, Delia—it's here." Her hand shook as she held it out to show Delia.

It was the same as Brooke's, the name Maîtrise and the

address in the tiniest raised letters on the elegant vellum. "It got bent," Delia noticed, handing it back.

MJ stared at it as if it were the Rosetta stone. "Now you."

"I'm not so sure I'm ready for this," Delia said, removing the shoe box from her bag.

"It's not a commitment. C'mon," MJ urged.

Delia chewed her lower lip as she took out the shoes. "Oh, they're gorgeous." She slipped her hand into the left one and held it up. "Nothing here. Maybe I'm just not mistress material."

"Delia!"

"Okay" She shook the right shoe, and the card fell out onto her lap. "Oh!" She hadn't expected it, honest to God. And now . . . now—

Delia handed it to MJ, her hand shaking a little.

"Exactly the same. And *it's* bent in one corner, too."

Delia's eyes widened. "That means something, then."

"Right, like admit one for Mistress Maintenance 101?"

"Something like that. Oh, Lord—now what?"

"We do it, is what! We do what Brooke did and we find our own lavish lovers—immediately. It works for me."

Delia looked a little uncertain. "I'm not ready yet."

"Then I'll be the next to go—tomorrow. I want to start the process *now*. Only—Delia?—you have to come with me to the door . . ."

* * *

Brooke was bone tired, boneless altogether. Thane was pumping the barest dribble of spunk into her exhausted body.

"Crap," he muttered, easing down beside her. "Effing penis can't produce."

"I think you produced it out," Brooke said.

"I want more."

She didn't say anything. His penis, still distended, dark, and huge, was at rest between his long legs and she ought to leave it alone, but she couldn't. She was fascinated by it, the size, the color, the heft, the taste. But he was wrung out even more than she.

He'd ordered room service again, but it sat on the table. He hungered solely for her body, and about the only way he hadn't fucked her was her standing on her head. She couldn't imagine what might come next.

He grabbed the house phone. "Get me a digital camera," he barked into the headset and slammed it down. He ran his hand over her buttocks, down her crease, and began stroking her mound. "I can't stop feeling you up."

"I don't want you to," she murmured contentedly as he fingered her cleft. He knew just how, too. The gentle spread, the lightest of caresses on the most naked part of her, the delicate penetration of his fingers . . . "*Yes* . . ." she sighed.

A knock came at the door. "Leave it on the effing floor," Thane shouted, still rhythmically thrusting his fingers.

Brooke reached for his penis; there was nothing like fondling it while a man was fingering you.

Her orgasm was a radiant light spreading from her center outward, soft and enfolding, just as he reached his full solid potential.

"I want that effing camera."

He bolted off the bed and she watched him, six feet of older naked man with a huge, dark, thrusting man root, and the stride of a man who knew exactly what he wanted and where he was going.

How much more could she give him today, in hopes that he'd want an endless amount of *more*, when she'd given him practically everything already?

Lord, she didn't know. But if he was commanding cameras to fulfill his fantasy of photographing her nipples, maybe she should draw the line there, saving that for next time.

Maybe.

He looked damned determined. Every part of him looked determined. There was something about this fantasy that just thickened and engorged him in a wholly different way. He *really* wanted that picture of her nipples, and he stood at the foot of the bed, hard, jutting, and implacable.

Be smart—don't give him every fantasy the first time. What did she have to lose, since she was a little ambivalent about him? *If you do everything on the first date, what's left for him to anticipate?*

"Sit up, Brooke, I want those nipples."

That was a command. She rolled onto her side and sat up. Immediately he reached for her nipples.

She stayed his hand. "I think we should leave this fabulous fantasy for next time."

"Really?" He was eyeing her nipples, which were taut with fondling.

"If there is a next time," she said daringly.

"And why is that?" That was the displeased CEO voice, the one that was accustomed to having everything he wanted done instantly.

"Because next time, I'll jack you off on my nipples and you can photograph them coated with your cum."

She felt the tremor of excitement lance through his body.

"I want it now."

"Next time," she said, knowing there was a touch of satisfaction in her voice. "Because if there *is* no next time, what's the point of my acceding to your wishes now?"

He gave her a long, considering look. "A little bitchy, Nipples. I offered you two days."

"You didn't say when, Thane. They could be a year from now or ten years from now. And I would enjoy another date just like this one, soon. I'd also like a good full-on shot of your penis—if it fits in the viewfinder."

He made a snorting sound.

"Tit for tit?" she murmured.

He laughed, a good, strong, appreciative laugh, and pushed her downward, murmuring, "Now you're in *my* viewfinder," entering her again before she even hit the bed.

His cell phone rang. It was nearly four o'clock, they were both exhausted, and he had allowed her to tease the camera away from him, to keep until the next date.

He spoke guardedly into the phone, then flipped it off and dropped back onto the bed.

"Crisis at home," he said briefly. "Do you mind?"

"Not at all, Thane. I know you have another life."

"And as much I hate it, I have to go. Come here."

She took his thorough blunt kisses, his sensual fingering of her nipples—whatever he wanted before he banished her from this luxurious aerie back to real life without him, without his limitless lust for her body.

His cell sounded again. He wrenched his mouth away and flipped open the phone. "*What?!*" He calmed down. "All right. I'll be there in fifteen minutes." He looked at his fingers, still busily playing with her nipple even as he'd been talking. "Well. That's that."

He got up, leaving her nipples feeling bereft that he had ended his caress so abruptly.

"The limousine will take you home, Brooke."

She nodded.

He grabbed his clothes and went into the bathroom. She heard the shower run. Ten minutes later, as she was picking at the cold chicken on the table, he was dressed and ready to go.

"I'll call," he said, dropping a hard kiss on her mouth.

"That's what they all say," Brooke teased.

"But you're the one with those pointed nipples," he said, tweaking one again. Then, without looking back, he walked out the door.

Chapter Thirteen

MJ was a languorous puddle of sexworthy flesh. Every nerve ending in her body felt feminine, soft, deliciously manipulated. She didn't want to move a muscle. She wanted to luxuriate the whole afternoon and let the magic hands of whoever was attending that station knead and nurture her. To enjoy the perks of the Mistress Club after passing all the stringent tests, and uttering the correct password—*control*.

"I like seeing a new member so content," Vanessa told her. "That's the whole point of Maîtrise. But now it's time for us to visit the lounge, yet another benefit of membership. So if you'll set aside the robe and put on this bra . . ."

MJ reluctantly swung herself off the couch of cushions. Vanessa handed her a wisp of a black cutout bra.

"It hooks right in front, MJ. Like that. Now just tuck your breasts into the cutouts—there—it's amazing. Every woman's nipples immediately get hard in that bra. And I've stolen your garter belt and stockings—I noticed the stockings during our interview. Very classy and sexy, MJ. So, if you would?"

MJ would; she couldn't take offense that Vanessa had just

appropriated her underthings when Vanessa was handing her a mile-high pair of sandals that consisted of two patent leather straps and a four-inch heel that was a pure off-the-charts mistress mule. She slipped into them and took an unsteady step.

"Perfect," Vanessa said. "This way."

She led her to the bank of elevators, and almost immediately one of the doors opened.

"Harold," Vanessa said in surprise. "MJ, this is Harold. Harold, this is MJ."

He was so tall that even MJ in her sky-high heels came only to midchest. He had the most piercing eyes, a firm handshake, salt-and-pepper hair. He was older, late fifties perhaps, and he was barefoot and dressed casually in an expensive silk shirt and tailored slacks.

MJ caught her breath as he took her hand, and she licked her lips as he said, "MJ," in a deep, commanding voice. He looked at Vanessa and then back to her. "MJ . . . I'm on my way to my dressing room. Join me."

He gripped her hand more emphatically, almost demanding that she acquiesce.

Instantly, she became supremely aware of her nakedness, of the way her stockings and garter belt framed her bush, the heat of her distended nipples, the hardness of his hand holding hers, and most imperatively, the force of his strength and will.

He looked at her like he *knew* her, knew the drive in her, the need in her, the desire in her. And more than that, he looked at her as if he could give her exactly what she wanted.

240

"MJ?" Vanessa said delicately. Perhaps there was just an edge to her question, as if she would be extremely displeased if MJ said no.

"I . . ." Her voice caught. "I'd love to."

Harold smiled, took her hand, and drew back into the elevator. "Vanessa."

She raised her eyebrows as the doors closed.

MJ started shaking. This was it, this was the goal, this was . . . so soon . . . too quick? And this was an older, more experienced man who would not ill use her, who would understand her needs and cater to them in a way that would allow her to cater to his desire.

She hoped. *Women always hoped.*

But did it matter? He kept looking at her nipples, at her bush. When the elevator stopped, she thought her heart might stop, too.

"Don't be afraid," Harold said, taking her hand and leading her from the elevator to his dressing room. He opened the door to a room that was as opulent as a sheikh's tent—the bed covered in lavish bedding, the walls draped in ivory silk, soft pillows, soft carpet underfoot, soft lighting, even softer music.

His hard hands, drawing her tightly to him.

"Undress me, MJ."

She'd known this was coming—but this fast, this soon? "MJ!"

She couldn't deny him. His hands were so strong, so confident, and he wanted this from *her.* Her hand shook as she unbuttoned his shirt and his trousers, which he shrugged off and let fall to the floor. He was naked beneath his clothes, his penis strutting up hard and alive against her belly.

"Fuck me."

She couldn't breathe.

"MJ—" A slight impatience that ramped up her desire.

She knelt, she kissed the engorged head of his penis, and she felt her insides go molten at how hot he was—how massive, how thick with his need for her mouth, her tongue, her lips. *This* was what she had missed: surrendering that part of her that could submit only to someone stronger than she.

And he *was* so strong, so certain of what he wanted, so adamant that *she* was the one to give it to him, guiding her frenetic sucking and stroking with his clever, hard, demanding hands.

She hadn't expected it would be this fast, this easy . . . that this most expert older man could just look at her and know that sucking off his long, strong sex was the stuff of her dreams.

Or maybe his. He convulsed in her mouth fast, unexpectedly. All it took was the intensive wet suck at the head, and he was there, filling her mouth, making her take it, take him wholly into her, orally and completely.

And then he slipped to his knees and looked at her in a sultry sheikh-hero way from under his lids. "I want more. What are you going to do to pleasure me?"

Her voice stuck in her throat. He pushed her back gently onto her rump and spread her legs. "I want your cunt."

Not *I want cunt . . . I want YOUR cunt. Her* cunt. He was looking at her, wanting *her.* She licked her lips that were still sticky with the taste of him.

"MJ . . . Your cunt is wet, my penis is hard. I want more."

She nodded and watched as he grasped her hips and tilted her body so that he was angled just at her cleft. And then he plunged, and she was so hot and he was so hard that their coming together seemed a perfect symmetry.

Why not? She had given just as much of her naked body to one-night bar bangers with half as much heft and finesse. This was easy, easier even than before—with *him*. The one whose name was never to enter her consciousness again in any comparisons with anyone else ever.

And this . . . was breathtaking. She felt delicate and feminine, enfolded by him, consumed by him in the way he lowered his body onto hers, covering her completely, his chest hair scraping her nipples, as he cradled her hips and pumped himself into her, as he kissed her with abandon and spurted thickly deep inside her.

"I'm claiming you," he muttered roughly into her ear. "Do you know what that means?"

Her body twinged at those thrilling words, but she sensed he wouldn't want her to have known.

She whispered, "No. I don't."

"It means your name is entered in my little black book, and then your body is mine to do with as I wish, until I decide if I want to keep you. No other man can approach you until I release you. I wouldn't give you a choice, but Maîtrise requires that I do. Do you want to be claimed?"

"Yes," she whispered.

"By me?"

"Yes, Harold." She could barely get the words out, breathless at the thought that he wanted to claim her this quickly.

"And you stay with me. No lounge, no spa. No one sees you except me until I say so."

"Yes, Harold." He was rocking his hips hard against hers; his mouth took hers, hard and tight, and he began thrusting in rhythm with the violence of his kisses.

She wrapped her silk-shrouded legs around his body and welcomed his ferocious pumping, welcomed his fierce kisses, his masterful claim, his volatile sex. Everything about him, she welcomed and wanted with the same ferocity with which he was taking her.

Yes, Harold, yes. Just like that—and that, and I'll stay with you forever . . .

"Okay," Delia said to Brooke that night as she fretted over the fact that Thane had not called, "so now it's MJ who's missing in action."

"I'm sure someone found her at Maîtrise, just as you predicted. Don't worry; obviously she's in good hands. This is what we wanted, and now we've all found it. And if MJ was approached as I was, and claimed already, then that's good."

"But she has to go back to work tomorrow. And the rent's due on her apartment, and I'm scared to death Baines is hanging around, and who knows what will happen if she goes back there."

"We'll figure all that out. Maybe she's been claimed, maybe her prospective lover is keeping her with him a little longer, maybe overnight. You didn't think that was such a bad thing when Thane claimed me."

"No, I didn't," Delia admitted. "You're right. Only I have to work the afternoon and evening shift tomorrow, and visit the Maîtrise doctor. So I won't know anything unless MJ calls. How did this get so complicated, when it was supposed to be fun?"

Brooke shrugged. "I don't know. You know, Lonita told me not to be dumb, but I *was* with Thane. I went against my every mistress mandate."

"What did you lose, really?" Delia asked. "There isn't a guy on the planet who'd call back this fast. And he offered you something."

"And I gave him everything—and look at where I'm sitting now."

MJ was sitting in Harold's lap with his slack penis cushioning her buttocks, his strong, clever hands idly exploring her nether parts and lulling her into a drowsy state of adoration while he asked desultory questions about her life.

Like, did she work? He didn't want her to work. He wanted her to give his needs priority, to give him complete access to her and as much sex as he could fit into his schedule.

The idea thrilled her—not working, just waiting for him and all the pleasure that came with his demanding needs.

He caressed and stroked her body, he kissed her, and in between his hot, hard kisses he told her what he expected and what he wanted.

He wanted everything. It was so simple that she wrapped her arms around his neck and whispered, "Yes, Harold," to everything he said.

He thumbed her nipples, pulled at them and twisted them lightly as he told her what he liked, how she must comport herself, how she must dress for him privately or in public.

"Never cover your nipples when we're together. Never hide your cunt, even when I'm not here. I want them available all the time."

"I'd adore that, Harold," she murmured hazily, seduced by his masterly manipulation of her nipples.

"These are mine."

She swallowed hard. This was familiar territory, yet it was different. This wasn't Dallan Baines, this wasn't a selfish, self-centered son of a bitch. This was an older man, an experienced man who knew what he was doing and how far to push her.

"My nipples are yours."

"And your cunt."

"All yours, Harold."

"That pleases me." He squeezed her nipples simultaneously and her body jolted with pleasure. "*They* please me."

"I'm glad, Harold."

He made a sound in his throat. "I have to make arrangements—to tell Vanessa and get things started. I own your sex now, you understand that."

"Yes, Harold."

"You're with me now."

"Yes, Harold."

"While I go speak to Vanessa, you telephone whomever you need to notify that I will be occupying your time and your cunt from now on."

She was breathless with excitement. "Yes, Harold."

He pointed at his clothes. "Dress me."

"Yes, Harold." She climbed off his warm lap, his hot sex.

"No, wait—fuck me again, first."

She knelt between his legs and took him to her mouth, and then paused with his shaft head just grazing her lips. She lowered her eyes and smiled a secret smile to herself before she obediently murmured, "Yes, Harold," and took him into her mouth.

Delia called Brooke at her office the next morning. "MJ called."

"Good. Where is she? What's happening?"

"She's with Harold . . . Hanson, I think she said. A sophisticated and experienced gentleman whom she met right out of the spa at Maîtrise. She's going to stay with him, and she wanted us to pack up her apartment. She's breaking the lease."

"Whoa!" Brooke breathed. "She's *staying* with him . . . already? No I'll call you? I'm knee-deep in envy."

"She said to just pack up the clothes, and she'll get a service to clear out the furniture and things."

"She'll get a service?" Brooke said in disbelief. "Wow, Mr. Gotrocks must be a pushover. One day with him and she's talking richspeak. Well, she doesn't have much in the way of furniture. Did she say what we're supposed to do with her clothes?"

"No."

"Then we'll pack everything in my big rollie suitcase. She sound okay?"

"Ecstatic."

"Wow—that's great. Can we do it this evening?"

Delia made a sound. "Like my calendar's bursting."

"It could be . . ." Brooke said slyly, knowing about all the ongoing offers and solicitations that Delia received at the restaurant.

"I'm *so* done talking to you. I'll meet you at MJ's around seven."

She rang off, and Brooke went back to her endless arrangements of tours and timetables.

That night, she and Delia made short work of packing up for MJ.

"What if Baines shows up again?" Delia said worriedly, more than once.

"He's a dead issue."

"Bet he doesn't think so."

"MJ didn't say if she'd gone back to work, did she? Because she'll need her clothes."

Delia straightened up, her eyes wide. "Yes, she did. She said she's giving notice."

"Holy . . . shit. She's *what*?!"

"Harold doesn't want her to work."

"Oh, my God." Brooke fell into a chair. "Is this a wet dream or what? I want to step in her stilettos right *now*. Management to mistress in one day?"

Delia continued packing and shot her a lancing look.

"What did *I* do wrong?"

Delia forbore telling her. And in fact, it was better that Brooke was so immersed in her distress over MJ's good luck, because Delia was coming to that secret drawer that was full of MJ's secrets.

"You want to look in the hall closet?" she asked Brooke, and Brooke obediently got up and rifled through the closet, pulling out coats and jackets and miscellaneous sweaters and shoes while Delia palmed all of MJ's sex paraphernalia that she would never want Brooke to see.

What was she thinking, to ask them both to do this packing?

She tucked the leather bras, the cuffs, the thrall collars, the sex toys deep into the piles of clothing in the suitcase, then tucked everything Brooke brought to her on top and all around them.

There, your secrets are kept, MJ. I hope this guy will be good to you.

Then they locked up, carried the suitcase downstairs with some difficulty, and hailed a cab.

"No Baines sightings," Brooke said with satisfaction.

But Delia wasn't so sure he wasn't lurking somewhere. And when she turned to take one last look at MJ's building, she could have sworn she saw a man standing there, watching the cab pull away.

Wednesday, Brooke's cell rang first thing in the morning.

"Nipples," his voice said.

She nearly dropped the phone and grasped for composure. "Thane."

"Don't be coy. You're damned glad I called."

"Am I?" *Son of a bitch.*

"Have lunch with me."

"I really don't know that I should."

"No games, Nipples. *I* know. Limo will pick you up at noon."

He disconnected.

She shook her head. *Limo will pick you up. I'll send a car service.*

I am the service, *for God's sake. I service well-heeled heels like Thane Bohansson.*

What was she thinking? He'd called, and that's what she'd longed for.

She rang Delia. "He called."

"Ha," Delia said.

"Do *not* say, 'I told you so.'"

"Okay, he called. And?"

"Lunch today. Limo to come."

"Oh, you're the high flyer now. A limo as opposed to a pedestrian car *service.*"

"And not a limo *service,* either. *His* limo. Oh, God, I look like hell."

"Then you'd better go and make sure you don't look like hell."

"Okay, details later."

It was a quarter of twelve at that point. She didn't have time for anything but a fast fix in the ladies' room, damn him. And that uniform of a suit—no room for creativity there. Damn damn damn . . .

She had on fresh makeup, a sexy silk blouse, and sexier high-heeled pumps—all quick purchases in the hotel store—when the front desk called to say her car had arrived.

The deskman gave her a look that spoke volumes as she left the lobby.

Oh, Lord, she'd have to run that obstacle course when she returned. The car was waiting with the chauffeur ready to open her door.

Lunch-hour traffic was insane, which only heightened her apprehension. They drove uptown to the East seventies and down an elegant tree-lined street with end-to-end brownstones. At the corner was an elegant, modern apartment building with a circular drive.

"The chauffeur turned into it and said, "Mr. Thane is expecting you. Apartment 10G."

She felt shaky as she pressed the button in the elevator, utterly bewildered about why he had summoned her. *He* wouldn't live here; that would be insane.

The hall was carpeted and painted in a soft rose color, with wall sconces providing just enough mute light so she could see that apartment 10G was at the far end.

The door was open and she walked into a flood of sunlight in a long, wide living room. The kitchen, which was open to the little foyer where she stood, was neat and compact and efficient, and to her right was a hallway.

She peeked into the kitchen, which had a dishwasher, a microwave, a refrigerator, a stove, and more counter space and cabinets than she would have guessed. Down the hall was a spacious bedroom with a big closet. Farther down there was a bathroom and a stacked laundry, and a larger second bedroom with a futon already set up, and a private bath.

Thane Bohansson was standing by the window, waiting to pounce.

"About damned time," he said, grabbing her and kissing her. "This is your place now. Our place."

"What?!"

"I want your nipples that bad. You owe me that photograph of them, by the way."

She felt shell-shocked. The place was bare, freshly painted, sparkling and new, quite wonderful in the realm of New York City apartments.

This was mistress territory. *This* was the luxury apartment provided by the lover who wanted his sex convenient and on his terms. This was the goal of *her* Mistress Club.

But so fast? This quick?

Why not? Was she not gorgeous, intelligent, firm, flexible, and fuckable?

"My decorator will take care of furnishing it; it'll be ready Friday."

She stared at him.

He took her palm and dropped in the keys. "You'll move in next week. Anything you don't like, change. Keep working or not, but be ready to accommodate me whenever I want to fuck you. That means lunch, after hours, before breakfast. I can give you Tuesdays and Thursdays, and plan for me to stay overnight."

She couldn't quite catch her breath; it was all too overwhelming.

"I'd rather you didn't work," he went on. "Then I could take my time when I feel like a fuck—like now."

Oh, Lord, how fast this was going! She couldn't grasp it all, she could barely breathe.

"I set up a little checking account for you. The bank's around the corner, across the street. You'll sign the cards, everything's done. I'll send up groceries once a week. That's it. I'll see you next Tuesday, five o'clock sharp. And there's the main disadvantage of your working: We could be fucking all day, instead of a couple of hours. Think about it, Nipples."

"I will," she whispered. All day? She swallowed hard. "I'll be here."

"Move in Monday. Maybe I can squeeze into you before breakfast."

The door closed. Her knees were so weak that she had to sit down.

I'm a mistress.

She felt heart-stopping panic. *I'm a mistress.*

And I still don't know if I want it to be him.

"Of course you're going to move in there," Delia told her. "Don't get nuts. You're getting everything for what we routinely give away. A well-heeled, well-endowed penis is handing it to you, and you're quibbling about his *looks*?"

"I know, I know. But—what if there's someone better out there?"

"Better looking, you mean?" Delia asked. "Don't be an ass, Brooke. Just do it and see what happens. You said the sex obliterates every hesitation, once you get started."

"Yeah. In the dark."

Delia was helping her pack. It was Saturday and they hadn't heard from MJ since she'd called Delia last Sunday, but they knew the apartment had been emptied and was now for rent. That was pretty final.

MJ's sudden disappearance was pretty final, come to that. She hadn't known where she was going to be living, so they had no way to find her.

Delia made a sound. "Well, MJ's with someone, and you didn't see her quibbling about him. She's reaping all those rewards you're turning up your nose at."

"And maybe hers is Prince Charming rather than the frog," Brooke said.

Delia looked disgusted with her. "By the way, what are you doing with this place?"

"I'm going to keep it—maybe sublet it if I can, unless you want to move here?"

Delia gave it some thought. "Tell you what, I'll stay at least until next weekend, because who knows what will happen after my interview with Vanessa."

"Right. Because your Prince Charming is going to walk right through that spa door."

Delia shook her head. "You'd better reread that Mistress Code, girl. Thane might be a frog, but he's also Prince Charming—for now."

MJ was purring with contentment. Harold had set her up in the sweetest little one-bedroom apartment in the Village. It had an efficient little kitchen looking into the long living room, a balcony, a nice-sized bedroom that accommodated a queen-sized bed, a little den, and a luxurious bathroom where she could soak to her heart's content when Harold was done having sex with her.

It was all perfect. She didn't have to go anywhere, do anything. All she had to do was keep herself perfumed, stroking soft, pliant, naked, and ready for Harold. She didn't even, technically, need clothes. He provided everything. *Everything*. All the forbidden, luscious, constricting, and cutout undergarments that she had ever coveted.

She had a thrall collar encrusted with gold. The leather corset she wore was strewn with gold studs. The bondage straps were decorated with diamonds. All for him and the delicacy with which he dominated her.

He could give her three days, Monday, Wednesday, and Saturday. She understood. He had a family, a wife, a job. Sometimes he snuck in early in the morning and made her submit to his demands. Sometimes he sat like a potentate in a special chair that he'd found for her living room. It had a cutout seat so his big balls could dangle freely and she could easily burrow between his legs to feast on them. It had stirrups for her where she hooked her heels to spread herself to give him utter control of her sex. It had restraints to keep her hands from interfering with anything he wanted to do to her.

He was gentle and firm with her both. She liked it best when he just held her down and pleasured her, but the covert implements were her secret excitement, her forbidden need, and he catered to that desire in her, too.

He liked inserting things into her, too, soft flexible eggs, objects that vibrated and penetrated front and back. He liked her blowing him off while he did her by vibrator, and he especially liked coming on her body.

"This is why I need you ready for me all the time," he whispered as they lay on the bed one morning after a furious bout of coupling. He pushed against her bottom, rock hard again and nudging into her crease. He began sliding his shaft between her buttocks, using it like her cleft.

She moved to keep rhythm with him; a minute later, he spurted into her crease.

"Crap. A teaspoon of milk; what good's that? MJ! Make me hard again."

"Yes, Harold."

She loved making him hard. She tried to be inventive about it, too. He had the biggest, hardest, pumpingest shaft she'd ever had, and she loved playing with it. She couldn't guarantee that would increase his semen production after so many hours of sex, but she knew that was what he wanted: a hot deluge erupting like a geyser, a monument to his virility. And he'd want to see it—he wouldn't want it pouring into her mysterious, dark womanhood.

The trick was to concentrate on his luscious balls, sucking them until they got tight and hard, and only then paying attention to his bull of a penis.

That was the secret with Harold: paying attention. Giving him what he wanted, then gratefully taking his reward for pleasuring him thoroughly. She loved the way he bullheaded his way into her in his purely male, take-possession way. She loved everything he did to her. She loved everything he gave her.

She was getting and giving in huge measure, because Harold was huge, in all ways. And how lucky was she to have found him almost on her doorstep at the Mistress Club?

I am a mistress, she thought as she climbed between his legs and delicately spread them apart. *I've got everything Brooke ever said we wanted. I'm getting all the sex a woman could want and all the perks: my own apartment, I don't have to work, and I own a bull of a man who pleasures me exactly the way I want to be pleasured.*

It was a stunning thought.

I really am Harold's mistress . . . she bent her head between his legs, her lips and tongue just grazing his saggy balls . . . *and I'm mistress of Harold right now.*

Chapter Fourteen

Delia decided to channel her inner Grace Kelly for her follow-up visit to Maîtrise and wore a white silk halter top draped with necklaces, a narrow taupe skirt that kissed her knees, cinched with a wide suede belt, brown suede open-toed shoes, a taupe envelope pocketbook tucked under her arm, pearl button earrings, and a slubbed silk topper thrown over her shoulders.

Her blonde hair was spiky with gel, and her makeup was more intense than usual, emphasizing her ingenuous blue eyes by rimming them with kohl.

"What do you think?" she asked Brooke, who was packing the final few things she would need when she moved to the apartment the next day.

"I think you need an escort."

"I'm trying to *find* an escort," Delia said. "Do I look approachable?"

Brooke grinned. "Every woman looks approachable when she's naked."

With that, Delia went out to catch a cab to Maîtrise.

It wasn't long before she was entering the living room.

Vanessa entered from the door on the far side of the room with her hands outstretched.

"I'm so pleased to offer you membership in Maîtrise," Vanessa said. "You'll be such an asset. Shall we go to my office?"

There, she went into the logistics of the club's confidentiality statement.

Delia signed.

Vanessa gave her the questionnaire. "Take your time, Delia."

"Thank you." It was what she expected, the answers obvious, as Brooke had described.

"Well, then. It's time to show you your dressing room. Here's the key."

At that moment, the door opened and a tall, vital man burst in. He was dressed impeccably in an expensive hand-tailored suit, and his accessories were perfectly matched. "Vanessa!"

"Sonny, what's the problem?"

"I . . ." He looked at Delia and his voice caught.

"This is Delia. Delia, this is Sonny Hanes."

Delia stood and held out her hand. "I'm so pleased," she murmured as he took her hand and held it in his warm bear grip.

"Delia." His voice was warm, gravelly, and rather shell-shocked. He turned to Vanessa. "Forget everything. Convince Delia to have lunch with me."

Vanessa raised her eyebrows. "Really, Sonny. You know better than anyone that we don't—"

"Let Delia decide. She can always come back later."

Vanessa sighed. "Delia, I'd like to introduce you to Mr. Sonny Hanes, a prominent businessman in the city, who would be delighted to take you to lunch if you'd like to go out with him."

Delia stared into his dark eyes. He had such a strong face and such a masculine presence. He was obviously a man who knew what he wanted and how to go about getting it. He would be a terror in business, she thought, and equally demanding in bed.

Here was a challenge, right at the start. What harm could lunch do?

"I'd be delighted," she said, smiling up at him. God, he was tall.

"Good. Let's go, now."

Out on the street, Sonny asked her, "Where would you like to eat?" He hailed a cab, gave the driver an address, and helped her in. "Anywhere you want to go. Or if you wouldn't mind, maybe you'd like to have lunch at my apartment."

Whoa, stud man, Delia thought. Talk about starting off at a gallop.

"I'll call my man."

His man? She looked at him consideringly.

He looked at her chest, at the satin slide of material that draped over her already stiff nipples, and then he looked at her. "Which would you prefer—a lot of pretty talk or straight shooting?"

"That depends on what you want to shoot, Mr. Hanes."

"I want to shoot my wad all over your nipples. Call me Sonny."

She swallowed. "That's pretty up front."

"Are you kidding? My up-front ejaculated the minute I walked in the door and saw you."

"Sonny," she said chidingly. That really was too much!

"Feel me." He grabbed her hand and slid it between his legs. His penis was hot and hard, and the fabric was wet just below the zipper.

He was obviously a client of Maîtrise, obviously well-off, and obviously instantly intrigued with her. She just as easily could have met him in the lounge as in Vanessa's office, and she didn't have to get naked to see he wanted to have sex with her.

As Brooke had always counseled, she was double protected, and to seal the deal, she wasn't put off by his power or averse to his unrefined looks.

A man dressed in Burberry always looks handsome.

He looked very good to her after her enforced celibacy, a vigorous man who could offer her something.

Like a nice, probing kiss that he deepened as she let herself respond and arch her body into it. His kiss was quite nice, restrained for a man who'd already jacked off and was again hard and humping her hand.

"Apartment," he muttered, his tongue in her mouth.

"Apartment," she agreed and opened her mouth wider.

They made out until the cab drew up at Ninetieth Street and Park Avenue.

By then, she was breathless and aroused in a way she'd never thought would happen again. Maybe this wasn't happening. Maybe this was a fantasy: being kidnapped by a virile, well-heeled man right out of the harem, and utterly seduced by his blatant desire for her.

This happened only in dreams. Yet Sonny was taking her hand, his own hand shaking slightly, and leading her into a building with a canopy and a marble-floored lobby. Leading her into the elevator, his gaze tight on her breasts and licking his lips in anticipation of how they would look naked, how they would feel when he fondled them, how they would taste when he sucked. All that concentrated male attention on that purely feminine part of her made her feel incredibly aroused and desired.

"Here we are." He opened a door and ushered her into an elegant living room furnished with plush sofas and chairs.

He drew her to the sofa, took off her jacket, took her bag. Ran his hands down her bare arms, barely able to control his hot, pulsating lust.

"The minute I saw you, I knew I couldn't let Vanessa get her hands on you. A beauty like you—you don't need to be powdered and primped. You need someone to adore you. Let me do that, Delia. Let me adore you."

His mouth came down on hers, and they slowly sank onto the couch.

This was so much better than a bar bang, even if she only got lunch out of it. That was more than she'd gotten in a long time, barring her night with Bill.

And it was so much nicer when the man kissing you knew what he was doing. Luscious when he knew how to expertly finger your nipples to make you hot to be naked for him. Arousing as hell when he knew where to caress those places that made your knees weak.

He eased up on his long, demanding kisses to whisper, "Jack off . . . nipples . . . blowing."

She unhooked his belt and unzipped him, foraged for his throbbing manhood, and pulled it into her hands.

He groped for the fastening of her halter top, his tongue still moving inside her mouth, and when he couldn't find it, he ripped her blouse down to her waist and pulled back to see her breasts.

"Oh, God, your breasts. Oh, baby . . . look at those nipples! Fuck the clothes; give me those tits right now."

She bent over to grasp his shaft and rubbed the underside against her nipples, first one, then the other, back and forth and forth and back, while he threw his head back, grasped her shoulders, and moved his hips in rhythm with her.

Then he shoved himself between her breasts, thumbing and squeezing her nipples as he pumped fast and furiously, stiffened, and spewed.

"I'm claiming you."

She was shocked. "What—?"

"I claim you. Your name will go right into my little black book before anyone else sees you. Nobody else is going to have you. You're *mine*. I'm calling Vanessa right now."

She played innocent. "What does that mean, claiming me?"

"It means no one else can approach you now, no matter how interested he might be, until your name is removed from my black book."

"I see." She closed her eyes and gave herself over to the massaging feeling of his fingers and the scent of his sex. She needed more, but she wasn't quite sure how to jack it out of him on this short acquaintance.

She opened her eyes and gave him a reproachful look. "You know, today was my first day at Maîtrise, and you high-jacked me before I even got a chance to meet any other members or to explore any possibilities there."

"You mean explore other penises. You don't have to. No one there can give what I can."

"Oh, I can't imagine anyone with a harder, thicker, more semen-filled penis," she said.

He stared at her through hooded eyes.

"But a well-hung shaft may not be everything," she went on. "There are certain intangibles."

"It always comes down to that. So what do you want?"

She sighed and patted his penis. "I really enjoyed your ejaculating on me, Sonny. And I really love how you kiss. You have such a commanding tongue, I can just imagine how it would feel between my legs. But—how exactly does it work when a man claims a member of Maîtrise?"

"It means what you think it means."

"So, I come here?"

"You *live* here for my convenience, Delia. And I fuck you whenever I want to, whenever I have time."

She smiled angelically. "I'm to be a convenience. I see. Of course, we might not be a good fit for each other," she added, preempting him.

"Thus the period of claiming," he said roughly. "We know that my penis fits nicely between your breasts. Shall we see how my tongue fits in your cunt?"

She caught her breath. "I can't wait to explore everything, Sonny. But I need to know what else comes with the apartment."

"By God, you *are* a little tit bitch." But his penis had spurted to life again at her flexing her power.

She hungrily eyed his burgeoning length. "Well, then, just take me back to Maîtrise, and I'll continue with the membership process. You don't need to buy me lunch. Although"—she slid her hand down his shaft—"I could lunch on him pretty nicely."

He looked at her hand on his manhood; he looked at her breasts.

"Everything comes with the apartment, including an allowance for food, clothes, and maintenance. No pets. No friends poaching on my good nature. No other men. Total access to your cunt all the time; I have the key and I like to fuck early *and* late—but my schedule will allow me regular visits only Friday and Sunday. If you don't work, there will be more time to fuck. If you don't like the terms, we're done."

"I work Friday nights. I won't give up my job."

"You meet men there?"

"Every night."

"No other men, any way, anywhere."

"Let's just see if we fit before I upend my life for you, Sonny. Which I'm perfectly willing to do, by the way. I like being sexed by a well-hung man more than almost anything else. But you haven't taken me yet."

His gaze narrowed on her breasts again. "True enough, my little tit bitch. I'll call Vanessa."

She encircled his shaft with her fingers and squeezed upward.

"I can think of a couple better things to do right now, Sonny. I'm not going anywhere. I'd love it if you'd enter my name in your black book and claim me. And I accept all of your terms."

Delia helped Brooke move into the apartment Monday evening. The decorator had done her work. One hundred thousand dollars had been dropped at Bloomingdale's for the softest of suede sofas, down-cushioned club chairs, a selection of British colonial antiques in the living room and bedroom; everything from sheets to silverware had been provided, and Delia was open-mouthed with astonishment.

"Wow," she said as she opened the kitchen cabinets to a set of expensive china. "Wow," as she examined the Cuisinart pots and appliances, the Bunn coffeemaker, the apartment-sized Viking stove and Sub-Zero fridge. "Oh, my God," as she walked in the bedroom and saw the huge bed, the cozy sitting area, the enormous walk-in closet that already contained expensive male clothing, the plasma TV built into the wall.

"Dear heaven—you couldn't afford this in a thousand lifetimes," she said.

Brooke sank into one of the living room chairs. "I need a drink."

"You need to give up your apartment, since I'm not going to use it. This is . . . this is heaven! You're never going to leave here."

Brooke took a deep breath. "There was nothing here Wednesday," she managed to say. "*Nothing*. Well, a futon for fucking, but we didn't. How could he do this in just five days?"

"Money did this in five days," Delia said practically. "Brooke, wake up—we're mistresses! We're being kept by men who can afford to pay to play. What else could you want?"

"I don't know. I guess I'm just in shock at how fast things are happening."

"Well, I gave notice today on my apartment. I'm moving into the Park Avenue apartment—oh, I love saying that—at the end of the week. I'll call you then, okay? Because you're going to be in the middle of a period of adjustment here, adjusting to limitless luxury and frequent-flyer fucking." She paused as she opened the door. "Sounds good to me."

The apartment seemed absolutely empty the minute Delia left, and Brooke wondered how Delia could be so upbeat about the realization of their goal while she, who had pushed and browbeaten them into it, felt hesitant and unsure.

What have I done? She wandered from room to room, touching the furniture, examining everything in the fridge, feeling the silk robe, the finely tailored worsted suit hanging in the closet.

You've done exactly what you set out to do—you've become a mistress to an extremely wealthy and powerful man. An extremely older, physically shapely, not terribly handsome, wealthy and powerful man who's as virile as a twenty-year-old.

Why was the question of his looks so important to her?

She shouldn't have any qualms. The goal had been met.

Besides, this is not forever. This is for now.

She heard the click of the lock and she froze, then whirled around to see Thane easing into the foyer.

"You're here. I'm glad. I have a present for you."

"Thane, this apartment is more than enough," she said, coming to him. "This is spectacular!"

"You like it?"

"I'm overwhelmed."

"Good. Did you check the dresser drawers?"

She shook her head. *The games have begun.* "Shall I now?"

"Humor me," he said as he guided her to the bedroom.

She opened the top dresser drawer and found it full of frothy lingerie: lace, see-through, cupless corsets, an open-crotch fishnet bodysuit . . . this man had plans.

"Did you give notice at work yet?"

"Not yet."

"Give notice, Nipples. I want that time for fucking."

No choice. He had paid for her, and this was his price. "You're right, I will."

"Good. Now—get naked."

Wow, he was on fast-forward today. And he expected her to strip with him watching. Fine. She'd taken off only her work jacket and pumps, and naked would be sexier than jeans.

He watched her as he lounged in one of the commodious

bedroom chairs, stroking his naked shaft. No coy belly-dance moves for her tonight, but it didn't matter. Anything she did aroused him, as his hard penis made it clear.

She knelt in front of the chair, ready to service him.

He pulled her up to straddle his thighs. "Your present." He gave her a tiny box. "One condition: You promise to wear it all the time."

"How hard could that be?" she murmured.

"As hard as my penis, Nipples. Open it."

She removed the cover. Inside was a fine gold chain, perhaps forty inches long, with gold satin loops at either end.

"It's lovely, Thane. What is it?"

"The loops stretch to fit around your nipples."

Her breath caught.

"Remember, you promised to wear it all the time, everywhere. To keep you focused on me."

He meant it. She swallowed convulsively.

"And to keep your nipples hard for me."

This was a game she must play, like it or not. "And to keep you lust-hard for me," she murmured, "imagining my nipples that hard for you under my everyday clothes. Are you sure you want me to stop working?"

"I'll dress your nipples," he growled, spreading the loops around his little finger, then plucking her nipples to hard points so he could slip the loops over the tips.

The compression was whisper soft, not tight as she'd expected. He instantly creamed, a full spume of hot semen.

He draped the chain around her neck so that it fell between and below her breasts, then looped up to her nipples.

"I'll never get tired of looking at your nipples dressed like this."

She didn't want him to. Her doubts had vanished; she was shaking with the erotic need to feel him between her legs. All she saw was his penis. To be so rampantly desired by a penis like his was worth his demands, his lust, his gift of gold, his sexual vigor.

"Take me *now*," she whispered, shifting upward so that he could guide himself inside her. "All I want is to drown in your cream."

"I have a better idea. I want that photograph of your nipples—the one promised me on the second date."

He reached into his jacket pocket and withdrew a camera. His ferocious gaze devoured her nipples, and his sex strutted to life again. "He's jacking up again pretty fast—so let's take a couple of shots of your nipples erotically chained."

A month later, MJ called Delia and asked her to send her clothes to her new address in the Village. "We have to have lunch," MJ said. "I miss you guys."

"Is he good to you?" Delia asked

"He's good and he gets it, and he doesn't abuse it."

Delia let out her breath. "So you can actually leave the apartment?"

"I can do whatever I want," MJ said.

"Even better. So, when shall the ladies lunch?"

MJ named a day, and two weeks later they convened at their old haunt, the Park Avenue Café. There was a new maître d' who didn't know them, a new crowd, more limos.

They fit right in, arriving by cab and limo themselves, dressed opulently, everything the best and most costly their lovers could afford.

"We're mistresses now," Brooke whispered as they were seated.

"Harold," MJ sighed. "Oh, my apartment, the sex . . . who cares about anything else?" She looked beautiful, brilliant, faintly punk with her slicked-backed red hair, her black, gauzy see-through blouse, leather skirt, onyx chains and rings, stiletto Gucci boots, and highly kohled eyes.

"No, Thane—unbelievable sex, unbelievable penis. You can't imagine," Brooke whispered. "I shop Madison Avenue exclusively." The sweater was so tight that she'd risked Thane's wrath by removing the nipple loops for lunch; the skirt was a classic plaid; the jacket buttery suede, matching the knee-high riding boots.

"But I haven't told you all about Sonny," Delia interposed. "The apartment, the stamina, the wall-to-wall sex." She wore a curve-revealing, burgundy jersey Yves St. Laurent dress cinched with a three-inch black belt, and the beautiful suede shoes from Images.

"Oh, God," MJ breathed. "We really did it."

"We really did it," Brooke echoed. They'd given up jobs, apartments, just about everything to be kept by these lovers who demanded their time, their loyalty, and their bodies.

And they were happy. MJ glowed. Delia looked more relaxed, and Brooke couldn't imagine how she looked after being ridden by Thane almost to oblivion last night.

They ordered their usual fish, salad, and coffee. The food

almost didn't matter. Just the fact they were together again was important and, as Brooke pointed out, "It's not going to be a regular thing any more. Our lovers are the priority now. But I've done something you might be angry at me for."

"Never," MJ and Delia protested simultaneously.

"I didn't give up my apartment."

"*What?*"

Brooke drew a deep breath. "Well, you know what a bitch it is finding an affordable place. And I thought, if something went wrong, if something didn't work out for one of us, we wouldn't be stranded. We'd have somewhere to go."

"And who's paying for this?"

"I am. Now that we're mistresses, I have no qualms about tapping my personal resources. And I thought it was important to have a backup."

MJ rolled her eyes. "You have no idea. Harold and I—"

"I know," Delia interrupted. "It's the same with Sonny and me. This isn't a fly-by-night affair. This is the real thing. He's so good to me, our sex is so vigorous—I can't tell you how many times a night—"

"Yeah, me too," Brooke put in. "Last night, all night—Well, anyway, you know how cautious I am; I always have to have contingency plans. So you just have to humor me on this."

"Fine, if it makes you feel safe," MJ said.

"Well, I propose a toast to Brooke, whose imagination and foresight got us here," Delia said, lifting her water glass.

"Hear, hear." They tapped glasses.

"To the Mistress Club," Brooke said, lifting her goblet again. "And long may we keep our lovers."

* * *

Thane was inside her again the morning after her lunch with the girls. "God, Nipples—there isn't a cunt like yours in the world, so hot, so tight, so *mine*."

She was getting used to him, his looks, his body, his needs. It wasn't that onerous, since he was with her Tuesdays and Thursdays generally, although sometimes he popped in at odd times to check if she was wearing her nipple loops and to pop his penis in for a quickie.

He spent an inordinate amount of time fondling her nipples. He was fascinated by them, and his fascination was a pure pleasure for her. And he loved the nipple loops, couldn't get enough of looking at her dressed in them.

He told her that he carried those pictures, which were also blown up and propped up in the bedroom, everywhere. *Her* nipples, from every angle, compressed by the satin loops, slick with his semen, pointed and proud to be coveted by him, and so desired that he had to have them with him everywhere.

When he wasn't there, she exercised, read, watched TV, shopped, and went to museums, always notifying him where she would be just in case he stopped in. Just in case he needed that five-minute respite for release.

She supposed that his intensive surveillance was just a precaution; he was protecting himself and his investment. It amused her to think that their sex time was an investment for him. And that he felt he had to ensure that another man wouldn't try to claim her or even put a sexual move on her.

"God, Nipples, if they ever knew what was under your clothes . . . I can't take that chance."

She never could convince him that the thought of his sex drove any other man right out of her mind. She could endure almost anything for the pleasure he gave her, for the pure erotic thrill of his existence in her life.

Sometimes she thought she was in love with his manhood. Often, it struck her she really *was* living the mistress life.

She talked to Delia sometimes, but not often to MJ. MJ was cloistered with her Harold, wholly immersed in and insane about him, and not willing to go into detail about their sex life.

MJ said only that they had sex often. He treated her right, not like that freak who'd almost destroyed her life. Harold was amazing, strong, deliciously demanding, and totally loving.

She didn't tell them that Harold was every bit as controlling as Dallan, only he was a master at it. She was deeply in love with everything he did to her, but she couldn't admit that either—or that her world revolved entirely around the moment he would arrive at the apartment and dominate her. She loved him and she didn't care what anyone might think or say.

Delia was practical enough to know that there wasn't much she could do about it. MJ would have to just work the thing out herself. If she crashed—well, Brooke had wisely kept her apartment for just such emergencies.

Not that Delia needed looking out for. Sonny was a handful in every possible way, but she wasn't deeply invested in him.

And maybe that, more than anything else, kept him coming back: that he couldn't quite get a handle on her, even with all the sex, all the erotic play, his cute little sex nicknames, his lavish gifts. She was still a little bit removed, as if she were enjoying it all from a distance.

It was probably the best stance to take. Hadn't Brooke cautioned them never to fall in love with these guys? Never waste your time on anything that doesn't get you something in return. Be aloof, elusive, and mysterious. Have no expectations, and you will be given everything: apartment, allowance, clothes, jewelry.

And now I'm a mistress of a powerful older man who can't get enough of me. And I love having sex with him, and taking care of him.

And that was enough . . . wasn't it? . . . for now.

Chapter Fifteen

Another perk of being a mistress was that Brooke ate at the best restaurants. Actually, she ate *from* the best restaurants, because Thane always arrived with a catered dinner.

The advantage of his bringing food was that he could get naked immediately. Although she really would have liked a night out, she understood that he couldn't take his mistress out in public without attracting attention.

But the isolated intimacy came with unexpected consequences. To her dismay, as fall verged into winter, she started wanting more and more of his time. She wanted him *all* the time, even though she'd always known that wasn't possible.

How had this happened? This was not proper Mistress Code. This was female hormone code, built into the DNA. *The more he's with me, the more he must want to be with me, just like I want to be with him.*

Shit. I hate this.

Worse, he kept bringing gifts—lingerie, shoes, clothes— bribes, she thought, even as she swore that all she wanted was him.

"You have all of me I can stuff into you," he told her.

"It's not enough," she whispered.

"It is what it is," he said callously. "And you waste fucking time even talking about it." The worst thing was to waste fucking time.

MISTRESS CODE ADDENDUM

A mistresses does not complain.

A mistress is grateful for every moment and twists her-self into a pretzel, mentally and physically, to accom-modate her lover.

A mistress's purpose is to please her lover and to never make demands.

A mistress eliminates the words "when will you" from her vocabulary.

As in, when will you come again? When will you have more time for me? When will you be available for the holi-days?

Oops. *Banish the word "holiday".*

Blast the Code.

She called Delia. "What are you doing for Thanksgiving?"

"Same as you, I guess."

"Then let's get together and do a turkey. At the apart-ment."

"I'd rather eat out. And I was thinking that if Thane finds out you kept that place, he'll absolutely believe you're doing someone on the side."

"Damn, I never thought of that."

"Get it sublet, then. Something short term that won't raise his suspicions."

"I'll think about it. Anything from MJ? Should I call her?"

"Call her. Harold must have family obligations on Thanksgiving, too."

But MJ wasn't answering her cell. She was swimming in an orgasmic miasma, her body strapped in gold-studded leather, suspended from a ceiling harness with her legs spread apart and Harold naked, prone, and massively erect beneath her, fondling and stroking her wide-open cunt. "Ah, my Surrendra, there's no one like you."

"No one like *you*," she whispered. "Harold . . . Harold—" She was breathless with the need for penetration. "*Please,* Harold . . ."

But he waited . . . and waited . . . and just when she thought she would never feel him inside her, he got to his feet, pulled her legs around his waist, and drove between her legs.

It was so much better when her cleft was level with his hips. She loved that harness; with her legs spread so wide, it intensified every feeling. And she loved the bull-nosed way he took her. He had an unchained lust to drive as deep into her as a man could go. How could she not love that he wanted her body that much?

By the time he was done with her, she felt boneless and sated, yet yearning for more of his rugged possession. And then he enjoyed standing there afterward, embedded in her, and she felt so connected, she really believed that if he removed himself, she would lose a vital part of herself.

"I have a present for you," he said when they were cleaned and dressed.

"Oh, Harold." He had been too generous already. "I can't imagine anything I want more than you."

"I know that," he said, handing her a wrapped box. "So this is for the times when I can't be here to fuck you."

She opened the package and unwrapped the tissue to find . . . a penis. A pliant latex penis, the size and thickness of his. She held it up and gave him a dewy look. "Thank you, Harold."

"My pleasure, Surrendra. Would you like to insert my penis now? Let's try it."

He washed it first, coated it with jelly, and then slowly prodded it between her legs. She gasped as it penetrated, shocked at how full she felt, how thick and realistic it was.

"Wear it until I come back." It wasn't a playful suggestion; it was a command.

She lowered her eyes. "Yes, Harold."

He was looking at the hunk of latex between her legs and getting visibly hard beneath his trousers, and she thought it was better that he hadn't seen her satisfied smile.

The thing Delia loved about being a mistress, besides the blow-away sex, was the fact she could indulge herself with all kinds of froufrou and see-through lingerie, satiny gowns that flowed and draped like water, and sexy little high-heeled mules, which she always wore when she was at home. Even though Sonny had her scheduled for only two days, he might walk in the door at any time of any day or night.

She liked to have tidbits for him to nibble on before he nibbled on her, and she always stocked his favorite wines and beer because she liked taking care of him.

She liked to be occupied, as well. Sonny must never think she was sitting around wishing he would come. That would be a deal breaker, if he believed that he was the center of everything for her.

Delia understood perfectly that she had to have an inner life that had nothing to do with him, and she reveled in the fact that all this leisurely indulgent activity was interrupted for obscenely delicious sex.

It was the best fantasy world ever. Delia never wanted it to end.

Plus, her apartment was delightful. She kept plants on the terrace, she tried new recipes in the kitchen, she kept the place beautifully clean—and once in a while, she felt bored.

But once a week, without her having to do a thing, groceries arrived from Dean and Deluca and fresh fruit and veggies from Citarella. This was sheer heaven. Who needed more than this?

She didn't need presents or tokens of affection, and he rarely brought them. But one day, he handed her a little box.

"Sonny." She put it aside, put her arms around him, and began kissing him. What was better than kissing him?

"Go on, open it."

She was wearing a silk dressing gown so whisper thin that she might as well have been naked. She sat down, crossed her legs so that the hem fell back and her lower torso was bared, and opened it.

Inside were a pair of heart charms dangling from three thin, interlocking wire circles. There were no posts—not earrings. She held one up. Gold, at any rate.

"Sonny?"

"Nipple adornments."

"Oh, Sonny . . ." she murmured as she shrugged out of the dressing gown, looked at him from under her lashes, and slipped one on.

His body jolted. She slipped the second one over her other nipple.

"Spread your legs right there, I'm coming in." He ripped open his belt and pants, and ripped down his zipper as she purred, "It's like a little Sonny caress on my tit."

He barreled between her legs, then lifted her against the wall.

She wound herself around him, whispered sweet luscious things in his ear. He was so big, the nipple rings were so erotic, he was so generous, so filling . . . She knew everything erotic to say to a man like Sonny; every way to tweak and twist his earlobe, his mouth, his tongue, how to hold him and cradle him even as she was his erotic plaything, so irresistible that he couldn't hold himself back.

The nipple rings fell from her breasts as they sank onto the floor and kissed and coupled until morning.

MJ did not join them for Thanksgiving dinner, which they had at the Union Square Café.

"Why not?" Brooke had said. "Why not somewhere high profile, elegant, festive, and familylike. Even if it costs the earth."

Delia was worried about MJ.

"You're always worried about MJ. What is it about her?" Brooke asked.

Delia hedged. "Can't you guess?"

Brooke raised her neatly plucked eyebrows. "She gets too needy?"

"Think about that bastard Baines."

"He was just a shit. A controlling, freaky shit."

"Yeah, and?"

Brooke's expression sagged a little. "Oh. Don't tell me— MJ *wants* a controlling shit to run her life?"

"Pretty much," Delia said. "And I guess she found one."

"At Maîtrise?"

"It takes all kinds. I don't think we're talking hard-core S and M, and I'm praying this guy knows how to wield his power in a way that she won't get hurt."

"She did say he *might* see her tonight."

"And *might* is the operative word. We *live* on operative words. Call you, hope, might, just in case, maybe I'll come . . . you know the drill. He probably *won't* come, but that's the nature of that game: to hype her up so much that when he shows, she shows her gratitude in unimaginable ways."

Brooke held up her hand. "Please. My appetite."

"Well, let's be candid here. How much do you give up for Thane, and how much do I give up for Sonny? Don't they make demands? Aren't there things they want that you'd never have done for anyone else?"

"For itinerant sex? Never. But yeah, there are things . . ."

Like the giant photographs of her nipples hanging over her bed—as if he was a teenager with a porn magazine, except his porn was in his bed and on the wall.

"Right," Delia agreed. "So who's to say MJ's things aren't as valid as the things we do, in the interest of keeping the interest of the men who can afford anybody and anything they want."

"Yeah. I hadn't thought of it like that." *We're things* . . . "But somehow it doesn't ease your worry."

"Because MJ is obsessive about this secret. She thinks it's aberrant, and she really believed there would never be anyone else who—"

"Guess she was wrong."

"I hope she guessed right," Delia said

"Did *we* guess right?" Brooke looked around at the couples and families and the soft holiday ambience. "Are we going to be alone at Christmas, too?"

"Uh-oh—something's getting to you."

"Isn't it you?"

"Hell, no," Delia said emphatically. "This is the best fantasy. He can come or go as he wants to, as long as I get the apartment and the perks. I don't care if he can't make the *family* holidays—I'm not family. I'm the holiday treat."

"That's how I thought I'd feel about it, but now I'm not so sure."

The waiter interrupted them, setting down oval plates of turkey, trimmings, vegetables, and gravy.

"Yum," Delia murmured, digging in. "Okay, why aren't you sure?"

Brooke inhaled deeply. There was nothing like the aroma of turkey and stuffing. It was comfort food for her in a family that never offered any comfort. She had always spent Thanksgiving with her best friend, whose mother invited over the "abandoned" teens—the ones whose families were separated, in transit, in conflict.

"Because sex begets wanting more sex. The more we have sex, the more I want. I just want it all the time. It goes against everything I ever believed. Totally *not* Mistress Code."

"You're in love with his manhood."

"Shut *up*. No, I'm not."

They ate in silence for a bit.

"You *so* are."

Brooke made a sound. "And you're not—with Sonny's, I mean?"

"Better his man root than him. I'd be destroyed if I fell in love with him. No, a couple of nights of bed bumping are fine with me. Along with all the goodies."

"Okay, so I just have to train myself to look at it like poker night. Penis poker. And I'm the one who antes up."

"And it's natural, on the holiday that reeks family and apple pie, that you'd feel like the shadow wife. Do you ever think about his other life?"

"Do you?"

Delia shook her head. "Honest to God, I'm fine with it. Like you said: Get what you can, while you can. Sonny's willing to give, and I'm willing to get. It's perfect for me—for now."

Brooke leapt on that. "You see? For *now*!"

"You never thought it would be forever, either."

Brooke looked at her. "I wonder if the families know."

"Please—they have to. Their husbands have a regular excuse to be away from home two nights a week? What else could it be?"

"I sometimes think they're skulking around spying on us. If they're not, they should be."

"And I think it's just the opposite—that the Mistress Club is set up to guarantee the family never gets a whiff of what they're doing. These guys cover their tracks like a blizzard. Vanessa is the lion at the gate; there's no way anyone gets past her. You worry way more than I do."

"Of course I do; I'm contingency girl. I want that escape route ready when this whole mistress thing explodes in my face."

Brooke disliked those huge nipple photos, but there they stayed, affixed to the headboard. They drove her nuts because she had to look at them, too.

But how did you tell your lover that you didn't like him looking at pictures of your nipples?

You didn't. Humoring him was part of the price. Whatever Thane wanted, he got. Even pictures to carry around with him.

"I want those nipples erect for me every minute."

"That's impossible; they get irritated. They need a break because you never give them a rest."

"Thank God I have pictures. They're always hard in the

pictures. I'll just fondle the pictures instead of your nipples."

He was incessant about her nipples, even when he was mounted and rocking deep inside her. Sometimes she didn't know what more she could give him. Sometimes she wondered if *he* was getting enough.

Was he getting bored? Restless? Nothing had changed. But she kept wanting more, and then she started thinking that maybe tomorrow this whole thing could come to an end altogether.

Maybe—maybe—maybe—

A mistress's life was all about maybes and questions, all keeping her off balance, every answer an unknown.

MJ had discovered one thing about wearing a latex penis: You had to be naked. It didn't work if you were clothed, or even erotically dressed.

But you didn't need anything else except a man's length to fill that heat between your legs. She was loving that sensation maybe even more than Harold had intended.

My little secret . . .

She loved it too much. She was curled up in a chair, just enjoying the thick, filling feel of it, and the way her nipples tightened with arousal and her whole body felt thick with erotic heat.

"So, you're enjoying the penis."

She jolted out of her erotic reverie. "Harold!"

"Harold's been good to you while I've been gone."

Why did he seem displeased? A little spunk is needed here, she thought.

"Harold is exactly where you decreed he should be."

He shrugged out of his jacket. "I did, didn't I? Is he as good?"

"He's not real," she said instantly. "How could something plastic ever be as good as real? Or any penis be better than yours?"

"The stupid thing can't fuck you. It can't feel you up inside with its fingers, the fucking stupid thing."

God, he was angry, like she'd been enjoying it too much. Which she had—stupid stupid stupid.

He pulled the dildo from her body and thrust his fingers inside her, deep, deep inside, as if he wanted to come out the other side.

And suddenly it was over. His anger wound down, and he carried her to the bed and set her down—well, not gently— and joined her, covering his face wearily with his arm. "Don't talk."

Dumb dumb dumb, loving that thing too much. Loving *his* thing too much. *Do not not not fall in love,* even with his manhood. *Brooke should add that to the Mistress Code . . .*

MJ didn't move a muscle, holding herself so tensely that she began to tremble. And she had to go to the bathroom. Maybe he was asleep? Pretending to be asleep? Nothing would surprise her, given his mercurial reaction to her following his express command.

Well, she wasn't going to pee in bed. She swung her legs over the side, then carefully padded around the bed, the chair, and his discarded jacket on the floor.

She picked it up to place it on the chair. There was a curious weight to it, like there was something in one of the pockets. Normally, she wouldn't have cared.

But today—shit. This was too tempting. She didn't know him—not at all, not after tonight's jealous display over a dildo. So if there was anything there . . .

She inserted her fingers into the right-hand pocket. Bingo. There was something tucked in there, like a pocket diary or a superthin wallet.

She thought men like him used the latest electronic gizmos. Maybe when you were juggling a mistress, a business, a married life, and a community life, you couldn't afford to be electronically tracked. And you probably couldn't afford to put anything in writing, either.

There was something else there. She picked it out carefully and slipped into the bathroom.

What was this?

Tiny photographs, maybe one inch by one inch square. But not a person.

A nipple?

Whose nipple?

Two, three pictures of someone's nipples in close-up, one with something surrounding the nipple, one with some slick residue on it.

She felt sick. *These are not me. Whose nipples are they? I can't ask. I can't tell. I can't stand it.*

I'd flush these down the toilet, but he'd know I found them. But how can I go on from this moment, knowing about them?

I want to kill her. Who is she? Don't tell me; I just want to kill her.

She wanted to tear the photographs to microscopic pieces and make them not exist.

How I can live with this? I thought, I thought—

Stupid, what did you think? A man with his appetites . . .

You don't even know those pictures aren't his wife.

Okay, it's his wife; I can live with that.

But they're so erotic, so tiny and clandestine . . .

She tiptoed back into the bedroom and slipped the pictures back into the jacket pocket, shielding the maneuver with her body.

It's his wife . . .

But if he adores her nipples so much, why does he need me?

She slipped into bed, trembling with uncertainty.

Because you do things with him she never would.

Really, it's his wife.

"You take the best care of me," Sonny whispered to Delia one evening shortly before Christmas, while they wallowed in afterglow.

"I should hope so." She trailed the little heart charm across his hairy chest—she liked a man with lots of hair on his chest—and looped it around his nipple and licked and sucked it. His body shivered, sapped as he was, and she smiled that infuriating little smile that intrigued and annoyed him.

The second charm she squeezed onto his penis head. The

slit barely showed through, just enough so she could lick and nip at it, just enough so that all that attention made him stiff and pulsing all over again.

She knew he liked her, liked her nurturing, her imagination, and their sex. She liked him and their sex. It was a perfect symbiotic relationship. Lots of sex, no regrets. She couldn't imagine what Brooke was worrying about.

But as Christmas approached, she also knew that he'd be spending a fair amount of time with his family and his various community obligations.

So what she needed to do, she thought idly, was to slip a little reminder of *her* in a jacket pocket, where a man invariably reached for his keys or some change, so that he wouldn't forget her. Some little Delia thing, just to remind him . . .

Like maybe one of the nipple rings.

"Good God, Delia, you could make a snowman hot and hard."

While he showered, she slipped the ring charm into the pocket of his Armani suit. Oops, there was something there. A pocket diary . . . and little pictures. Of . . . nipples?

Three little pictures of some exhibitionistic whore's distended and adorned nipples. Nipples that were not hers. Hard, pointy nipples, looped and chained in one picture, naked in another, and in the third, coated with some slick substance. Goddamn him, she knew what *that* was.

"Delia!"

She started. God, if he came out and saw her with these . . . She slipped them back into his pocket and opened the bathroom door.

"Yes, Sonny?" in her most sugary tone.

"I need a fuck now."

She took a deep, quelling breath. "That's what I'm here for."

But not for nipple pictures, she thought furiously.

Now what do I do? But there was no question. She slipped into the slower, closed the door, and fucked him.

Thane was swimming in her: He didn't have one drop of semen left, but he was still hard and didn't want to waste the erection.

"Christmas vacation is coming," he reminded her.

"I'm aware." Brooke hadn't wanted to think about his family and that he might have to allocate time to them during the holidays.

"Good. It might be two weeks until I come again."

"If you can take it," she said lightly. "Not coming, I mean."

He shimmied himself deeper. "Right now, I don't think so."

"I'll be here." What else could she say? To personalize it more would be to risk pushing him away, she was sure of it.

How did mistresses do this?

There was nothing in the Mistress Code about holidays or hormones. And it wasn't as if she didn't know about his wife and family. Googling him had provided minimal details. He had a socialite wife, scads of money, lived in a nearby suburban town, had two grown children, and was a pillar of the community—facts couched in fuzzy terms so no idle surfer could home in on specifics.

She'd been content with that before, but *home for Christmas* was so Norman Rockwell. Normal and familial and exclusive. It excluded *her*.

How could he go off and leave her for two weeks when he could barely contain himself the two days he gave her?

Don't think about it. Give him something to remind him of you. Something small . . . The nipple loop chain. It fit in the palm of her hand, it would take up no space in his jacket pocket, and when he found it, maybe—

"Brooke! Come back, I'm feeling creamy."

"Then let me have it, to sustain me for the time you'll be gone."

And he did, a riptide of an orgasm. He'd barely squeezed out the last drop when he said, "I have to go," and headed for the shower.

This was her chance. She eased out of bed, removed the loops and chain, and slipped them into his jacket pocket.

But wait—there was something in there—his day calendar, yes, but, oh, God—her nipple pictures were right in his jacket pocket—*and*—three thin interlocking wires with a charm suspended from them. What on earth would you do with—

She looked at her nipples, placed it on her right nipple, and looked at herself in the mirror. A nipple charm? For *whom*?

It hung, gently suspended from her nipple tip. *Don't forget me . . .*

No. She shook her head. No, he was too consumed with *her*. Her sex, *her* nipples, her—

Wasn't he?

The thing glittered and glistened as she moved; it would entice any lover to focus there.

Damn him to hell.

No, I won't believe it. He got it for me. He's going to give it to me, something to remember *him* by for these two weeks—

"*Nipples!*"

The bastard, calling me that when—"Yes, Thane?"

"I need a fuck."

She wanted to kill him. She wanted to drown him in the shower, him and his heartless, insatiable manhood. She slipped the pictures and the nipple ring back into his pocket, and did the only thing she could: She went into the bathroom and let him have his way with her.

Chapter Sixteen

He lived in a nine-bedroom mansion in Pelham Manor that overlooked Long Island Sound. It had two parlors, an estate-sized dining room, a family dining room, a restaurant-sized kitchen with the most up-to-the-moment professional appliances, and two family rooms—one was his office, and a smaller one his wife, Rae, used as her office and to entertain friends.

There was stone loggia the width of the house that stepped down to the now snow-covered lawn, which swooped right to the water and to his rarely used private dock.

He loved his house. It was the symbol of everything the name Thane Bohansson meant, everything he'd accomplished.

He was a man of brazen appetites. He hadn't gotten where he was by being namby-pamby; his wealth was secured in covert accounts under numerous company names and corporate aliases, Sonny Hanes and Harold Hanson among them. Naturally he'd placed his alter egos' biographies on the internet as CEOs of two of those dummy corporations. That was what the damned thing was for—to aid and abet sharp businessmen who knew how to work the system.

And to deflect nosy women. Of course they all checked on him; he knew that from experience. But he loved nosy young women. He loved them fresh, firm fleshed, beautiful, and still untouched by the exigencies of trying to make it in the city. While they were still sexually voracious. He couldn't take those experienced, emotionally needy, snotty-assed models and would-be actresses anymore. God, what luck that Brooke had mentioned to Vanessa that she had two friends and that they were as young, untried, and hot as she was.

Of course he had to have them. It was so simple to set up an alias with each: apartments on opposite sides of the city, the demand they give up their jobs to be always available for him. That subterfuge was the cost of doing business, a mere entertainment expense for his proud and rigorous penis.

It was so simple for Vanessa to set it up, as she always did in return for his generous remuneration, so that he could preempt them before they were seen or touched by another man's hands.

MJ—an absolute dream of a submissive. And Delia—he rather liked that faint elusiveness in her, and that combination of sexpot and earth mother. And Brooke—where could a man find a more delicious hole than one that loved being fucked solely for the sake of being fucked?

He had been in orgasmic heaven for the past six months. Three gorgeous, nubile penis pumps. Hot, smooth flesh, tight, wet pussies . . . it occupied his mind all the time.

He didn't know how he was going to contain his lust while he was home. Maybe he'd sneak off and surprise them all as a Christmas treat.

No, he couldn't wait that long. Well, he'd just have to find a whore in town. Home for the holidays and blasting off already—he stripped, changed, and went to find a fast fuck.

An hour later, Rae entered their bedroom.

Ah, my ghost has been here.

She caught glimpses of him now and then, drifting in and out of her life. She'd been married to him for thirty years now, and she was well aware that she had bartered her body and her family name for big bucks and ultrarespectability. She had her showcase house and all the other trappings, the trade-offs women of her social status made in order to stay married to high-powered men. She just didn't have *him*.

But it was a nice life. She knew nothing; didn't want to know anything. It would be much more difficult if she did know, and not having to deal with that merciless sex was a blessing.

And it wasn't that she wasn't attractive or sexual. It was just that Thane was Thane, and he couldn't be controlled by a hundred of her. He needed a harem. He was a pasha under the skin, who lived to be serviced by a long line of different young women salivating for the chance.

So she let it all slide, because it never intruded here, in her Shangri-la.

The kids were grown now. Egan and Alaina were nice kids, in spite of their father, polite, successful, and devoted to her. She didn't need to protect them anymore; she was free to do anything she wanted now.

She could throw extravagant parties, shop the Paris runways, take the corporate jet anywhere in the world, or sail their lavish yacht to Monaco. She had personal shoppers, the current trendy decorator, and houses in Biarritz and Tuscany if she was bored in Pelham.

She had lots of friends, she'd had several particular male friends, and Thane didn't care because it never intruded in *his* life.

But here he was for his mandatory Christmas appearance, because she yearned for some small degree of normalcy. But, as ever, there was no normalcy. He'd come and gone, leaving his semen-soaked clothes on the floor like a naughty little boy thumbing his nose at her.

Moments like these, she hated him and she hated her life.

She picked up his trousers, went through the pockets, and stuffed the pants in the cleaning bag; picked up his jacket, delved in the pockets, and—took out the day calendar, the little photographs, the looped chain, the triple-wire heart charm. Rae sank onto the bed, her hand shaking, every alarm bell clanging in her head: *intrusion, intrusion.* After carefully placing the items on the white duvet, she girded herself to open the calendar.

It was one of those wallet-sized books that had a week's worth of notations every two facing pages.

Thane's handwriting was like hieroglyphics, but she was used to it and easily deciphered three sets of initials plotted out each week for the last six months: npls on Tuesday and Thursday; srdr on Monday, Wednesday, and Saturday; d'a on Friday and Sunday. Next to each set of initials was a number and sometimes a notation.

Wednesday: srdr 5 hrs. Tuesday: npls 4 fd. It looked like he was keeping a cryptic diary of . . . what? She didn't want to think of what it was.

She tossed the diary onto the bed and picked up the wire. Not an earring. She dangled it from her fingers. Maybe the post was broken?

But the gold chain was something else; it was like an eyeglass holder, of a length that could only dangle uselessly down around the groin . . .

Was *everything* to do with Thane so overtly sexual?

She picked up the little pictures and her heart stopped. Nipples. Some fucking slut's naked nipples, close up, pointed and hard. They posed with the stretchy loops of the chain around them in one picture and were coated with . . . Damn his evil soul!

He couldn't.

He didn't—

She took the photographs to the window. The sick son of a bitch bastard, carrying pictures of some whore's naked nipples where anyone could find them—*npls* . . . now she understood the diary entry.

A sex diary, a nipple necklace, pictures—this was obscenely intruding in her life, even if she'd found the items by accident.

She didn't know what to do.

She wanted to castrate him, to hang him by his hairy balls until he screamed for mercy. But that was illegal.

She burned to make his sex life miserable. Maybe she could find out who these damned whores were and destroy them, personally and professionally.

There had to be something she could legally do to punish Thane. Their son Egan was a lawyer—he'd know what to do.

MJ gave in to temptation and went back to her old neighborhood, back, in her heart, to a time when things were simpler and she hadn't been betrayed like that.

She just couldn't get it out of her mind or heart: There was someone else in Harold's life. Even though he'd treated her like she was the special one—damn it, she *was* the special one.

She felt cold and dead inside. She'd thought Harold was . . . but what *was* he? He was a man who loved dominating her as much as she loved being controlled, and he'd given her a gorgeous apartment and three days a week of his time. So what was her problem? Having the perfect man in her life?

Could the perfect man want a submissive little nobody *seven* days a week? His need for sex was so off the charts that one single woman couldn't hold him. Still, it was a knife in the heart to know that Harold had other relations with other women that didn't include bondage. Maybe she'd thought it would go on forever because he was so perfect for her.

She had no idea what she would do. Would she even tell him she'd found the photographs, accuse him of—of what?

He was her master for now, not forever. By the nature of it, her time as his mistress was limited. He might grow tired of her, or she'd grow bored with him—something would ease the high-voltage sexual tension.

Without those photographs, she would never have known about this. So forget them. Forget those nipples that were so extraordinarily hard. Think of them as erotic pictures for a supersexed man who needed to be in charge. She should be grateful he was still with her.

She walked around the block where her apartment had been. Everything looked smaller, as if Harold's world had so enlarged hers that by comparison everything had shrunk.

Then the door of the building opened, and a familiar figure stepped out.

"Dallan?"

He whipped around. "MJ?"

"What are you doing here?"

"I rented your old apartment for . . . business purposes."

There was something in his eyes. This was too odd, him taking her apartment. Unless he had a mistress stashed up there. She didn't feel a pang at the thought. "I see. Well . . ." She turned away.

"MJ—" His voice was hard, harsh, commanding.

"I'm with someone else," she said bluntly.

"With? Meaning what?"

"I'm his mistress."

"Like you were with me?" he said aggressively.

She had to end this. Obviously it stuck in his craw that she'd left of her own volition and he'd had no control over that. Now he was trying to control this moment, perhaps trying to get her to admit that she still wanted him.

"More than the way I was with you," she said curtly. "More of *everything* exactly the way I like it. Good-bye, Dallan."

"MJ!" His voice was tense with suppressed fury. She turned away abruptly and dashed across the street, knowing he was watching her. The quickest escape was a cab.

A moment later she hailed one, unaware that he had grabbed one, too.

Delia paced back and forth in a fury, although the practical side of her wondered why she was so angry. She wasn't invested in him. She didn't care about feelings, or how often he had sex with her.

So what's your problem? He didn't swear sexual loyalty to you.

It just seems like such a violation—his other life intruding into *my* life.

No, it didn't. You were the one intruding in his pocket.

Enough. Call Brooke. She'll figure out how to cope with this.

"So here's the problem," Delia said three hours later, over a plate of raviolacci, sun-dried tomatoes, and goat cheese. "No—if I start telling you, I'll lose my appetite."

"Okay," Brooke said, "eat first, regurgitate later."

"Ewww, yucky visual." Delia looked at MJ, who was picking at her tuna and balsamic salad greens. "MJ, wake up."

"I'm going to be lousy company tonight."

"Not after you hear my sad story," Delia assured her. "Come on, eat. We've all got shore leave for a few days, right? We don't get much time together, so let's enjoy it."

"You're right," MJ said, heaving a huge sigh.

"Oh, brother," Delia muttered. "Well, I'm here to *eat*." She dug in, and so did Brooke, who had ordered the double-cut veal chop.

"All right, the shrink's office is open," Brooke said finally. "But let's order coffee and dessert first. We deserve dessert since we've all been abandoned for the holidays."

"Seduced and abandoned," MJ murmured sotto voce, and said suddenly, "I saw Dallan today."

"Jeez Louise—*how*?" Delia demanded.

"I went to the old neighborhood, and you know what? The effing bastard rented my old apartment."

"Shut *up*. Why the hell would he do that?"

"I don't know, but it was weird in a really bad way. He said it was for business. I told him flat out I was someone else's mistress and that my lover was more to me than he ever was." She heaved another sigh. "God, what a stupid thing to do."

"So why did you?" Delia asked.

"Because . . . oh shit, I'm going first? I thought this was about your problem, Delia."

"It doesn't matter."

"No, you go first." MJ's expression was stubborn.

"All right. Well, you know that my attitude about this mistress stuff is pretty much take it or leave it. And I was never curious about Sonny's wife, his family, any of that. But the other night I found something, and it upset me. And I don't understand why."

"What did you find?" MJ asked.

"Little photographs . . ."

MJ made an odd sound.

Delia went on, "Three photographs of a particular body part—"

Brooke's cup crashed to the saucer.

"Nipples," MJ whispered, "right? Three different little pictures of some other woman's nipples."

"How did *you* know?" Delia demanded.

"I found pictures like that, too."

"*Shit!*" Brooke's voice was shaking. "The bollocking son of a bitch!"

"What? *What?*" Delia demanded.

Brooke could barely get her voice in control, or her fury. "I found something, too."

Delia looked at her oddly.

"A heart charm suspended from a circular wire."

"What?!"

There was a hard moment of silence and then Brooke spat out, "That effing shithead was fucking all of us!"

"No!"

"How? *No! Not* Harold—"

"Oh, you don't think the legendary Thane Bohansson couldn't have alter egos? That son of a bitch! That frigging son of a—he was fucking all of us!" She slammed her fist down on the table. "When did that bastard find time when he was with me Tuesday and Thursday . . . and mornings and nights in between?"

Delia looked shell-shocked. "Friday and Sunday for me."

MJ whispered, "Monday, Wednesday, and Saturday."

"*Three* days? He gave you *three* days? That frigging horny rat bastard." Brooke stood abruptly. "I can't frigging believe this. We've been together six months, he's fucking me to oblivion, *and* he's fucking my best friends behind my back?" She pulled out a handful of bills and threw them on the table. "God almighty. You all should have known . . ."

"Oh, yeah, Sonny Hanes and Harold Hanson sound a lot like Thane Bohansson," Delia intervened, trying to keep some calm. "How the hell could we have known?"

"Hell-O—Thane . . . Hanes—Hanson, BoHANSSON. Well, to hell with all of you and to hell with him. Don't ever call me again." She stalked out of the restaurant.

MJ bolted to her feet, tossing her share of the bill onto the messy pile of money. "Harold loves *me*," she hissed. "He's *not* Thane Bohansson, and I never want to see you again, either." She stalked off, too.

Delia stared at the money, stared at the empty chairs, and tried to get a handle on what had just happened.

Thane Bohansson had truly screwed them all over—and he probably didn't give a shit about it.

But . . . the pictures. How did Brooke know about the pictures? She hadn't been shocked. Because . . . because those were her nipples in the photographs.

* * *

She called Brooke that night.

"I'm not talking to you," Brooke snapped and flipped off her cell.

Damn. Delia tried MJ.

MJ didn't answer.

She called Brooke again. "This is stupid," she spit out before Brooke cut her off without a word.

Brooke was just going to let their friendship slip away because of a stupid male?

She tried calling again.

"Brooke—"

"Don't call me." *Blip.*

Damn. She rang MJ again.

"I'm going to kill him," MJ breathed into the receiver. "Don't ever call me again."

Jeez, was she the only one with a level head here? They were *mistresses* for God's sake. They were conveniences, receptacles, adornments—so why were Brooke and MJ acting like he'd taken some unbreakable vow to be faithful? He was breaking his own marriage vows, for God's sake; how could they be shocked and resentful that he screwed around on *them*?

The bottom line had always been what he was willing to put out in exchange for them putting out. Which was considerable. Everything else was irrelevant.

But her live-and-let-live philosophy was sorely tested late that night when a body fell down heavily next to her on the bed.

Half asleep, she almost called him Thane, but she caught herself.

"Sonny? What—? I thought—"

"Don't think," he muttered thickly. "Spread your legs."

She spread her legs and he poled into her, into the hotbox that he owned and paid for.

"I'm a regular Santa tonight." He flexed his shaft. "I like giving presents . . ." He buried his face in her neck and licked the curve.

It took all her control not to freeze. Santa, delivering flyby fucks?

Just enjoy the sex. Forget about the rest.

It was the dead of night and Brooke awakened with a start. Someone was feeling her up, a hot finger probing for her clit, and a hot mouth closed over one nipple.

Shit shit shit—what do I do now?

He grew insistent with his caress, seeking her deeper. "Nipples!"

She couldn't pretend to be asleep now that her body was fully awake and disgustingly aware and responsive. "Thane!" She nearly choked on his name.

"Santa's in the house, and he's hungry for nipples."

She swallowed hard. Deny him? Do as he said?

He flicked on the nightstand lamp and Brooke looked up at him kneeling over her. He was engorged, his eyes a little glazed, and maybe he was a little drunk.

"Dance for me, Nipples."

Does MJ dance for you? Does Delia?

This was no time to be weighing her Midwest morality against her mistress mentality.

307

He burrowed another finger into her cleft. "Now, Nipples."

She danced, using every belly-dance move she could summon up half asleep. He'd paid for this private performance, after all, and if he got a lap dance later from Delia, well, he'd paid for that privilege, too.

His own damn private harem.

As she danced, he stroked himself and stoked her until ripples of hot pleasure slithered through her and spilled onto his fingers.

He pushed her down onto the bed. "You're the only one who does it for me."

Only one of how many?

Don't go there.

"Take it, Thane," she whispered. "My Christmas present to you."

God, I hate myself.

It wasn't Harold. It *couldn't* be Harold. MJ kept telling herself that, though it didn't reassure her.

God, she missed him. It was Christmas Eve, and she wanted him desperately. She was angry at herself for going to her old neighborhood, despised herself for prying into Harold's pockets. And she would *not* allow that abortive dinner last night to destroy her peace of mind.

"Surrendra."

Was she imagining his rasping voice? It was so early in the morning, maybe three o'clock. She struggled up onto her elbows. "Harold?"

"It's Santa, baby, here with his bag of goodies . . ."

Oh, goody—

She was sore when he left before dawn. He had used her body ruthlessly, in the most forbidden places that brimmed with unexpected, explosive pleasure. This time he had done things to her that were so off the charts, so unspeakably pleasurable, that the fact it was Christmas slipped away from her as she wallowed in the reverberating sensations.

I'm the one, and he's not someone named Thane or Sonny, and whenever he wants my body, I'm his to do anything with that he desires.

Her cell rang sometime in the morning. She idly picked it up, thinking it might be Harold. But no—nosy Delia.

Do not want to talk to you ever again, she tapped in text message mode and sent it. There. Now it would be just her and Harold.

Christmas morning.

Delia cooked. It felt homey to be cooking, even alone, on Christmas Day. She wanted to invite Brooke to come over, but Brooke wasn't answering her cell. MJ was a lost cause altogether.

She made a roast chicken, stuffing, gravy. She baked a carrot cake with cream cheese icing, a whole big sheet of chocolate chip cookies. She made coffee in her expensive Bunn machine. And then she sat at her table, one person at her dinner for six, staring out the window at the falling snow and wondering if she had fallen too far for redemption.

* * *

Christmas morning.

A long time ago in the big house in Pelham, Christmas had had the veneer of a joyous family holiday. But no more: Thane's attitude was pretty much one foot out the door.

Of course Egan and Alaina always made the best of it, for her sake.

But Christmas Day was just the four of them together, opening lavish and usually meaningless presents.

Rae had it running like clockwork so there would be no gaps, no awful silences. At nine o'clock, everyone would have coffee in the small family room—*her* room, the cozy room that overlooked the loggia and the Sound. There, the Christmas tree was set up, music would be playing softly, and they would sit for an hour and pretend they were a cohesive and loving family.

Could she pretend today? Knowing what she knew?

She put on her Christmas Day robe, beautiful ruby-colored satin with antique lace at the collar and cuffs, and went down the hallway and knocked on everyone's doors. Then she went down to the kitchen.

"Coffee's ready, ma'am. And Danish, toast, muffins, eggs, sausage, and home fries *en buffet,* as you requested," this year's chef reported. The resident chef prepared the same breakfast buffet every year, even though Rae tended to change chefs yearly, depending on her level of irritation with life.

"Thank you." This chef had been with them something like six or seven months, and she had been wondering whether to let him go. But that was a decision for another day.

She heard noises upstairs, her children—children no more—scrambling to be the first downstairs.

That was what *her* Christmas was all about.

She pushed open the door to the family room, to the stunning vision of the tree, highly decorated and glowing softly in the dim light, the soft music already playing as she had instructed, the scent of coffee from the side table set up with breakfast goodies, to the pile on the floor of . . . of . . .

She screamed. And couldn't stop screaming. She heard footsteps, she heard Egan's and Alaina's voices—heard someone call the police.

Omigod, omigod. Thane.

She screamed his name as they led her out of the room, her perfect room, her perfect Christmas, and her perfect husband dead on the floor.

Chapter Seventeen

The news broke that night.

Delia decided to watch TV, since there wasn't much else to do when you were all alone Christmas night. She settled onto her pillow-piled bed with coffee, cookies, and the remote.

Brooke turned on the TV just to have noise in the apartment; the comforting presence of sound made her feel less alone.

MJ turned on the TV when she realized that all her pining for Harold would not bring him to her on a night when he obviously had family obligations.

CNN had it first. *This just in: media magnate Thane Bohansson was found dead in his home Christmas morning . . .*

They'd found a picture from very long ago, maybe twenty years.

MJ screamed, because it *was* Harold.

. . . Thane Bohansson, rumored to be the power behind the powers that be, the influential owner of hundreds of media outlets, newspapers, cable stations, and satellite radio, was found dead this morning in his home—

A picture of a stately mansion on the Long Island Sound, taken from the water, flashed on the screen.

—by his wife. The family was in residence for the holidays—wife Rae; son Egan, a lawyer and chief operations counsel to the corporation; his daughter Alaina, an artist—

Their pictures on screen, one after the other: the elegant wife, as gorgeous as any mistress; his son, handsome, with just a hint of his father's jaw and eyes; the daughter, the image of the mother.

—and a skeleton house staff. Police not ready to call it homicide. Autopsy scheduled. Funeral arrangements to be announced by the family.

A family that Thane had chosen to disrespect and ignore, with his stable of sex dolls, Delia thought.

The legendary Thane Bohansson. The ruthless Thane Bohansson. The obsessively elusive mogul who owned the media . . .

His wife had no inkling of his secret inner cravings, MJ thought—the cravings in him that only *I* serviced. How can I bear it? What am I going to do?

What will happen now? the pundits demanded. *So much at stake. Is Egan Bohansson competent to take the reins? And what about his wife?*

All the things Brooke had never wanted to know about him were now shooting full blast across every network, for all the world to chew on. The social register life, the cars, the servants, the appalled neighbors.

No one had seen anything; the neighbors were aghast something like this could happen. They told whoever would listen that Egan was a partner in the prestigious Westchester law firm that was counsel to his father, that Alaina was an artist in Manhattan, that they were good kids, devoted kids.

That Rae Bohansson was active in the community; that Thane sat on the boards of local organizations and was an elder of the church. They were convivial people, charitable people. They did not appear to be estranged.

But how could that be? Delia wondered, watching the coverage. How could he have kept up with family and community obligations and still have the time for three full-time mistresses?

She feared that was the thing that was going to come bubbling up, erupt to the surface, and wash them all in the toxic muck of public exposure.

She wanted more than anything to call Brooke and MJ, but neither was talking to her.

I have nothing.

The sudden thought stunned her, because for these six months, she'd sincerely believed she had had everything she wanted—for now.

But what none of them had seen was that Thane had isolated them in a golden cage, cutting off jobs and friends with his demand that they devote all their time to him.

They'd never thought about what might happen if there *were* no Thane.

And now they had nothing—not even each other. And sooner or later, someone was going to come knocking at the door and tell them to leave. What did abandoned mistresses do?

Each of them watched the endless coverage, periodic updates by the impatient crime-scene detective, Nick Galligan, which said the same thing in fifty different ways. Autopsy pending. Nothing to report. Ongoing investigation. Assiduously pursuing leads.

And what about his secrets? How much of Thane's sexual life would become public knowledge and how soon? The media were digging right now.

It was only a matter of time until they got to his mistresses, MJ thought, terrified. She had been with Harold-Thane into the wee early hours; what if the police questioned everyone who'd seen him between Christmas Eve and the morning his wife found him?

What do I do? How much of the truth do I really have to tell?

Nothing—until someone knocks on your door.

All she could do was watch the endless loop of Harold-Thane's life playing over and over, a train wreck about to happen.

Breaking news . . .

The autopsy results crawling across the screen of a dozen news stations—Thane Bohansson, death by asphyxiation, signs of strangulation—*homicide.*

"Shit shit shit! My life isn't enough of a mess, I have to get effing buried in Thane Bohansson's *murder*?" Nick Galligan popped an antacid pill and glared at his captain. "Crap. I thought this was going to be a nice cut-and-dried heart attack."

"Cute touch, leaving the body as a present under the tree," Tom Farris said. "Somebody thought that was funny or symbolic or something. And the A-list of somebodies was right on the scene."

"Crap. A year's salary says they've all got A-list alibis." Nick stalked out of the station house.

He didn't want to go back to the Bohansson house, with the robot family going through the robot motions of pretending grief and loss. No one would know anything, everyone would lie, and he'd have to untangle everyone's self-interests to get anywhere near what really happened.

Forensics hadn't found anything that wasn't expected: The whole family, the chef, and a maid had all been in the room at one time or another over the past week and Christmas morning.

Bohansson had spent time in his bedroom and in the guest bedroom but had conclusively been strangled—to immobilize him—and killed in the family room. There were signs of a struggle, which indicated that whoever had attacked him had been as strong, or stronger. Probably two males, because one had immobilized him while the other had smothered him.

No blood, no trauma except for the marks around his neck.

It was too clean. Too neat. Bloodless—like *them.*

Nick didn't like it, and he didn't like the family. They were too helpful, too reasonable. They weren't as shaken up as they ought to be—though he'd bet that come Friday, they'd be dissolved in tears as the TV cameras rolled.

He felt itchy. There was something deep beneath the skin here, and he was going to have to scratch hard to make it bleed.

The elegant and composed Rae Bohansson brought him into her husband's large office, pretending confusion at his presence since they'd been questioned in depth the morning the body was discovered.

"But now we have a murder to investigate," Nick said, watching her expression. Not a twitch. "Now we're talking about all those things you see on TV: motivation, alibis, and where were *you* at two that morning?"

Her eyelids flickered.

"So, where *were* you at two in the morning?"

"Sleeping, Detective. Weren't you?"

"And I'll bet this house is so well built and so well insulated, you couldn't hear an explosion if it happened—am I right?"

"Something like that," Rae said. "I told you everything I know, Detective Galligan. I was up a little after eight. I had given staff previous instructions to set up our traditional Christmas breakfast before seven, to start the music, to light the tree. I knocked on everyone's door, came downstairs, and then I walked into the small family room and saw Thane lying there dead."

"You assumed he was dead before even checking to see if he were alive?"

"He was heaped up under the tree at a very odd angle, Detective."

Nick made a sound. "You don't sleep together."

"We do share a bedroom. But he'd gone out, so I assumed he'd slept in the guest room so as not to disturb me when he returned."

"And where might he have been that night, that he wasn't home and wouldn't have wanted to disturb you?"

Her gaze slewed away from his. "Thane was always having meetings at all kinds of crazy hours. He could have jetted off to Europe or he could have been working in this very office, and I wouldn't have known which."

"But he wasn't here. So, where?"

Her lips thinned slightly. "I don't know."

She knew.

But he got nowhere with her, or Egan and Alaina. They knew, too, his gut was certain. But they were as tight-lipped as their mother.

Nor could Egan be terrorized by the threat of Nick poking around in the business books or his father's personal life.

"I'll tell you what you'll find, Detective."

"Really—*that* you'll tell me?" God protect him from lawyers, especially rich ones, ready to eviscerate whoever got in their way.

"You'll find everything in tip-top shape, is what you'll find." He said it gently but with a smug certainty Nick wanted to choke out of him.

He took a shot from the ongoing rumors. "What about the mistresses?"

There was just a flicker of something in Egan's eyes. "I don't know what you're talking about, Detective."

"I expect the books will do the talking—those hidden expenses for jewelry, clothes, furs, apartments, the usual tawdry stuff."

Egan shrugged, his expression . . . attentive. "Get your warrant and send in your clowns."

The good son, protecting the father, the secrets, and the lies.

So be it. Nick called Farris the minute he left the house. "Get the paperwork now, and our best guys onto those corporate books immediately—screw the holidays."

Nick was looking forward to the eleven AM funeral service on Friday at a Park Avenue church. Seeing the people who attended the funerals of the powerful and famous told you a lot about them, and about the deceased. Family, friends, business associates, satellites, hangers-on, status seekers, the slime and the sirens—they'd all be there.

As he predicted, it was mayhem. The press jamming the stone steps of the church, talking to the CEOs, CFOs, and COOs of every major corporation and media conglomerate in the world who expressed their condolences to the TV cameras. The family swathed in black, the limousines, the lines, the pissed and the predatory, the insiders and the ignored.

Nick roamed the fringes of the crowd, listening to snippets of conversation. He brushed against an elegant black-haired woman dressed in a black couture suit who was so striking that everyone's eyes were on her. He watched as the TV cameras followed her, looking for pay dirt, or just dirt.

Watched her rebuff a nicely rounded blonde and turn away from another woman, a tall, slim redhead. All beauties among three dozen or more beauties scattered among the six-deep crowd of people who couldn't fit into the church.

"Hey, Nick!"

Crap. It was Dev McDevitt, ace reporter, dressed like an ad in Men's *Vogue*, trolling for gold-plated gossip.

"What do you know?" Dev asked casually, joining him.

"No comment."

"Huh. Did you know they're taking bets in Vegas on whether Egan Bohansson has the *cojones* to juggle the shadow corps and manage the legit operation?"

"Trust me, he's got his daddy's balls. But off the record, our boys are trained in CPA *ninjutsu*."

"Really? Can I anonymous-source that?"

"Hell no. You'll need CPR if I catch a whiff of it."

"Okay. Here's another quid pro quo: I found out about the mistresses."

Nick went very still. Dev could be bluffing. "What mistresses?"

"I knew something was up," Dev said with that little *gotcha* lilt in his voice. "Nick, you've got to let me in on this. Everyone's digging, and since *I* found out Bohansson was knee-deep in mistresses, they're all going to be on my tail."

"Dev, you write for the *Post*," Nick said. "Page Six is but a slip of the tongue into deep shit, and I don't have my waders on today."

"Let me tag along, then."

"Not happening."

Dev's gaze skimmed the crowd and settled on the stunning woman in black whom Nick had noticed earlier. "Lots of ladies in mourning today." He cocked an eye at Nick. "I guess I'll start with those mythical mistresses."

"Go chase the mouse in the maze, my friend. I've got a murder to investigate."

The eulogy, sonorously piped through a loudspeaker to the crowd outside, extolled the scrupulous and brilliant businessman, beloved father, husband, community leader, and revered church elder, to the point there wasn't a dry eye anywhere. Still, there wasn't a soul there who wasn't reckoning the net worth of his estate at the closing bell.

Egan Bohansson threw up his hands. "You win. He had lots of extracurricular . . . activity, shall we say?"

It was the day after the funeral, and Galligan's crack team of accountants had gone through the books like wildfire. The *real* books—the ones they stashed in hidden vaults.

"How much is *lots*?" Nick asked.

"Over the years, or currently?" Egan asked with a touch of sarcasm.

Nick gave him a skewering look.

"Lots. He liked them young, a little experienced so they knew which way was up, but not so much that he'd be taken to the cleaners."

"And so you buried it all in the expense account under *cleaning bills*—and tailoring. Tailored to his needs apparently: apartments, checking accounts, clothing allowances. Let's get to the current concubines."

Eagan said resignedly, "Currently there are three. God knows how, but . . . there are three."

Christ, *three?* He'd been servicing *three* young sex-hungry mistresses, and the guy was sixty-something? Where had he found the time, the stamina? This guy should be in the *Guinness Book of World Records.*

"Who are they and where are they?"

Egan started scribbling addresses on an index card. "I don't know them. I'm evicting them all today." He tossed the card to Nick. "I hope you beat me to the door."

Brooke was in the throes of packing when the buzzer sounded and the dreaded words came through the intercom. *Detective. Police. Pelham.*

She dropped the receiver. *Don't panic!* You can't pretend you're not here, since you answered the intercom. *Think.*

See him. Be reticent: Less is more. You did nothing wrong. You have nothing to hide. Get it over with—and then *run.*

She took the receiver. "Send him up."

What would he be like? Rough, tough, grizzled, skeptical . . . Oh, God, what am I going to do?

There was a brisk knock at the door.

She wet her lips, swallowed hard, and looked at herself in the mirror. She wore Juicy Couture jeans, an oversized white shirt, and sneakers, with no makeup and her long, dark hair bundled into an untidy topknot. She hadn't been expecting anyone this morning; she'd just been planning to get herself out of the frying pan—now she was stepping into the fire.

She opened the door. The detective was tall, with reddish

brown hair and steely gray eyes. No uniform, slightly rumpled, as if he'd been up all night.

And he looked familiar. Why?

Nick said, "Mind if I come in?"

Pull yourself together. "Please do, Detective . . . ?"

"Nick Galligan."

Right, the one giving the updates on TV. He flashed his badge and handed her his card, and wandered into the living room while she looked at it. "Nice place."

"Coffee?" This felt surreal, too like a social call. He wasn't her nice neighbor next door; he was a piranha sniffing for blood.

"Sure." He looked into the closest bedroom. "Hmmm . . ."

Hmmms were *not* good. She poured the coffee, and set out accompaniments on the pass-through counter.

He was in the back bedroom now, where all her clothes were strewn around and her suitcases were very much in evidence.

"Going somewhere?" he asked politely as he came back to the kitchen and picked up his coffee, which he took black. Of course.

There was something about him that rankled her. The skeptical way he was looking at everything, the cynical way he was looking at her across the counter. The man who stood for truth, justice, and morality was judging her over a cup of coffee.

"The gig's over," she said succinctly. "So ask your questions and let me get on with it." Those eyes, that voice—they grated on her. She hated him. Hated Thane. Hated her fantasy that had become a nightmare.

"So what's your story?" He wasn't browbeating her, he was being polite, and yet she felt pinned to the wall.

Or maybe that was her own guilt.

"I was Thane Bohansson's mistress for six months. Now he's dead and I have to move out and move on."

"And how did that all happen?" Nick asked. "I mean, a girl doesn't come from—where are you from?—and just fall into the arms of someone like Bohansson."

Brooke took a deep breath. "It was a plan," she said, deciding to omit any reference to her friends. "To come to New York and become a mistress to a big-bucks kind of guy who could afford to support me."

Nick put down his cup. "Christ."

He hated it, she could see. Older guys always hated stuff like this, and he had at least fifteen years on her. He was annoying and judgmental, and she wanted to annoy him as much as he was irritating her.

"Why not? Women my age give it away, anyway. So I figured why not get something in return for my youth and looks? A business arrangement with no commitment, no regrets, no mess. When it's over, a clean break and you walk away with your stash."

"Crap," Nick said succinctly. "Because you're in a mess now, lady. And you're not walking away from it cleanly or with any kind of *stash*."

"Yeah, well, I didn't think the guy would die."

"And just where were you, Christmas Eve?"

She looked up at him, her eyes flashing. His gaze was steady, his expression impassive.

"Here," she said.

"Alone?"

She didn't want to tell him. But the doorman might have seen Thane, or a neighbor . . . "No, he was with me for a couple of hours late that night."

"Were you aware there were other mistresses?"

Her heart took a flying leap. Now what? She felt cornered; she felt like he'd been waiting to spring that on her, but she couldn't tell how much he knew or if he was just fishing. And he just sat there with his coffee and that steely gray gaze, watching and waiting.

"Not at first," she whispered finally.

He nodded. Waited a beat. "Do you know them?"

"Do *you*?"

"I have their names right here." He tapped his jacket pocket. "Delia Parry. MJ Branden." She made a strangled sound. "Did you say something?"

"I said I don't want to answer any more questions," she said.

His eyes never wavered. "About them, you mean?"

"About anything," she said tartly. "Without a lawyer." Oh, God, where would she get the money for one?

"I don't blame you. But—well, let's see where we are. You came to New York with the express intention of hooking up with some rich guy who'd support you in return for sex. You'd been with Bohansson for six months, were with him Christmas Eve, and—do I have this right?—only recently found out that he was supporting two other mistresses?"

"Yes."

"Then that's it. Oh—I don't suppose Christmas Eve was the very moment you found out about the *others*?"

"No."

"Of course, we only have your word for it." He moved away from the counter. "I wonder what the other mistresses will say? I need your forwarding address, by the way."

"I don't know yet," Brooke said, crossing her fingers.

"Oh, so you didn't keep that apartment on the West Side?"

Trapped again. She swallowed. "I did."

"Good. Then you'll be there."

"Only if I have no other choice."

"Can't go home to Mommy and Daddy, can you?"

How much did the bastard know about her life?

"Not now," she said viciously.

"Good. I'll be in touch."

The door closed behind him, leaving Brooke feeling terrified.

She needed a lawyer. She had to warn Delia and MJ. What difference did it make now, that Thane had screwed them, too? What if the police manufactured a conspiracy among the three of them to murder Thane?

After all, they were the easiest targets, the ones without the alibis, the ones without connections and family and support. She had been alone with him that very night, and maybe Delia and MJ had been, too. The police wouldn't even look for any other suspects with that on the table.

She had to do something. She'd gotten them into this, and she couldn't let them take the fall.

* * *

This was starting out to be a very bad morning for Delia.

There was a sneak alleging he was a reporter on her doorstep, and the expected but unpleasant eviction notice. She had to be out that day, taking only her personal possessions. She wondered how Egan Bohansson's lawyers defined *personal possessions* and if he'd be waiting right outside the door.

Her cell rang. She flipped it open and read the ID. "Brooke!"

"Yeah. Listen, we're in deep shit here. I just got a visit from the detective on the case."

"Oh, God."

"They know a lot. They know too much—about me, the fact there were three mistresses—"

"Yeah, I know. I just got an eviction notice."

"Oh, Jeez . . . me, too. Look, Delia—you and MJ have to get over to my old apartment as soon as you can. I don't care about all that Thane shit anymore. One of us could be arrested for murder! And the media is going to fry us if we don't stick together."

"I know. A reporter's outside my door right now."

"Get rid of him and get hold of MJ. We have to *talk*."

Delia punched in MJ's number as she threw things into a suitcase.

MJ, answer the damn phone!

MJ picked up on the third ring. "I don't—"

"Don't you hang up on me, hear?" Delia barreled over her protest. "Forget all your Harold shit. We've got bigger problems to deal with, like the police and press. Brooke wants us at her old apartment as soon as possible. Did you get your eviction notice?"

She could hear MJ swallow and then whisper, "Yes."

"If you are not at Brooke's by three, I'm coming to get you and I will break down the door, MJ. That bastard screwed all of us, and he's still doing it from the grave. They could arrest us for murder, MJ. *All* of us," Delia went on relentlessly. "We have a better chance to survive if we stick together. Are you getting this, MJ? Are you packed to go?"

A long pause, then a sniffle. "I'm packed. I just didn't know where to—I didn't know what to do . . ."

Thank God. Delia let out her breath. "Well, I'm telling you what to do. Go to Brooke's. I'll be there soon."

Brooke banged the gavel on her dining table. "I hereby call this meeting of the Mistress Club to order."

The apartment was stuffy and smelled of disuse. Brooke had gotten hold of two racks for their clothes and two air mattresses, and bought some groceries and takeout for dinner.

"This is our brand-new life," Brooke told them. "Though Detective Galligan hasn't caught up with you two yet, trust me, he'll find you—even if you *can* technically claim you didn't know you were being investigated.

"So here's the thing: *We* have to find out who killed Thane, and why. Otherwise we three become the top suspects, and they don't have to look anywhere else. When Galligan finds out we know each other, we'll be shark meat for the police and the press." She looked at them both, one to the other. "He knows about this apartment."

"Oh, hell." Delia.

"It gets worse." Brooke slumped in her chair. "I was with Thane that night."

There was an instant dead silence that lasted an ungodly long time. Then MJ jacked up from her chair, almost as if she were going to attack Brooke. "*I* was with him."

Delia grabbed her wrist and forced her back down to her seat.

"So was I," Delia said softly.

"Oh, brother," Brooke muttered. "And Galligan asked me if we knew each other. Now he can add the fact we all slept with Thane that night to the growing list of motive, means, and opportunity he has filed under *mistress* . . ."

"I'm leaving," MJ said.

"You're not going anywhere," Delia contradicted sharply. "You have nowhere to go and no idea how bad this looks. We all saw him that night."

"And now we've got to make a plan," Brooke said.

MJ's laugh bordered on hysteria. "You think you can solve the murder by making another damn *plan*?

"If not for my *plans,* we wouldn't have this apartment and you'd be out in the street," Brooke retorted angrily.

"Children, children, let's stop squabbling," Delia said, holding up her hands. "We don't have much time. So, Brooke, what's your plan?"

"We have to figure out who killed Thane," she repeated.

"Piece of cake," MJ muttered.

"Look," Brooke said, "it could easily be one of the family. I mean, maybe his wife found out about the mistresses. Maybe Egan was tired of his father squandering all that money, his inheritance, on prurient pleasures. Maybe Thane came on to one of Alaina's friends. Or maybe a girlfriend of Egan's got an invitation to Maîtrise—hey, maybe Thane was the money behind Maîtrise! What if that girlfriend told Egan about it, and he decided to put an end to it. And that's just *five* possibilities the police will never investigate."

"So what do you propose we do?" MJ asked.

"We keep an eye on the mother, Egan, and Alaina. I don't know what we're looking for, but we have to do something, and watching them is a logical place to start. So tomorrow, I'm going to Pelham. Delia, you take Egan. MJ, Alaina. Maybe we'll find out something."

"You think?" MJ asked skeptically.

"I *think*," Brooke said impatiently, "that if we sit on our butts, nursing our grudges and doing nothing, we'll all be arrested tomorrow for conspiracy to commit murder."

Chapter Eighteen

They'd dressed in jeans and sneakers, and Brooke had found three hats that would obscure their faces. She'd rented a car to drive out to Pelham, and they were minutes away from walking out the door when the buzzer rang.

Brooke froze. "Shit." She took a deep breath. "Don't move." She went to the window. "Oh, Jeez, there's at least one reporter down there. How did he find this apartment? Damn it. Now we have to sneak out of here."

"Is there a back door?"

"I think there's an emergency exit in the basement. Let's go before anyone else shows up."

The emergency exit unfortunately let out on the front of the building. It would be pure luck if someone didn't notice them slipping out like thieves. Brooke took a deep breath, crossed her fingers, and pushed open the door.

Once they were down the block, their precautions seemed melodramatic. No one even looked at them on the street, or at the garage. There was no all points bulletin and no one had frozen Brooke's credit card, so the car was no problem.

After she drove off, MJ and Delia hopped a bus to Midtown. When they saw the headline on a fellow passenger's *Daily News,* they froze.

MISTRESSES, MAYHEM AND MURDER.

Delia pulled her hat lower and whispered to MJ, "Oh, my God, this is a nightmare!"

"Yeah. What good will this surveillance do now?" MJ asked.

"At least we're doing something. Where's Alaina's studio?"

"Madison Avenue. I'll just window-shop the area all day and hope I learn something before I freeze to death."

"My plan's pretty vague, too. I'll figure it out when I get there, I guess. Here's my stop," she said as the bus stopped at Fifty-seventh and Fifth. "See you later."

But MJ had no hopes for later, or that today's must-do-something was better than doing nothing at all.

By late afternoon, Brooke couldn't see the point of trailing Rae Bohansson any farther. She'd spent the morning at home, had gone to a local spa for an exercise class and a massage, and had spent the rest of the afternoon at her club, where she'd lunched with sympathetic friends and attended a meeting. Then she'd returned home and stayed there.

She'd made no calls, met no mysterious men behind the coat room, had no interaction that seemed suspicious. After all, she was in mourning, and Rae Bohansson always observed correct form. She wasn't going to do anything that attracted undue attention.

Brooke headed back to Manhattan and was just about to enter the garage when a car blocked her way.

"Hey!" Her heart dropped. Galligan—oh, damn.

He turned, double-parked, and motioned her to enter the garage.

"I thought we were done," she said as he pointed to his car. His unmarked car, thank God.

"We've barely begun. One hardly knows where to start, even. Let's see . . . where are Ms. Parry and Ms. Branden?"

Did he know? How did he know? How *much* did he know? How much truth, how much omission?

"Why are you so certain I know the answer to that question?" she asked as he pulled into the stream of traffic.

"You have an apartment—very wise; I admire a woman who keeps her head and plans ahead. You're all friends, and they have nowhere else to go. The only conclusion is, they're with you."

Damned Sherlock. "They're out," she said curtly.

"They'll be back, then?"

"Let's hope."

"Let's wait," he said, "and we can get some other questions out of the way."

Worse and worse. He circled the block to make certain the paparazzi weren't lurking. "Lucky for you that they haven't figured it out yet, but I bet they'll be here in full force tomorrow morning. And this is a lousy fortress; no escape route. Do you mind if I call you Brooke?"

He clipped on his ID tags and parked.

Inside, he said, "This place is a lot smaller. Hmm . . . excess clothes, deflated air mattresses—looks like the other ladies *are* staying with you."

He gave her a faint smile. "Any chance of some coffee?"

Brooke made it, then handed it to him across the counter dividing the kitchen from the living room. She stayed on the other side of the counter.

"So what exactly do you want to know, Detective?"

He straddled the stool at the counter. "Everything. From the beginning."

She was scared to death of him. She needed her heart to stop pounding and her hands to warm up and for that icy look in his eyes to not be fixed on her. "Why?"

"Well, I'm just fascinated by this whole mistress thing. Three young women who are best friends, one old dead guy who's been doing all three of them . . . Kind of heartwarming, actually, keeps it in the family, so to speak. And since you're the one who apparently came up with the idea, you're the one I'm going to focus on for the moment."

"I want a lawyer."

"I'm not here to arrest you. If you'll just answer the damned questions, it'll make life easier for both of us."

"There's nothing to tie us to his death other than the fact we were his mistresses."

"This is true—on the surface. And it's true that none of you rented a car Christmas Eve or morning. But there are trains. There are killers for hire . . ."

"And there is entrapment."

"I don't do things like that. I wish to hell I didn't have to do this, too, but I need to know how you met Bohansson."

Her insides prickled. "Why?"

"Prurient curiosity. Why do you think?"

"Maybe you're on the hunt," Brooke retorted venomously. "You're just about that age." Oh, God, why had she said that to him? What was it about this man that was driving her so crazy?

"Oh, that's good. And what age is that, Brooke?"

"I'm sorry. That was a rude thing to say."

"But so true. I *am* just at that age where some sexy young thing could flatter me into supporting her and giving her expensive gifts in return for certain *personal* favors. But I doubt Bohansson was that easy."

Brooke couldn't tell anything from his expression. His gaze was steady on hers. He took a sip of his now cold coffee and waited with the patience of a hunter. He looked like he'd *been* on the hunt for days, too—grizzled, wrinkled, tired, determined.

"No, he wasn't that easy. *I* was."

A hard silence fell. He didn't like that, nor did she like saying the words.

"Right. You came to New York with that express purpose . . ."

"Yes."

"All three of you?"

"Yes. Right after graduation."

"How long did it take?"

"About a year."

"Where would you meet someone like Bohansson? You don't run in those circles. You're not a model, an actress, or a groupie."

"No. There's—" the words stuck in her throat; it sounded

so . . . she didn't know what it sounded like. "—an intermediary."

He didn't say a word, just looked at her with those steely moral eyes.

"He was there. He was interested, we dated. He made the offer. I said yes," she finished.

"A fine romance," he murmured. "No kisses?"

"That's none of your business."

He hadn't asked about the intermediary yet; she was scared witless he would ask.

"So painful to talk about, I know. Those billionaires dying on you, when you had such a good thing going. Only it was also going on with your two best friends, and you didn't know. When exactly *did* you know?"

She swallowed hard. "Just before Christmas."

"Interesting. You find out he's doing your friends, and then the guy is killed. Can't blame a man for connecting dots A, B, and C."

"We didn't talk to each other after we found out."

"So maybe one of you took him out in revenge."

"How? When? With what? He was a big man, Detective . . ."

Nick's eyebrows went up. "So I've heard."

Her frustration level escalated. "Are we finished here?"

"But I'm having such a lovely time. And I want to meet your friends *and* hear more about this intermediary."

"I'm not saying another word."

"Then can I have more coffee?"

"Get it yourself." She stormed out of the kitchen just as

she heard a key in the lock and voices. Damn! MJ and Delia. And no way to warn them that Galligan was here.

She blocked his view as they pushed open the door and motioned imperceptibly over her shoulder.

Delia's eyes widened. She got it immediately. "Hello," she called, shrugging off her coat. "Who're you?"

The blonde at the funeral. Nick remembered her clearly as he got up to shake her hand. And the slim redhead. Of course; that was why Brooke had seemed so familiar. "Nick Galligan, Pelham Police. Which one are you?"

"Delia. That's MJ. And obviously you've become way better acquainted with Brooke."

"The whole point of the exercise," Nick said, going into the kitchen for his coffee and then taking the stool that Brooke had occupied. "Anyone want coffee? It's fresh."

As if he'd made it. Irritating man. *Enemy* man. Brooke stalked off to stare out the window as Nick eased into questioning Delia.

Bless Delia with her ingenuous air. No one could ever think she had secrets or sorrows.

"Look," Delia said, in response to his question about the day they'd found out Thane was screwing all of them. "The guy went to all this trouble to take on aliases, to fake a business biography for each of them, to set us up miles away from each other, and to keep us so occupied that we had no time to compare notes every day. That was his game. As for me, how much more fun could life be than a really well-heeled guy buying you an apartment and clothes and having great sex with you? You don't get into the guy—you just make him happy.

"So when we figured out he was involved with all of us, it didn't make a difference. He played it that way because he could, and I'd agreed to the rules. So what else do you want to know?"

Nick looked a little nonplussed at Delia's nonchalance. "MJ?"

"I was devastated," MJ said tensely. "That's all I want to say."

"So devastated that you didn't want anyone else to have him?"

"How could that be? He was married."

Nick nodded. "But spending a lot of time pretending he wasn't."

"There was no pretense," Delia said. "We all knew it."

"And our knowing it, regardless of our reactions, is still no proof we had anything to do with his death," Brooke put in from the window. "So I think we're done here. If you'd please leave?"

"Get yourself a lawyer, Brooke. I'll be back soon."

As Nick closed the door behind him, she turned to Delia. "I *hate* him. I despise him. I never want to see him again. And I need you to tell me what happened today before we talk about *him*."

They all crowded around the counter, taking the last of the coffee.

"*I* want to talk about him," Delia said slyly. When Brooke sent her an exasperated look, Delia gave her knowing grin.

MJ said, "I didn't turn up anything. Alaina runs her studio, talks on the phone a lot, doesn't have many customers,

340

teaches a class on the premises, and takes a two-hour lunch break. Although today, she ordered in. So basically, I got lots of exercise and my feet are frozen."

Brooke outlined Rae Bohansson's day. "I think she's not going to do anything out of the ordinary that would be noticed. At least not until the mourning period is officially over."

"Same with Egan," Delia said. "He's going to be in meetings from now until Easter, with the transfer of power. They brought lunch in, and he was playing musical conference rooms all day long."

"And how do you know that?"

"I snuck into the reception room. There were so many people waiting to see him, I was just one more, and I'm sure he didn't know who I was. Or he was too busy to notice."

"So the day netted a big fat zero," MJ said dispiritedly. "We need a lawyer. Except we can't afford a lawyer. We might as well just hand ourselves over to Galligan."

"Now wait a minute," Brooke intervened. "He can't prove we've done anything except sleep with the man. If Galligan thinks we were in collusion to kill Thane, then *he* has to prove that we got together sometime in the wee hours of Christmas morning, somehow got to Pelham, got into the house, got him down to that family room, and then attacked him. Do we look like we could immobilize a guy as big and strong as Thane Bohansson?"

"I can think of one way," Delia murmured. "But, be that as it may, I think I know a lawyer. I used to kind of flirt with

341

him at the restaurant." She bit her lip. "I wonder . . . Except it'd have to be a pro bono thing."

"Don't wonder. Let's get hold of him before Galligan turns up on the doorstep again."

Egan Bohansson went on the attack in the local media that night, detailing the cautionary tale of three mistresses—the three of hearts, or diamonds, depending on how you looked at it. Three sexually voracious women giving an aging but powerful old man back his youth, his virility.

"Those women, those leeches—they should give back every dollar the old man spent on them," he spat at the cameras when reporters cornered him in front of the Bohansson building.

"Those gold diggers should rot for destroying our family," he responded to a question from Fox News via a remote. "Taking advantage of an old man, faking everything from orgasms to their concern for him. They should fry in hell. And he gave them everything—he was a gullible old man, looking to reclaim his youth."

Media spin, the whitewash cycle running full blast.

"It was a midlife crisis. He'd never hurt my mother like that." Alaina, on *Larry King Live.* "You know how those powerful older men are—they think they can control everything, even growing old. What kind of women would take him for everything they could get? They're prostitutes, and they should return everything he paid for."

"We're sitting ducks," MJ said to Brooke as they watched the performance that night.

The escalating pressure from the press in just one day was daunting. It was like a tsunami crashing over West End Avenue.

Doorbells ringing, importuning shouts, bribes to the managing agent, the super, the mailman. Cells going off constantly. A ladder braced against the building that almost reached their second floor, and a camera appearing just above the windowsill to try to catch a shot of someone, something, anything.

Ben Osias, Delia's lawyer acquaintance, was as precise and pinstriped as Galligan was rumpled and random: tall, gray haired, elegant, with snapping black eyes and a rich, deep voice that was deceptively gentle. He agreed to meet them at the apartment the next morning in spite of the media mayhem outside.

He arrived at eight and elbowed his way through the throng without answering one question.

"First things first," he said as he took off his coat. "Give me a dollar." Delia promptly did. "Now you officially have me on retainer."

Brooke herded them to the dining table, and Ben took a legal pad out of his briefcase while Delia served coffee and made introductions.

"Tell me what's going on," he invited.

"What do you know?" Brooke asked him.

"What everyone else knows: not much. There are no immediate suspects, no forensic evidence, three mistresses, and lots of speculation."

"The detective, Galligan, questioned me yesterday for the second time," Brooke told him. "I bet he's got a notebook full of follow-ups now." She looked at Delia, who was looking at Osias with an odd expression on her face, strangely silent.

MJ spoke up. "It's just that we all pretty much have the same story: We were all with him Christmas Eve—"

That caused a slight tremor in Osias's calm demeanor. "All three?"

"As near as we can determine, Brooke was first, then Delia, then me. One after the other."

Only MJ could have told him that with a straight face, Brooke thought. He looked a little confounded, which he hid behind raised eyebrows and taking some quick notes.

"We think the police think we conspired to kill Thane when we discovered he was *with* all of us," MJ went on, parsing her words carefully.

"Did you?"

"No! It's true that we found out about each other being his mistress—or rather, Brooke deduced it—and we were upset . . ."

"How could you not know?" Osias asked curiously.

"He used different names," Brooke answered. "And he'd sequestered us in different parts of the city. He wanted us individually available at all times, which meant quitting our jobs and giving up pretty much everything else. In return, he kept us very nicely. No money changed hands, but we got clothing and food allowances, a checking account, and other . . . nonmonetary remuneration."

Osias made a noncommittal sound. "So all the police have is your voluntary admission that Bohansson was with each of you that night, and that you found out at some point that each of you was a . . . *particular* friend?"

"Which could be motive enough in their eyes," Brooke said bluntly, "since *we* are friends. So they're probably thinking betrayal and revenge."

"Um-hmm. How did you all come to meet Bohansson initially?"

Brooke told him about her idea of a Mistress Club, then her discovering the real Mistress Club, and how Thane had met each of them.

Osias gave a low whistle. "Okay. Well, I think we're fine for now. You're correct in assuming Galligan's not finished with you, but until he can prove you went to Pelham that morning and somehow got into the house, he has no case. So the fun and fire is going to be all about the public's fascination with the fact that a sixty-eight-year-old, notoriously mysterious mogul had the juice to service all three of you. Pardon my bluntness."

It sounded awful coming from him in that rich dark, voice of his.

"So if it all gets really out of hand, we could write a book?" Delia asked.

"Oh, at the least. Shall I look into it?" He couldn't quite hide his ghoulish relish at the thought.

"Ben!"

"Or sell your story to the tabloids or *People.*"

It was nearly nine before he was done taking notes.

"Watch out for the reporters," Osias warned them. "They were five deep an hour ago. This is *not* a good situation. You have no back alley and no way to get out of this building since it takes up the whole corner."

"We'll use disguises."

"I don't think you'll get away with it."

"There's a basement exit," Brooke offered.

"Forget that; they know about it already."

"We have no money for hotels," MJ added stiffly.

"Let me think what to do," he said as left them. "I'll call Delia later."

He got them out later that morning at a coordinated moment when the police had cleared the street of the media for fifteen minutes. Which didn't mean cameras weren't snapping and rolling as they were hustled into a police car, or that the reporters' assumption wasn't that they were being arrested.

Precautions were taken that they weren't followed as they were driven to an obscure hotel, where their names were not on the register and they were given a small suite to share on the top floor.

They were to have their meals from room service, or if they wanted groceries, they were to notify the concierge. They were not to leave the hotel for any reason for the time being.

"Forget that," Brooke said, after Osias had left. "We're still on the case."

They had the luxury of two beds and a TV in the bedroom, and a living room with a sofa and a second TV. There was a tiny kitchen with a sink, an undercounter fridge, a microwave, a hot plate, and a supply of coffee, hot chocolate, and packaged snacks.

"Just like home," MJ said. "Dibs on a bed."

"You both take the beds, since you had the air mattresses," Brooke said. "I'm going to figure out how to get out of this place."

Delia didn't try to stop her; she'd feel better knowing they could escape the hotel, too.

Brooke came back with groceries and Chinese takeout, which Delia and MJ wolfed down instantly.

"Okay, here's the deal," Brooke said. "There's one elevator on the tenth floor where you can transfer to the other side of the building. So tomorrow we're going to scope out Alaina again. We'll be clothed up to the eyeballs, in this cold, so no one will know."

She had plotted their escaping the hotel with Delia leaving first, then MJ, all of them hatted and scarved, with collars up around their faces, ready for the freezing wind. They would separate, go east, and meet near Alaina's Madison Avenue gallery, and keep an eye on her.

Outside they immediately saw the screaming headlines.

WHERE ARE THE MISTRESSES HIDING? WHAT ARE THEY HIDING?

DESPERATE MISTRESSES ON THE MOVE

THE MISTRESSES, THE MONEY, AND THE MOGUL

SEX SECRETS OF THE BILLIONAIRE'S BIMBOS

The headlines followed them right to Madison Avenue.

It was eleven-thirty; the lunch crowd was beginning to flow. The streets were a little more crowded, making it easier to blend in. Cabs edged toward the sides of the street; lunch menus went out in front of restaurants.

The sky got darker. A thin shower of snowflakes flurried down.

The minutes ticked by. As the lunch crowd emerged from the surrounding offices, MJ kept looking at her watch wondering where Brooke was—she hadn't appeared yet.

Nothing would happen today, Delia thought in despair. Alaina and her family were walking a public tightrope and wouldn't do a thing that wasn't scripted. She would do only whatever Thane's media specialists told them to.

Damn. They were no match for the Bohansson media machine. There would be nothing to find now, nothing they could do or change. She waved to MJ, who shook her head and pointed back at the gallery.

Oh, God . . . please, a little luck, a little break.

Delia edged closer to the corner and saw Alaina, swathed in mink to the tips of her perfectly coiffed blonde hair, locking the front door of her gallery. As Alaina turned east to cross Madison, Delia motioned to MJ.

MJ nodded and scurried across the street, and they melted into the lunchtime crowd behind Alaina Bohansson.

Things got more complicated when Alaina entered a restaurant two blocks farther east. There were no unreserved seats available, so she and MJ squeezed themselves in at the bar.

"She's back there," Delia murmured. "We just have to see if she's with someone."

"I'll go to the ladies' room," MJ volunteered. "Let's get drinks to make this more realistic."

They ordered Cosmopolitans, speculated about Brooke's absence and made idle chitchat about the crowd for ten minutes, then MJ slipped away. After a few minutes, it felt to Delia like MJ was taking forever. How did you do reconnaissance in a crowded restaurant? How close could MJ get to Alaina's table, anyway?

Delia took another sip of her drink. What if Alaina knew who MJ was and she got caught? What if this was the worst idea in creation?

And then MJ was there, signaling to the bartender. She threw some money on the counter and urgently took Delia's arm. "C'mon."

"Why the rush?"

"Because—" MJ pushed through the crowd until they got outside.

"Because—" She looked behind her as she rushed Delia down the street. "I couldn't see the guy Alaina was with since his back was to me, but I got near enough to hear his voice. And I think . . . how crazy could this be? I think she was having lunch with Dallan Baines."

Chapter Nineteen

When MJ and Delia returned to the hotel, they found Galligan and Osias there with Brooke, who looked extremely irritated.

"What the hell did you two think you were doing?" Galligan demanded furiously when Delia finally burst in the door. "*Everyone* wants to know where the hell you are, and you're sashaying all over Midtown, out in the open? Jesus! How soon do you think it will be before the vultures track you down here?" He threw up his hands. "I give up. I won't even ask what you were doing."

"And we won't ask what you're doing, either," Delia said sweetly.

"So where are we?" Brooke asked tightly.

Galligan gave her a long, steely look. "Nowhere. Unless you're holding something back."

Why did she have the feeling there was another meaning to those words? "You know everything, Detective." Except about Maîtrise. "So *you* prove how we got to Pelham, how we got in the house, got Thane down to the family room, and subdued him before he could shout for help. Otherwise, there's nothing more to talk about."

Nick sighed. "Ben?"

"There's nothing more you can do, Nick, except keep them out of sight."

Nick snorted. "Yeah, I can see how well *that* went." He looked at MJ, who was huddled on the couch by Brooke. There was something in her face . . . she was on tenterhooks, waiting for him to leave.

And Delia was acting just a little too perky.

"We should get going," Osias said. "Ladies."

Brooke went to the door. "Thanks, Ben." She opened it exaggeratedly wide for Galligan. "Detective?" She obviously couldn't wait for him to leave.

"Was it something I said?"

She slammed the door hard behind him and stormed back into the living room. "That man!"

"Tell me," MJ said, still shaken by her discovery. "It's no fun barging in on you two going nose to nose like a WWF smackdown."

Delia said, "We couldn't figure out what happened to you."

"Galligan caught me locking up. I couldn't slide out of it. Too many questions, most of which I avoided. I was trying desperately not to have to talk about Maîtrise. And I was going crazy trying to picture what was going on with you guys."

"After today," MJ said to Brooke, "I'm with you: we have to do something. Alaina was having lunch with Dallan Baines."

Brooke sank down onto the couch, speechless for a moment. "Call Osias."

"But if it turns out to be nothing—"

"But how could it?"

"I don't know. But tomorrow I'm going to follow him."

"But from where? He could be at his home or at his Midtown place—"

"Or he could still be at *my* old apartment," MJ finished. "We can't go to Westchester, but maybe Delia can hang out at Grand Central in case he spent the night at home. You could stake out the Midtown apartment, and I'll keep watch on mine. His."

"Yeah, we could do that. God, if Galligan finds out . . . You really want to do that?"

"Yes. I'm totally dumbfounded that he and Alaina Bohansson know each other. And why would he have rented my old apartment? That was so creepy."

"Then we'll go find out—and hope to hell Galligan doesn't catch us."

The three slipped out of the hotel at daybreak.

"Are we nuts?" MJ asked, worrying now that she'd thought it over a bit.

"Just let's do it," Brooke said encouragingly. "I mean, we didn't expect to find out anything yesterday and we found an unexploded bomb."

"Right. You're right. Okay."

They separated, and MJ took the bus downtown thinking this *was* nuts, but it was too late to back out now. After she got off the bus a block away from her former apartment building, she grabbed a paper with the howling headline MISTRESS MADNESS and ducked back into the bus kiosk.

She could see the building and wouldn't look suspicious with an open newspaper in her hands. Unless someone noticed she'd been standing there, pretending to read for hours.

But that wouldn't happen. Dallan wouldn't be at this apartment. Her whole idea was stupid. It was seven o'clock, hours to go yet. And it was so damned cold. . . . This really was a dumb idea.

By eight she was freezing and just about to give up, when she saw him. She punched Brooke's number on her cell. "He's here. He's leaving."

"Go get him."

He was getting a cab. She raced into the traffic and hailed her own, frantically trying to keep Dallan's taxi in sight as she followed him uptown. One red light and she'd lose him. The light turned yellow—"Keep going!" she told the cabbie. "I'll tell you when to stop." She got out two twenty-dollar bills in case she had to jump out and run. West thirties now, forties, then his cab turned east on Forty-second Street.

"Turn here toward Grand Central." Oh, God, how did detectives do this?

Down Forty-second Street . . . "STOP!" She tossed the money at the driver, catching a glimpse of Dallan disappearing into Grand Central.

Then it was a race. Down the ramp, where the hell could he be going?

He didn't need a timetable. And she had no time to call Delia, who was somewhere roaming around inside.

He was heading toward the Lexington Avenue side of the station. To—where? The train to . . . *Pelham*? She crossed her fingers and ducked into the end car three minutes before the whistle sounded and the doors closed.

She took the thirty-minute trip to Pelham at the premium on-board fare, then took a cab to the Bohansson house just in time to see him heading around to the rear entrance.

What?

She blew out a long breath. This didn't make any sense.

"Lady?" The driver was looking at her in the rearview mirror. "Are you staying or going?"

"I'm going," MJ said, taking out her phone. It was nine-fifteen. She called Delia, Brooke, and Osias to meet her back at the hotel.

Nick showed up, too, at Osias's invitation, with McDevitt tagging along.

"Dev's useful sometimes," he told Osias. "A reporter, true, but a man with helpful sources and some imagination, who isn't averse to drawing gut conclusions and proving them in ways we don't want to know about."

Osias nodded his okay. "But everything's off the record."

"I don't operate any other way with him," Galligan said grimly.

Brooke had ordered up coffee and Danish from room service. They pulled up chairs; Brooke poured the coffee and handed out the pastries, and Ben and Dev took out notepads.

MJ looked around at all of them. "I guess this is my story. I'll start at the point after we found jobs here. One of the patrons of the store where I worked—well, we struck up a conversation, which led to a date, and subsequently to a . . . relationship. I broke it off after a while, and not very long after that, I met Harold Hanson or, rather, Thane Bohansson.

Her face crumpled a little, then she went on. "Everything was fine until two weeks ago. It was the holidays and I was feeling lonely because Harold had said he wouldn't be seeing me for a couple of weeks. So I kind of wandered down to my old neighborhood, feeling some nostalgia for the way things used to be, and, I guess, for this other guy who really was— bad for me.

"So he was the last person I expected to see that day, and there he was, coming out of the building where I used to live. He said he'd rented my old apartment, which stunned me. He said it was for business purposes. I told him I was with someone else now, and I got out of there as fast as I could. I think he followed me, but I can't be certain.

"Anyway, after Harold's—Thane's—death, Brooke was thinking that of all the family, Alaina wasn't as likely to be watched as closely as her mother or brother, and if we somehow kept an eye on her, we might . . . I don't know. I don't know what she thought we'd find. But we *did* stumble on something. Alaina was having lunch yesterday with Dallan Baines—the man I had that first relationship with, and who now seems to be living in my old apartment."

She took a deep breath. "Which might mean nothing, but it *was* odd. So this morning"—she slanted a look at Galligan's impassive face—"we staked him out. Brooke went to his Midtown apartment; Delia went to Grand Central; I was at the old apartment. I saw him there and followed him onto a train to Pelham and to the Bohansson house. I saw him go in the back way."

"Whoa," Dev murmured, furiously writing things down. "Dallan Baines, huh?"

"Dev," Galligan said warningly.

"Let me ask the questions," Osias said. "MJ."

"What?" Her voice was a little sharper than she intended.

"Pretty fast work." He sounded skeptical.

"We didn't expect anything to happen; it was just something to do because we felt so confined. Really, that's all there was to it."

"How long were you with this Baines guy?"

"Several months."

"You were his mistress?"

MJ gave him a killing look. "Yes."

"Who broke it off?"

"Me."

"Why?"

"I wasn't happy."

"Why?"

She wanted to strike him; his tone was too kind.

"He was too demanding," she said finally. "About *everything*."

"And you hadn't seen him at all since your breakup—until that day?"

357

"No."

"You don't know if he spied on you?"

"No."

"And you had no idea he had any connection to Alaina Bohansson before yesterday?"

"No."

Osias nodded. "Okay. What else do you need, Nick?"

"Something to make sense," Nick growled.

"I can do some digging," Dev said, pulling out his laptop. He tapped away for a moment, then: "Let's see—Baines runs around in those upper-strata social circles, and he's known for keeping company with beautiful young women. Usually models. Sometimes daughters of business acquaintances."

"At last, a reason we need Page Six," Nick murmured.

Dev ignored him. "He's married, has a couple of kids, lives in South Salem. Corporate officer in a law firm. Has an apartment in Midtown—no, *had* an apartment in Midtown. Huh. Wonder what that means. Wonder how he met Alaina Bohansson. I bet someone knows. I'll go back to the office and do some heavy research."

Nick said, "Here's one thing: There's no one connected with the Bohansson family named Baines."

Brooke suggested, "What if he has an alias? I mean, Thane had two."

"Taking another name is not that easy to do," Osias said, "but it's possible. He has connections."

"Still off the record, Dev," Nick said warningly, as Dev made a note.

"Got it. If he's operating under another name, I'll find it."

He gathered up his gear and winked at Delia. "See you. And I'd love to see *you* again," he added in a lower tone, just to her.

"He'll find it," Nick said as the door closed. "Meanwhile, what do you think?"

"I think you're wearing us out," Brooke snapped.

He fixed those steady eyes on her. "Oh, I think you were well-worn already, Ms. Sarrett."

She made a movement, almost as if he had struck her.

"That was low. Sorry." But he didn't look or sound sorry.

Brooke grabbed her coat and stalked out the door. Delia followed, shooting Galligan a furious look over her shoulder.

"Son of a bitch!" Brooke was raging mad, punching the elevator button. "That fucking son of a—"

"Hey hey—"

"That *bastard*—Shit!"

Delia rubbed her arm, trying to calm her.

"I'm not going back in there," Brooke fumed as the elevator doors closed behind them.

"Of course not. We'll just walk for a while."

"I want to *hit* something. I want to *smack* him! I—" She charged ahead of Delia out of the elevator.

Delia grabbed at her arm. "Hey, slow down. Did it ever occur to you that he's totally thrown by you, in a good way?"

Brooke came to a screeching halt. "*What?*"

"The way he looks at you—"

"Oh, God, another older guy? Forget it. I'm not doing the mistress thing again."

"I don't think he's a mistress kind of guy," Delia said gently.

"He's up to no good, in every way."

They stepped out into the icy cold air.

"Damn, I didn't take a hat."

"C'mon, just walk, you'll warm up and cool down."

"What he said was unforgivable."

"And that's what I mean," Delia said. "All those sparks flying around."

"No, that was hellfire and brimstone." Brooke walked faster, tucking her arms around her waist. "He's that kind of guy."

"He's the kind that makes you think about home and hearth and family Thanksgiving, and all that good stuff."

Brooke blew out an impatient breath. "Well, I'm not that kind of girl." She'd been thinking maybe she *was* that kind of girl, but never with someone like him. She was sick of him judging her. "Enough. It's ridiculous."

"If you say so." They turned down Broadway, where they could duck into a store or a restaurant if necessary. "God, it's cold."

Suddenly it seemed as if there was more of a crowd than usual, and then came a shout—"Hey! It's the mistresses!" And people started running, swarming around them.

Delia grabbed Brooke's hand just as someone pushed her, hard, into the oncoming traffic, with Delia falling on top of her.

Brakes slammed, drivers shouted; people pulled them up, brushed them off. "The mistresses, the mistresses." It went through the crowd like a match set to tinder.

"You okay?" Delia asked.

"Yeah. Somebody pushed me."

"God. Let's go." They broke from the crowd and dashed into the oncoming traffic with four or five people following them.

"Oh, God, we're going to die," Brooke panted as she skirted one brake-slamming cab after another.

"Light's green, lady!"

"The mistresses!" someone shouted.

"Hey, get in," the cabbie called. "I'll take you places you've never been before." He pointed to them as they dashed to the opposite side of the street. "It's the mistresses . . ."

They wheeled in the opposite direction and ran south this time, then west, where the traffic on Riverside Drive could hold up a driver and buy them some time. East again, toward Broadway—

"We'll never get back to the hotel," Brooke panted. "How stupid . . ."

Delia looked back. "We're okay. Walk slowly, head down. Maybe we should separate?"

"Hey! Delia!"

She whirled involuntarily. There was a car edging up to them, the man inside motioning to her.

"It's Dev," she said.

He squealed to a stop. "Get in. The press is swarming all over the city, looking for you."

"We know." They scrambled into his Mini Cooper.

"You know, you've *got* to tell your story sometime," Dev said, pulling from the curb and nearly sidewiping a cab. "They're crucifying you everywhere."

"And we thought he was an ally?" Brooke said mordantly. "Turns out he's looking out for his own interests, too."

"And what could we tell you to offset any of that, anyway?" Delia asked, noting almost automatically that he was wearing Versace, a fact that had been lost on her when they were in the hotel suite. What kind of reporter dressed to the nines like that?

"Oh, I don't know. You were coerced, blackmailed, held as sex slaves against your will."

Delia rolled her eyes. "No comment."

Dev shot a bemused look at her. He'd been drawn to her the minute he'd walked into the hotel room. She didn't look so slick or sleek you could bounce a dime off of her, but she didn't seem like an innocent, either. He didn't know what to make of her, and he was usually pretty quick to sum up a person.

Brooke was all edgy and defensive, sharp and intelligent, and much angrier than Delia. But then, Galligan had been pushing her buttons big time. He was acting pretty edgy himself and was much more obnoxious than usual . . . especially with her.

"I don't get you three," he said, maneuvering down Central Park West toward Sixty-fifth Street.

"There's nothing to get, Dev. The story is what it is."

"No, you didn't take the guy for a fortune. You're not dripping in furs and diamonds, driving in limos all over town."

"Oh, but we converted it all to cash and it's in my Swiss bank account," Brooke put in sarcastically.

"It's probably all in Egan's Swiss bank account," Dev said. "What the hell were you doing out in the open, anyway?"

"No comment," Brooke said, staring out the window at Central Park.

Which meant Nick had said something that set her off. "Okay. Well, I'm taking you back to my place for the moment. We'll call Nick and tell him. I can do what I need to do from home."

"I get it," Delia said. "He's kidnapping us to get the exclusive. How do we know this isn't a ploy?"

"You have to have a friend in the press, Delia, or they'll bury you alive."

"We're as good as dead anyway," Brooke said.

"We can reverse that. I can help."

"What a nice guy. Of course, that just might kill the book deal."

"Jesus—book deal? I was hoping—"

"That you could ghost it?" Brooke asked abrasively.

"You know what? Talk to Galligan. He'll tell you I'm not half bad."

Delia made a disgusted sound. "The wolf has been disguised as a lamb and is finally showing what big teeth he has."

"Delia—"

"Just let it go. Call Galligan. We need to know this little pickup is legit."

Dev lived on the top floor of a Federal town house in the east twenties. It had two bedrooms carved out of the middle of the floor-through; the kitchen, bath, and dining area, with fireplace, overlooked the garden in the rear; and the living room, with fireplace, faced the street. One corner held Dev's home office and a small conference area with a round table and four chairs. He barely had room for a couch and his obligatory big-screen TV.

But the apartment was scrupulously neat and meticulously furnished without screaming designer names.

They called Galligan and told him about the pushing incident. While they waited for him to arrive, Dev pounded his sources and Delia made coffee. Delia liked the apartment; felt comfortable rummaging in his narrow galley kitchen while Brooke sat at the oak dining table and stared out over the trees.

"Look," Delia said, "we really don't know if someone *pushed* you. The crowd was surging to get close to us, so—"

"I felt two hands just below my shoulders, and they pressed very hard against my back."

"Okay. But why?"

"I don't know. General mistress hatred?"

"Hey, come in here." Dev had turned on the TV and there they were, running from the crowd not an hour ago as the anchor intoned, "The mystery of the missing mistresses . . . seen running from the crowd on upper Broadway. They subsequently disappeared and no one has been able to find them . . ."

"I could get a million dollars for the secret of your location right now," Dev said in a melodramatic voice.

Delia looked appalled.

"Only kidding," he said as the buzzer sounded. "That's Galligan."

As Delia admitted him, Dev called out, "Seen the news?"

"Yes. And you've been salivating, haven't you?"

"Not at all. Delia promised me dibs on the book."

"Dev!"

"Where's MJ?" Brooke asked.

"Osias took her to his office for the time being. I don't think it's a bad idea to separate you three, anyway." He turned to Dev. "Let's sit down. Okay, first things first—Brooke?"

"There's nothing much more to tell. We were walking down Broadway, and someone recognized us and the crowd started coming at us, and someone in that chaos pushed me hard into the oncoming traffic."

He stared at her for a moment, his expression inscrutable. "Dev?"

"Lots of goodies. Bet you know all this stuff already."

"Maybe not. What have you got?"

"Not only did Baines give up that much-desired Midtown apartment, he took a leave of absence from his job."

Nick nodded.

"But *he* didn't rent MJ's old apartment—someone named Ian Baen did." Dev looked at them. Nick clearly knew; Delia and Brooke were dumbstruck.

"And here's the fun part," Dev continued. "My sources tell me that Ian Baen and Alaina Bohansson have been dating quite seriously." He went on, "Baines is said to be very obsessive, and by MJ's account, very controlling."

Nick jumped in. "So it's conceivable that he killed Bohansson because MJ had left him to start an affair with him. But you can't just walk up to a larger-than-life guy like Bohansson and stick a knife into him. You have to plan these things. You take a leave of absence. You remove yourself from your former life. You take an alias. You rent your former lover's apartment, a step that keeps the goal in mind every minute of the day. You somehow worm your way into the family."

"And since he's a serial adulterer, why not seduce the guy's daughter?" Dev put in.

"Or," Nick said, "the *coup de foudre*. You go to *work* for the family, where you can easily become acquainted with and then seduce the daughter. It's the European royal scenario: the princess and the chauffeur thing."

"And here comes the big finish. The Bohanssons hired a new chef six or seven months ago," Dev said. "His name is Ian Baen."

"Tall guy, very fit, very good-looking and smooth. Any of you know him?" Nick asked.

Delia answered, "No. MJ kept him all to herself."

"And so he'd want to hurt Brooke because . . . ?"

"Not just Brooke, both of us. We both convinced MJ to ditch him."

"You think it's that simple? I think there's more to the story. So here's what we're doing: Dev is going to guard Delia like the bulldog he is, and Brooke is coming with me."

Brooke prickled up instantly. "The hell I am. I'm going back to my place."

Nick shook his head. "The reporters are still camped out there. Nope, you're coming with me. And whatever I don't know yet, you're going to tell me—tonight."

Chapter Twenty

"If you browbeat me, I'm not going anywhere with you," Brooke said defiantly, but Nick just elbowed her out of Dev's apartment.

"Relax. I can be as metrosexual as the next guy."

Brooke made a disbelieving sound. "You think?"

They came out the door onto the highly desirable tree-lined street.

"Well, Miss Mistress, we've still got a few missing pieces of the puzzle." He opened the passenger-side door of his car for her.

Uh-oh. She'd be getting into tight quarters with him. Too close to him and his acid comments. And with Delia's observations overlaying her own fraught feelings about him, things were going from difficult to worse in a New York minute. "No browbeating," she warned.

"Oh, yeah, I forgot that part." He climbed in and turned the key.

"You don't forget much," she muttered.

"No, I don't—like the business about an intermediary that you skated around." He roared out into the street and turned north on Third Avenue while her body froze with apprehension. "I think we have to stroll down that avenue, Brooke."

"I'd like not to turn onto that avenue altogether."

"Lots of dark alleys, huh? Just the kind I like."

"I'm not going there. Dark alleys are scary. *You're* scary. You scare the hell out of me."

"Yeah, me too," he muttered.

"And you have enough on Baines to arrest him for something."

"Oh, sure. Big, angry man plotting to get revenge on the skinny girlfriend who dumped him. I love it. Except for one thing. It took two to kill Bohansson. Someone held Bohansson down, someone else snuffed him out," Nick said brutally. "So who else was angry enough to kill him?"

"One name leaps to mind," she murmured. "Alaina."

"What about his wife, or Egan?"

"What about them? And where are you taking me, anyway?" she demanded as she noticed he was heading north up the West Side Highway.

"My house."

She quelled the funny feeling in her gut. "That's pretty exofficio, Galligan."

"Well, if someone kills you, it'll be pretty *officio*—and obviously Egan's gunning for you. You three can't fight his money and his reach or his people. So it's better to have the three of you separated. The Thane Bohansson effect, we'll call it."

She felt like the interior of the car was heating up like a

sauna, *she* was steaming up like a sauna, and that the last place she was safe on *any* level was with Nick Galligan.

He turned off the interstate at Pelham and drove through a residential section near the Metro North tracks before he turned into the driveway of a small Cape Cod house.

A tiny house with barely any lawn or driveway, the tiniest vestibule that put you into the living room with one step, three steps to your left was a dining room, and beyond the living room to the left was a short hallway. Brooke asked to use the facilities and found the bathroom down the hall, along with two small bedrooms—one an office, the other slightly larger: his bedroom, furnished with an antique four-poster bed, a dresser with a small TV, and a night table. A wing chair in the corner with a floor lamp, and a table piled with books and magazines beside it. An Oriental rug on the floor.

She heard him moving around in the kitchen, and she returned into the living room. Here was a cushy modern sofa, more floor lamps, softly lit now, and another Oriental rug. There were antique accessories—a blanket chest as the coffee table, a massive old coffee grinder converted to a lamp, sitting beside a club chair and ottoman in the far corner, an old painting over the fireplace. There was also an upholstered rocker between the front windows, and shelves filled top to bottom with music and a mini CD player on the wall beside the door. A steel-stringed guitar rested on the ottoman; there was a wall of books opposite the door, and no TV. The surroundings fit him and she didn't feel uncomfortable, but she didn't want to analyze why.

He came in with two cups of coffee and set them down on the blanket chest. "Okay. Intermediary time."

Shit. "Nice house," she said, perching on the edge of the sofa. He sat on the chest and handed her the coffee, made exactly the way she liked it.

She slanted a startled look at him, and in that moment she saw what Delia had seen: the bafflement, the resistance, the hunger, the restraint, the desperate wish that her choices hadn't been so heedless. She saw the difference between a hedonist who had only wanted to play the game by his rules for his ongoing pleasure, and a man whose sole goal was centered all on the woman he had chosen.

This thing between them had everything to do with her—what made her *her,* the mystery of her, and his need to know everything about her that complemented the opposite things in him.

The spark, the attraction had nothing to do with body parts or sex, though that was there, too. It scared her how much he knew, how much he saw.

But she understood too that he was a romantic under the skin, and he wanted to believe. He almost could believe because he wanted it so much. But for his own moral peace, he had to push her away because any relationship for him was not a cavalier display of power. And he knew, the way a real man knows, that she knew it and she knew the reasons why too.

But what did she know about *him*? He loved music, played guitar, was a voracious reader, made good coffee; he was neat, tenacious, irritating, sarcastic, blunt, and, on every

372

level, exciting. But these were superficial things; she didn't know what lay beneath—except one failed marriage.

But when she looked at him, she felt enfolded. She saw warm, cozy nights, shared days, energetic kids, and picket fences. She saw the kind of man a woman would want to marry . . .

And that was the moment she fell in love. She wanted to be perfect for him, though the reality was that she would always be an imperfect sinner and that wall would always be there. An insurmountable barrier.

"My ex-wife got everything," he was saying. "This was all I could put together afterward. Damned lawyers. I hate intermediaries. Speaking of which, want to talk, Brooke?"

Intermediaries . . . She mentally shook herself back to the cruddy business of what she'd done that was probably so unforgivable that nothing could ever happen between them. *How stupid am I? But how could I know these feelings would blindside me like this, and it would be so different than I imagined?*

"Okay." He moved the guitar and sat on the ottoman. "Here's where we are. Three unbelievably beautiful girls come to New York, and in this incredible fairy tale, they all hook up with the biggest money pot in the nation, unbeknownst to each other. I wouldn't believe it if I hadn't heard it with my own ears. And every time we try to get at just *how* three really inexperienced girls from out of town got together with I-Own-the-World Bohansson, we get this fuzzy explanation about an *intermediary*. So now it's time to hear about the intermediary."

Brooke's heart dropped a hundred feet. This would seal the deal. He'd despise her more than he already did, and he'd bury whatever nascent feelings he had about her deep in his cold case files forever.

"Brooke—?"

Was there a little compassion there? Did she *have* to tell him about the dual Mistress Clubs—and everything else? If she even looked at him, her heart would be in her eyes and it would just be another disaster.

It was a disaster anyway, so she might as well tell him. It just seemed so unfair that fate should finally show her what she really wanted, and then ruthlessly take it away.

He simply waited and waited, so she finally told him. Everything. From the day in the diner when she conceived her Mistress Club, to the moment at Images when Marielyce opened the door to Maîtrise for her.

Counting the components: two Mistress Clubs, three incipient mistresses, six months of being kept and controlled, one dead lover, and one skeptical detective listening to her long, sad story with such a remote look in his steely gray eyes that she was ready to curl up and die.

He should have known, Nick thought. Egan Bohansson had flat out told him about his father's penchant for the young and wide-eyed. But there hadn't been only three; there'd been dozens over the years. And the question he *hadn't* asked was where Bohansson was getting those mistresses. Where did a man of his wealth, stature, and elusiveness traffic in that kind of young, unused flesh?

He creates Maîtrise.

Nick shook his head—it was so out of the realm of anything in his life. But Brooke and MJ and Delia had lived it, and had, by Delia's account, enjoyed everything that came with it. How did a man get past that? Could *he* get past that? And why was he even thinking about getting past it?

He'd had enough of Bohansson and of everything that had ever touched him. Including...

Her—so young, vibrant, gorgeous, and defiant, crumpled up like the past six months' experience had eroded her inside. It was always going to be there for him, and he was too old to waste time wishing it weren't so.

"Brooke." She reluctantly looked at him. "Don't cry—I can't deal with that, or that kind of pain. You *will* mend. Only I'll always see the cracks—and God help me, that will shatter you one day."

She lifted her head, held back tears by sheer iron will, and said in a quavering voice, "One other thing. I had thought that someone with a hell of a lot money owned Maîtrise. Maybe even Thane—just to fill his bed."

"Yeah. I got that, too," he said. "I'll look into it."

"Okay," she whispered.

"It will be," he said. "It's going to be okay."

The next morning they convened again at Dev's apartment to strategize.

"I think we need to get Baines out in the open," Nick said. "He's sitting back thinking that everything's good, that one of you is bound to be arrested, and he hopes in particular that it's MJ. So instead, what if MJ goes out in the open? If

MJ goes back to Maîtrise to find another well-heeled guy, wouldn't that set him off?"

MJ said, "It could. He had a thing about how women treat their men. If he thought I was being cavalier about Thane, now that he's dead, he could go a little crazy."

"It's the crazy part I don't like," Delia put in. "It's too risky."

"No," MJ said. "I want to do it. Otherwise they're going to hound us forever, and we'll never have a life. How dangerous could it be?"

"We'll be with you every step of the way," Nick said. "Ben would arrange it—a carefully orchestrated glimpse so the media's on your heels, then over to Maîtrise and see if something explodes."

"I'll do it," MJ said.

"We'll set it up for tomorrow," Ben said. "The sooner the better, while the tabloids are still screaming for blood."

MJ did it up to the max the next morning. Dev had brought a selection of sultry clothes from Brooke's apartment, including skyscraper heels, and she put on full battle makeup.

"How's that?" she asked.

"Attention grabbing," Dev said. "So here's the drill: We've got manpower following us and staked out around Maîtrise, so if there's a situation, we can deal with it. Your job," he told MJ, "is to hook the reporters and get to Maîtrise. Our hope is that Baines gets the word, follows you there, and something happens."

"Got it."

"Probably nothing *will* happen, though," Dev reassured her.

"I'm not worried," MJ said, but she knew Delia and Brooke were. "And I have my dressing room key just in case."

"We're going with you," Delia said to Dev.

He brought the Mini Cooper around and they crowded into it. The plan was for MJ to be seen near Brooke's apartment, where some reporters still hung out, hoping that Brooke would return. After that, it would be luck and some of Dev's contacts to draw whatever news posse was scouring the city to catch up with her.

He stopped the car across the street from Brooke's building where, as predicted, about two dozen media people had cameras and microphones trained on the windows and front door.

"Okay, this is it." MJ opened the door.

As soon as she was on the sidewalk, Dev drove up a few feet and then honked the horn. Immediately all eyes swiveled to him, and then to MJ, who was posed looking wistfully at the building.

"It's a mistress!" someone shouted. "Let's get her!" They instantly folded their cameras and equipment and started coming across the street. MJ waited till the optimum moment, then hailed a cab.

Dev zoomed behind her cab, keeping an eye on her, and flipped open his cell. "Hey, Grogan, I've got a bead on a mistress. Going south from West End Avenue and that apartment. Call the others. I'll keep you posted."

The chase was on, culminating in a crowd of reporters converging on the building that housed Maîtrise, banging on the front doors, storming through them, and aiming a storm of questions at the doorman.

"Where's the mistress? Did you see her? Why is she here? What is this place?"

Before he could stop them, half the horde had breached the interior doors and was swarming into the elevators and up into the private sanctums of the rich.

MJ had ducked into her dressing room, but even that was no safe haven. The reporters would be there in minutes, unless they were too taken by what they found in the spa and lounge.

Above her, all was pandemonium. It was a gold strike, a career-making story, a far better story than the mistresses—which would take most of the pressure off her, Brooke, and Delia.

She didn't know whether Dallan had taken the bait and followed her here, but she wasn't about to go look for him. It was time to leave.

She peeked out of her dressing room, debating which way to go. The elevators were full with photographers, cameras, noise. The stairwells, too. Maybe she should go to Vanessa's office and hide out there. The door wasn't obvious, fitted into the paneling, and maybe there was some other way from there to leave the building.

She eased her way downstairs, past the reporters swarming up the back stairwell who were too focused on the story of Maîtrise to really take notice of her.

She found the living room surprisingly empty, though it had been gone over thoroughly—obviously there was nothing of interest there, or someone would be there with a camera and a crew.

She went to the far side of the room, where Vanessa always seemed to appear by magic, and scanned the paneling for the door. There was a little brass knob embedded waist-high in the one of the panels. She pushed it, it swung open, and—

"So *there* you are," Dallan said.

She froze.

"I've been waiting for you, MJ. *We've* been waiting for you. Do come in."

She made an impulsive movement to turn, but he grabbed her arm and yanked her inside, where Alaina Bohansson was sitting behind Vanessa's desk.

"Here's the last of them. We'll kill them all, and then his monstrous evil will be wiped off the face of the earth."

"I'm going to burn everything out of existence," Alaina said. She stood, held up both hands, which were full of the little black books, and dropped them into a wastebasket. "Here they all are." She came out from behind the desk and set the wastebasket by the door. "All the whores. All the girls. All going to die." She motioned to Dallan, who pulled MJ to the door. "*You're* going to die, MJ. For abusing Ian's trust and for fucking my father."

MJ felt pure heart-stopping terror and knew that despite the precautions surrounding her, she was going to die.

Alaina flicked a lighter. "He was a fucking shit, and you're a stinking whore." She bent to light the contents of the basket, and MJ leapt, propelled by horror and fury.

She crashed into Alaina, who dropped the lighter and fell back onto the floor as a flame whooshed up behind them. Dallan screamed, and smoke and flames poured out of Vanessa's office as MJ pummeled Alaina, who had turned into a scratching, writhing animal.

She couldn't hold on much longer.

Everything was whirling, the smoke had filled her lungs, and the effort of containing Alaina felt like it was crushing her heart. Alaina was breathing fire . . . or was that her imagination? Or was that Dallan, singed and staggering out of the flames, in tandem with the wail of fire engines, the pounding of footsteps, and screams and babbling voices suffused with fear, voices calling out, calling her name, the fire getting hotter, Alaina almost rolling her over onto her back. MJ fought back, Alaina's wild determination to punish and destroy no match for her own determination to live and survive. She jammed her smoke-racked body down hard on Alaina's and kept her pinned to the floor.

Dev wrote the exclusive story, the one about the poor little rich girl whose daddy slept with girls her age. How, growing up, she'd always felt in competition with her father's paramours. How she'd vowed to make him pay someday.

And then there was the other story, the one about the middle-aged middle manager who liked to dictate and dominate, who lost control of his mistress to another man.

That man, Dallan Baines, and that daughter, Alaina Bohansson, were two points ready to converge, the lust for revenge of one poised to feed the demand for retribution of the other.

And so Dallan Baines concocted his master plan whereby he assumed the identity of Ian Baen, master chef, got hired by Rae Bohansson, and began his seduction of the very willing Alaina Bohansson.

Theirs was a six-month affair, linked by their hatred of Thane Bohansson and Alaina's determination to do something to punish her father for his outpouring of money, time, and attention on all those other young women. Dallan Baines had only thought to take his own secret revenge, and suddenly he was presented with a lover, a plan, and a partner all in one blow.

The plan was simple: Alaina would lure her father to the small family room, where Ian/Dallan would grab him from behind and keep him in a chokehold long enough so that Alaina could have the sadistic pleasure of snuffing out his useless life.

They'd almost gotten away with it, and they *had* destroyed his pleasure palace, his reputation, and his name. The tabloids had a field day identifying those who were caught at Maîtrise, though none of them were the notorious three mistresses.

Alaina and Baines were awaiting trial. Case closed.

Brooke banged her gavel on the living room table.

"I hereby call the last meeting of the Mistress Club to order."

It was so good to be home, and even better to be able to go out in public without causing a frenzy. She'd gone back to Chicago for the month after the sensational arrest of Alaina Bohansson and Dallan Baines. MJ had stayed here at the apartment, and Delia had gone to Maine to contemplate her life.

Now they were together again, and everything was different. Everything had changed. They had changed.

"So I went back to school, to the diner, and it was so weird," Delia said. "I felt like it was a million years ago. I can't even remember who I was back then."

"Yeah, I thought that, too, when I went home," Brooke said. "I didn't tell Mom and Dad half of what happened. They've finally decided to sell the apartment and go their separate ways, so that was sad. And after our experiences— well, everything seems kind of sad right now."

"Not for me." Delia smiled. "Dev and I are—"

"That's great! But you were in Maine."

"I never said I was alone."

"Wow," Brooke said enviously. "He doesn't have *any* problem with the whole mistress thing?"

"He's kind of fascinated by it, actually. But then, he's much younger than Nick Galligan."

"*Who?*" MJ asked, her ears pricking up.

Brooke sighed. "Galligan."

"No! No shit."

"*No*, period," Brooke muttered.

"Anyway, Dev and I will do the book," Delia said. "Ben's already shopping an outline and a couple of chapters with publishers, and we'll see what happens. So I'm okay."

"I'm okay, too," MJ said. "My family's probably been rabidly devouring all the coverage and pretending they don't know me, but that's okay. That's how it's always been. And I made a decision while you guys were gone."

"What was that?" Delia asked.

"I like being a mistress."

There was a long silence, and then MJ went on, "I like what I like, and I think it belongs in a mistress relationship, not a plain old vanilla marriage. I was deeply in love with Harold, and I want to find another man just like him. So that's what I'm going to do."

"Well. Okay." Brooke was a little nonplussed by her certainty. Certainty was enviable. She wished she were certain about anything. "That was the purpose of having this last meeting: to try to get those happily ever afters going."

"New apartments and jobs," Delia put in.

Brooke nodded. "I drained my bank account paying the rent on this place all those mistress months. A job sounds good to me."

"Nick'll come around," Delia reassured her. "It takes a while for older guys to wrap their minds around it."

"It'll take *me* a while, too. And now, let's go out to dinner to celebrate old friends and new beginnings."

Delia moved out two weeks later to be with Dev. MJ followed the next month, having hooked up with a lover who was willing to keep her.

That left Brooke alone, keeping herself busy while trying to sort out her life.

The problem was, love clobbered you. It came out of nowhere, and it was always the least likely man—like one much older than her. Yet after meeting him, no other man seemed right for her.

It was crazy. It shouldn't work like that.

And all the slinky sexy tricks she knew could never seduce him. They had nothing to do with love and everything to do with power, manipulation, and control. That had been her life for six months, and how could he be certain about her motives or her honesty after that? She was envious that Delia could just step into something bright, hopeful, and new.

But Delia had handled the thing right: no investment, no regrets. And MJ was happy, too, making that monumental decision to yield to her nature and return to the mistress life.

They were happy, while she, the instigator and cheerleader, was burdened with a confused conscience and an unrequited love.

MJ was not in love; MJ was in happy bondage. And Delia was not in love. Delia was deep in "like" with a mischievous, overgrown boy whom she could take care of.

Will I ever find someone who's perfect for me?

She took a temp job just as spring was blooming—mindless work that involved filing, sorting, and delivering airline tickets. Penance for her cupidity. Time to ruminate on her stupidity.

Spring was the perfect time of year to begin over, with everything flowering, the crisp fresh air, bright blue skies, couples strolling in the park . . . Well, seeing all the couples in love wasn't so great.

Now she yearned for love the way she'd formerly yearned for control. Love had nothing to do with control.

She'd thought she knew all the answers—she knew nothing.

I'm not ready for someone like Nick yet. I have to grow up. I have to learn what being in love really means.

So when she walked out of her office late one afternoon, the last person she expected to see was *him*.

Her heart stopped; she felt a heady joy with a hundred darts of pleasure zinging through her; she went weak and nearly dropped her bag; she wondered how she looked, she didn't care . . . She wasn't aware she had come to a full stop until people jostling her propelled her forward again.

And then she couldn't speak. *God, I am such a baby. This is* not *mature, worldly woman behavior.*

All she could say was, "Hi."

He was looking at her oddly with that steely gaze. "Hi, yourself. Before you ask, Delia told me where you work and verbally chewed my ass for not calling sooner."

Brooke gave him a skittery smile. It seemed inadequate to say, good to see you, but, God, it *was* good to see him.

"So I thought, maybe you could take off your hair shirt now."

Instantly she prickled up. "What about yours?" she threw back.

"Mine comes with being the one who's supposed to be the adult in the situation. Except things keep getting in the way."

"Yeah? What things?"

"Stupid male things. Let's walk."

They turned uptown on Fifth. It was a perfect spring day, the sky blue, the breeze gentle, the air sweetly scented, and Brooke couldn't find a thing to say. They headed up toward the park, their silence oddly companionable.

As they passed the Plaza and the horse-drawn carriages lined up on Fifty-ninth Street, Brooke asked, "Are you planning a carriage ride?"

"God, no. I don't do carriage rides. I'm too old."

"You keep saying that."

"Well, I *am* too old. And you're too young—but more than that, you're experienced way out of my league, and it stinks. I don't like it, I don't want it, but I'm tired of fighting it anymore." He glanced down at her stunned expression.

"I love you," she whispered, not cowed for a moment by that faintly off-putting speech.

"Oh, shit."

"Yeah, I thought the same thing." She was on firm ground now. He *was* a romantic, he'd waited till spring, and he'd come for her in spite of every reservation. "Love's a bitch. So why are you here?"

"To tell you it's not going to work. That we're two different worlds, two different generations, and we have nothing in common. And you know nothing about the hellish toll my job and my hours take on a relationship—"

"Blah blah blah," she murmured under the litany of *nots,* but deep beneath that, she caught the fleeting glimpse of the battle he'd had with himself to even come to her. If he wasn't in love with her, he was very close to it, in spite of everything that had happened, and he'd needed this time and distance to come to grips with the rest.

And so had she.

He stopped and looked down at her, and that look was there again—the one she'd lived on for months, the one where she'd first recognized the profound way he knew her, saw her, and wanted her, the look that erased the past and gave them a future.

He said, "And I came to tell you that I want to try."

He took her hand, and his grip was so warm and firm that something moved deep inside her, because his taking her hand like that was the commitment.

"Where are we going?" she asked breathlessly.

"We're not going to dive into bed."

"No." That wasn't what this moment was about, despite the heat crackling between them.

"*Yet.* And no kissing."

"Yes, kissing," she said.

"Nope, kissing leads to bed."

"No, there needs to be kissing," Brooke said emphatically.

He stopped again to look at her. "Maybe." He bent his head, touched her lips, a soft, tender kiss.

"Kisses will do," he murmured. "And dating. I'm old-fashioned that way: We'll get to know each other before we fall into bed."

"I know everything *I* need to know."

He smiled faintly. "Not everything, Brooke. And there *is* something to be said for a little restraint and anticipation."

"I can't imagine what," Brooke murmured.

He took her hand again and they started walking across Fifty-ninth Street to the park entrance. "There's no rush. I'm not going anywhere and I'm not in any hurry."

Brooke made a faint sound.

He stopped and kissed her again, a real kiss this time, a kiss that made her knees weak and everything inside her reach for him.

"We need to talk," he murmured. "And later, *after* we talk, I'll show you the value of all that restraint and anticipation."